TALK OF THE TOWN

Tracie Howard and Danita Carter's sizzling debut, *Revenge Is Best Served Cold,* broke "exciting new ground in African-American fiction" (Kimberla Lawson Roby). Now they're back—and so are their invincible heroines in a sexy new novel of romance and wealth—Manhattan style.

Morgan Nelson is working 24/7 to get her fledgling party-planning company, Caché, off the ground. Dakota Cantrell is busy turning heads and landing fat commissions in the upper echelon of mostly white, mostly male Wall Street. But the professional lives of these two best friends are about to take an unexpectedly personal turn.

If dealing with a string of mysterious business mishaps wasn't stressful enough, Morgan discovers she's pregnant—and for the first time, she has begun to doubt her husband's fidelity. A hot-shot record executive, he's suddenly putting in a lot of late nights with an attractive colleague. As always, Morgan turns to her rock—Dakota—who opens her checkbook and offers her shoulder. But Dakota has troubles of her own: a man who seems too good to be true and a secret she's kept from Morgan that could save or destroy Caché.

continued . . .

Tracie Howard
AND **Danita Carter**

TALK OF THE TOWN

NEW AMERICAN LIBRARY

New American Library
Published by New American Library, a division of
Penguin Putnam Inc., 375 Hudson Street,
New York, New York 10014, U.S.A.
Penguin Books Ltd, 80 Strand,
London WC2R 0RL, England
Penguin Books Australia Ltd, Ringwood,
Victoria, Australia
Penguin Books Canada Ltd, 10 Alcorn Avenue,
Toronto, Ontario, Canada M4V 3B2
Penguin Books (N.Z.) Ltd, 182–190 Wairau Road,
Auckland 10, New Zealand

Penguin Books Ltd, Registered Offices:
Harmondsworth, Middlesex, England

First published by New American Library, a division of Penguin Putnam Inc.

First Printing, November 2002
10 9 8 7 6 5 4 3 2 1

Ⓝ REGISTERED TRADEMARK—MARCA REGISTRADA

Library of Congress Cataloging-in-Publication Data:

Carter, Danita.
Talk of the town / by Danita Carter and Tracie Howard.
p. cm.
ISBN 0-451-20703-3 (alk. paper)
1. African American women—Fiction. 2. Female friendship—Fiction. 3. New York
(N.Y.)—Fiction. I. Howard, Tracie. II. Title.

PS3603.A777 T35   2002
813'.6—dc21   2002070275

Printed in the United States of America
Set in Sabon
Designed by Ginger Legato

This book is dedicated to my partner and other half, Scott Folks—without his love, support and unwavering belief in me, my life would not be nearly as meaningful, interesting or fulfilled.
This one's for you, baby!

Tracie

I'd like to dedicate this book to the ancestors —for without them there would be no us.

And to my parents, Bill and Alline, who taught me through their fifty-year marriage that it takes more than saying, "I Do," to make a partnership last.

Danita

1

Sure, a Saturday spent shopping the designer outlets in Woodbury Commons with Dakota was one of Morgan's favorite weekend activities, but a Sunday antiquing in Connecticut with her husband was a very close second. They'd left the city before the crack of dawn en route to Chester, Connecticut. Retracing the two-hour trek late in the afternoon, Morgan decided it had been well worth every mile. The back of the Range Rover was full of things she couldn't live without, including a pair of early-nineteenth-century candelabra, a period antique English Chippendale mirror, and a cylindrical marble foyer table.

As they headed south, back into Gotham, as Miles liked to call Manhattan, new tracks from his hot girl group, Ecstasy, blared through the SUV's custom speaker system. Morgan often referred to their cars as stereos on wheels. The Jaguar had twenty-eight speakers embedded into its interior and a subwoofer took up most of the trunk. The Rover was no exception, so the base line was strong on the group's yet-to-be-released single, "You Make Me High."

"Let's stop by the office," she yelled over the song's hook.

"What?" Miles strained to hear her as his head bopped along to the record's groove.

"I said, let's stop by the office." She had to practically scream to be heard.

Miles found the remote and lowered the volume. The fact that he had a remote control in the car, when the buttons were but an arm's reach away, was not lost on Morgan. She'd seen Miles spend twenty minutes looking for the remote in the media room, rather than push a button himself. Boys and their toys. She simply shook her head.

"I'm sorry. Now what did you say?"

"We should stop by the office and drop off the table on the way to Midtown." Morgan's new office was in an apartment building they'd bought in Harlem's tree-lined Hamilton Grange neighborhood. It boasted magnificent hand-carved ornamentation and exquisite metalwork. The interior, which was still undergoing restoration, was being returned to its original glory. Like the rest of Harlem, its beauty had been hidden under years of neglect. As a labor of love and a quest for a good investment, Morgan and Miles had spent the last eight months, not to mention several hundred thousand dollars, restoring its elegant cut-glass chandeliers, rich cherry and mahogany paneling, marble fireplaces, and elaborate moldings. Not to mention updating the electrical wiring and plumbing.

When they reached the lower-level garden apartment, which was Morgan's new office, she noticed a piece of plastic covering a section right above eye level. "What's that?"

"I don't know. Let's see," Miles answered, with a twinkle of mischief in his eye. Removing the strip he revealed shiny elegant cursive brass lettering that spelled CACHÉ, the name of Morgan's company.

"Oh, Miles, it's beautiful!" Morgan cried.

"I'm glad you like it, baby." Miles smiled.

"Now it feels like a *real* office," she said, still smiling broadly. Reaching him on tiptoes, she pulled his face toward hers for a series of teasing kisses. Before long their tongues locked in a sexy duet. He picked her up and carried her over the threshold and into the office. He laid her on the sofa before tasting her lips, neck, then trailing southward, planning to christen the new office in style. Things were just heating up when the doorbell rang.

"Who is that?" Miles asked, annoyed at the unwanted intrusion. The doorbell was an old-fashioned model that sounded like the "bbbbrrriiing, bbbbrrriiing" of a rotary phone. On the third ring, he begrudgingly lifted himself from the sofa.

"I don't know, but it'd better be good." Morgan quickly composed herself, smoothing her thin wheat-colored cashmere sweater and adjusting the drawstring of the matching pants. She was five foot eight, svelte, with a glowing chestnut-brown complexion. Her hair was cut boy short, giving her an exotic and sexy look that men never failed to notice.

"Hurry back," Miles said pleadingly. Still very much in the mood, he admired her figure as she headed to the front door.

"Hey, Morgan!" an excited voice exclaimed as the large mahogany double door opened.

"Lisa, hi. What are you doing here?" Lisa was Morgan's new operations manager.

"Just thought I'd stop by and take a look at the new office. Plus, I was in the area anyway." Morgan had just hired Lisa a few weeks earlier. They'd been working out of Morgan and Miles' East Side apartment, waiting for the final touches to be completed on the Harlem office.

Smiling tightly, Morgan replied, "Lisa, I appreciate your enthusiasm, but the job doesn't require weekends, unless of course there's an event." Morgan was hoping that this would end the doorside chatter so that she and Miles could pick up where they had left off.

Ignoring Morgan's hint, Lisa walked past her into the brownstone's foyer, gazing up at the intricate crown molding and stained-glass windows. "Plus, I've been anxious to see this place," Lisa said, doing a complete three-sixty as she took in as many details as one spin allowed. "It's incredible!"

"Thank you," Morgan said modestly, while groaning inside.

With the feel of Miles' hot kisses still fresh, Morgan stood impatiently at the door with her arms folded. Oblivious, Lisa gazed wide-eyed around the grand foyer. Her wonderment was halted by Miles' sudden appearance in the hallway. "Hi, Lisa," he said, with next to zero enthusiasm. Miles was six foot one, with a swimmer's build, and chocolate-brown good looks. The kind of man who made a girl want to taste him all over.

"Miles, how are you?" she gushed. "I love your place! It's fabulous!"

"Thank you."

Finally sensing that she might have interrupted something, she said, "I'm sorry to just drop in. I am *sooo* excited about Caché and working for Morgan." Lisa turned and smiled at her boss. Lisa, a single mom in her late twenties, had a figure that prechild was probably awesome, and was pretty good even now.

Morgan graciously offered, "Since you're here, I may as well show you the office."

"Just a minute," Lisa said, turning to head back out of the doorway, returning in seconds with a little boy, who looked to be about three years old. "This is my son, Justin." The little boy stood shyly, affixed to his mother's leg.

Morgan stooped to greet him, a large smile suddenly appearing on her face. "Hi, Justin." She held out her hand for a little-boy handshake. After appraising her, Justin held out his little hand and shook hers.

"What do you say to Mrs. Nelson?" his mother prompted.

"Hi," he said, peering up in her direction.

"How old are you?" Morgan asked, taking in the cute little boy.

"Four," he answered, holding up three fingers.

He was adorable, Morgan thought. "Miles, meet my new friend, Justin," she said, turning to face her husband.

Miles knelt on one knee to greet the slight little boy. "Hey, buddy? You watch any good football games today?" he teased.

The little boy smiled and said, "I'm a quarterback." He made a little muscle by bending his arm at the elbow.

"I can tell," Miles said, gently squeezing his small bicep. Miles was so good with kids. Morgan couldn't wait to have one of their own. Last year, Miles had surprised her while on vacation with the news that he too was ready to start a family.

"Enough of that, Mr. Universe," Lisa said, patting him on the head. "I'm sure Mr. and Mrs. Nelson have a lot to do today."

"Before you leave, let me give you the ten-cent tour," Morgan offered again. She led the way down the corridor. The office had thirteen-foot-high ceilings and an entrance out onto the back garden. To the left was a small bathroom with a cubelike shower stall, and to the right was a small closet and a galley kitchen. The main room featured two handsome mahogany desks, a sofa, a pair of file cabinets, and two chairs coupled with a cocktail table. It wasn't huge, but it was elegant and would be very chic once Morgan put the final touches on the decor.

"How many apartments are in this building?"

"Including the office, there are four," Morgan answered.

"I can't believe you guys aren't going to live here. This place is awesome!"

"It was time to separate the business from our personal lives," Morgan explained, "so we'll stay in the East Side apartment."

Getting Caché off the ground had put enormous pressure on their marriage, and not just because of the home office. Morgan's initial partner had turned out to be a con man, and his chicanery had cost her day-job as vice president of marketing for Global Financial, as well as a sizable amount of money. Miles had warned her about the phony Blake St. James, but she hadn't listened. She vowed never again to let business interfere with her marriage. Besides, the brownstone was an investment, and rentals in Harlem were beginning to yield substantial returns.

Sensing that Lisa wasn't leaving without assistance, Miles grabbed his coat to signal the end of their little tour. Picking up on his cue, Morgan said, "Shall we?" She headed for the door, grabbing her pea coat and Hermes bag on the way.

As they headed up the sidewalk, Lisa turned to her son before opening the passenger-side door to her ten-year-old Celica. "Say good-bye," she coached Justin, who waved gamely. "Good to see you, Miles. Morgan, I'll be here bright and early tomorrow morning!" She stopped and turned to Miles. "By the way, did you read Talk of the Town today?" Private Affairs was the scandal column in the *New York Gazette*. It often broke titillating stories about celebrities.

"No, I haven't." It wasn't Miles' favorite section of the paper. He was an executive at a major music label, and some of his artists invariably ended up in it.

"Rumor has it that Carmen is swinging both ways and her lesbian partner is her publicist." Carmen, one of Miles' female vocalists, was married to a macho rapper. Lisa had the paper tucked under her arm and showed it to Miles in case he didn't believe it.

The only comment he made was, "Don't believe everything you read."

"Just thought you might want to know," she said. "Until tomorrow."

Miles waited for her to get in the car and start the rattling engine before he asked, "Are you sure about her?"

"Of course, Miles," Morgan answered. "You know how thoroughly I checked her out." They walked to the SUV and got in. "And besides," she added, "she's not my partner. She's my employee."

"I hear ya," Miles said warily. "Cute kid, though."

"Yes, he is. But didn't he seem a little small to be four years old?"

As they drove through Harlem on the way home, it was impossible for Morgan not to draw comparisons, since the two locations were so close, yet so far. Back in the twenties, Harlem had jumped with entertainers like Cab Calloway, Duke Ellington, Louis Armstrong, and Ma Raine and leading dances like the boogie-woogie, turkey trot, and the big apple. Morgan remembered a quote by Rudolf Fisher, "Negro stock is going up and everybody's buying." Eight decades after the Harlem Renaissance, as they drove down 125th Street, it looked as if Negro stock had crashed and burned. Within one city block was every form of urban decay, from the pencil-thin, crack-addicted pregnant woman, to the young, prison-bound hardhead trading in drugs and human currency.

Instead of growing and thriving, post-Prohibition Harlem had flat-lined, with no life support. Gone were the successful black-owned businesses and blocks of grand brownstones owned by black professionals, entertainers, painters, authors, and philosophers. Until recently these once magnificent homes were so devalued they couldn't be given away.

While they were stopped at a red light, a man approached the window of the SUV yelling, "Yo, my brotha!" He was a stumbling slackard, stinking of Boone's Farm. "I got five chirren at home. Can ya give a brotha a coupla dollas?" He looked as if the sheer effort to keep his eyelids open was nearly insurmountable.

Miles knew that even if there were five children at home, any money he gave would never make it that far. He leaned out of the car window and looked his "brotha" in the blood-shot eyes. "I'll tell you what, my man," he said, motioning toward the grocery store at the corner. "Why don't I meet you at ShopRite and I'll buy your family some food?"

Not knowing what to make of this unexpected offer, the man began stammering a series of incoherent excuses. "A'ra, a'ra, you know, man, I gotta run, you know, uumph . . ." He blinked furiously while backing away from the car as if it were suddenly contagious.

Miles shook his head. "The saddest thing is that he proba-bly does have five kids somewhere."

As they continued down 125th Street, Morgan said, dis-couraged, "If the rest of Manhattan looks like a movie set, Harlem is still the back lot."

Signs of change were cropping up, though. Home Depot was building a superstore; Magic Johnson had opened movie theaters. And enterprising investors continued to buy up block after block. The only problem was, as Morgan saw it, many of these fabulous brownstones were being gobbled up by Caucasian pioneers eager to stake out their new frontier, gobbling up the last piece of the Manhattan pie.

Reflecting on the gulf between the haves and the have-nots, Morgan couldn't help but think about Lisa climbing into the old battered car with her son in tow, while she and Miles tooled between their Manhattan real estate in a eighty-thousand-dollar truck. But it wasn't just the price and condition of Lisa's car that bothered her as they drove down Park Avenue; instead it was her son. His clothes were threadbare and a couple of sizes too large for his small body. It left Morgan with a feeling of despair, because at four years old, he was already being cast as one of the have-nots.

2

The trading floor at SBI was pure pandemonium. Tech stocks were once again causing the market to react like the Cyclone at Great America, with dizzying highs one minute and plunging lows the next. Dakota Cantrell's eyes were transfixed to one of three flat-screen monitors on her desk, tracking the escalating price of the IPO that had just opened for trading. Dakota was a sales trader for Swiss Bank International, one of Wall Street's major players. Her commanding voice gave her a presence far beyond her petite five-foot-five-inch frame, which served her well in the testosterone-dominated financial industry.

Being in the business for most of the get-rich-quick nineties, and witnessing the rise and fall of the dot-com craze, had taught Dakota one thing: Keeping her eyes glued to the monitors was vital when tracking a highly volatile initial public offering. A few top portfolio managers, who had millions of dollars under management, had been allocated shares of the Hunt Pharmaceuticals IPO at the preopening price of eight dollars. Ten minutes after it opened, the stock was already up forty points. Being allocated shares of a hot stock before it went public was such a political game, she thought. The heavy hitters were sure to win.

"Dakota, line two!" yelled Paul, one of her coworkers.

"Dakota here," she snapped into the receiver.

"Dakota, Armin. I want to buy another fifteen hundred shares while it's still trading below sixty."

"You got it. At the pace this stock is moving, it won't be long before it reaches a hundred." She rapidly scribbled the new order on a trade ticket and time-stamped it on both sides. The pace was fast and furious especially in the morning, due to the six-hour time difference between New York and Switzerland, where most of her clients were based. "I'll call you back with the execution." Dakota hung up and yelled over to the OTC trader, "Todd, I need to buy another fifteen hundred shares of Hunt, and give me your best price."

Todd never looked in her direction, just yelled back, "Stock ahead."

"Don't bullshit me and try to hold the stock until the price ticks up," Dakota shouted. She knew some traders tried to fatten their P & L by widening the spread of a stock, then selling it at the higher price and keeping the difference.

"Would I do that to you, D? Look, take a thousand at a quarter and five hundred at a half."

"That's more like it." Dakota hit the speed dial to Switzerland. "Armin, you bought an additional fifteen hundred shares at an average price of $48.3334."

He sounded very pleased. "Thanks, Dakota. I'll talk to you later. Oh, I had a great time when you were in town. We'll have to do that again soon."

Dakota had just gotten back from a trip to Switzerland to visit a few of her favorite clients, and of course she'd stopped off in Paris to visit a few of her favorite couture houses. "So did I, but the next time you have to come to New York so I can return the favor."

"Will do. Maybe before the end of the year."

Two other phone lines lit up at the same time. "Gotta run. I'll catch you later." She pushed line two. "Dakota here."

That's how the day went, how most of her crazy days went. By the time the closing bell rang at four o'clock, the IPO had reached a high of two hundred forty points. Dakota looked at the trade tickets on her desk and sighed. She had written at least a hundred orders. She labeled and rubber-banded the tickets, then dropped them in the telex box to be processed by operations. After a tumultuous day, Dakota's nerves were frayed and needed soothing with a perfectly mixed martini or two.

"Hey, D, how about a drink?" asked Paul. "Some of us are going over to the Bull and Bear."

Though Paul was one of the coolest white boys on the floor, she wasn't in the mood for a pissing contest, which usually took place with traders exaggerating about how much money they made that day. Preferring instead a friendly face, she politely declined Paul's offer and picked up the phone to enlist her girl Morgan in a drink before their mysterious meeting with the real Blake St. James.

Morgan and Dakota had known each other for years. They had met at Morgan's cousin's wedding in Atlanta and immediately formed a bond. Though they had grown up in different regions of the country—Morgan in the grassy hills of the Peach State and Dakota on the South Side of the Windy City—they had a lot in common, especially loving all the possibilities that New York City had to offer. Like reinventing yourself in a completely different profession. Or finding designer evening gowns at a deep discount at a sample sale on Seventh Avenue. Or being on the guest list on opening night for a hot new restaurant. But despite all they shared, there was one thing that Dakota could never claim. And that was the guidance of loving parents. Hers had been killed in an automobile accident when she was a child. Although her grandmother, Nana, provided a good stable home, Dakota was on a perpetual search for love. Which in part explained her many failed relationships.

"Good afternoon, Caché."

Dakota didn't recognize the voice on the other end. It must be the new person Morgan had hired. "Is Morgan available?"

"May I ask who's calling?"

"Dakota," she said, a little put off by the woman's officious tone.

"Dakota who?"

"Look, just tell her Dakota is on the line. Trust me, she'll take the call."

The voice on the other end exhaled loudly into the receiver, then snapped, "She's on another line."

Firing back at the heifer would get her nowhere fast. Dakota remembered what her grandmother always said: "You catch more flies with honey than with vinegar." Sweetly she asked, "Can you please tell her Dakota Cantrell is holding?"

Dakota heard the loud click of the HOLD button in her ear. "Damn, she could have said, 'Hold on please.' "

After a few moments Morgan picked up. "Hey, girl, what's going on?"

"Who the hell was that? Cruella De Vil?"

"My new operations manager." Immediately concerned, Morgan whispered, "Why? What did she say? Was she rude?"

Dakota didn't want to get the new girl in trouble already. Plus, it was partially her fault. She was accustomed to Aimee, Morgan's old assistant at Global, who had always recognized her voice instantly. "No, forget it. I was just calling to see if you want to meet for an early drink."

Morgan's voice sounded ten times brighter as she said, "Sounds like a plan. Where to?"

"How about Asia de Cuba? Say around six o'clock."

"See you then," Morgan said. "And don't forget, Blake invited us to dinner at eight."

Asia de Cuba, on Madison and Thirty-seventh Street, was in one of the fabulous Ian Schrager boutique hotels. The decor as well as the cuisine was Asia meets Cuba, hence the name. Even after going home to change for dinner, Dakota still arrived first and headed upstairs to the bar. She sat at a table along the perimeter that looked down into the dining area. The long, slender thirty-six-seat communal table was the focal point of the room and billowy white drapes dramatically covered the walls, giving the room a sophisticated, tropical feel. When the waitress came by, she ordered a dirty martini with Belvedere for herself and a glass of cabernet sauvignon for Morgan. Settling in, she began to check out the scene below.

Garden-variety businessmen in generic blue, gray, or black pinstripe suits were wooing model-thin waifs with their expense accounts. A group of black-clad cool boys, whom Dakota assumed were ad execs from Madison Avenue, were holding court in one of the white leather booths. And to round out the scene, she spotted a daytime heartthrob from *All My Children* with his entourage in tow, trying to look incognito in conspicuous dark aviator glasses.

"I see you're busy people-watching," Morgan said, sitting down.

"One of my favorite sports," Dakota chuckled. "I ordered you a cabernet."

Over the first round of drinks they caught up. High on Morgan's list was her overeager office manager showing up out of the blue on Sunday with her little boy and interrupting the groove session she and Miles were having.

"Please tell me you've checked out her background thoroughly and she's not some whacko from *America's Most Wanted*," Dakota commented. The last time Morgan had partnered with someone, it had been an unmitigated disaster.

"Trust me, after Mr. Tyrone, I've checked her up one side and down the other. I don't think the KGB could have done a better job."

Not fully convinced, Dakota asked, "Where did you find her?"

"An employment agency that Miles recommended. Sound Entertainment uses them on a regular basis."

Dakota peered over her cat's-eye glasses, still in doubt, then said, "Well, I can't wait to meet Ms. Thing in person. I'm a pretty good judge of character."

Morgan wanted to say, *Then why did you let your ex-fiancé play you like a fiddle from the Grand Ole Opry?* Parker Emilio had also worked for SBI, but quit out of embarrassment when Dakota caught him in a very compromising position with another woman. But that was water under the bridge, so instead Morgan said lightly, "Come by the office one day next week. You can meet her and also see my new space." She suddenly rapped the table with a light knock.

"Speaking of meeting people. Why do you think Blake wants us to come by for dinner?"

"I don't know. But I'll tell you one thing," Dakota said, raising her eyebrows, "I'm not too anxious to go back to that penthouse. Not after our last visit."

"Whatever he wants to discuss with us, we'll find out soon enough," Morgan said, taking a nervous sip of her wine. "You don't think he'd want to press charges against us, not after all this time."

"Oh, no," Dakota quickly put in, "he wouldn't do anything like that." She looked up at Morgan. "Would he?" That was the last thing Dakota needed. She had too much on her plate as it was. The market was in a slump and as a result her numbers were lower than last quarter's. And to make matters worse, her grandmother had begun to complain about a recurring ache in her side. Which was totally unlike Nana, who was as strong as an ox and other than a common cold had never been sick a day in her life. Dakota couldn't bear the thought of her grandmother having a serious illness. She tried to convince herself that this was just a normal sign of old age, while urging Nana to get a thorough medical exam.

Morgan glanced at her watch. "We'd better get the check," she said, looking around for the waitress.

"Yeah, heaven forbid we should keep his lordship waiting," Dakota mused, trying to shake off the nervous feeling in the pit of her stomach.

It was surreal walking through the impressive double doors of the Fifth Avenue penthouse. Rich splendor and impeccable taste suffused the six-bedroom bilevel apartment. The last and only time Morgan had glimpsed these splendid digs was last year when she and Dakota had stormed the St. James fortress demanding settlement of the debt owed by Blake, the son of Dr. Richard St. James. But like Alice trapped in Wonderland they found they'd followed a bounding rabbit down a deep and twisting hole. They had been shocked to learn that the tall, charismatic man that she and Dakota had befriended—

and she had ultimately gone into business with—was not Blake St. James at all. Instead, he was Tyrone, the son of the St. James maid, Mattie. It turned out that Tyrone was a master at impersonating the very rich, and had masqueraded as the real Blake, a wealthy, trust-funded man about town.

That day, blinded by fury on the way in, and dazed by shock as she stumbled out, Morgan had failed to fully appreciate the magnificence of the antique chandeliers, eighteen-foot-high ceilings, priceless rugs, and other accoutrements of old-money living. By many standards she and Miles lived "the life," but by *any* standard the St. James family *was* "the life."

Mattie led Morgan and Dakota past the stately marble foyer, down a hallway-cum–art gallery, and into a magnificent drawing room. The room had deep cranberry silk walls, which set off an original Picasso that hung strikingly over an imported Italian marble fireplace. The room's elegance was rivaled only by the floor-to-ceiling view of Central Park. Gazing at the grand piano set on a slightly elevated platform, Morgan envisioned the fabulous parties for United Nations dignitaries that Tyrone had so vividly described. Now she knew why his accounts felt firsthand. He was not the son of the great Dr. St. James, but was undoubtedly there along with his mother, Mattie, as help.

Once they were settled into a Queen Anne love seat and a Louis XV chair, Mattie asked, "Would you like cocktails before dinner?"

As they gave their requests, Morgan sensed Mattie's hesitance to make eye contact. It then occurred to her that the maid was probably embarrassed by the trouble caused by Tyrone, her only child. To put her at ease, Morgan said, "Mattie, I am so sorry about everything that happened with Tyrone."

Relief washed over the older woman's face. "No, Miss Morgan, I'm the one that's sorry. I shoulda known that that boy was upta no good, as usual," she said in a soft Southern accent.

"You had no way of knowing," Dakota added. "He managed to fool all of us."

Morgan thought, All of us except Miles. Though he hadn't known the extent of Tyrone's ruse, Miles had been wary of him from the start.

"I never woulda thought that boy would try to imperson-ate Master Blake." Mattie shook her head and retreated to get the drinks.

Once she left, Morgan and Dakota glanced at each other nervously. They had no idea why they had been summoned to the St. James home. They had both received phone calls from an assistant with the mysterious invitation. It had occurred to them that since Tyrone had shamelessly used Dr. St. James' name to add credibility to his and Morgan's company, that perhaps he harbored some residual anger toward Morgan. Not to mention the fact that the last time they were here, Morgan and Dakota had both mouthed off at him.

Just then, the doctor's son, Blake, appeared in the doorway adorned in a rich burgundy velvet smoking jacket, black shirt, and black slacks, accented by his signature ascot, also in black. Striding gracefully across the antique Persian rug, he greeted them with firm but warm handshakes.

"You both look splendid," he said, displaying a perfect set of white teeth. Morgan wore a black Armani wool jersey cocktail dress that tastefully displayed her tall yet volup-tuously slender figure, accented with a strand of creamy Miki-moto pearls and spiked pumps. Dakota had changed into a slate-gray Gucci dinner suit with black whip-stitching, a black silk chiffon blouse, and black patent boots.

"As do you," Dakota replied, raising an eyebrow in appre-ciation of Blake's dashing ensemble. She and Morgan had often discussed what a waste of a fine man it was for Blake to be gay. But unlike Tyrone, the real Blake wasn't the least bit flamboyant. He had just the right amount of bon vivant.

"I trust that Mattie has taken care of you both."

"Only the best for the ladies, Master Blake," Mattie said as she walked briskly back into the room, carrying a silver serving tray with cocktails and caviar on water crackers.

After Mattie left the room, Blake proposed a toast: "To Tyrone." Dakota and Morgan looked at each other questioningly. "Though his morals were faulty," Blake went on, "his taste in friends was indeed impeccable. So, to new friends, regardless of how our paths initially crossed." With a twinkle in his light brown eyes, Blake raised his martini glass to his guests.

"To new friends," Morgan and Dakota said, joining Blake as they all clinked crystal glasses. With the ice broken, they chatted. Morgan told Blake about Caché's progress, and he had just started telling them about his new art gallery when Mattie appeared to announce that dinner was served. Blake, taking each lady by an arm, headed down the hallway past a dimly lit library into an awe-inspiring formal dining room. At its center was a large chandelier with hundreds of intricately cut crystals. Two gold candelabra rose from a cream linen-covered table, their flickering flames enhancing the faint glow from dimmed antique wall sconces, which highlighted yet more priceless art. The radiance bounced off the fine Baccarat wineglasses and goblets, onto English silver flatware, and caused the bone china to appear luminescent.

Morgan and Dakota sat on one side and Blake on the other, leaving the fourth setting at the head of the table empty. As they settled into their Biedermeier dining chairs, Dr. St. James entered the room, wearing a cashmere sports coat over brown wool slacks, an eggshell cotton pique Brioni shirt, and an earth-toned paisley tie. His presence was casual, but dignified and quietly commanding.

"Good evening," he said, bowing slightly to the ladies.

"Dr. St. James, it's a pleasure to see you again, especially under more pleasant circumstances," Morgan said, blushing at the memory of their first encounter.

Settling into his place at the head of the table, Dr. St. James replied, "I must say, it's not every day that two beautiful young women barge into my home making demands of me." Chuckling, he added, "Though that wouldn't be *all* bad."

"Depending on the demands," Blake teased his father. "I'm not sure that Mom would echo those sentiments."

"Speaking of my wife"—Dr. St. James turned to Morgan and Dakota—"she sends her regrets. Unfortunately she had an emergency at the hospital." Blake's mother was a highly regarded neurosurgeon.

The dinner started with a sumptuous potato leek soup and endive salad, followed by rack of lamb, with wild mushroom risotto and baby carrots with braised artichokes. To accompany dinner was a magnificent Chateau Lafitte Rothschild.

As they ate, Dr. St. James turned to Morgan. "How are things going with Caché?"

At the mention of her company, Morgan stiffened. But she was determined to be absolutely honest with the St. Jameses. They deserved nothing less. "Not bad. Especially considering the rocky start. Since Tyrone's scheme was uncovered, it's been difficult convincing clients and prospective clients that Caché is in fact a reputable company. I'm trying to be optimistic, but it's a long hard road ahead to rebuild."

"You might have guessed that's why I asked you to dinner this evening . . . and I trust I can speak openly of business matters in front of Dakota?"

Here it comes, Morgan thought, tensing. She nodded.

"I have to tell you, after that debacle I did some investigating of my own. What I discovered is that you ladies are indeed the upstanding citizens that you appear to be—unlike our duplicitous Tyrone." He leaned back, swirling his wine. "At any rate, I've felt partly responsible for the undue hardship you've suffered, however unwittingly, because of my family."

"But, Dr. St. James—" Morgan started.

He held up his hand to silence any interruption. "So I'm considering making a monetary contribution to Caché."

Morgan was stunned. "Dr. St. James, you really don't have to do that."

"It's not a done deal yet, and of course it would be an investment for me," he said. "There are certain stipulations, however. My accountants would have to assess your P and L over a two-quarter period. If things look promising, then I'll not only support Caché financially, but also share some of my contacts to increase your business."

Later, as Morgan and Dakota descended from the penthouse in the private elevator, Morgan turned to Dakota and said, "Well, one thing's for sure. You never know what to expect when you walk into that house."

"You can say that again," Dakota said, shaking her head.

"Now all I have to do is spend twenty-four hours a day getting Caché off the ground." Morgan smiled, suddenly infused with so much energy she was ready to go right back to the office and get started tonight.

3

"Miles, Rodney's on line one. Are you in a meeting, out of the country, or just plain ol' unavailable?" asked Lauren, Miles' quick-witted assistant.

Depressing the INTERCOM bottom on his five-line phone, Miles answered, "Let's really shock him. Put him through." Why put off the inevitable? he figured. Rodney Jones was not likely to go away. The man was like the sheen on polyester—he was all over you.

Rodney's voice blared through the phone. "Yo, my man, what's up!"

"Just workin', man," Miles answered, leaning back in his black kid-leather swivel chair, resigned to a waste of a good five minutes. "So what can I do for you?" he asked, crossing his ankles and resting his Gravati-clad feet on his glass-topped, kidney-shaped desk.

"No, man, it's what *I* can do for *you*. Now I know the last eight groups I've brought to you weren't quite right." That was an understatement, thought Miles. The last one, a group called Yo Boys, Rodney had sworn was the next coming of the Jackson Five. Somehow, he overlooked the fact that a full set of teeth was a minimal requirement for speaking, let alone singing. "But now I got this hot new rap group called the Hang Gang, and, man, they the next Fugees. But hey, seein' is believin'. They gone be in the open mike at Nell's on Thursday. You down?"

"Rodney, you know Jeff handles A and R now, and he makes the decisions on all new talent," Miles patiently explained. He had no doubt that the "hot rap group" Rodney was pushing was more than likely a band of juvenile convicts who thought a rap sheet was a prerequisite for stardom.

"Yeah, but you da head nigger in charge. You tell him what ta do. Right?"

"Rodney, I appreciate the flattery, but it doesn't quite work like that. You need to talk to Jeff, and if he likes the group, then we'll talk. I'll have Lauren transfer you. Hold on." Before Rodney could conjure a lame response, Miles was giving instructions to Lauren.

Even so, Miles felt a little sorry for the guy. Rodney was a record industry relic: a cagey warhorse who, in spite of his old-school ways, still deserved a measure of respect for discovering and managing some of the hottest artists of the seventies and eighties. So, toothless talent or not, most executives still took his calls.

Miles reflected on the many changes that had swept through the music industry, turning rap from a niche product into a mainstream driver of popular culture. In fact, the majority of hard-core rap music was purchased by lily-white suburban kids hungry for a dose of the reality that their parents couldn't run from fast enough. They even emulated the walk and dress of those who sang it, without fully understanding rap's origins. Not knowing that the shuffling pimp shoulder-dipping walk they mimicked started in jailhouses when shackled inmates were unable to walk straight, and the baggy jeans that sagged below the waist were a result of convicts being denied belts that could be used as weapons.

Despite the many changes in music, over the last fifteen years Miles had done well. He made his name in R&B, but he also recognized and knew how to capitalize on the emergence of rap music. His office was a testament to his many achievements. It was like a hip but elegant living room. Art deco

Barcelona chairs sat opposite his desk, and a deep cranberry crushed velvet chaise was set off to the side flanked by sleek glass and Italian mahogany coffee tables. His windows over-looked Madison Avenue, directly across the street from Tommy Mottola's domain in the Sony building. In case any-one mistook his stylish office for a SoHo lounge, his walls were adorned with gold and platinum records further validating his stellar success.

The latest addition was a gold record for Ecstasy's smash hit single, "Name That Thang." This was Miles' latest master-piece. The group currently had more heat on them than a rocket launcher. They had already won two Soul Train Music Awards, and there was even talk of multiple Grammys. Their videos were in heavy rotation on all of the major and local cable channels. Press on the girls was unbelievable. And to top it off, sponsors were lining up to offer endorsement deals for everything from designer clothing to upscale cosmetics. The national tour that Miles was planning would push them over the top, setting up another set of gold records for their next two singles.

The morning was taken up with meetings, which covered everything from the photo shoots and videos, to finance and release schedules. Finally, in the afternoon Miles was able to return the slew of phone calls from earlier in the day.

Number one on the list was the manager of Ecstasy. "Cee-Cee, what's up?" Miles asked, wanting to get right to the point. Cee-Cee was an uncle of one of the girls, and had no business skills whatsoever. He was just along for the party. His only experience in the music industry was by way of his portable transistor radio. And from the looks of him, it seemed stuck on a golden oldies station. Cee-Cee was the last of a dying breed. He was a true mack's mack. He always had a two-toned pastel derby for every outfit, and when he really wanted to make a fashion statement, he would pull out two-toned pastel gaiters to match. For accent, he wore rings. One on each finger.

"Yeah, I just got the tour plan and looks like y'all left out a few things."

Miles doubted it. He had gone over those plans meticulously. But he said, "Oh, yeah, what would that be?"

"Well, the girls want to take a few folk on tour wit' 'em."

Miles had heard this line before. "I've been more than generous by going out of my way allocating a family member for each girl, a manager, makeup artist, hairdresser, and stylist," he said patiently.

"And they be real grateful, but a'ra, you see, they was thinking of a few other peoples."

Smelling trouble brewing, Miles slowly leaned forward. In measured tones he said, "Who, might I ask?"

"Just a few of they friends, a'ra, you know, they posse."

"How many?" Miles asked, fighting to maintain composure. The last thing he needed right now was an artist relations problem. Even though Ecstasy was the hottest group out, the girls were also very young, immature, and to use Cee-Cee's vernacular, "ignant."

"Twelve. That be foe apiece," Cee-Cee answered, doing the math for Miles.

"Twelve!" Miles almost screamed. "You've got to be kidding. For a national tour that would cost over a quarter million dollars. Now, if they want to pay for it out of royalties, that's another conversation. But frankly, I'm not sure that I'd even allow that. I also have a fiscal responsibility to the girls."

"The girls want they posse wit' 'em, and I think they done made enough money for Sound Entertainment that y'all oughta pick up the tab."

"That's just not possible," Miles said, definitively.

"Course it is, and if it isn't, then you can call off dis here tour."

"You've got to be kid—" Dial tone. Fuming, Miles yelled into the intercom, "Lauren, get Cee-Cee back on the phone. Now!"

When the call finally came back through, Cee-Cee's greeting was: "Dis here contract says dat Sound Entertainment is 'sponsible for all costs 'sociated wit promotin' these here records. And dis is a cost of promotin'."

Staring disaster in the face, Miles retreated momentarily.

"Cee-Cee, since this sounds more like a contract issue, I'll be happy to discuss it with the girls' attorney." It was useless negotiating with anyone who still wore a dripping jheri curl. No way he'd let Cee-Cee derail the masterpiece that he'd so carefully put together.

"Yeah, well you do dat," Cee-Cee said, and slammed the phone down in Miles' ear.

"Some people," Miles said to himself, shaking his head. With both hands he rubbed his temples, trying to release the pressure of an oncoming headache.

"Looks like you're havin' one of those days," Phillip said as he strolled into Miles' office. Phillip Anderson was Sound Entertainment's V.P. of Marketing, and Miles' best friend. He also had the undeserved reputation of a ladies' man, given his prominent position and sexy good looks. Phillip was a bona fide Brooklynite, born and bred in Bed-Stuy. He was six feet three, with dimples set into honey-dipped cheeks and a physique that rivaled Morris Chestnut's. In fact, he was in a monogamous relationship and was one of the most honest people Miles knew.

"You have no idea. What's up?"

"Just stopped by to see if you've met Vic Pellam, the new corporate senior vice president of A and R." Phillip sat in one of the Barcelona chairs. Though Miles hired his own Sound Entertainment staff, the corporate office for the parent company, Millennium Music Worldwide, also hired senior executives who served as adjunct resources for each of the five labels. And since Ecstasy had all the makings of a huge success, this Vic Pellam had been assigned to help out.

"No, but I have a three o'clock with him," Miles said as he gathered papers for the meeting scheduled to start in ten minutes.

Phillip raised an eyebrow, smirked, and said, "Oh, you do, do you?"

Miles never looked up from his desk, so he didn't notice Phillip's expression. "Yeah, I do. What's his name again?"

"Vic Pellam," Phillip answered.

"That's right. Well, Vic and I are going to be working on Ecstasy's tour together."

"Man, are you in for a surprise," Phillip said as he headed for the door.

"What are you talking about?" Miles asked, finally looking up.

"Just buzz me after the meeting," Phillip said, and walked out smiling.

Miles gathered budget reports, color glossies of the girls, as well as a proposed tour schedule, and brought them over to the oval granite conference table, which was near the rear of his office. Just as he was settling into one of the six leather swivel chairs, Lauren's voice came through the speaker loud and clear. "Miles, your three o'clock is here."

Miles pressed the TALK button on the speakerphone: "Show him in." Thinking he might need his Palm Pilot for the meeting, Miles headed back to his desk. He heard the door open and without looking up said, "Come on in and have a seat at the conference table." He picked up the Palm, turned around, and . . . stopped dead in his tracks. Miles was not one to stammer, but he had a hard time formulating a coherent sentence. "Uh, uh . . ."

Vic Pellam was drop-dead gorgeous, a cross between Vanessa Williams and Beyoncé, with long strawberry blond cascading hair and a spectacular five-foot-nine-inch frame. She had boobs the size of overripe cantaloupes, which were on full display in a low-cut sheer blouse, and skintight python-print leather pants, which accentuated her shapely hips. "Hi, I'm Victoria Pellam," she said, extending her hand. "But everyone calls me Vic."

He had automatically assumed that Vic was a guy. Still, he quickly recovered, shook her hand, and introduced himself. "Welcome to the team."

"I've heard your name often during my career in the industry," she said, flipping her hair. "I understand you are the brainchild behind the slick digital video Ecstasy's working on."

"That would be me," Miles said, trying to keep his eyes

off her beckoning breasts. "Let's have a seat and I'll bring you up to speed on Ecstasy's tour plan."

He took a seat at the table and Vic sat beside him, a little too close for comfort. Miles could smell the Gucci Rush perfume she wore. The scent was familiar because his wife Morgan wore it from time to time. He thought about moving to the other side of the conference table, but decided that would be silly. After all, she was just another colleague. So why did he look down at her left hand and notice it was bare of rings?

Miles was a polished professional, though. For the next hour he kept them chartered strictly on business. They went over everything from personal appearances to tour budget and designer fittings.

At the end Miles asked, "Why don't we schedule a follow-up meeting for next week?"

Vic reached into her briefcase and took out her Palm Pilot.

"Is that a Palm V or VII?" Miles asked, noticing.

"VII," she said, turning it on. "I see you also have a VII."

"Yeah, I love it. Really keeps me organized."

Vic had already observed how sharply he dressed. He was wearing a taupe knit shirt tucked neatly into tan slacks with a brown crocodile belt. She had a hard time imagining him being unorganized, Palm VII or no.

With the meeting wrapped up, Vic walked to the door. Glancing up, Miles couldn't help but notice her heart-shaped rear, which topped off the overall package.

No sooner had she left than Phillip came sauntering into Miles' office again. "Well?" he asked with a mischievous gleam in his eye.

"Well what?" Miles asked, knowing full well what Phillip was talking about.

"What did you think of Ms. Victoria's secrets?"

"Thanks a lot for the warning," Miles said, walking over to his desk.

"That woman's body should be registered as a weapon," Phillip said, slouching into one of the seats in front of the desk.

"You should suit up," Miles remarked. "You're still a free agent." Though Phillip and Paula, an entertainment attorney, had been together for a couple of years, the subject of marriage never seemed to come up. Miles had often wondered if they were right for each other.

"Not really. Besides, I'd have to hire the entire WWF to guard that body. Man, I like 'em fine, but she looks like she should be *in* one of our videos instead of making them."

"Yeah, she is fine," Miles finally agreed. "But—"

"Butt is right! Did you see hers? Man!" Phillip exclaimed, flicking his wrist as though he had touched something piping hot.

"Man, you need to stop. What I was going to say is, even though she's all that, my heart belongs to my wife."

"Aw, isn't that sweet?" Phillip teased.

"Anyway, what's up with you and Paula?" he asked, wanting to change the subject.

"Man, it's cool." They were considered one of the "perfect couples." The entertainment attorney and entertainment executive. Long-term commitment, no children, no drama.

"So when are you popping the big question?"

Phillip looked distinctly uncomfortable. "Soon."

Though he didn't show it, Miles was surprised by his answer. "Take your time. It is a big step."

"Try, it's like leaping into the Grand Canyon."

"It's not that bad. Plus, Paula's a great girl." And she was. Not to mention the fact that she had an excellent pedigree. She'd gone to exclusive private schools before attending Ivy League undergrad and law school. Besides, both of her parents were judges, so she was the perfect buppie—even according to the BAP's handbook.

"I hear ya," Phillip said, sounding less than convinced. "But I don't envy you."

"Why?"

"I wouldn't want to work so closely with Vic," Phillip said, raising an eyebrow. "Because, you know, temptation can be a bitch." He didn't really think that Miles needed warning; he just couldn't help teasing him.

Miles leaned forward and looked Phillip dead in the eye. "Like I said before, my heart belongs to Morgan."

Phillip got up to leave. "Yeah, okay. Be strong, my brother," he said and fake-pimped out of the office.

Miles had long since hung up his notched belt. "She can't hold a candle to Morgan," he told himself, "but nevertheless, it is a good thing I'm a strong brother."

The intercom buzzed, interrupting his thoughts. "Miles, Morgan's on line one," said Lauren.

What a relief. "Hey, babe, I was just thinking about you." It was comforting to hear his wife's sweet voice.

"Oh, really? What were you thinking?" Morgan purred into the phone.

"That I'm the luckiest guy in town."

That made her even happier. "What brought on this sentiment?"

"Oh, nothing. Can't I compliment my wife?"

"Anytime you like," she said. "I was just calling to see how your day's going."

"It's been interesting," Miles said, not realizing how interesting it would soon become. After all, tours took a lot of planning.

4

"May I help you?"

Dakota stopped short of the doorway as a cinnamon-hued woman with high cheekbones stood blocking her entrance. "Excuse me?" Dakota said, checking out the five-foot-eight-inch Amazon, from her cheap pleather shoes to her too-tight polyester suit and home-styled hairdo. "I'm here to see Morgan Nelson," Dakota said, taking a challenging step forward.

"If you're here for the fund-raiser, it hasn't started yet." In a commanding, no-nonsense tone the woman added, "Come back at six o'clock."

Caché had been commissioned by Black Diamonds Entertainment, a networking organization for urban professionals, to plan a fund-raiser at the Studio Museum in Harlem. Though Caché was not a catering company, Morgan had jumped at the opportunity to lend her expertise to one of Harlem's oldest establishments. The Studio Museum, on 125th Street, had been a fixture in Harlem for more than thirty years, showcasing the work of such masters as Romare Bearden, Jacob Lawrence, and Faith Ringgold, among others. It also housed a vast permanent collection of more than sixteen hundred pieces.

Dakota was taken aback. "Excuse me?" Who was this woman? "And you would be?"

"I'm Lisa Burrows, Caché's operations manager." Then mimicking Dakota, she asked, *"And you would be?"*

No sooner had Lisa introduced herself than Dakota had a flashback to their first conversation. She had never made it by Morgan's new office, so she hadn't had the pleasure of meeting Ms. Thing in person. She extended her hand. "I'm Dakota Cantrell. We've spoken over the phone."

Lisa's left eye tightened as if recalling the rude telephone exchange. Then she extended her hand and gave Dakota a limp, barely there handshake. "So you're Dakota," she said, giving her a scrutinizing once-over.

Dakota ignored the sarcasm in Lisa's voice and walked past her into the museum. "Wow, the space looks great."

The gallery was painted a rich charcoal. Three-foot-square bleached white canvases provided a stark contrast against the deep gray walls. The fund-raiser was being held for the artist-in-residence program the museum sponsored. Mounted on each canvas were miniature brackets holding replicas of the original art. The monotone theme was carried over to the buffet. The centerpiece was a cascading arrangement of white tulips and rare black roses. Silver tiers dripping with faux pearls held oysters in a rich truffle sauce. Black olives surrounded soft white Camembert and water crackers. Osetra caviar nestled in crème fraiche on pumpernickel toast points lined the perimeter of the buffet. Waiters were preparing crystal flutes of champagne garnished with white grapes instead of strawberries to complete the picture.

As Dakota reached for a toast point, Lisa appeared at her side. "Do you mind? I don't want to disturb the arrangement of the buffet."

"Oh," Dakota said, feeling like a chastised two-year-old. Trying to save face, she asked, "Where's Morgan? Is she here yet?"

"She's in a meeting with the curator," Lisa said curtly.

Dakota wasn't the most patient person on the planet, but she was willing to chalk up the woman's rudeness to pre-opening jitters. "Since I'm early I might as well pitch in. What can I do?" she said, pushing up the sleeves to her jacket.

"Nothing. I wouldn't want you to get that pretty little outfit dirty," Lisa said, commenting on Dakota's beige Calvin Klein pantsuit.

"What the hell is your prob—"

Morgan walked up with a clipboard in hand. "Hey, Dakota, when did you get here?" she asked. "Lisa, this is my best friend, Dakota," she said, oblivious of the tension between the two women.

"We've met." Lisa glanced over at the buffet and said, "Where are the cocktail napkins? Let me check in the kitchen. I'll be right back."

"Don't hurry," Dakota mumbled.

Morgan watched Lisa depart, then turned to Dakota. "What was that about?"

"Your girl Friday isn't feeling me," Dakota said, rolling her eyes.

"What did you say to her?" Morgan asked suspiciously. She knew that Dakota could be abrupt when she was staking out territory.

"What makes you think it was me?"

"Because I know you. You probably . . . Oh, no!" Morgan said, looking up from her clipboard. "You didn't say anything about her Payless shoes, did you?"

Dakota looked insulted. "Of course not. Just because I like Gucci, Pucci, and Fiorucci doesn't mean I'm a fashion snob."

"Yeah, right."

"Don't forget I grew up wearing Sears and Robert Hall. I didn't get my first pair of leather shoes until I graduated from elementary school. So there, missy," Dakota said, feeling vindicated.

"You're preaching to the choir, Ms. Prada," Morgan said knowingly. "I know you checked her out from head to toe."

Dakota grinned, refusing to admit that Morgan was right. "I'll take the Fifth."

"Anyway, despite her brusqueness, she actually has a great aptitude for detail. Besides, she's a single parent and can't afford to wear four-hundred-dollar shoes like some of us,"

Morgan said, motioning toward Dakota's stunning Robert Clergerie pumps.

"Well, maybe it's time for a raise," Dakota quipped.

"Ha-ha, very funny. But seriously, Dakota, I want you guys to get along. Lisa and I are going to be working very closely together. You heard Dr. St. James. If Caché is profitable over the next two quarters, it could not only mean more dollars but incredible contacts. And Lisa is going to help me get there. It would just simplify things if there isn't any animosity between you guys." Morgan glanced over at the front door and noticed people had begun to file in. "We'll talk later. Let me go welcome the guests."

Just wait until the honeymoon is over, Dakota said to herself, rebelliously taking the toast point she had been denied earlier. A heifer with that attitude was bound to cause problems.

Soon the museum was filled to capacity with an assortment of urban professionals—entrepreneurs, bankers, artists, doctors, and restaurateurs. Dakota milled about the room talking to people and networking. She overheard an ebony-toned man dressed neatly in slacks and a sweater ask a woman, who she assumed was a banker, about financing a restaurant in Harlem.

"I've received a deluge of applications for commercial loans over the last quarter. And most of them were for restaurants," said the woman.

"Sounds like Harlem is nearly oversaturated with restaurants."

Especially soul food, Dakota thought.

"That's an understatement. White folks are even starting to serve up Southern cuisine in Harlem."

The man hissed, "I tell you, we can't have nothing."

Dakota wanted to join in the conversation, but didn't want to get on that bandwagon. That topic was a thorn in her side. The Caucasians in her grandmother's South Side Chicago neighborhood made a grand exodus to the suburbs in the sixties, only to return forty years later, trying to take over. The same thing was happening in Harlem. Just the night before, she had seen a segment on HGTV showcasing a reno-

vated brownstone on 137th Street that a white yuppie couple
had bought for a song. Instead of getting riled up, she meandered back to the buffet and made a plate of the tasty hors
d'oeuvres.

"Well, what do you think?" Morgan asked as she made her
way through the crowd, holding a glass of mixed fruit juice.

"From the looks of things, I'd say it's a success. Maybe I'm
in the wrong business."

"Don't give me that. You love Wall Street."

"Not lately, especially since the Dow doesn't know
whether to hibernate like a grizzly or charge like a bull. Anyway, here's to your business. If it always works like this, I'm
sure it will thrive," Dakota said, tapping her cocktail plate to
Morgan's glass.

"Cheers," Morgan said, taking a sip.

Suddenly she could feel the fruit drink settle in the pit of
her stomach. She grimaced and handed the mixture to
Dakota, saying, "Hold this. I'll be right back."

Morgan hurried through the crowd, made a swift left
down the hall and into the ladies' room. Once inside the safety
of the stall, she leaned over the toilet bowl with the overwhelming urge to retch, but nothing came up. She came out
of the stall, went to the sink to freshen up, and rejoined the
party.

"Are you okay?" Dakota asked. Looking at Morgan
closely, she added, "You look a bit green around the gills."

"I haven't eaten since this morning, that's all. By the way,
where's Lisa?" Morgan said, changing the subject. "I haven't
seen her since she went to check on the napkins."

Dakota didn't say a word. She just raised her eyebrow as if
to insinuate that Lisa was probably somewhere goofing off.

Morgan reached toward Dakota's plate, took an oyster,
and popped it into her mouth. Just then Lisa joined them.
"Where have you been?" Morgan quizzed.

"We're going to run short of champagne, so I went over to
PJ Liquors and picked up a few cases. The owner is a friend of
mine, and he agreed to deliver it cold, bill us, and take back
what we don't use," she said, handing the invoice to Morgan.

Morgan looked back at Dakota and gave her a wink. "Good work, Lisa." Yet as she took another sip of the fruit juice, she felt her stomach do another somersault. "I don't know what it is, but this juice just isn't agreeing with me. I'll be back in a minute," she said, dashing off toward the ladies' room again.

Five minutes passed, and Morgan still didn't return. "Maybe I should go and see if she's okay," Lisa said, concerned.

"*I'll* go," Dakota said firmly and walked away before Lisa had a chance to challenge her.

"Morgan?" Dakota called out. A few ladies were primping in the mirror, putting on lipstick, spraying perfume, and combing their hair. "Morgan, are you still in here?" Just as Dakota turned to leave, she heard a gagging sound coming from the handicap stall. She tapped lightly on the locked door. "Morgan, is that you?"

"Yeah. Can you wet a paper towel and hand it to me?" Morgan said from behind the door.

Dakota proceeded to hold a few towels underneath the faucet, then tapped on the door again. "Here you go."

"Thanks," Morgan said as she finally opened up.

"What's wrong? Are you okay?" Dakota asked when she saw Morgan's ashen face.

"I don't know. It must be the juice," Morgan said, dabbing her forehead.

"But you only had a few sips. Maybe you're coming down with the flu or something. Do you have chills?"

"No," Morgan said weakly.

"Maybe it's the oysters," Dakota said, offering another diagnosis. "Do you want to go to the emergency room?"

Morgan waved off such a drastic idea. "No, I'll call my doctor in the morning, if I'm not feeling any better."

"Well, let me call you a car. You don't look so good."

"I hate to leave, but the party is well under control. I think I should go home and lie down." She leaned against the sink. "Lisa has to leave by ten-thirty to pick up her son from the baby-sitter. Do you think you can cover for me?"

"No problem. I'll stay and make sure all the loose ends are tied up."

"Thanks. I really appreciate it," Morgan said.

Dakota took out her cell phone. She dialed a car service, gave them the address, and arranged for an immediate pickup. Helping Morgan to a leather bench near the door, she said, "The car will be here in about fifteen minutes."

"How did you manage that? It usually takes at least thirty minutes for a car, even longer uptown."

"I have a house account through SBI. As much as we're billed per month," she said darkly, "they ought to give us a chauffeur-driven Bentley."

"Dakota, I don't know what I'd do without you," Morgan said, resting her head against the wall.

"You know, maybe you should call Miles so he can look out for you."

"Hopefully he's home by now," Morgan said, glancing at her watch.

Dakota bent over and kissed Morgan on the cheek. "Feel better. I'll call you tomorrow," she said, then walked out.

Left alone, Morgan reached in her evening bag, took out her cell, and called home. After the fourth ring she hung up. She then dialed Miles' mobile, but got his voice mail. Morgan checked her watch again and decided to call his office on the off chance he was still there. She was caught a bit off guard when his assistant picked up his direct line.

"Hi, Lauren, is Miles there?"

"Uh, no, he's at a dinner meeting."

"Really?"

"Yeah, with Vic Pellam, our new V.P. of A and R."

"Oh, yes, I do remember Miles mentioning him."

"It's not a—"

"Morgan, it looks like you're needed for one last thing," interrupted Dakota, sticking her head in the door.

"Lauren, I have to run. No need to leave a message. I'll see him at home."

5

Freddie Hudson, a native New Yorker, loved the second and fourth Friday of the month, since that was payday for most people. Which translated to payday for him, since he was a pickpocket. In the afternoons he would stroll from his low-rent apartment on Lenox Avenue down to Midtown Manhattan where full pockets were plentiful. Freddie meandered in and out of the crowded sidewalk nabbing wallets of innocent victims along the way. His long nimble fingers were the perfect tools for the trade. He stood on the densely populated corner and waited for the light to change. He glanced down at the man standing in front of him and noticed his wallet riding up out of his right back pocket. Freddie knew he had exactly forty-five seconds to lift the wallet before the light turned green. Men were easy marks, since most of them carried their wallets in their back pockets, ready for the taking. Freddie took off his suit jacket and draped it over his arm for cover. He then took a step closer to his victim. He shifted his eyes to the right and to the left, making sure he was in the clear. New Yorkers were accustomed to close contact, so a gentle nudge at a crowded street corner was no cause for alarm. Freddie used the crowd to his advantage and in one swift motion swiped the wallet out of the man's pocket just as the light changed.

After a few more especially nice scores, Freddie took a

break and stood at the window of one of the upscale boutiques along Madison Avenue, hoping he had enough to buy the navy gabardine suit on display. He self-consciously glanced down at his three-year-old wool blend suit, bought on sale at Syms. Freddie put on the jacket and ran his hand along the sleeves, trying to smooth away the permanent wrinkles that were a result of constant wear. He inhaled, stood up straight, and marched into the store with major attitude. He found the suit that was on display in the window. Not looking at the size, he lifted it from the rack and held it against his chest.

"May I get that in your size?" asked the snooty clerk, noticing the sleeves were two inches too short.

"Forty-two long," Freddie said, matching the clerk's superior tone.

The clerk quickly found the correct size. "Follow me," he said, heading toward the fitting rooms. "Do you need a shirt and tie with that, or maybe a mock turtleneck?"

"Just the suit for now," Freddie said, thinking he had better really count his contraband before selecting anything else. Once inside the privacy of the fitting room, Freddie emptied his pockets of the stolen wallets. He riffled through each one. Inside were the usual suspects—credit cards, cash, driver's license, and pictures of kids. Most of them contained crisp twenties, fifties, and hundred-dollar bills. Except for one wallet that yielded only plastic. Credit cards could be the kiss of death, since most people reported the cards stolen before the end of the day. He counted the cash. "Damn, all I got is six hundred and twenty dollars." He then looked at the price tag. Twelve hundred dollars. Freddie looked at the array of credit cards—green, gold, and platinum. Stupid bastards probably didn't even realize the cards were gone yet. He decided to charge the suit. What the hell.

"Is everything all right in there?" asked the salesman, interrupting Freddie's thoughts.

"Just fine. Can you please bring me a black mock turtleneck? And do you have a tailor on the premises?" Freddie said through the slats of the door.

Sensing a fat commission, the clerk promptly changed his rude tone. "Yes, we certainly do, sir. Would you need the suit altered today?"

"Yes, I'd like the slacks hemmed as soon as possible. I only have thirty minutes. Is that possible?" Freddie said.

"Uh, no problem," the clerk said. "I'll send him in immediately."

"Thank you." Freddie fanned out the stolen credit cards in his hand. He selected one and took a Bic pen out of his breast pocket and began to practice the signature. Once he felt confident with the forgery, he stuck the card in his wallet along with the cash.

After forty minutes Freddie was fitted with his new suit, now hanging perfectly from his six-foot frame. Freddie's masculine good looks often attracted women. Little did they know that he desired exactly what they did—men.

"Will this be cash or charge?"

"Charge," Freddie said confidently as he handed the salesman the stolen platinum card. He stood there with an outwardly unconcerned look on his face, though inside he felt that delicious feeling of his nerves jangling like electrical wires. The clerk swiped the card and waited for approval. Freddie's palms began to sweat. Beads of perspiration sprouted across his brow. He began to fidget until he heard the cash register printing out a receipt, confirming he had gotten away with his caper.

"Sign here, Mr. Collins," said the unsuspecting clerk.

Freddie scribbled the signature, picked up the bag containing his old suit, and sauntered out the door. Once outside, his stomach began to calm down. Then it gave a loud growl, signaling its need for nourishment. Working always made him hungry. Freddie approached a trendy restaurant and was just about to go in when he noticed an easy mark with his blazer flapping in the wind as he hailed a taxi. Freddie could see the imprint of a wallet in the man's back pocket. His victim never even turned around as Freddie ever so gently brushed his backside, lifting his wallet at the same time. "He's gonna be surprised when it's time to get out and pay the driver," Freddie chuckled as he walked into the restaurant.

"Will you be dining alone?" the host asked haughtily.

"Unfortunately," Freddie smirked. "Where's your men's room?"

"Second door to your left."

"I'll be right back," Freddie said.

Once inside the rest room stall, he went through his ritual of checking out the wallet, expecting to find the usual. But among the green, gold, and platinum cards was an American Express Centurion Card, black with platinum trim and embossing. "Damn, this must be some new shit." Little did Freddie know that the Centurion card was the new primo status symbol, offered by invitation only to a select group of American Express platinum cardholders and arriving special delivery in its very own scented box.

"This dude must be loaded." Freddie searched the wallet for family pictures, interested to learn more about this man. But instead of the wife and kids in stiff mannequin poses, he found a beefcake photo of a muscular chocolate hunk. He was propped up on one elbow, twirling a purple g-string around his index finger. His legs gaped open, exposing a perfectly erect twelve-inch penis. Freddie turned the picture over and stamped in black ink was a telephone number, "1-900-SOL-POLE." Next to the picture was a gold-wrapped Magnum. "My kind of man," he murmured, slipping both the condom and picture in his wallet. He added the cash to his stash, which made his bounty for the day over a grand. He continued to search through the wallet and found a business card. "I think I'll mosey on over after lunch and return his wallet."

"Care for a cocktail before lunch?" asked the waiter, handing Freddie a menu once he was seated.

"Do you have Champale?" Freddie said, forgetting he wasn't back in the 'hood.

The waiter looked perplexed. "Excuse me?"

"I mean champagne," he quickly corrected himself.

"Of course. A glass of Moët & Chandon? And would you

care for bottled water?" the waiter asked in a tone that implied anything else was totally gauche.

Freddie picked up on the tone and said, "Yes, please."

"With or without gas?"

Did he just ask me if I had gas? Freddie wondered. "What did you say?"

The waiter explained, seeing his unsophisticated patron had no clue. "Gas is the European term for sparkling water. Without gas is basically your flat mineral and spring waters."

"Damn, who knew water could be so deep? I'll try the gassy water. Thanks for dropping that little bit of science on me, man."

"Excuse me?" This time it was the waiter who was clueless.

Freddie chuckled. "It means thanks for the information."

"Oh. I'll be right back with your beverage."

Freddie pondered the incredibly confusing menu. Most of the entrées he couldn't even pronounce. And the prices were astronomical. It was a good thing he had some extra loot.

"Have you decided?" asked the waiter as he placed a small bottle of Pellegrino and a glass of Moët on the table.

Freddie looked at the menu again and decided to ask about the specials, thinking that way he could at least hear what was being offered.

"Our soup du jour is a consommé of scallops and leeks. Our fish today is sea bass, grilled to perfection with a sprig of rosemary and drizzled with a lemongrass aioli."

"Perfect. I'll have that and a salad."

The waiter came back in record time with a minute crock of consommé and about six leaves of lettuce with two cherry tomatoes on a decorative plate. Freddie looked at the soup and salad and thought, Damn, somebody ought to be shot, charging fifteen dollars for this little-ass bowl of soup.

The waiter reappeared in fifteen minutes with his entrée. "Can I get you anything else?"

"No, thank you. I'm fine for now." Freddie pushed up the sleeves on his new blazer and chowed down. Gourmet cuisine had a more appealing taste when he didn't have to use his own money to pay the bill.

"Would you care for dessert?" the waiter asked as he removed the empty dishes.

Freddie wanted dessert and another drink, but was anxious to return the wallet. "No. Just the check."

The waiter handed him a black leather case with a little bow. "Thank you."

"Sixty-five dollars?" Freddie spurted, looking at the bill. "It's a good thing I went to work today." He chuckled and put seventy dollars in the leather case and walked out, never noticing the waiter's disdain at the less than ten percent tip.

He cut over two avenues and strolled down Lexington until he came to Gallery Row, a block famous for its diverse art galleries. Freddie checked for the address on the business card. When he reached the building, the windows were covered with thick brown paper. The place appeared to be closed. He walked closer and noticed that the door was ajar; he pushed it open and walked in. He found himself in a sterile-looking space with stark white walls, minitrack lights, and high-gloss hardwood floors. An abstract sculpture on a marble pedestal caught his eye. He stopped in front of it, trying to figure out what it was made of.

"Looks like solid gold, doesn't it?" asked a voice from behind him.

Freddie turned around and looked into the eyes of the most beautiful man he had ever seen. He was about five-eleven with warm, sexy eyes, and full lips that complemented his mocha complexion. He was dressed impeccably, in a suit so stylish and expensive-looking that Freddie's new clothes felt drab and ordinary by comparison.

"It sure does," Freddie said without breaking eye contact.

Walking around to the other side of the sculpture, the man said, "Well, it's actually a gold-leaf overlay." He ran his hand over the sculpture. "We're not officially open yet. This is the first piece to arrive." Extending his hand he said, "I'm Blake St. James, the owner."

"Freddie Hudson." Freddie shook Blake's hand and held it a little longer than he should have. "Actually, I'm here to return this," he said, handing over the wallet.

Blake was ecstatic. "Thank you so much. Where did you find it? I've been looking all over the place."

"On the sidewalk not far from here. You must have dropped it," Freddie lied.

Blake looked inside the wallet, checking for any missing items. All of his cards including the black Centurion Card were there. The cash of course was gone. He looked inside the fold of the wallet for the picture of his private dancer. And felt a rush of embarrassment when he didn't see the lewd photo.

"Is everything there?" Freddie asked, seemingly concerned.

"Uh, uh, yeah. Everything's here except the cash, of course. How can I ever thank you?"

Freddie gave him a wink. "Maybe you can buy me a drink sometime."

"It would be my pleasure. Are you a collector?" Blake asked, then added, "Nice suit," admiring the three-button navy suit, but noticing that the rest of his outfit didn't quite measure up, especially the worn brown loafers.

"Thanks, and no, I'm not an art collector. Not yet, at least." Freddie chuckled, thinking he was too broke to collect stamps. "But I am in the market for a small but tasteful piece."

"Let me show you this charcoal by a local artist. It just came in and is moderately priced but very well done," Blake said, walking to the front of the gallery.

Freddie followed behind, checking out Blake's tight butt with each step. When they reached the piece, Freddie was a bit surprised. It was a drawing of two men lounging nude in each other's arms. Is he trying to tell me something? Freddie wondered.

"This is an original line drawing by Channer. Let me check the price," Blake said, flipping through his clipboard. "This must be your lucky day. It is selling for only seventeen hundred."

Freddie swallowed hard and said, "Dollars."

"You have to admit, that's a bargain considering it's an original Channer."

"Absolutely. Let me think about it for a few days," Freddie said, keeping up the charade. He was close to cracking up at the thought of buying a stupid sketch for that much money. It looked like something done in elementary school.

"Well, here's my card. And feel free to call me anytime for that drink . . . I owe you one."

"I'll hold you to that," Freddie said with a grin and walked out. This was without a doubt his lucky day. But he wouldn't blow it by calling too soon. He knew what to do in this situation—arrange for another "accidental" meeting. To reel in rich prey, he was going to go slowly, one step at a time. "Now," he mused aloud, "I got to find myself a good, cheap camera."

6

Morgan and Lisa spent the entire morning putting finishing touches on Caché's new office. It had been painted a deep, warm butterscotch and the trim, moldings, and ceiling medallion were accented with a glossy cream. Their crescent-shaped desks were highly polished mahogany, and each was placed under a recessed light, in the corners opposite the window. The sofa, covered in brown brocade, along with matching chairs, was put opposite the desks under the five-panel window. In the room's center, directly under an art deco light fixture, sat the marble foyer table from Connecticut holding a graceful human-form abstract, carved from Shona stone.

As the operations manager for Caché, Lisa was responsible for the tactical-level execution of all event plans. She'd previously served as the personal assistant to Juan DeVille, one of New York's premier chefs. So she came with a well-stocked Rolodex of chefs, waiters, and floral and set designers. And what she lacked in sophistication she made up for in ambition and scrupulous attention to detail.

Morgan had been understandably nervous about bringing someone else into Caché in light of Tyrone's trickery. Not only did she call every reference twice, she put feelers out to the "black, read, and write club," an unofficial network of educated black people with often only three degrees of separation between any two of them. When those efforts yielded nothing suspicious, she hired a private detective. She'd learned that Lisa had Justin in her early twenties and with no husband or support had worked hard to care for the boy, raising him virtually alone with the help of her elderly grandmother who sat with him after preschool. Morgan admired her for that, and worked out flex-hours for Lisa so that she could be home with Justin on the afternoons when she had a party to work in the evening.

Her only flaw was a touch of moodiness. Most days she was as chipper as a head cheerleader, but at times you'd think that someone had moved her cheese. Morgan attributed her mood swings to the stresses of being a single mother. And as long as it didn't affect customers and business, it was a small price to pay for her efficiency.

Over the last month, Morgan began to trust Lisa to tend to crucial details that could make or break the company. During Fashion Week, at a small cocktail party for a couture designer, Lisa discovered slight but noticeable smudges on the crystal stemware during her pre-event check. While the client looked on, she had the staff hand-wash and -dry all four hundred glasses, helping to spread Caché's reputation for uncompromising excellence.

After moving furniture about all morning, Morgan suddenly felt a wave of light-headedness, causing her to grab the desktop for balance.

"Are you okay?" Lisa asked, quickly at her side.

Blinking rapidly, Morgan answered, "Yeah, I'm fine," though she held steadfastly to the desk.

"You don't look so good," Lisa said, frowning as she cut her eyes at Morgan.

"Oh, gee, thanks," Morgan replied sarcastically.

"No, I don't mean it like that. It's just that your color is a little blotchy."

"It's probably from moving all of this furniture and the files," she said, dismissing the wave of nausea that had just rolled past.

"Are you sure?" Lisa grabbed Morgan's hand and led her to the sofa.

"I'm positive." But before Morgan could sit down, she was forced to make a mad dash for the bathroom to save the beautiful Tibetan rug they had just laid down.

Tentatively tapping on the door, Lisa called out, "Morgan? Morgan? Are you okay?"

Through the door she heard a weak, "Never better." Finally opening it, Morgan looked like she'd run a marathon without proper training. She walked gingerly back toward her desk chair. "I don't know what's wrong with me."

"Listen, honey, I'm no doctor, but have you considered that you might be pregnant?" she asked.

"Pregnant?"

"Yeah. You know, it's the thing that happens sometimes when opposite sexes do the . . . you know."

"Pregnant?" Although she and Miles had agreed last year to start a family, the fact that they might have succeeded never occurred to her. But with her hectic schedule of parties, renovations, and moving, it was no wonder.

"Lately you've been eating like a refugee, and now you're light-headed and throwing up. Seems pretty obvious to me," Lisa proclaimed.

"Pregnant?" Morgan was still taken aback by the idea. As a nebulous notion pregnancy was one thing, but the idea of actually harboring life was quite another.

"Yeah. You know, it's the only time when one plus one equals three."

"Wow!" was all Morgan could say. She felt dazed. "Wow, pregnant."

Later Morgan felt like the cat who'd swallowed the canary, only it was staying for nine months. Unable to hold the secret a moment longer, she picked up the phone to call Dakota. "You feel like some shopping this weekend?" she asked casually.

"Girl, that's like asking a fish if it wants a swim. Of course I do. Where?"

"I was thinking about Veronique or maybe Liz Lange."

"What?" Dakota had been expecting Morgan to suggest a jaunt to Woodbury Commons. "Why would we go there?

Don't they sell maternity clo—" Before the word found its way out of her mouth, the implications had materialized in her brain. "Aahhhhh!" she screamed. Morgan could hear the ruckus as Dakota jumped up and down in her loft apartment, delighted for her best friend. When she finally calmed down, she fired off a series of questions: "When did you find out? Have you told Miles? What did he say? How far along are you?" All in one breath.

After Morgan stopped laughing, she answered, "This afternoon. No. So he hasn't said anything. And about six weeks."

"Wow!" Now Dakota was speechless.

When Miles walked through the door of their posh East Side apartment, he was surprised to smell the aroma coming from the kitchen. Morgan had many talents, but cooking wasn't one of them. Besides, with their schedules, when their housekeeper didn't double as cook, eating out or ordering in was always more convenient.

"Morgan?" No answer. "Morgan?" He followed his nose through the foyer, around a curved hallway, past the living room. Every recessed light was out, so the only source of illumination sparkled off the East River and danced into the apartment through the wall of windows. Making his way toward the formal dining room, Miles began to feel as though he'd stumbled into the wrong apartment. But it was their dining room, only it was lit with a dozen candles. They were on the table, on the buffet, and all across the expansive windowsill. And there sat Morgan shining brighter than all of them combined.

Miles expectantly set down his Prada briefcase. "So what's the occasion?"

"Does there have to be a reason?" Morgan asked coyly as she removed his coat and strolled to the hall closet. Her silk kimono was slit thigh-high along each side, so the back panel swayed seductively.

"Well, no . . ." he answered. Pulling out Morgan's chair, he noticed a third place setting. "Who's joining us?" he asked, disappointed that it wasn't the intimate dinner for two he had envisioned.

"Our guest is already here," Morgan said, bursting to tell Miles her exciting news.

"Where?" Miles asked, looking around. He was now sure that he'd entered the twilight zone. Either that or Morgan had been working *way* too hard. "I don't see anyone."

"That's because he, or she, is in here," Morgan said, smiling broadly as she rubbed her still flat stomach.

Miles was as confused as Morgan had been earlier that day. "There . . . ? A . . . a . . . baby?" he managed to stammer.

"Yes, a baby," Morgan said, enjoying his response.

"You're pregnant?"

"Yes, we're having a baby! Baby," Morgan said, standing to hug Miles and to steady him, since he looked light-headed.

"Wow!" Miles said, repeating what seemed to be the word of the day.

While they ate dinner, the nursery was decorated, names were debated, an Ivy League school chosen, and careers considered. They were both so giddy from the notion of a child that neither had much of an appetite.

When she stood to clear the dishes, Miles bounced from his seat. "What are you doing?" he asked, alarmed.

"I'm clearing the table," Morgan answered, puzzled.

"You're pregnant. You shouldn't be lifting anything," he insisted.

"Miles, I don't think a serving platter constitutes heavy lifting. Remember, I'm pregnant, not sick. Women have been having babies for centuries. It happens every day."

"Yeah, but they weren't having *my* baby." Sticking his chest out, Miles boasted, "I knew one of my backstroking little spermozoids would make it to the Promised Land."

"Okay, Mandingo," she said, sticking the plate into his hands. "Why don't you help me put away the dishes and maybe you too can visit the Land of Milk and Honey?" she added seductively.

Pulling her close, Miles kissed her so tenderly that she first thought she had imagined the sensation. It wasn't until his warm tongue began its probing that Morgan knew the dishes would have to wait for later. They blew out the candles and made their way through the darkness upstairs to the bedroom. Once they reached the master suite, also lit by flickering candlelight, Morgan felt consumed by a deep, spiritual love that seemed to burn more intensely with the knowledge of their growing child. As she savored the comfort of Miles' protective embrace, she could hear his heart's strong, steady beat. Closing her eyes, she imagined the beating heart of the new life they'd created. Reaching up to cup his face, she pulled Miles close to taste him, picking up where they left off downstairs. Not breaking away, she removed his necktie and began unbuttoning his shirt. As she released each button, her passion grew. She planted wet kisses that trailed her busy fingers, leading to Miles' belt, which she made quick work of unfastening.

"Let me," he whispered softly before probing her ear with his tongue. He led her to the California king-sized bed, where he tugged at the sash of her olive kimono, opening it like a cherished present that had been wrapped in the most exquisite paper with the silkiest satin ribbons. As he finished undressing, Miles stood over Morgan, looking down at her with a reverence for the life that she now carried.

It was his turn to shower her with kisses, and he made it a downpour. He covered every inch of her smooth, succulent body, slowing his course only to pay homage to Morgan's full and even more sensitive breasts.

She moaned, enjoying every breath and lick. Every sensation traveled from her nipples to her groin. His tongue was a lightning rod, bringing intense pleasure.

In no hurry, he made slow and sensual love to Morgan. Not the intense, forceful blur that accompanied their sex on nights when they were driven as much by lust as by love. No, tonight he gave her all of himself—heart, body, and soul—leading them both down a winding stream and over a beautiful fall.

As they lay holding each other after the waves of pleasure had passed, Morgan closed her eyes and dreamed of pink-and-blue skies.

7

Dakota leaned back on the four-foot-long leather headboard of her bed and decided to languish there for another twenty minutes, since it was only ten and she wasn't meeting Morgan and Miles until eleven. Those two were getting a head start on baby shopping and were probably already at ABC Carpet & Home buying the entire infant department. Dakota rubbed her flat belly and felt a twinge of melancholy. She was overjoyed for her friends, but at the same time she wished she could be nurturing the seed of the man she loved. There was only one problem—there wasn't a man in the picture, on the canvas, or anywhere on the horizon. She pulled the covers over her head. "What the hell is wrong with me?" she mumbled. She decided to ask herself two of Dr. Phil's questions she remembered from seeing him on Oprah: "What's working in my life?" She thought about it for a moment, then peeked her head out of the covers, looked around her beautiful bedroom, and said aloud, "My career." The second question, "What's not working in my life?" was a bit tougher to face. Dakota thought long and hard. She wanted to be real with herself. "My inability to find a man I can trust and who will love me unconditionally. Obviously I keep choosing the wrong guy." She felt tears beginning to form as she shouted into the empty apartment, "What the hell is wrong with me?"

Suddenly the phone rang, jolting her from her pity party. "Hello," she said, trying to disguise the tears in her voice.

"Are you still asleep?" Morgan asked.

"Just groggy. I dozed off," Dakota lied. She didn't want to be the cloud that darkened Morgan's day.

"Aren't you meeting us for brunch at Odeon?"

"Yeah," she said, looking over at the clock. "Oh, shit," she said.

"What?" Morgan asked, alarmed.

"It's already ten-thirty. Aren't we supposed to meet at eleven?"

"Well, I was calling to tell you to make it twelve, because Miles and I are still at ABC. Girl, you wouldn't believe their selection!" ABC Carpet & Home was one of New York's most fabulous home-furnishing stores. Actually, it was more than a furniture store—it was more like a smorgasbord for the rich and famous, selling not only high-end furniture, but also ornate chandeliers, imported rugs, fine linen, designer jewelry, and unique clothes for women and children.

"Okay, let me run, I'll see you later," Dakota said, throwing back the damask comforter and jumping out of bed. She decided that if she hurried she'd have just enough time to pick up something for the baby. Shopping always put a smile on her face. She showered in record time, ran into the large walk-in closet, and threw on a black sleeveless turtleneck, jeans, and black Tods with the matching shoulder bag.

With her somber mood behind her, she hurried over to the South Street Seaport Mall. It was basically a tourist trap, but it was nearby and would serve the purpose for today. She found Baby Gap on the directory and went in. Dakota quickly browsed through the adorable baby clothes, frowning. She wanted something more striking than a dainty little yellow jumper, booties, or receiving blanket. So she decided to look at the clothes for toddlers. "Oh, isn't this the cutest thing?" she said, holding up a miniature tan-and-black leather bomber jacket. It had BABY BOMBER written in small block letters on the back.

"Do you have a gift box?" she asked the salesclerk.

"We sure do," said the perky teenager.

Dakota paid for the jacket and rushed outside to look for a taxi. Fortunately, there was one cruising by. She flagged him down and hopped in the backseat.

"West Broadway and Duane," Dakota instructed. She was glad they had decided to meet in Tribeca, which was only a ten-minute cab ride from the Seaport. In no time the taxi let her out in front of Odeon, a restaurant famous for its brunch.

"Table for one?" the hostess asked.

"No, I'm meeting friends," Dakota said, scanning the room for Morgan and Miles. "Oh, there they are." They were sitting near the back wall, looking over the menu. Pink multi-colored ABC shopping bags were spilling over onto the chairs that belonged to the adjoining table.

Miles stood up to give Dakota a hug. "Hey, D, how you doing? Let me move some of these bags."

Dakota surveyed the collection and began to laugh. "So tell me, what didn't you buy? Does ABC still have a kids department left?"

"Girl, you've got to see this," Morgan said, reaching into a bag. She took out an ivory sleeper with lace trimming.

"Wow, that's beautiful," Dakota said, touching the fabric. "It feels like imported cotton. I tell you, your baby is going to be the best-dressed kid in town."

"We just couldn't resist," Morgan gushed.

Dakota's friends were beaming with joy. A special joy that could only come with the anticipation of a firstborn child. "Well, I couldn't resist either," she said, handing Morgan the shopping bag from the Gap.

"What's this?" Morgan said, opening the box. "This is too cute! Look, Miles."

"Oh, wow. His first leather jacket. Thanks, D."

Morgan gave her husband the eye. "Who said we're having a boy?"

He smoothed away the look with a kiss. "A guy can hope, can't he?"

During brunch the three talked about everything from nannies to nursery schools. About the pros and cons of raising a child in Manhattan versus the virtues of living in the suburbs of Long Island or Westchester or New Jersey. They were waiting for coffee when Miles spotted a familiar face at the bar. "Hey, there's Phillip," he said, and motioned him over.

"Hey, man, what's up?" Phillip said, giving Miles some dap. He leaned down and kissed Morgan on the cheek.

"Are you here alone?" she asked.

"No, I'm waiting for Paula." He looked at his watch. "I tell you, if she were ever on time, it'd be a news flash," he chuckled.

"Well, have a seat while you wait," Miles said, clearing more space. "Phillip, this is our good friend Dakota Cantrell."

Phillip shook Dakota's hand. "Pleased to meet you."

"Likewise," Dakota said, checking him out. There was a lot to see. He was a cross between Denzel and Taye Diggs. He wore faded jeans, a long-sleeved T-shirt, Timberlands, and a Brooklyn Dodger's baseball cap. He was handsome in a sexy-rugged kind of way.

"How do you two know each other?" Dakota asked.

"Phillip is my V.P. of Marketing," Miles explained.

"When I came aboard I was a little green, and my man Miles gave me the rundown on the infrastructure. He taught me who to schmooze and who to lose," Phillip laughed.

"Stop already," Miles blushed. "So did I hear you're going on the road with N2Deep?"

"Not sure. Paula and I are supposed to be on vacation that week. That is, if she can break away from the office." He chuckled again, but Dakota couldn't help noticing the hurt or annoyance that flickered in his eyes. This Paula must be some kind of fool, she thought.

Miles and Phillip began to talk shop, which gave Morgan and Dakota a chance to chat. Dakota hadn't seen Morgan since the fund-raiser at the Studio Museum. Morgan wasn't showing yet, but had that undeniable glow of a mother-to-be.

"Girl, I thought you had a stomach flu that night," Dakota said.

"I know. Even though Miles and I had been trying, it took me by surprise. You know the stories you hear about a couple trying for years and nothing. I didn't think we were exactly candidates for the fertility clinic, but I didn't think it'd happen this soon."

Dakota picked up her mimosa and saluted her. "Congratulations again, Morgan. I know you're going to make a great mother."

"Thanks, and you're going to make the perfect godmother," Morgan said, hugging her.

As they were embracing Dakota heard a loud female voice talking on a cell phone. It was coming closer. "No, I didn't approve the contract. It has too many loopholes. . . . Yes, loopholes that are in your favor. . . . No, no . . . Look, I can't . . ."

Dakota looked at the woman, who was now standing beside their table. She had long wavy dark hair curled in a loose flip, dark piercing brown eyes, and a small pouty mouth. She looked rather like some intense little animal, maybe a mongoose. Dakota was ready to ask her to tone it down a notch when Phillip stood up and kissed the loud woman. She mouthed the words, "I'll just be a second," and turned away from him to finish her conversation.

"Sorry, I'm late, honey," she said, finally putting her phone away. "Harvey called just as I was about to walk out, and I have to tie up this contract before I even *think* about going on vacation."

"What else is new?" Phillip said quietly. "Paula, this is Dakota, a friend of Miles and Morgan's."

"Hi," Paula said abruptly, then turned her attention to Morgan. "Girl, congratulations. Phillip told me you were pregnant. I couldn't even *imagine* being pregnant now. How are you going to work and have a baby?" She didn't give Morgan a chance to answer, but just kept on talking. "Girl, with my schedule I barely have time for a relationship. Do you know how *draining* babies are? And not just on your time and energy, but the *expense*!"

Phillip didn't say anything, but Paula read the look and said, "Aw, baby, you know I love you. We'll have kids someday." She brushed his cheek with a kiss and he seemed content. "Let's go to our table. I'm starving."

"It was nice meeting you, Dakota. I'll see you guys later." As Phillip led Paula toward the hostess stand her cell rang, and she began her loud talking once again.

Watching Paula handle her business while ignoring Phillip, Dakota thought, As crass as she is, I'm surprised she even *has* a man. And for the third time that day she wondered what the hell was wrong with her.

8

Since Miles' troubling conversation with Cee-Cee several weeks earlier, he had been on the line constantly, strung between Ecstasy's attorney and his own legal department. The issue had to be resolved since commitments had been made to sponsors who wouldn't think twice about suing Sound Entertainment if the concert tour was canceled. In addition, such a public blunder would do little to instill confidence in his superiors.

As he sat mulling over the sticky situation, he was interrupted by Lauren. "Miles, Rick's on line one." Rick was the head of the sales department. He was more than likely calling to complain about either the promotion or publicity departments. Both, he felt, failed to keep him adequately apprised of their projections, causing him undue hardship. Sometimes Miles felt like he ran a nursery instead of a three-hundred-million-dollar record label. "Put him through." Bracing for more drama, Miles said, "Rick, what's up?"

"Miles, you're not going to believe this."

"What are you talking about?" Miles asked, impatiently leaning back in his chair.

"I just got the latest report from RIAA, and Ecstasy's single has gone platinum! And in record time!"

"Platinum! Yesssss!" Miles screamed, jumping from his

chair. He pulled his fist aggressively to his side, pumping it like a testosterone-driven athlete after a victory.

"Miles, this is tremendous. And the next two singles as well as the album are also clipping along at an unbelievable rate," exclaimed the near breathless Rick.

"Rick, this is great news. Keep me posted."

As Miles hung up, Lauren peeked into the office, drawn by his scream. "Are you okay?" she asked, not sure whether it was good news or bad.

"I am more than okay, I'm king of the world!" Miles said, imitating Leonardo DiCaprio, with arms spread at the bow of the *Titanic*.

"I know that," Lauren teased, "but what's all the excitement about?"

"Ecstasy's single went *platinum*!"

Having seen the project from its inception, when Miles was the head of Marketing, Lauren had a complete appreciation for what it had taken to get the group to this level. "Congratulations!" she said, giving Miles a big hug.

"*God*, this is great. I couldn't be happier," Miles said. Maybe all of the drama he endured was worth it after all.

"In that case, this is probably a good time for me to ask you for a favor," Lauren said cheekily.

"Shoot." Lauren was so efficient, loyal, and reliable that anytime would be okay for her to ask for a favor, especially since she rarely did.

"My son is in his school's play tonight. So can I leave early, say about five-thirty?" Lauren was a single mom who took care of business at home and at work. With the help of her mother she held down a demanding job, and sent her son to a private school. Miles admired and respected her determination.

"No problem. In fact, why don't you cut out around four-thirty? I have that four o'clock meeting, and after that, it's reports and paperwork. You can catch up tomorrow."

"Thanks, Miles."

"Don't mention it." Lauren was usually in the office well

past seven o'clock, the official closing hour. She sometimes stayed even later than Miles, who almost never left before eight-thirty. So letting her go early was a no-brainer.

Just before four o'clock, Lauren announced Vic's arrival. Miles was anxious to discuss a resolution to the Cee-Cee situation and hoped that with Corporate's backing all could be worked out.

As Miles stood to greet her, she surprised him by reaching one arm around his waist for a hug. Miles understood why, when champagne materialized from behind her back. "I think congratulations are in order," she said. "I just heard on my way over that Ecstasy's gone platinum, so I ran out to grab champagne to celebrate!"

Vic was all smiles and curves. If Miles had to guess, he'd say she was about 38-25-39. Her development went beyond the brick house straight to multidwelling status.

"How thoughtful," Miles managed. "Let me have Lauren put that on ice."

"Actually, it's freshly chilled. So why don't we start our meeting with a toast?" she suggested.

Miles grinned as she removed two champagne flutes from her Marc Jacobs satchel. "Someone's prepared," he said.

"In my previous life, I was a girl scout." Vic smiled in return, giving Miles the full benefit of Chiclets-perfect teeth. She expertly uncorked the bottle of Dom Pérignon with immaculately manicured hands. Her long red nails were in stark contrast to the natural, closely cut, and buffed manicure that Morgan wore. Though Vic was a traffic stopper, she really wasn't Miles' type, for he had always preferred a more elegant, exotic beauty. Even so, he could definitely appreciate Vic's charms.

She deftly poured two sparkling glasses of champagne. Handing one to Miles, she fixed him with her light green eyes and said, "To Ecstasy."

Miles was momentarily caught off guard. He hesitated for a beat, before realizing that she was referring to the group— not the sensation. He joined her in the toast. "To Ecstasy. May the success continue."

After taking the first sip, he decided to use the pretext to segue into the point of today's meeting. "Vic, speaking of continued success, I'd like to make one thing clear. My goal is not to celebrate one platinum single and a national tour. Although that's great, I plan to make the girls superstars, the next coming of Madonna." Looking at her in all seriousness, Miles continued. "Right now Ecstasy's at a critical juncture in their career. 'Name That Thang,' though a great record, does have a novelty element to its success. So unless it is followed by solid hits, which is in part a by-product of good marketing and promotion, they could easily instead be the next one-hit wonder."

"You're right, Miles," Vic said, her demeanor transforming from party girl to executive in record time.

"I'm glad we're on the same page," Miles said, now ready to plow down the row he'd just prepared. "So to that end, I view every dollar spent as an investment in their future, and future sales. And honestly, I can think of much more lucrative ways to spend a quarter of a million dollars than on increasing the girls' entourage. In fact, based on past promotion-to-sales ratios, for every dollar spent on promo or marketing, the return is quadrupled."

"Interesting," Vic said, leaning toward him. As she did, Miles could not help noticing the way her ample frontage strained mightily against the thin silk fabric of her V-neck sweater.

Bravely ignoring it, he continued. "On the other hand, I also understand the girls' need to have the support and encouragement of their friends. So I propose we both put aside the fine-tooth combs and contracts and consider a compromise."

"I'm all ears," Vic said, settling back into the deep recesses of the sofa, her large breasts now propped high on her chest.

"What I propose, in lieu of spending a quarter of a mil to have twelve 'friends' traipse across the country, is to have Corporate chip in to finance a splashy celebration party once the tour reaches New York. That way the girls get to floss for their friends, who we can give the VIP treatment, and we all

benefit from the press surrounding such a large-scale event."
Caught up in the idea, Miles said, "Consider this. By spending
a quarter of a million dollars on this type of advertising, we
could generate approximately 1.2 million dollars in additional
sales."

"That's an interesting compromise," Vic admitted.

"To put it in even more simple terms, ask the girls if they
would rather travel through a grueling tour with three
'friends,' or make an extra three hundred thousand dollars
each," Miles offered, holding up both palms, as if to say, *Case
closed*.

"Good point," Vic concurred.

Miles smiled. Though his argument was sound and certainly seemed fair, truth be told, he had already padded the
advertising budget for such a party in the event the girls did
go platinum. But of course Vic didn't know this, and Cee-Cee
and the girls probably couldn't even spell budget.

Putting the final piece in place, Miles said, "Since Cee-Cee
is not hearing a word I'm saying, why don't you set up an ap-
pointment to pitch the idea to him?"

"Not a problem. I'll call him first thing in the morning."

"That's great. Now that leaves us with only about sixteen
other things to discuss."

After another couple hours and several glasses of bubbly,
they were both settled into the soft recesses of the couch. Vic,
relaxed, had removed her Blahniks to tuck her feet underneath
her, and Miles loosened his tie as they continued to sort out
the remaining issues.

They were both so mellow and involved in conversation
that neither of them saw nor heard Morgan open the door to
Miles' office. Knowing that he was working late, she had
planned to surprise him by bringing in takeout for dinner.
With Lauren missing from her desk and light clearly coming
from under the door, she headed in. She found Miles leaning
into a voluptuous light-skinned, green-eyed woman, both
with champagne glasses in hand. "Excuse *me*," Morgan said,
after the initial shock wore off.

Also surprised, Miles jumped from the sofa, nearly knocking the champagne bottle from the table. "Morgan! Hi, baby, what are you doing here?" he said, making his way across the room to her.

"I'd planned to bring dinner for you, but I see that you have company," she said evenly, her eyes shifting from Miles to Vic, who was attempting to slide covertly back into her heels.

"No! In fact, we—we were just finishing up," Miles stammered as he glanced back at the scene from Morgan's doorway point of view: sexy woman in tight sweater, empty bottle of champagne for two, and bare feet. Not a pretty picture. Trying to repaint the situation, he said, "Morgan, this is Vic, corporate V.P. of A and R. Vic, this is my wife, Morgan."

Shoes on now, Vic stood and walked over to shake Morgan's hand. "Hi, Morgan, it's a pleasure to meet you."

"Likewise," was all that Morgan said as she fumed inwardly. She had thought that Vic was a man, since Miles had never said anything to make her think otherwise.

Turning to Vic, Miles said, "Vic, I think we have most of the main points covered. I'll have Dave in legal draw up an addendum to the contract that spells out the terms we discussed."

"Great. I'll look forward to getting the draft," Vic said as she turned to retrieve her jacket and satchel.

"I'll leave a message for him to call you first thing," Miles said.

"Okay. See you later and congratulations again." Walking past Morgan and Miles, she proceeded down the hall. Her well-endowed bottom swayed back and forth, sending a message of its own.

"What was that all about?" Morgan asked, her arms folded tightly across her chest.

Miles had started gathering his things. Without pausing he said, "Nothing."

"So I find a woman, shoes off, on my husband's couch sipping champagne, and you tell me it's nothing?" The edge in her voice made it clear that to her it was a lot more than nothing.

"Vic heard about Ecstasy's album going platinum on the way over for our meeting and picked up a bottle to celebrate. It happens all the time."

"Why didn't you tell me that Vic was a woman?"

"Since when have we discussed the gender of my staff and coworkers?" The best defense was always a good offense.

"Maybe we should start now if private evening chats over champagne are in the plans," she shot back.

"Morgan, you're overreacting."

"I hope so," she said, fixing him with a stern gaze, "because I'd hate to think that now that I'm pregnant you've already started looking at other women."

"Don't be silly," Miles said, reaching out to hug Morgan.

"Trust me. There's nothing silly about this." She dislodged herself from his embrace and headed out the door.

9

Dakota could feel her stomach flutter as the plane descended over the skies of Chicago. A while after the pilot released the landing gear, she felt a thump indicating a successful touchdown. Looking out the window at the familiar surroundings of O'Hare Airport, she realized her discomfort had nothing to do with the flight, but instead with the phone call that preceded it.

She had been well into the trading day when Patricia, her cousin who lived with their grandmother in Chicago, phoned. Tricia, as she preferred to be called, had moved in with Nana when she decided to enroll in cosmetology school, giving up her tiny apartment and her day job at Target.

"Hey, Kota, you busy?"

"What's up?" Dakota asked, with a bit of an edge. She was always suspicious when Tricia called, because nine times out of ten she wanted something.

"Don't worry. I don't want nothing," Tricia answered. "It's Nana."

Alarmed, Dakota sat up in her chair, tossing aside the trading tickets that moments before had consumed all her attention. "What's wrong?"

"She in the hospital," Tricia said matter-of-factly.

"What happened? Is she going to be okay? What is the doctor saying?"

"Damn, give me a chance to answer the first question first," Tricia said, making a *tsk* sound.

Exasperated, Dakota looked up toward the ceiling. When was the bickering ever to stop? "Look, this has nothing to do with you and me. It's about Nana."

Their feud had started the day, so long ago, when Dakota moved in with Nana. She was in grade school when her parents' car was sideswiped by a semitruck and they were killed instantly. Tricia was jealous because of the one-on-one attention Dakota had gotten from their grandmother, something Dakota never understood. She would've preferred to have been raised by her parents—not to slight Nana, who stepped in and became both mother and father. Dakota in return despised Tricia's work ethic or, more accurately, lack of one. She never kept a job longer than six months, and expected the family to fund one cockamamie fantasy after the other. Her latest pipe dream was going to cosmetology school so that she could open her own beauty shop. On the surface, the goal seemed fine. The only problem was, Tricia had no plan—no start-up capital, no client base, and no prior experience in operating a business. But that was the norm for her, free-falling without a parachute.

"Look, she in Mercy. Why don't you call and give *them* the damn third degree?" Tricia hissed.

"I'll do that," Dakota said, and slammed down the receiver. She counted to twenty, picked up the phone, and instead called her travel agent to book a seat on the next available flight to Chicago.

When Dakota deplaned, she thought about renting a car, but didn't want to waste time at a rental agency. Instead, she hailed a taxi outside baggage claim. In New York she usually took a taxi or car service to and from the airport. But in Chicago either family or friends had always played the role of chauffeur. Arriving solo had never bothered her before. But as Dakota stood in the taxi queue she watched people greet each other with bear hugs and kisses and she realized how alone she actually was.

On the way to Mercy Hospital, which was about ten miles

south of downtown, Dakota noticed some changes in her old hometown. Gone were the once-dilapidated buildings on Taylor Street, replaced with three-hundred-thousand-dollar town houses. The area surrounding the hospital had once been a warehouse district, but now the warehouses were converted lofts. Everyone had woken up and realized how boring the suburbs were, Dakota thought with some dismay.

Once the taxi pulled up in front of the hospital, she hurried out and rushed through the revolving doors and made a beeline to the information desk. "I need a pass to see Anna Mae Cantrell," she said, nervously tapping her nails on the counter.

The information attendant slowly typed the name into her computer, then used her index finger to scan for Nana's name. "She's in room seven-ten, bed B," she said at last, handing Dakota a laminated yellow day pass.

On her way to the bank of elevators, she walked past an eight-foot-high marble statue of the Virgin Mary, one of the many religious icons left over from when the hospital was run by an order of nuns. Seeing it, Dakota whispered a silent prayer. When the doors opened onto the seventh floor, two orderlies in puke-green scrubs rushed a patient into the elevator, hemming her into a corner. Startled, she looked down at the semiconscious person lying on the gurney and could feel her face turning the color of those scrubs. Hospitals always made her nauseous. Dakota hit the button marked OPEN DOOR and escaped before losing her lunch. She walked past the nurse's station and down the hall toward 710. When she reached the room, Nana was lying flat on her back, hooked up to IVs and a heart monitor. At the grim sight Dakota was suddenly paralyzed with fear. She stood in the doorway for a few seconds, unsure of what to do.

Finally she called out softly, "Nana." No response. She called again, this time a little louder, "Nana." Still no response. Her heart skipped a beat as she hesitantly tiptoed over to the bed. When she looked closely, though, she realized Nana was merely asleep. Breathing a sigh of relief, Dakota sank into a chair near the window to wait. Soon the blue waters of Lake Michigan outside attracted her attention. The lake was like an ever-changing chameleon: steel-gray and stormy one day, smooth as glass with a tropical blue-green glow the next. Dakota remembered summers at the beach playing Marco Polo in the water with her friends and picnicking on the sand. Chicago had the best beachfront of any major city except of course Los Angeles. Dakota looked out over the water and felt it calming her. Before long she had drifted into a doze.

"Kota. Baby, what you doing here?"

She heard the faint voice through her sleep, jumped up, and rushed to Nana's side. "How you feeling?" Dakota asked, touching her grandmother's forehead for signs of a fever.

"Nothing for you to worry about. Like I said before, what you doing here?"

"Tricia told me you were in the hospital. Thought I better come and see for myself exactly what's going on."

"And what do you mean by that, Ms. Smarty Pants?" Nana's voice was hoarse.

Dakota turned to the nightstand, poured a cup of water from the plastic pitcher, and handed it to her. "Well, we both know you have a habit of leaving out details when it comes to your health."

Nana slowly drank the water, cleared her throat, and said, "Since when did you become my momma?"

"Who else is going to take care of you?" Dakota joked, trying to lighten the mood.

"Tricia is here," she said matter-of-factly.

Dakota's lighthearted tone soured in a flash. "Oh, like she's responsible."

"You need to give her a break. She been doing really good in that there hair school."

"That's her problem. She's always getting a break." Dakota saw a pained look cross Nana's face. She didn't need to hear this. "Look, I didn't come here to talk about Tricia. Why are you in the hospital? What did the doctor say?" Before Nana could answer, Dakota added, "And tell me everything."

Nana sighed. She knew her granddaughter's impatience all too well. "Well, I was in the kitchen cooking, and all of a sudden I started seeing these little black dots. At first it was just a couple. Then it seemed like they was everywhere. The next thing I knew, I had passed out. Tricia found me on the floor and called the paramedics."

Dakota could feel tears welling up in her eyes. She couldn't bear the thought of her grandmother passed out on the floor. Nana was her rock. Dakota's mind began to reel with horrifying scenarios. What if Nana was seriously ill? What if she had some dreaded disease?

Nana looked up and saw Dakota's distress. "Now don't start no crying. I'm going to be just fine."

"If you came here to punk out, you could've stayed in New York."

Dakota swung at the new voice coming from behind her. Tricia was her first cousin, but they looked more like sisters. They had the same almond-shaped eyes and the same sun-kissed cocoa complexion. Tricia was taller by two inches and wore her thick hair past her shoulders. Tricia prided herself on being different from Dakota, which explained why she took on the around-the-way-girl persona.

Still sniffling, Dakota said, "This is between me and Nana."

"You've always wanted it just between you and Nana," Tricia said, mocking Dakota's highbrow tone. She tossed her fake Prada knapsack on an empty chair and continued. "But I'm on the scene now, and I gots everythang under control."

"Since when did you have *anything* under control? I'm the one who—"

Tricia butted in. "*I'm* the one who called the paramedics, when you was out hobnobbing with your uppity-ass friends."

"Okay, watch your mouth," Nana warned.

Tricia walked over to the other side of Nana's bed. "Sorry 'bout the cussing, but she pisses me off, coming in here power-tripping."

Wearily Nana picked up the remote and pressed a button, raising the back of the bed. She took another sip of water then cleared her throat again. "I want y'all to listen real good, 'cause I'm only going to say this once—stop the bickering. I'm not always going to be around to keep the peace between you two."

Dakota and Tricia, standing on opposite sides of the bed, glared at each other, but both held back from firing off accusations. Lying between them, looking old and frail in a hospital bed, was their grandmother, pleading for them to come together.

Looking squarely at her cousin, Dakota spoke first. "Tricia, I'm more than willing to call a truce, if you are."

Tricia shifted her weight from one leg to the other, and rolled her eyes toward the ceiling as if pondering the proposition.

Trying to seal the deal, Dakota added, "After all we are family."

"Yeah, al'ight," Tricia said, finally conceding.

"Mrs. Cantrell," a doctor said briskly as he entered the room, breaking the tension between the two cousins.

"Yes?"

"Your EKG came back normal."

"Praise the Lord," Nana said.

"But we want to run a few more tests."

"What kind of tests?" Dakota asked sharply.

"Excuse her, Doctor. This is my granddaughter from Manhattan," Nana said, as if that explained Dakota's abruptness.

"I'm concerned about my grandmother."

"It's just routine," the doctor said vaguely.

"I don't mean to be rude, but you're really not telling us much."

"We're going to run a liver-enzyme test and an ultrasound," the doctor mumbled, consulting the chart. Finally, he seemed to focus on who he was talking to. "Well, visiting hours are just about over. We should let Mrs. Cantrell get some rest."

Dakota wasn't going to be brushed off like that, but Nana said, "That's right. Y'all go on home. I'll see you tomorrow."

Dakota bent down to give her a kiss. "I'll be here first thing in the morning."

"No need to rush. I'm not going anywhere," Nana chuckled.

"Good night, Nana," Tricia said, getting her kiss in too.

Dakota and Tricia went down the elevator and walked to the parking lot in silence. Since they were little girls Nana had always been the buffer between them. Now that they were left to their own devices, there didn't seem to be any urgency to fight.

"Where are you parked?" Dakota asked.

"Over there," she said, pointing to the back of the parking lot.

When they reached Tricia's orange '78 Opal, Dakota said, "I didn't know you still had this car."

"Sorry it's not up to your standards," Tricia snapped.

"That's not what I meant," Dakota apologized.

"Whatever."

"All I meant was it still looks good," Dakota said, trying to keep the peace.

"It runs good too—that is, when it's not in the shop."

They both laughed. Well, Dakota said to herself, at least this is a start.

10

"Morgan, Yvette from Vanity Media's on line one," Lisa said, after depressing the HOLD button.

"Regarding?" Morgan hated picking up a call cold, especially when she had an assistant who was supposed to buffer and sort through them. She felt it was a direct reflection of status to have an assistant who manned the gate. Even if there was only one person behind it. Over the past several months, Lisa's judgment about what to handle herself and what to give to Morgan seemed to be oddly less and less reliable.

"I don't know." Lisa never looked up from the papers on her desk.

"Do you mind finding out?" Morgan snapped. It was the weirdest thing, she thought. Earlier that morning Lisa had bounced into the office like an elf on Christmas Eve, all perky and helpful. But after getting a mysterious phone call, which she practically whispered through, she turned into Scrooge. Not that she was rude, just not on the ball.

"She said Ken wants to schedule the meeting that you two discussed last week."

Morgan had run into Ken Ridley at the Essence Awards the previous week. He was the CEO of Vanity Media, which owned several urban magazines.

"You've got my calendar. Book it."

One thing that Lisa didn't seem to understand was that, even though it was a two-person operation, there were certain conversations that Morgan didn't need to have. And setting up a meeting with Ken's assistant was one of them.

Lisa put the phone back to her ear and depressed the HOLD button for the second time. "Hi, Yvette, I've got Morgan's schedule right here. What time works for Mr. Ridley?" After running through the few options on his hectic calendar, they set a date. "You're on for dinner, at seven-thirty. Where should I book the reservation?" she asked Morgan, who was scanning the current issue of *Bon Appétit* for interesting menu combinations.

"Call Frank at Il Cantanori. The food is great, I know we'll get good service, and you can actually have a conversation there." So many of the trendy restaurants in New York were more about hip, well-dressed patrons and deafening noise levels than they were about food. In some, the waiters had more attitude than the guests. "Also tell Frank that I want my favorite table in the main dining room. The one in the corner."

Lisa picked up the phone again, and then she hesitated. "For how many?"

"Two," Morgan replied, trying to remain patient.

"Don't you think I should come?" Before Morgan could say no, Lisa plowed ahead. "I'm only concerned about you," she said, fixing Morgan with a maternal look. "Pretty soon you won't be able to hold every client's hand. You won't have the energy, and once the baby comes, you won't have the time. So the sooner clients and prospects become comfortable with me, the better the transition." When Morgan still didn't answer, trying to process this new switch, Lisa continued. "Besides, if Ken knows me as your right hand, it's more likely that he'll give us the business. He'll be familar with someone besides you who is responsible for the details."

Morgan wasn't persuaded. Though it was certainly a business meeting, Morgan also wanted to catch up socially. She and Ken had met six years before when she worked with the

Atlanta Committee for the Olympic Games and he was running *Volume* magazine. "Reserve a table for two," she said, "but you can join us for a drink first."

"Oh, um . . . I just remembered that my grandmother has a church dinner tonight and can't watch Justin," Lisa said. "But . . . I could join you later, say about nine, for dessert."

Morgan sat back, thinking that Lisa's request, and her forgetfulness, were rather odd. But she was probably right about demonstrating a show of force. It was important for Ken and other clients to see that she had capable people behind her. Especially when the news of her pregnancy got out. She nodded to Lisa, and returned to her work.

Il Cantanori, an Italian restaurant in Greenwich Village, was one of Morgan and Miles' favorites. It was located among a block of brownstones fronted by pricey, elegant antiques stores. When Morgan walked through the door, Frank, the manager, immediately greeted her with a big hug before holding her at arm's length to check the status of her impending delivery.

"Look at choo," Frank said in his straight-up Brooklyn accent. "Ya look faaaaabulous! Now ya know other women are gonna hate ya? As if they don't already. How can you be five months pregnant and still look so sexy? You tell me?"

From the moment Morgan discovered that she was expecting, she vowed on her collection of size-four designer wear not to ever let pregnancy be an excuse to pack on pounds. Her sandy brown complexion, which was always flawless, now had an extra glow. She rubbed vitamin E and olive oil on her tummy to ward off stretch marks, she ate only the healthiest foods, and she continued to do a light workout, as directed by her doctor. So far, so good.

"Thank you, honey," Morgan purred, favoring Frank with a dazzling smile and dancing eyes before turning around for him to remove her brown cashmere coat. Morgan was equally fastidious about her maternity wardrobe. She'd recently told Dakota to have her committed to an out-of-state asylum if she was ever caught wearing stretch pants and some dowdy burlap-bag cut shift. Tonight she wore a Diane Von Furstenberg wrap dress and a double strand of Tiffany pearls with a pair of three-inch Gucci sling backs.

Morgan strolled behind Frank as he led her to her favorite table. Il Cantanori was a cozy, intimate restaurant. Not too small, but not a whole lot of open space, except in warm weather when the front window retracted to provide access to a quaint outdoor patio. The first dining room was clustered with candlelit tables, where everyone from Harrison Ford to L.A. Reid and Sarah Jessica Parker were likely to be seen. The crowded bar separated the front room from an even cozier back dining room, where Morgan liked to hold court.

While she settled at her table, another regular came over to say hello. Betty was one of the most elegantly dressed women that Morgan knew. She knew how to make simple elegant.

Betty leaned over to give Morgan kisses on both cheeks. "Well, don't you look marvelous!"

"I'd have to say the same about you. Love that bag." Betty carried a vintage Chanel patchwork purse that emanated style.

"If I thought pregnancy would look that good on me, even I might give it a try," Betty teased.

Just then Ken appeared. "Sorry I'm late," he said, leaning over to hug Morgan.

After Morgan made the introductions, Betty left them to their dinner. Ken was tall, with a light complexion and dark wavy hair. Many women found him very attractive, but he was also very married, which didn't always stop the ladies, as Morgan well knew from her brief encounter with Miles' hot-to-trot new V.P. Morgan had been burning mad, but she smiled to herself now, thinking about how incredibly sweet and attentive Miles had been to her ever since, calling twice a day and always coming straight home after work, usually with flowers, dinner, and plenty of good old-fashioned loving that made her feel like the luckiest and most cherished woman in the world.

Focusing her attention back on Ken, she thought how appropriate it was that he had recently been named one of *Peo-*

ple magazine's fifty most attractive men. "So tell me about the day in the life of a media mogul," Morgan teased. She was happy to see Ken getting his accolades for years of hard work.

"Being a mogul isn't all it's cracked up to be, especially when ad revenue is at a ten-year low and investors are scarce."

"If it were easy, I'm sure you wouldn't be interested."

"That's true," he said, flashing his trademark shy-boy smile. "So how are you?" he said. "Besides pregnant."

"I'm good. The pregnancy has been easy so far. But of course starting and growing a company is no walk on the beach."

"Who are you telling?" He laughed.

"Sometimes I feel like I take one step forward followed by two backward." She and Lisa were making progress, but they really needed a marquis client in order to get to the next phase.

"Hang in there. It just takes perseverance." He had always been a good sounding board for Morgan, but tonight she needed him as a client.

"You're right. It also takes the right partnerships. For my business, that's everything."

"It sounds like you're on the right track. I hear that you handled the listening parties for Pink and Eve."

"I did, but what I need now is a marquis client. A company that gives high-level parties frequently, and that gets media attention. Who else but Vanity Media? People are still talking about *Heat*'s launch party."

"Yeah, it was fly." He seemed surprised that she would compliment a competitor's performance.

"I would've made it even better," Morgan challenged, leaning back in her chair.

"Do tell," Ken said, delighted to take the bait. Just then the waiter came over to tell them about the specials.

After the dinner orders were placed, Morgan let him have it. "First of all I would've added a fashion component, particularly since some of your most important advertising will be from fashion houses."

He sat back in his chair thoughtfully. "That's an interesting thought. How would you do it?"

"By partnering with a top designer who has targeted the hip urban market. And there are plenty. Louis Vuitton, Christian Dior, Gucci—they all look to urban culture to drive mainstream notions of what's hot." Morgan took a sip of her mixed cranberry and orange juice, which she insisted be served in a martini glass. Leaning forward again, she said, "What you do is have an interactive fashion show. Have the models change clothes behind lit screens so that you see the form as a shadow. Then have them emerge in runway-style exotic couture. Make it sexy! They could mix with guests, dancing and bringing the drama."

"That's a hot idea," Ken said, nodding his head.

"Only one of many," Morgan said confidently.

They continued to discuss concepts, right through dinner. Morgan ordered her usual, the calves liver in a buttery wine-infused gravy with fresh baby green beans. Ken, a meat-and-potatoes kinda guy, had the rib eye with mashed potatoes and asparagus. As they were ordering dessert and coffee, Morgan caught a strong whiff of Bobbi perfume, which was her favorite scent two years ago. Looking up to see the source, she saw Lisa. A whole new Lisa, wearing a too-tight black dress with a plunging neckline, spilling a set of 38Cs that looked lethal. Oddly, Morgan had never noticed them before. It was as if they had been unleashed.

"Hey, Morgan!" Before Morgan could respond or make introductions, Lisa had turned to face Ken. "You must be Ken Ridley," she gushed.

He stood to greet her. "I am. And you?"

Before Lisa could say anything, Morgan interrupted. "Ken, this is my manager, Lisa Burrows, whom I mentioned earlier."

"Yes. Please have a seat," Ken said, motioning to the chair across from him.

"Lisa and I thought it'd be a good idea for you to meet her since she will be responsible for much of the execution of your events." Having been trained in sales at Xerox, right out of college, Morgan was a believer in the assumptive close. Let him tell her that she *didn't* have the business.

"That's a good idea." Turning to Lisa, he said, "Morgan and I have been discussing some fashion ideas for our *Heat* parties. I'm excited about the direction."

Leaning so far across the table that her boobs could have been dessert, Lisa said, "I'm really happy to hear that we'll be working with you." She smiled at Ken as though she wanted to lap him up like a dish of crème brûlée.

Embarrassed and eager to shift the attention, Morgan said, "Ken, why don't you give us an overview of your circulation numbers and demographics for each magazine?" As he took them through each publication, Morgan could see out of the corner of her eyes Lisa unconsciously licking her scarlet-covered lips. What on earth had happened? Had she created a monster? This sort of approach would bomb with Ken.

After dessert, Morgan called for the check and feigned fatigue to bring a speedy end to the evening. Still not getting it, Lisa said, "Why don't you go ahead home? You've been running all day and I'm sure baby Nelson is ready for a rest."

Aha. So this was what Lisa's inability to make it for drinks was all about. "Better yet, why don't we all call it a night?" Morgan stood, leading them to the front of the restaurant and giving Ken a hug before his driver opened the door of the waiting town car and Ken slipped inside.

Once she and Lisa were out of earshot Morgan stopped in her tracks and turned to face Lisa. "What is with you tonight?"

Still glowing from her proximity to Ken, Lisa gave her an innocent look. "What are you talking about?"

"Lisa, you acted as though you thought Ken was dessert."

"I was just being friendly."

"If you'd been any nicer, I would've had to pry you off of him."

Now Lisa looked wounded by Morgan's words. "I'm sorry. I was just trying to help."

Morgan shook her head as she kept walking toward

Broadway. She didn't get Lisa. Earlier that same day she had gone through her depressed stage. Now tonight she had turned into Mae West. What the hell was going on? She flagged a cab that they shared. It dropped Morgan off first, but she gave Lisa a twenty to cover the rest of the fare.

11

The day after her arrival in Chicago, Dakota called her boss in New York to let him know that they were still waiting for test results, so she would like to take a long weekend. He was aware that Dakota had been raised by her grandmother, and told her to take as much time as she needed. Surprisingly, she and Tricia were getting along. An entire evening and not one fight.

"Hey," Tricia said as she walked into the room.

The small kitchen was charming, with original appliances from the 1950s. Crisp white curtains framed the window above the aged porcelain sink. Dakota loved the chrome knobs on the antique stove, gleaming in the morning sunshine. The sight of the knobs brought to mind Saturday mornings when Nana would wake her up bright and early to scrub the entire stove, with special attention paid to those knobs. Nana would say, "Chile, I paid too much money for this here stove to have dirt take it over." Dakota smiled at the thought, then turned to Tricia. "Good morning, you want some breakfast?"

"Yeah, thanks. What time do you want to go to the hospital?"

"When I come back from the grocery store. I'm making catfish and spaghetti tonight, just in case the doctor discharges Nana. You know how she likes fish on Friday," Dakota said optimistically.

"You think they gonna let her go?" Tricia said, sitting at the yellow Formica dinette set.

"If Nana has anything to say about it, I'm sure they will."

Tricia watched as Dakota moved about the kitchen making mushroom omelettes, bacon, biscuits, and coffee. "I didn't know you could throw down like this."

Dakota filled Tricia's plate with an oversized omelette oozing with cheese, two biscuits, and two pieces of bacon, then placed it in front of her. "I like to cook, but I don't have the time in New York, so thanks for indulging me."

"I should be thanking you, 'cause this is really good," Tricia said, her mouth now full of food.

Dakota couldn't believe her ears. Tricia had never once in her lifetime given her a compliment. Maybe they were finally making a breakthrough.

Even so, she wasn't pressing her luck. She thumbed through the *Sun-Times* as she ate, lingering on their stock columns. Soon she finished her breakfast and began to clear the table.

"I'll do the dishes, since you cooked."

"Okay," Dakota said, once again taken aback. "I'm going to run to the store. Do you want anything?"

"No. You can use my car if you want."

Dakota decided not to push the envelope. "Thanks, but I need to walk off some of this food."

Since Dakota had flown to Chicago straight from work, the only clothes she had were on her back. She walked down the hall from the kitchen into Nana's room and turned on the light. The room was painted the same Pepto-Bismol pink that Dakota had known as a child. Nana's bureau was filled with jewelry and various bottles of perfume. In the corner sat a snapshot of Dakota's parents. In the picture her mother was proudly showing off her engagement ring. She had a broad grin across her face, as she held on to Dakota's father. Nana had told her that the picture was taken a week before her parents' wedding. Dakota looked closely at the picture and wondered if Nana had kept her parents' wedding rings. I'll ask her when she comes home, Dakota thought. She felt an odd tingle being in Nana's room looking for clothes. One Halloween when she was nine, she went rambling through Nana's drawers searching for scarves and jewelry to complete her gypsy costume. Nana burst in, alarmed at the sight of her personal possessions strewn about the room. She sat Dakota down on the bed and told her to respect other people's private space and always ask for what you want before going hunting on someone else's territory.

She thought about asking Tricia for an outfit, but wasn't in the mood for miniskirts and fishnets. Then she remembered the silk jogging suit she had brought for Nana last year. She put on the teal floral pants and adjusted them to her waist with large safety pins. She zipped up the jacket and rolled up the sleeves. One glance in the mirror told her she was a *Glamour* "don't." The black loafers were definitely out of place. Still, she was only going to the neighborhood store. Taking another look at her outrageous appearance, she said, "Maybe I'll just have to go by Biba Bis and pick up a few pieces." Biba Bis, an upscale boutique on West Superior, had some of the hottest clothes in the city.

Dakota half walked and half jogged to the grocery store two blocks away, wanting to hurry so no one would see her in Nana's clothes. Once inside the brightly lit store, Dakota quickly filled the grocery basket and made a beeline to the cashier. She was standing in line, blissfully among strangers, when she heard someone call out her name. She hesitantly looked to her left, hoping there was another Dakota in the store. Then she heard her name again. Standing in the next checkout lane was a tall, light-brown-skinned man with a goatee, waving to get her attention. She couldn't see his eyes because he had on rose-tinted horn-rimmed glasses.

Dakota pointed to herself and mouthed, "Are you talking to me?"

He held up his index finger, saying, "Just a minute."

They both paid for their groceries, and as Dakota waited for the clerk to bag her food, the mystery man walked over.

"Dakota Cantrell?"

"Yeah?" she said, still unaware of the handsome stranger's identity.

"Tristan Lewis," he said, taking off his shades. "We had English together in high school," he said, smiling.

Dakota looked into his dazzling hazel eyes and instantly remembered the little quiet boy in the back of class with the pretty eyes. He wasn't little anymore, and apparently he wasn't shy either.

"You probably don't remember me. I was a loner back then," he said, giving her a quick once-over.

She wished she had worn anything other than Nana's too big jogging suit. "I remember you," she finally said.

"Here, let me help you with that bag," he said as they walked out of the store. "Where's your car?" he said, putting his shades back on.

"I walked here," she said, feeling like a loser: no car, no dope sunglasses, and no fly outfit.

"Where do you live?"

Trying to redeem herself, she said proudly, "In New York," knowing most people were impressed with the mere mention of the Big Apple.

"What a coincidence. Me too," he said. "I'm here visiting my parents. What are you doing in Chicago?"

"My grandmother is in the hospital."

"Sorry to hear that," he said. "Do you need a lift?"

"Sure."

As they drove down King Drive, Dakota stole glances at Tristan. He was pretty-boy handsome with wavy coal-black hair that accentuated his creamy complexion. He had to have a black book the size of the yellow pages. She looked at his manicured nails as he tapped the steering wheel to the music on the radio. Neat, and smells good too, she said to herself, inhaling his intoxicating scent.

"Hey, remember this song?" he said, interrupting Dakota's thoughts.

"Bodyheat" by James Brown pulsed from the radio. Tristan leaned over and turned the volume up. They began to sing in unison.

"We had a dance coordinated to that song," Dakota said, referring to her high school days as a pom-pom girl.

Tristan glanced over his glasses and smiled at Dakota as if recalling those days. "I remember you and your girls, prancing around school in those teeny-weeny skirts and tight sweaters."

"We did not prance, thank you very much." Dakota smiled mischievously, knowing that was exactly what they did. "Make a right at the corner," she said as they neared Nana's block.

Her house was located in Chatham, one of the oldest African-American neighborhoods in Chicago. The residents, most of whom were now elderly, hired lawn services to maintain the wide strip of grass in front of their homes. Nana's saffron-colored brick house was set between two massive oak trees. Flowerpots, which overflowed with petunias in the summer, flanked each side of the concrete porch.

As they pulled up in front, a motley crew of neighbors was in place on the porch next door. Kevin lived with his parents and usually hung out with Jasmine, his overweight girlfriend, and J. B., his sidekick. They all gawked in the direction of Tristan's winter-green Volvo. Dakota knew the Spanish Inquisition was coming the moment she stepped out of the car.

"How long are you going to be in town?" Tristan asked, oblivious to the onlookers.

"For at least a few days. Why?"

"Let's get together for a drink tonight," Tristan said, taking off his shades and pinning her with those mesmerizing eyes.

Dakota looked skeptical, then reasoned, Why not? It's just a drink. She tore off a piece of the brown paper bag and wrote down her cell number.

Tristan took the paper, folded it, and stuck it in the car visor. "I'll call you around seven."

"Okay. Thanks for the ride," Dakota said cheerfully, and got out of the car.

"Hey, Kota," Kevin yelled from the porch next door.

Here it comes, she thought, looking over at the three musketeers. Did they ever work or did they just hang out all day?

"Wasn't that Tristan from school?"

"Yeah, it was," she said, and kept stepping.

"Wh-what you d-doin' ho-hoo-home?" J. B. stuttered.

Not wanting to elaborate, she simply said, "Nana's in the hospital."

"Oh, is she going to be okay?" asked Jasmine, sucking on a watermelon Jolly Rancher.

"She'll be fine," Dakota said, and dashed into the house.

Tricia was sitting in the living room. "Kota, you ready to go to the hospital?"

"Let me change into my suit, since it's the only decent thing I have to wear."

She soon had the groceries unpacked and her good clothes on her back. She and Tricia got in the car and started off. Her neighborly trio hadn't budged an inch. On the way to the hospital Tricia asked, "Who was that in the Volvo?"

"Tristan Lewis. We went to high school together. He's in town visiting his parents. We're supposed to hook up later."

"He sure is fine," Tricia said, licking her lips as if he were a delectable dish.

Dakota asked, her voice full of humor, "Were you doing a Nana, spying through the curtains?"

"Basically." Tricia chuckled. "Where does he live?"

"New York. Can you believe that?"

"What a small world—for you."

"And getting smaller all the time," Dakota said.

When they reached Nana's room, she was watching *The Young and the Restless*, her favorite soap. Tricia and Dakota knew to take a seat and wait until the commercial break before starting a conversation. Finally the theme music came on indicating the end of the show. Dakota turned and touched Nana's hand. "Hey there, how you feeling? Has the doctor been in yet?"

"I'm okay for an old lady. How y'all making out?" Nana asked, looking over at Tricia.

"It's all good, Nana," Tricia said, moving closer to the bed.

"Does that mean y'all getting along?"

"Yeah, Nana, we getting along fine," Dakota confirmed.

"Excuse me, ladies," the doctor said, entering the room.

"Did you get her test results back?" Dakota asked anxiously, even before the doctor had a chance to open his chart.

"Not yet. The lab's backed up. I should have them in a day or two," he said, directing his conversation toward Nana.

Dakota began to pace in front of the window, trying to hold her tongue. Yet she couldn't contain herself. This was her grandmother. "Can you put a rush on it?" she blurted out.

Nana shot her a warning look that read, Don't be disrespectful.

It was something about Nana's generation that revered doctors, putting them on unapproachable pedestals, Dakota thought. Hanging on their every word, afraid to ask questions, and heaven forbid they should ask for a second opinion.

"It wouldn't matter, because all the labs are understaffed," he said, seemingly annoyed with her persistence. "Mrs. Cantrell, the nurse will be in shortly to take your afternoon vitals," he said, again focusing his attention on Nana.

"Thank you, Doctor," Nana said meekly.

The moment he walked out, she turned on Dakota. "Why you talking to the doctor like that? He doing all he can." Nana then nodded toward Tricia. "You need to learn to keep quiet like Tricia. She didn't make one peep, not one. You could take a lesson from her. Living in New York has you acting rude and . . ."

Dakota turned a deaf ear on the rest of Nana's sermon, forcing her mind to go elsewhere, much as she did as a child. And that was exactly what she felt like, a twelve-year-old being scolded for talking in church. She looked over at Tricia, who had the biggest shit-eating grin plastered across her face. Dakota wanted to smack that stupid grin. Me? Take a lesson from *her*? Ha! she said to herself.

"Nana, you okay? Can I get you anything?" Tricia asked, posing as the perfect obedient child.

"Naw, baby, I'm fine."

Dakota wanted to vomit at the cloying sentiment between Tricia and Nana. Instead, she plopped down in the chair and stared out the window. It looked like a long afternoon of watching soap operas.

Tricia and Dakota drove home in silence, listening to the rumble from the loose muffler underneath the car. When they pulled up in front of the house, Dakota looked at the empty porch next door and was relieved that her childhood friends were MIA. As she got out of the car, her cell phone rang. "Hello?"

"Dakota, this is Tristan."

From the sound of his voice she had a feeling that he was canceling their date. Probably had a better offer, she thought. "Hey, Tristan," she said.

"Are we still on for tonight?"

Her mood brightened instantly. "Sure," she said, trying to sound cool and unconcerned.

"Okay, I'll pick you up at seven."

Dakota realized that she hadn't had a chance to pick up an outfit. She refused to be caught in another unsightly ensemble. "Can you make it eight instead?"

"Not a problem. See you at eight."

With no time to spare, Dakota asked, "Tricia, can I use your car?"

"Where you going?"

"I have to go downtown and catch Biba Bis before they close. Tristan and I are going out tonight, and I have nothing to wear."

Tricia was puzzled. "Why you going all the way downtown when you can borrow something of mine?"

Dakota could just imagine herself decked out in a tiger-print microminidress with four-inch platform shoes and fishnets. "Thanks, but I brought nothing with me, so I need to buy some clothes anyway," she said diplomatically.

Tricia tossed her the keys. "Suit yourself."

Once out on the road, Dakota had to admit that Tricia's Opal had some serious get-up-and-go. She whizzed past SUVs, semis and sporty little two-seaters as she revved up the

RPMs on the twenty-year-old relic. Twelve minutes flat and she was parking in front of Biba Bis. She walked through the glass door of the minimalist boutique and explained her dilemma to Debra and Albert, the owners.

"Debra, you have to hook me up," she said, a little out of breath from rushing. "I need an evening outfit and three or four casual pieces."

"Don't panic. I'm sure we have something for you," Debra said calmly.

Dakota had known Debra for years and trusted her impeccable taste. Debra showed her to a fitting room, and before Dakota could completely disrobe she was handed a dress through the plush curtains.

"Here, try this."

Dakota put on the dress and looked in the full-length mirror. "Wow," she remarked at her reflection. The black jersey dress draped her body, hugging curves she didn't know she had. Stopping just below the knee, the dress complemented her well-defined calves. She turned to get a rear view. Black leather strips were latticed across the back of the dress from the waist up.

"You like it?" Debra asked through the curtain.

"Like it? I love it!" Dakota exclaimed.

"Here, try these," she said, handing Dakota an armful of clothes and a pair of Ron Donovan black sling backs.

Dakota was meeting Tristan in an hour, so she wasted little time trying on each piece, expertly stepping in and out of slacks and buttoning and unbuttoning blouses, creating her own pandemonium like backstage at Seventh on Sixth, the semiannual designer fashion show in New York.

"You guys are lifesavers," Dakota said, bringing the clothes to the register.

Albert blushed modestly. "Glad we could help."

With her goodies in hand, Dakota rushed for the door, but not before kissing her friends good-bye. Her trek back to the South Side was equally as swift. Fortunately, traffic was light on a Saturday. Once she reached the house, she called out to Tricia, who was upstairs in her room. Dakota showered and changed into the sexy black dress. As she stood at the bathroom mirror applying makeup, she thought back to her high school years. She had stood before the same mirror applying Vaseline on her lips instead of the Groovy Grape lipgloss that Nana forbade her to wear. She remembered the eleven-thirty curfews after the school dances, which were always over at eleven o'clock.

Just as she was adjusting her earrings, the doorbell rang. "I got it," she nervously yelled out to Tricia.

Dakota opened the door and nearly gasped at the fine specimen before her. Tristan wore a pale blue ribbed sweater that fit snugly across his midsection, emphasizing his flat stomach, and black gabardine slacks.

"Don't you look all grown up," Tristan said, in a voice oozing with sexual overtones.

"What did you expect?" Dakota suggestively smoothed the front of her dress. "My pom-pom uniform?"

Tristan chuckled.

Dakota sashayed over to the cocktail table and picked up her purse and keys, and took her coat from the front closet. Once outside, Tristan escorted her to the passenger side of the car. She stood close behind him as he opened the door, and for the second time that day inhaled his intoxicating scent. Whatever he was wearing sure smelled enticing.

"I thought we'd go over to City Life," he said, starting the engine. "A friend of mine is playing tonight."

City Life was a neighborhood jazz joint that was packed every weekend. Famous musicians were known to drop by and play a set or two. Dakota and Tristan strolled in, looking overdressed. Most of the patrons were old-timers bopping their heads and snapping their nicotine-stained fingers in time to the beat. Tristan found a small intimate table along the wall.

"What can I get you to drink?" a waitress asked.

Dakota thought it best to stick with the basics. "I'll have a vodka and cranberry," she said, knowing this was not the type of place that served designer martinis.

Tristan asked her about her work and she told him about the trials and tribulations of working on Wall Street. "So what profession are you in?"

"I own an Internet company," he said proudly.

Oh, no, not another dot-bomb, Dakota thought, cringing to herself. She had seen so many Internet companies go soaring out of the gate the first day of trading, making the key investors millions only to go bust a year or so later because they had no real earnings.

"I know what you're thinking, but my company has a solid track record. We've been in business for more than seven years. We've developed a voice-recognition chip that will allow consumers to vote via their computer or over the phone. So there won't be another ballot debacle like the last presidential election."

The idea piqued her interest. "How would that work? What would prevent people from voting twice?"

He nodded as though he expected the question. "Just like no two people have the same fingerprints, every voice is also unique. The chip deciphers voice quality and patterns and would not allow that particular voice to vote again. There will also be other firewalls and personal identification safeguards in place like Social Security numbers, and so forth. As a matter of fact, I'm in negotiations with Microsoft—they want to buy the rights to the software."

So the class nerd was about to become the multimillion-dollar man. "Congratulations," she said, holding up her drink.

"Not yet. But hopefully I'll be celebrating in the very near future."

They continued to chat and listen to the music. By the last set, the combination of drinks and jazz had them playing footsy underneath the table like high school sweethearts.

"I'm leaving tomorrow, but I would love to see you in New York," he said, rubbing his knees against her bare legs.

Dakota searched Tristan's eyes, hoping they would reveal any hidden secrets, but all she saw was an extremely sexy man. Why not? she thought. He was a catch, and they had their hometown in common. "I'm listed," she finally said. "I'll be back in a couple of days, so give me a call."

"Well, I'll be sure to get the four-one-one on you, Ms. Pom-pom." He winked.

Suddenly Dakota wished she had taken his information. She hated feeling powerless, waiting on that proverbial phone call. But if she asked for his number now, she would reveal her insecurity, and she was far too cool for that. She would enjoy him tonight, she decided, and not expect to hear from him *ever*. That way she wouldn't have to worry about another man weaseling his way into her heart and then breaking it.

12

Morgan flipped down the car's visor to inspect the application of her lipstick in the lit mirror. "I couldn't believe her!" Morgan said after recounting Lisa's behavior at Il Cantanori the night before.

Miles scoffed at the idea of the Lisa he knew playing a sex vixen. "Are you sure she was coming on to him?" He just couldn't imagine it.

Morgan touched up her M•A•C Viva Glam lipstick before closing the visor. "I don't know what else to call the flurry of batting eyelashes, the heaving bosom, and that can-I-have-*you*-for-dessert look."

Laughing, Miles said, "Did you get the business?"

"Yes."

"Well, maybe you owe her a commission," he teased, steering the Jaguar XJE down Sixth Avenue.

Morgan playfully swatted him in the chest with her cashmere shawl. "That's not funny."

Miles put up a hand in surrender. "She was probably just trying to get her groove on," he chuckled. "Think about it. She's either hanging out with you and Dakota, the style mavens of Manhattan, or at home with an old lady and a four-year-old. She probably needs some adult male company and a little horizontal action."

"Well, she'd better find it on her own time." Morgan was

adamant. "I've had enough of business associates with emotional issues to last me a lifetime."

At this oblique mention of Tyrone, Miles' grin turned harder. Morgan's company was serious business, and he wasn't about to let anyone else trifle with it. "Did you speak to her about it?"

"I drafted a dress code this morning and went over it with her."

"How did she take it?"

"She seemed a little embarrassed, but I think she gets the point."

Miles reached over to hold Morgan's hand. "I wouldn't worry about it too much. She's a hard worker and she seems loyal. I'm sure she just needs more experience."

Miles was probably right, she considered. He was known for his level head and he also had a keen ability to size people up. While Tyrone was busy conning the rest of the world, Miles was the only person skeptical of him from the start.

When they reached the Apartment, a popular party spot, Miles pulled up and came around to open Morgan's door. She slipped her arm through his as the valet took his keys. At the entrance, their names were checked off the guest list for Usher's listening party. The cavernous club was candlelit and the crowd was downtown-hip. Morgan wore a long black jersey fitted halter dress, which cradled her sensuous pregnant form, with a matching cashmere shawl. Miles looked distinguished in a tailored black Dolce & Gabbana worsted wool suit that he and Morgan had picked up in Rome earlier that year. He wore it with a royal blue plaid shirt, European-style, with a black, rib-textured thickly knotted tie and a sexy five o'clock shadow. He attracted the eye of every woman they passed.

As they settled into the VIP section, they waved to Derrick and Susan Johnson, a well-known couple around town, who were chatting with publicist-extraordinaire CoAnne Wilshire, just as Vanessa Baylor, another good friend, stopped by to chat.

"It looks like pregnancy agrees with you," she said, giving Morgan a big hug.

"What about me?" Miles joked, turning to offer the profile of his midsection before also giving her a hug.

Just then his two-way pager buzzed for the umpteenth time that day. Morgan simply rolled her eyes. She thought the device, which many seemed unable to live without, was like a narcotic. Hordes of entertainment-industry types sat in restaurants and meetings waiting for their next hit, oblivious to the people sitting right in front of them. While Miles typed away with two thumbs, Morgan watched Usher take the stage.

His performance was brilliant and his new look was ultra-fly—oozing a little bad-boy sex appeal, which hadn't been a part of his earlier persona. He wore rose-tinted wraparound aviator sunglasses, a tight shirt with a wide collar opened to his abs, and tight flat-front bell-bottoms. The set started with his new hit single before he stirred the crowd with some of his older tracks.

Afterward, while many were trickling out, headed to the after party, Morgan and Miles mingled with friends and many of his colleagues. "Hi, Morgan, it's good to see you." Morgan turned to see Vic Pellam standing before her, wearing a broad smile and little else. Morgan cursed the day that spandex was discovered. Vic's excuse for a black dress looked as though it had come in a bottle and was poured over her body.

"Vic, how are you?" Morgan asked, masking her revulsion. After all, she'd gotten past the incident in Miles' office and Vic was one of Miles' most important colleagues.

"I'm great!" she answered a little too enthusiastically for Morgan's taste. "It must be difficult being pregnant and hanging out with this guy," she teased, nudging Miles, who was engrossed in a conversation with Arista Records' CEO Antonio "L.A." Reid and his beautiful wife, Erica.

Miles turned, saw Vic, and exchanged a hug with her. A little too tight, Morgan thought. Trying to keep it light, and hold her own paranoia in check, Morgan said, "Baby, are you just about ready to go?" She pinned him with a meaningful look.

Totally missing it, Miles resumed his conversation with L.A., while Vic barely stifled a grin.

Morgan wanted to smack him, then turn around and knock the smug look off of Vic's face. Vic whispered, "You don't have to worry about Miles going out alone. I'll keep my eye on him."

Morgan couldn't believe the woman's gall. She gave her a scathing look. "Trust me," she replied, "that won't be necessary."

Later, as they drove uptown, Morgan held her fury in as long as she could, before unleashing it on Miles. "You need to put that hussy in check."

Miles frowned, turned to her puzzled, and said, "What hussy?"

"You know who I'm talking about," she answered, folding her arms across her stomach.

"Morgan, we've been through this before—"

Turning to face him, she said, "Well, I thought we'd been through it, too." She could feel her blood throbbing in her temples. "But after all your bullshit reassurances about that little champagne tête-à-tête meaning nothing, your quote-unquote colleague tells me it must be hard to hang on to you because I'm pregnant, then goes on to tell me, to my face, that she's got her eyes on you." Just recounting it gave Morgan a fresh dose of anger.

"Morgan, I'm sure that you didn't have anything to drink tonight," Miles said, shaking his head, "but something has you delusional."

"Me? Delusional! Miles, for someone so smart, you are being incredibly stupid."

At that, he bristled. "Morgan, I think we should end this conversation. You obviously are emotional, and maybe it's because of the pregnancy. But it's still unfair for you to attack Vic. She is a colleague, and one I can't afford to have a bad—and unnecessarily bad, I might add—relationship with." With that, he gripped the wheel of the Jag and stared straight ahead..

"I may be emotional, but I'm not crazy. You'd better watch out for that bitch, because I certainly will be." She snapped her head to face the opposite direction, staring out over the East River.

They rode the rest of the way home in silence. After leaving the car with their building's attendant, Miles wrapped his arms around Morgan as they took the elevator upstairs. When they reached the apartment, she was still seething. He could tell by her stiff body language.

Miles turned her to face him. "Morgan, what are you worried about?" he asked gently.

"Nothing." The frown on her face gave a different answer.

"You know how much I love you, and I'm ecstatic about the baby." His earnest expression pulled at Morgan's heart.

"How much?" The beginnings of a smile started at the corners of her mouth.

Miles kissed her full on the lips. As things heated up she reached for his crotch for a test feel.

"You are such a flirt," Miles whispered.

"Just checking to make sure that I still had your attention," Morgan said, coyly pulling back.

"You'll always have my attention."

"No matter what?"

"No matter what," he said definitively.

"Even if I gained fifty pounds, and watched Jerry Springer all day?"

"The pounds I might overlook, but Jerry Springer could be a problem," Miles said, looking dead serious, before giving her that sly handsome smile.

Laughing, Morgan said, "So much for 'no matter what.'"

"Don't try to change the subject," Miles insisted, leading Morgan into the bedroom. He slowly undressed her.

While he nibbled behind her ear, she stirred beneath his hand. He savored every sensation. Then his kisses became longer, wetter, slower, and more probing as they moved farther downtown, stopping between the twin mounds of her breasts. Miles was a learned breast man. So he had landed in heaven, cushioned between clouds of full, soft flesh. With his head buried between them, he used both hands to firmly squeeze as much of her as he could. His eager mouth went from one firm nipple to the other, licking, kissing, and lightly pinching until he finally settled on one, sucking it deep and hard.

The intensity of his mouth stirred a hungry passion in Morgan. While Miles lavished attention on her full breasts, Morgan's right hand unconsciously wandered down over the life in her stomach, under her pink lace panties, and between her parted legs. She slowly massaged herself, causing a slow burn at her center. Still feasting, Miles removed his slacks with one fast hand, before following the trail that Morgan had just left. Pausing at her belly, he kissed the smooth rounded skin, before moving on to find her fingers buried in hot sex. He loved the sight of Morgan taking matters into her own hands, so he couldn't help but to stop and watch as she stoked the fire that he had started. Her hips rotated seductively as her passion burned hotter, her other hand urgently squeezing her left breast, adding fuel to the smoldering fire.

Unable to resist any longer, Miles kissed her there, fingers, flesh and all, his lips nudging away her hand so that he could lick, suck, and lap every inch of her. When she felt his hot tongue connect with her clitoris, then caress it over and over, she squirmed and tensed, before exploding in a powerful orgasm that felt like it would never end. Just as she was coming down, Miles moved over her, kissing her deeply on the lips with the taste of her own sex, then entering her gradually with his rock-hard erection. He teased her, never giving it all, only a few inches, before withdrawing again to fan the fire.

"Please . . ." she moaned, begging him for more.

"Please what?" he said, in a deep husky voice.

"Let me have it, baby. . . . Give it to me." Morgan's hips rose urgently from the mattress, eager to meet him more than halfway.

No longer able to refrain, Miles filled her completely in

one long, powerful thrust. The wet heat of her sheath triggered a fierce thirst that drove him like a parched man poised at a cold spring. While the sweat sheened his tensed body and mingled with Morgan's own perspiration, Miles took the plunge, shuddering with ecstasy as he released his seed into her warm crevice.

13

Dakota felt as if she were suffocating. Black dots began to cloud her vision, indicating the onset of a fainting spell. Her ears still rang with the doctor's words.

"Excuse me, ladies," the doctor had said as he entered Nana's hospital room.

"Did you get the test results back yet?" Dakota asked anxiously.

The doctor clutched his clipboard with a concerned look on his stern face. "We did, and—"

"And she's going to be just fine, right?" Dakota said.

The doctor flipped open his chart, thumbed through a few pages, then looked up and said somberly to Nana, "Your liver-enzyme test came back abnormal."

Dakota heard the word "abnormal" and instantly felt uneasy. "Exactly what does that mean?"

"Kota, let the doctor talk," Nana said.

"Our findings indicate that you have metastasized liver cancer, Mrs. Cantrell."

Dakota couldn't believe her ears. "But there is a treatment for it, isn't there?"

Finally he turned to Dakota. "The most we can do is administer drug therapy. The cancer has spread and it's inoperable."

His blandness, as though her nana was just another medical statistic, infuriated Dakota. "I'd like to have her transferred over to Northwestern for a second opinion."

Nana laid a hand on her forearm. "Wait a minute now, Kota. I'm not going to another hospital," she said flatly. "I'm too old to be traipsing around looking for a cure."

"Don't say that, Nana," Tricia said, tears welling up in her eyes.

"Doctor, if you can just give me something, 'cause I have a little pain in my stomach," she said, wincing.

"I'll have your medication increased right away." He turned and walked out the door.

He wasn't going to escape that easily. Ignoring Nana's call to her, Dakota headed out after him. She quickly caught up. Though she hated to ask the next question, she had to know what they were facing. "How long are we talking?"

The doctor stopped and abruptly faced her. "I don't like to quote time frames, because only God really knows, but I'd guess we're looking at three to five months. I'm sorry. I'll come back this afternoon with her discharge papers," he said, turning to leave.

"Why are you letting her go home if she's got cancer?" Tricia blurted out. She had followed on Dakota's heels.

"Basically, there's nothing more we can do here. With medication she can rest comfortably at home."

Dakota felt the hall closing in around her. This couldn't be happening. She looked over at Tricia. Tears were now flowing freely down her cheeks.

When they returned to Nana's room, she immediately saw their tears, even though Dakota had tried to suck it up. "Stop all that crying," Nana insisted.

Dakota sniffled. "Nana, are you sure you don't want a second opinion?"

"Baby, ain't no need for another doctor to be probing me. I figured something was wrong 'cause I been having pains for some time now."

"Nana," Dakota protested, "why didn't you tell me? We could have caught it before now!"

The old woman sank back on her pillows. "Baby, whether or not we found out about this cancer thing a few months ago doesn't really matter, 'cause when it's my time, the good Lord will take me home. And can't no doctor stop that."

Dakota didn't know what to do. Suggesting a second opinion was her only option, and since Nana had adamantly refused, she was helpless. The weight of the doctor's words were crushing her. She felt as if she were going to collapse. "Nana, I'm going to the cafeteria." She had to leave the room, compose herself. She had to be strong for her grandmother. "Do you want anything?"

"No, thanks, baby. I don't need anything."

As Dakota left the room, Tricia slumped down in the chair near Nana's bed. She blew her nose, trying to get her emotions in check.

Tricia and Nana sat in silence with only the background noise from the television between them. The nurse came in and gave her an injection of morphine. After a few minutes Nana began to slip in and out of consciousness. Tricia turned from the TV show as Nana mumbled incoherently, "Kota, is that you?"

"Nana, Dakota is downstairs. Can I get you anything?"

Nana didn't hear her. Instead she rambled on, "Kota, I . . . I . . . got to tell you something before I leave here."

Tricia eased to the edge of her chair. "Nana, it's me, Tricia."

"Kota, I want you to have . . ." Nana's voice faded.

This was what Tricia had always hated, the special closeness between Nana and Dakota. It wasn't fair. And why should Nana have secrets even now, when she was dying? "What are you talking about, Nana?"

Nana remained quiet, her eyes closed. Tricia thought Nana had drifted off to sleep until she began to babble, revealing the story in bits and pieces.

She must be hallucinating from the medication, Tricia thought, looking toward the doorway for any signs of her cousin. But if she wasn't, Tricia couldn't ever let Dakota find out.

With the next words out of Nana's mouth, Tricia knew she was telling the truth: "Kota, now that you know, I can rest in peace."

Nana drifted off again, and soon Dakota came back into the room. "How is she doing?"

"Um . . . the nurse came in and gave her some morphine," Tricia said nervously.

Looking at Nana resting, Dakota said, "It must have really knocked her out." Tricia was fidgeting, and Dakota gave her a curious look. "What's wrong?"

"Oh, nothing. I'm just sad, that's all."

The next morning, Dakota tiptoed down the hall around seven. She peeped into Nana's bedroom, expecting to find her sound asleep, but was greeted instead by an empty bed. That was funny. Nana had still been pretty zonked out when she was discharged yesterday. Dakota looked in the bathroom but still no Nana. Panic set in as she hurried down the stairs. Then she heard noises from the kitchen. She raced down the hall. There was Nana, dressed in her multicolored housedress, standing over the stove stirring a huge pot.

"Nana, what are you doing out of bed?" Dakota scolded.

Her grandmother's voice was clear and calm. "Child, I'm making something for this pain."

Dakota looked into the pot at the gook Nana had concocted. "What is *that*?"

"My momma used to make this for me when I was sick," Nana said, putting a large wooden spoon to her lips.

"But what is it?"

"Chicken broth, lard, rosehips, garlic cloves, and thyme."

"Ugh, that sounds gross," Dakota said, turning up her nose.

Nana put the lid on the pot and sat down at the dinette table. "I don't care how it sound. It always made me feel better."

"Nana, that's why the doctor prescribed pain medication."

"Them pills is okay, but ain't nothing like a little homemade brew."

Nana had lost a considerable amount of weight, Dakota noticed, looking sadly at her gaunt face. Her once-chubby cheeks had been replaced by sharp, protruding cheekbones. Her housedress hung loosely off her shoulders. "Nana, why don't you get back in bed? Let me finish up for you."

The Nana she knew would have never let someone else do her cooking for her. Yet now her grandmother seemed grateful for the offer. "All right, just put a little salt in it, turn the fire down low, and let it simmer for about an hour." She rose heavily to her feet and started out. "I'm a lay down and take a little nap."

Dakota did as instructed, then sat in the kitchen chair Nana had just vacated and began to cry silently. The house was quiet with Tricia at school and Nana upstairs, and soon Dakota let the floodgates open. She had held back for Nana's sake, but now it was her turn to break down. As Dakota was blowing her nose, the phone rang.

"Is this the Cantrell residence?" asked the male caller.

"Yes, it is," she said, not recognizing the voice.

"Is Dakota in?"

"This is Dakota."

"Hi, it's Tristan Lewis."

Surprised to hear from him, she asked, "How did you get this number?"

"I called your house, and when I got your answering machine, I called information in Chicago, hoping your grandmother was listed," he explained. "Am I disturbing you?"

"Not at all," she said, glad to have the distraction.

"How is your grandmother doing?"

Her tears returned, threatening to drown her. In between sniffles she told him about Nana's grim prognosis.

"How are you holding up?" Tristan asked with alarm.

Dakota's voice caught in her throat as she tried to fight back her emotions. "I'm sorry. I didn't mean—"

Tristan cut her off. "Don't be silly. You're going through a tough time. I know this may sound like a cliché, but if there's anything I can do . . ."

"I'll be fine," she said, trying to regain her composure.

"Listen, I can take a few days off and come back to Chicago in case you need a shoulder."

Dakota couldn't believe he was willing to drop everything to lend his support. Maybe he was one of the rare good guys. "I really appreciate your offer, but I'll be okay."

"You don't sound okay. Have you eaten?"

"No, I don't really have an appetite," she said, realizing she hadn't even thought about eating.

"Well, I understand that, but you can't run yourself down."

His concern touched her. "I know. I'll eat something later."

"If I were there I'd fix you a nice breakfast and give you a relaxing rubdown. Hey, I have an idea."

Curious, she asked, "What?"

"I want you to run a warm bath, with bubbles." He chuckled. "And if you don't have any fancy bath products, do what we all used to do and put dishwashing liquid in the water."

Dakota couldn't help but laugh, because that was exactly what Nana used to put in her bath when she was little.

"Do you have any candles?"

"I think I can scare up a few," she said, glancing around the kitchen.

"Well, light them, turn off the lights, get in the tub, and let all that tension drain away."

She thought about it for a second. "Actually, that's a good idea."

"Thanks. I only wish I could be there to wash your back," he said with a smile in his sexy voice.

"I just bet you do," she said, feeling her old self resurfacing.

"That's not what I meant. I just—"

"Yeah, yeah, I know what you meant."

"No seriously, all I mean is that you need a little TLC before you run yourself down." Then his tone grew huskier. "No hanky-panky, at least not yet."

"And what makes you think there'll be any in the future?" Dakota asked tartly.

"Don't dash all of my hopes. Listen, why don't you go take that bath and I'll check on you later?"

"Thanks," she said, and hung up the phone. What a pleasant surprise, she thought. She couldn't believe how caring Tristan seemed. He had appeared awfully slick before. Maybe she had him pegged all wrong.

She went into the bathroom with some candles she found in the kitchen. Tristan was right. The warm water and soothing atmosphere did ease the tension out of her body. Dakota climbed out of the tub and put on one of Nana's fuzzy terrycloth robes. Feeling renewed, she headed to Nana's room to check on her. Nana was tossing and turning, talking in her sleep.

"Nana, are you okay?" Dakota whispered.

"Kota, is that you?" When Nana turned over, she had a glazed look in her eyes.

"Yes, it's me. Can I get you anything? Do you want some of your soup?"

"I'm so glad I told you," Nana said.

Dakota had no idea what Nana was talking about. "Told me what?"

"I didn't want to leave here without you knowing. Now I can rest." Nana closed her eyes and started humming "Amazing Grace."

"Nana, know what?" Dakota shook her lightly. "Nana, what are you talking about?" But Nana just kept humming one verse after the other, as if Dakota weren't there.

Dakota walked out and pulled the door closed. "It must be the medicine," she said to herself as she went downstairs.

Nana's constitution was as strong as a weathered oak. The next morning she was up bright and early. Maybe her magic brew was working.

"Nana, where do you think you're going?" Tricia asked, standing in the doorway of Nana's bedroom.

"To the eleven o'clock service," Nana said, putting on her thick support hose.

"Did the doctor say that it's okay for you to go out?"

"Child, that doctor can't tell me when I can go to my Lord's house. As long as I got breath in my body, I'm a praise His name."

"But are you feeling up to it?"

"Child, I been going to church all my life and I ain't goin' stop now," Nana snapped.

"All right, all right. I'm gonna wake up Dakota so we can go with you."

"That'll be nice, baby, but y'all hurry up, 'cause you know how fast the main sanctuary fills up."

Nana, Tricia, and Dakota pulled in front of Trinity Church of Christ, which had been Nana's house of worship for years. The main parking lot was filled to capacity, so Tricia let Nana and Dakota out in front and drove two blocks down to the alternative parking area.

The morning parishioners were filing into the main sanctuary as Nana and Dakota entered.

"Mornin', Sister Cantrell," said the head of the usher board.

"Mornin', Sister Russell, how you doing?"

"He woke me up this mornin', and started me on my way, so I'm doin' good. Y'all come on down front while there's still room," she said, handing them programs.

"We're waiting for my other granddaughter," Nana said, looking through the crowd for Tricia.

"I remember Patricia. I'll send her down when she comes in."

No sooner had Nana and Dakota sat down than the choir dressed in brightly colored African-inspired robes marched in singing "Come Go with Me to My Father's House" accompanied by Reverend Wright on piano. Not only was the reverend an accomplished pianist, he was a dynamic minister, zealously preaching the word, even using modern slang to reach the young folk in the congregation. Nana looked at the program and saw today's sermon was from the Book of Job.

How appropriate, she thought. Job had much and lost much in his lifetime, but never lost his faith in God. Nana felt the same way. Even though her prognosis was grim, her faith never waned. Nana looked around the sanctuary at the ruby-colored pews, the beautiful stained glass, the mud-cloth-draped pulpit, and envisioned her homegoing celebration with the one hundred-plus member choir singing "Precious Lord."

"Kota, I want you and Tricia to make all my arrangements here at Trinity. I don't want to be laid out at no cold ole funeral home," Nana whispered.

"Nana, why you talking like that?"

"I don't want there to be no mistaking what I want, so I'm telling you now. And I don't want no carnations. I want some white roses and lilies of the valley."

Dakota looked down with tears in her eyes and said, "Yes, Nana, of course you'll have whatever you want."

"Thank you, baby," she said, patting her granddaughter's hand.

"Nana, you're not going anywhere soon," Dakota said, trying to ward off the inevitable.

"Hush up now so I can enjoy the service."

After church, once they were back home, Tricia went upstairs to change clothes, giving Nana a chance to have a little heart-to-heart with Dakota. "Baby, go on back home. You been here long enough. I'm a be all right. The Lord's preparing a place for me. We have to put our trust in Him and remember in Him we'll all have everlasting life."

Dakota knew she was right, but was reluctant to go. "I don't want to leave you," she sobbed, throwing her arms around Nana.

"Baby, I've had a good life and watching you grow into a strong independent woman has been my greatest joy," Nana said, tightly embracing Dakota. "I'm trusting you to look out for Tricia, 'cause she still hasn't found her way."

"I will, Nana. Don't worry," Dakota said, wiping the tears away with the back of her hand.

"I been feeling so good lately, ole Nana'll be here longer

than them doctors thank. Now go on and pack up your things."

Dakota turned to walk away. "Nana, I love you so much."

"I love you too, baby. Now scoot."

14

"Superstar!" Spence greeted Blake as he strolled into the gallery decked out in a black Prada high-cut suit, black textured shirt, and a black ribbed tie. Spence always looked as if he'd just strolled out of *Town & Country*. His skin had the perpetual glow of expert post-exfoliation.

Blake set aside the original prints he'd been assessing. He was pleasantly surprised to see Spence. "Hey, man. What are you doing here?"

"I was in the neighborhood, so I thought I'd drop in. I just showed a *fabulous* penthouse on Central Park West," Spence answered. "If only I had an extra nine mil lying around," he said wistfully, flipping his hand in the air.

He probably does, Blake thought, smiling at his friend. Spence was the in-the-mix real estate agent to New York's hip entertainment set. He'd sold homes to famous actors, actresses, studio executives, and NBA players. The fact that he was black and gay had never stopped him. Spence could charm the scales off a snake with his award-winning smile.

"When you close the deal, don't forget to hook a brother up," Blake said, slipping intentionally into street vernacular. "Every time you see a bare wall, think 'art.' Otherwise I could starve to death up in here in WASP land." Blake was teasing, but also serious. He knew that alliances like this one were how he would succeed in the lily-white world of fine art.

"Now you know I couldn't forget you. Every time I think bare anything, I think Blake." Spence had that coy gleam in his eyes that Blake knew all too well. He and Spence had dated for a while, but quickly discovered that they both like their mates rougher. In gay lingo, they were two bottoms, both needing a top.

"So who's the client?" Blake asked, showing Spence into his elegant but sparse office. Though the gallery wasn't officially opened yet, his office had been completed. The desk was a Chippendale, borrowed from the attic of the family's house in the Hamptons. It sat on an oval silk Persian rug, with hues of cranberry, pale blue, and chartreuse. The walls were painted a smooth eggshell in order to display a collection of contemporary art. On the wall opposite the vaulted entry hung an impressive abstract oil on canvas painted in 1935 by Arshile Gorky, called *The City*. The far wall boasted a series of photographs by the heralded photographer Lyle Ashton Harris. Using one of only five 20-by-24-inch developing machines in the world, his new Polaroid cross-process technique produced a patina effect reminiscent of nineteenth-century toned albumen prints.

Settling into an Italian-inspired mahogany guest chair, Spence crossed his legs so that a black square-toed Testoni shoe dangled off one knee. "Reggie-Regge, you know, the hip-hop mogul, owns Wrap Records? He also had a clothing line called Wrap Around."

"Vaguely," Blake answered. The name sounded familiar, but Blake's idea of pop culture was a quick jaunt over to the Met.

"Anyway, he's worth about a gazillion dollars and is insisting on something on the Upper East Side that screams money. I told him that the two concepts are diametrically opposed."

"Diametrically opposed? If you said that, I'm sure he had no idea what you were talking about." They both laughed.

"What time are you getting out of here?"

Looking at his watch, Blake answered, "In a couple of minutes, actually. I don't think I could listen to another Fifth Avenue trophy wife lamenting over the challenge of matching her artwork to her chintz."

"You'd better get used to it," Spence laughed.

"You'd think I would be, considering my mother's penchant for decorating."

"True. I forgot you grew up on Park Avenue."

"Yeah, but at least Moms also cared about things other than French lace."

"I know these women can be a royal pain, but grin and bear it. I have to every day. Come to think of it"—Spence cocked his head—"you're not even open for business yet, are you?"

"I'm not really, but Mom and Dad are sending a stream of referrals. I think they want to make sure when I move into my own place next week that I can support myself. In other words, they don't want me to come crawling back to the penthouse."

"You poor thing," Spence teased.

"You wouldn't tease me if you could hear some of these tacky nouveau riche wives."

"Don't be confused. Money is money. You can't also expect taste. You should hear Reggie-Regge's ghetto-fabulous baby-mamma waxing on about the benefits of four-color tattoos versus two-color."

Standing up, Blake said, "On that dreary note . . ."

"Hey, let's go over to the X-Spot and grab a drink." The X-Spot was a gay bar on Avenue D in Alphabet City.

"Let's do it," Blake said, grabbing his fedora as they headed for the door.

The X-Spot was so "inside" that from the outside a tourist would never know it existed. The only evidence was a small sign with the Roman numeral "X" hanging from two metal hooks. There were no marquees, lights, velvet ropes, or doormen. When Blake walked up to the thick dark metal door, he rang a discreet doorbell and waited to be inspected through a small peephole.

Passing muster, Blake and Spence gained entry into pitch darkness. A thick velvet drape was parted and they proceeded into a dimly lit speakeasy with low ceilings and rustic stamped-tin walls. Settling into comfy upholstered chairs snuggled up to a round marble-topped table, they were perfectly situated to see and be seen.

The waiter, a dark muscular clean-shaven type in tight black stretch pants and a fitted T-shirt, made his way over. "What can I get for you, boys?"

"I'll have a gimlet martini," Blake said, absently checking out the scene.

"The same, but with vodka and a splash," Spence said.

The club was a series of cozy living rooms, with low over-stuffed sofas, inviting chairs, and the soft glow of candlelight. Jill Scott's sultry voice drifted through the air, creating a nice mellow, intimate groove. After their drinks were presented on a gold-plated serving tray, Blake raised his glass to take a sip, but before he could wet his lips, he was interrupted.

"Blake! What a surprise."

"Hi," Blake said, somewhat caught off guard by the face that appeared before him. He couldn't remember the fellow's name.

Sensing his friend's dilemma, Spence chimed in. "Hi, I'm Spence Ellis." He reached out to shake the stranger's hand.

"I'm Freddie. Freddie Hudson," the slim man said, careful to enunciate properly.

"Nice to meet you," Spence said, giving Freddie the once-over.

"Same here. Do you guys mind if I join you?" Freddie asked, pulling up a chair before his question could be answered. He felt a surge of adrenaline. He'd trailed Mr. Money Bags and his sidekick, who also looked to be dipped in gold, from the gallery. This time he even had some shoes to match his designer duds.

"Of course not," Blake said. After all, Freddie's company could spice up the evening. "Excuse me," he said, motioning to the passing waiter, "would you bring our friend here a drink?"

A couple of drinks later, they were all pleasantly lubed and having a grand old time speculating on the backgrounds and sexual prowess of the bar's other patrons.

"I'll bet homeboy over in the corner is carrying a dangerous load." Freddie eyed a bodybuilder type with a knowing expression, taking a slow sip of his martini. His first meeting with a martini, over an hour ago, hadn't been love at first sip. But it was amazing how quickly one adapted. Now the potent drink went down smooth as silk.

"Don't be too sure of that. You know what they say about all of that working out?" Spencer half smiled.

"Do tell." Blake leaned back, enjoying this.

"Don't quote me, but something about pumping iron—especially if steroids are involved—causes a shrinkage of the family jewels."

Freddie wasn't buying it. "You don't believe that, do you?"

"There's only one way to find out," Spence challenged. "Are you man enough?"

Always down for a dare, Freddie rose from his seat and sauntered over to the six-foot-two, 260-pound cut of muscle seated at the bar. After several minutes of gesturing and posturing by Freddie, Spence and Blake noticed him shimmy closer to the heap of beef. Then Freddie leaned down and put his mouth to the other man's ear while his hand disappeared into his lap. A large toothy grin broke out across Muscle Man's face.

Show over, Freddie returned to the table to report he had firsthand knowledge that the testosterone poisoning rumor was greatly exaggerated. He leaned into Blake, whispering something naughty.

Blushing, Blake said, "Well, the mind *is* a terrible thing to waste."

Not missing a beat, Freddie shot back, "And so is a good hard-on."

15

Dakota's mood matched her outfit—black. She was slightly depressed. She still hadn't quite come to grips with Nana's condition. And she had had a bitch of a day. At seven-thirty in the morning, the futures were down, indicating the market was going to open in New York in negative territory. By nine-forty her screen was bleeding, with the Dow minus three hundred and the NASDAQ down one hundred fifty. There was panic selling all over the Street.

"Dakota, line two!" yelled Paul.

She put up her hand and twirled her index finger in the air, the signal for "I'll call back."

Paul relayed her message, then yelled back, "It's Juerg, and he wants you *now*!"

"Hey there, Juerg," Dakota said calmly, disguising the panic in her heart. "How are you doing?"

"How are my stocks doing? Tell me that. Then I'll tell you how I'm doing," he snapped into the receiver.

"Juerg, you know as well as I do that all this selling is just a knee-jerk reaction to that tech analyst over at Goldman forecasting negative earnings for the sector," she said, trying to calm her nervous client.

"That may be true, but my portfolio is still down thirty percent."

"All of your holdings are in solid companies with positive

earnings, so hold tight and let's not make any rash moves. We'll see what the afternoon brings."

"I know but . . ."

"But if you sell now you're going to lose more than thirty percent. Tell you what, if the market doesn't rebound by one o'clock, *then* we'll devise an exit strategy. Okay?"

"Well . . ."

"You trust me, don't you, Juerg?" she asked firmly.

"I do. I just hope you're right."

"I usually am." Dakota chuckled, trying to lighten up the conversation. "Talk to you this afternoon." She put down the phone, looked at her screen, then popped two Tylenols and said a prayer.

Fortunately for Dakota, the afternoon saw a market rebound. She watched as her screen of stock tickers magically transformed like a proverbial stoplight, from red to green. As promised, she picked up the phone and dialed Juerg in Zurich. Even though it was now seven o'clock in Switzerland, she knew he would still be in the office, eagerly anticipating her call.

Sure enough, he snatched up the phone on the first ring. "Juerg here."

"We're back in the money!" she said gleefully. "The Dow is up one ten and rising."

"Who's better than you, Dakota?"

"Not many." Of course, she was well aware that the Dow could have continued to plummet and this conversation would have had a totally different slant. Wall Street was schizophrenic. The market could change for no apparent reason in a blink of an eye. The only true loyalty the client had was to money, be it the dollar, yen, pound, or euro. As long as you were making it, they were taking it, she thought. Then you're a goddess. But let their portfolio lose a little profit and you're suddenly a bumbling idiot. "I'll speak to you tomorrow, Juerg."

Despite the Tylenol her head was still throbbing at four o'clock when the closing bell rang. The stress of the day had taken its toll on her nerves. Instinctively she picked up the phone to call Morgan for an after-work drink but hung up before the call went through. Morgan was alcohol-free during her pregnancy, and Dakota felt like having some serious drinks tonight.

She decided to go solo to check out the scene at the Hudson, the latest ultrahip Ian Schrager hotel on Fifty-eighth and Ninth. Formerly a residence for single women, the building had been completely gutted, transforming it into an eclectic lodge in the middle of the city, complete with mounted elk heads, exposed brick walls, a library with fireplace, a cutting-edge restaurant, and a private garden and cozy bar areas.

"Good evening," the handsome doorman said as he opened the door for Dakota.

"Good evening, yourself." She smiled. They must do their hiring from a local modeling agency, she mused.

Dakota stepped on the escalator that led to the lobby, and as she rode up she looked at the Lucitelike walls on either side. They were illuminated with bright chartreuse-colored lights, and made her feel as if she were going to a dance club. As she reached the lobby, she noticed the huge ornate chandelier, adorned with hologram pictures of lightbulbs, hanging above the registration desk. She decided to have a drink in the library, which was subdued compared to the other bar areas. Dakota took a seat at one of the empty game tables.

"What can I get for you?" said the attractive waitress.

"I'll have a dirty martini with Belvedere."

"Would you like to run a tab?"

"Why not?" she said, taking out her Platinum card and handing it to the waitress.

She looked around the room, thinking she was definitely in the land of the beautiful people. Everyone from the wait staff to the patrons was gorgeous and dressed to kill. The room looked more like a movie set than a bar. Dakota glanced down at her outfit and was glad she had worn her black knit jersey wrap dress and Louis Vuitton black-and-brown-check sling backs. As she took her first sip of her drink, she continued to people-watch. Suddenly her eyes landed on a familiar face.

Dakota motioned the waitress over. "Can you send him a drink on me?" she said, nodding her head in the direction of a strikingly handsome gentleman. She slid lower in her comfortable club chair and watched like a spy on a covert mission as the waitress took his drink order. He scanned the room, trying to determine who had bought him a cocktail. Seeing no one he recognized, he turned back to the bar and his drink.

Dakota motioned the waitress back over. "Can you do me a favor? Ask him for his cell number. Tell him the person who bought him a drink would like to call him."

"Uh, okay."

"But don't come directly back to me, because I don't want him to see me yet."

The waitress seemed uncertain, as if the task were too complex for her.

What an airhead, Dakota thought. She *must* be a model. She watched as the waitress took his cell number and walked back to the bar. Dakota composed a quick script in her head so she wouldn't sound like an idiot when she called him. Finally the waitress came back with the number. Dakota took out her cell and quickly dialed. She could hear his phone ring from across the room.

"Hello," he said in a sexy baritone voice.

"Hey there, handsome," she said, trying to keep from laughing. "Are you waiting for someone?" She wanted to determine if he was expecting someone before she revealed herself. For all she knew, he was waiting for his girlfriend.

"I'm not waiting for anyone. Just sitting here enjoying the drink you bought for me. I would love to return the favor, but I don't have a clue who you are, or for that matter where you are," he said, continuing to scan the room.

Dakota waited until he was looking in the opposite direction, then stood up and walked toward him. When she was standing only a few inches away, she said, "Hey there."

Hearing her voice come from his phone as well as his free ear, Tristan Lewis quickly turned around. "Dakota Cantrell! When did you get back?"

"Yesterday."

He clicked his phone shut, stood up, and gave her a tight hug. "How's your grandmother?"

"She's hanging in there. Thanks for asking." She remained in his embrace, inhaling his intoxicating cologne and lingering longer than she should have. "What is that scent?" she finally asked.

"Dunhill." He slowly released her. "Do you like it?"

I like you, she wanted to say, but merely said, "Yes."

"Here, have a seat." They moved over to a cozy leather sofa in front of the fireplace. He pressed his knee against her leg as they chatted and caught up since seeing each other in Chicago. "Have you had dinner yet?" he asked eventually.

Dakota didn't know whether it was the warmth of the fireplace or Tristan's nearness that was causing the heat to rise within her, making her palms sweat. "No, I haven't."

Her interest in him must have been mutual, because he straightened up. "I'll check with the hostess to see if we can get a reservation. I'll be right back."

Tristan headed in the direction of the Hudson Cafeteria, a high-ceilinged restaurant with communal tables and upscale comfort food, which was on the opposite side of the registration desk. Dakota watched him as he reentered the bar. She hadn't noticed before but he was slightly slue-footed, just enough to make his strut enticingly sexy.

"We're in luck. They can seat us now," he said, reaching for her hand and helping her out of the deep-seated sofa.

"I have to settle this tab," she said, looking for the waitress.

Handing her back her card, he said, "It's been taken care of."

So . . . he has a few tricks of his own, she thought.

They walked hand in hand to the restaurant, like old friends with a new agenda. "Right this way," said the hostess, showing them to their table.

"Would you care for a cocktail before dinner?" a waiter asked, once they were seated.

Before Dakota could answer, Tristan said, "We'll have a bottle of Veuve Clicquot."

"Yes, sir." The waiter smiled.

She was impressed. "Are we celebrating anything in particular, or is this just a champagne kind of night?"

"Both," he said coyly. "Remember the deal I was telling you about in Chicago?"

"You mean with Microsoft?"

"Yeah. Initially, I was going to take my company public, but since the market isn't receptive to IPOs these days, like it was a few years ago, I decided to sell to the big boys and not take the risk. I just closed the deal this week."

The waiter brought over the champagne and two crystal flutes.

"Here's to realizing your dreams. Congratulations!" Dakota said with a gleam in her eye.

Tristan clinked her glass. "Thank you."

It must have been the combination of the champagne and Tristan, because halfway through dinner Dakota was as giddy as a teenager on a first date. "So . . ." she said, smiling.

"Yeesss?"

"Why were you going to celebrate alone?"

He picked up her hand and kissed the inside of her palm. Looking into her eyes, he said, "Actually, I'd just finished a long boring meeting with my accountant and thought I'd have a quick drink before heading home. I'm glad I did."

His smile should be patented, Dakota thought.

She opened her mouth to speak, but words escaped her. Instead she let out a slight moan.

He held her hand close to his chest for a moment, before gently putting it back on the table, but keeping it covered by his.

The waiter approached and cleared his throat discreetly. "Would you care to see the dessert menu?"

"What I have a taste for isn't on the menu," Tristan said with a laugh, and Dakota nodded in agreement. "Just the check, please."

After settling the bill, Tristan extended his hand to her as she stood up. "Do you want to go over to Iridium and listen to some jazz?"

Now completely out of her black mood, she had a different idea in mind. "I'm not in the mood for jazz."

"What about a nightcap?"

"Yeah, I guess I could go for a port. What's in walking distance?" she said. "There's O'Neals' on Sixty-fourth."

"I know a place that's even closer," Tristan said, pressing the elevator's UP button.

Dakota was confused. "Does the Hudson have a roof garden?"

"Yes, but that's not where we're going," he said as the door slid open.

He pressed the button for the tenth floor, and as they rose he took out a room key.

"You're staying here?" she asked, surprised, knowing that he lived in the city.

Tristan encircled her waist, pulling her close. "I made a reservation when I reserved the table."

"Aren't we a smooth operator?" she said, falling willingly into his embrace. She felt an electric charge of excitement, yet at the same time didn't like coming across as so predictable. He must have been awfully sure of her to drop $400 on a room here! But then she thought, What the hell? You only live once. And she *had* known him since grade school. She pulled away, then sashayed out of the elevator and down the hall.

Tristan surveyed the curvaceous figure before him, watching as the clingy fabric of her dress outlined her hips.

Dakota turned around. "What room are you in?" she said, suggestively walking toward him and taking the key out of his hand.

"Ten-fourteen."

He snuggled up close behind Dakota as she tried to open the door. He ran his hand against her soft rear, checking for panty lines, but found none. He could feel an erection coming on and began to kiss the back of her neck. She fumbled with the key and dropped it. As she bent over to pick it up, he grabbed her hips with both hands and began to grind his now rock-hard erection into her backside.

Dakota was glad she had worn her black lace thong, which was now moist. She quickly inserted the key before somebody caught them in this lewd position, and opened the door. Once inside, she instantly pushed Tristan against the back of the door and began to unbuckle his pants, eager to check out his package. It had been months since she had even kissed a man, let alone had passionate sex. The alcohol had unleashed the desire that was already in her. Within seconds his pants slid to the floor and he stood there in a pair of snug sport boxers that emphasized his impressive package. She put her hands on the waistband and slowly stripped him of his underwear. Her mouth watered as she stroked his smooth, hot flesh. She dropped to her knees and took him into her mouth. She teased the tip of his penis with her tongue as she gently fondled his testicles. She then took the full length in her mouth and began to lick and suck him, slowly at first but gradually picking up the rhythm and intensity until she could taste his sweet juice as it began to ooze out.

"Oh, baby, you got skills."

"I want you to come for me," she murmured.

"What?" he panted.

She looked up into his eyes, while still stroking his penis with her hands. "I want you to come for me."

"Not yet," he said, sliding down to the floor, in between her legs. He flipped her dress off above her head and pulled her thong down over her hips. "Oh, I love a Brazilian," he said, referring to her completely waxed pubic area. He ran his large hand across the smooth skin, then planted wet kisses on her mound. The anticipation of what was coming next made Dakota gasp with desire. He began to suck her firm clitoris, driving her even closer to the edge.

Without taking his mouth off her, Tristan reached back for his pants, found his wallet, took out a Magnum, and rolled it onto his erect penis. He spread her legs wide with his muscular arms, then slowly entered her. They immediately found their rhythm, and before long were singing the same song. "I'm coming, I'm *coming*!"

As they lay on the carpet, drained but satisfied, Tristan pulled Dakota close to him. "Now that's what I call a nightcap."

She laid her head on his chest and could hear his heart beating. All the while she was thinking, What have I gotten myself into?

He reached down and began to massage her rear. "You're so soft." He then bent over and began to kiss and suck her breast. "I don't know what it is about you, but I want more."

Dakota looked down and couldn't believe her eyes. He was rock-hard again, as if he had never had an orgasm. "What are you on? Viagra?"

"Baby, I don't need no little blue pill. All I need is you," he said with a cocky grin and began to kiss her passionately.

Dakota laced her fingers in his curly hair and gave into her desires. It had been a long time since she had had such uninhibited sex. Her mind began to reel with thoughts of the last time she totally gave herself to a man—and the heartache it caused. A chill swept through her, almost like a premonition. Why couldn't she let relationships develop more gradually? Why did it have to be all or nothing? She suddenly felt like a fool to think that growing up in the same neighborhood would make a difference. Tristan was a player. She stopped kissing him.

"What's wrong?" Tristan asked, sounding a little annoyed.

"I think I should go," Dakota said, pulling away.

"You're kidding, right?"

"No," she said, searching for her underwear.

Tristan was not taking no for an answer. He began kissing the small of her back, using the roughness of his goatee to send chills up her spine. He trailed his tongue up to her neck, finding another of her vulnerable erogenous zones. He reached around, spread her legs, and gently played with her labia, causing her to moan.

Dakota tried to resist, but the good feelings were overwhelming. Against her better judgment she fell back into his arms. He scooped her up and carried her to the bed. He covered her breasts with soft wet kisses, until her nipples were firm. "I'll be right back," he whispered.

"Wait," she panted. "Where are you going?"

Stroking her stomach, he said, "To get another condom."

"Hurry up."

To her surprise, he said, "Don't worry. I'm a give you some more of this big dick."

Dakota didn't like his tone. It sounded so crude and selfish. She sat up and swung her legs over the side of the bed. I'll show him I can resist him and his *big dick,* she thought, standing up to leave. But her constitution weakened as she watched him slide the condom on over his long hard shaft and walk toward her. The man might be conceited, but he sure had the goods to back it up. Dakota sighed and fell back on the bed.

16

The New York Knicks were playing the Chicago Bulls at Madison Square Garden. The house was packed as New York fans prayed en masse for a shot at the playoffs. Miles and Phillip sat in their corporate seats courtside, cheering, berating, and cajoling their favorite team on to victory.

"Man, did you see that pass?" Miles screamed, rising from his seat, catapulted by the contagious surge of testosterone raging through the building. "That was nasty!" Greg Anthony, Chicago's veteran guard, had just executed a between-the-legs blind pass to Elton Brand, which resulted in a barreling in-your-face, chest-pounding slam dunk.

Miles was feeling a little schizophrenic tonight. Even though he wanted his Knicks to win, he also wanted his boy Greg to have a good game.

"Whose side are you on?" Phillip asked, looking around nervously. New York fans didn't take kindly to demonstrative cheering for opponents. Particularly when the guilty party was sporting a Knicks cap.

"Hey, man, I just want Greg to have a good game."

"Are you kidding? He can have one tomorrow night, but not here at the Garden. This is hostile territory." As if to punctuate Phillip's sentiment, the three-hundred-pounder wedged into the seat next to Miles shifted and glared at him. He looked as though the outcome of the game was the single most important event in his life, with the possible exception of scarfing down his next couple Big Macs.

Just then Greg passed their seats on the way to his bench, but not before stopping to salute Miles with a smile. This treacherous act caused the capillaries in Miles' seatmate's bulbous nose to engorge. He turned pointedly to Miles and stared at him.

"Yo, man, you got a problem?" Miles asked, meeting the stare straight on.

Before the man could respond, Phillip said, "Hey, man, you gotta excuse him. He and Greg are brothers. This is Miles Anthony. You understand. Right?" Miles rolled his eyes at the lame excuse, but his neighbor chilled out, while Phillip prayed that Greg would remain on the bench for the rest of the night. Greg didn't, but their neighbor, disheartened by Chicago's twenty-point lead with ten minutes remaining, rose to go.

"Well, the Bulls brought the noise tonight," Miles said.

"Let's not start that again," Phillip said as they went back to watching the game.

"Wow! That was a great give-and-go," a female voice said.

In what was the empty seat now sat Vic, wearing a Knicks cap with her ponytail hanging out of the back, a pair of asshugging, low-rider jeans and a white shirt with the collar up.

Phillip spoke first. "Vic, what are you doing here?"

"Just cheering on my team, though tonight it didn't seem to do much good."

"What do you know about a give-and-go?" Miles asked, a bemused smile on his face.

"I know my b-ball," Vic answered with a little challenge in her voice.

"I see," Miles said, impressed. Just then Allan Houston hit a three-pointer from downtown and the entire arena jumped to its feet, roaring—one mass of high fives and pumping fists.

Miles, marveling at the incredible shot, nearly got knocked off his feet as Vic grabbed him in a bear hug. "Yes!" she screamed, eyes glued to the court. Miles' arms involuntarily went around her to steady himself, and his hand connected with her firm, round ass. He quickly released her and stepped back, but not before she flashed him a knowing look and a just-admit-you-want-me smile.

Miles felt a rush of heat that had nothing to do with the other nineteen thousand fans. Phillip simply shook his head.

After the game, Miles and Phillip met Greg and some of the other players for drinks at Canteen, a too-cool below-street-level restaurant on Mercer Street at Prince. When the players walked in, they drew stares from every woman in the place. As if they wore homing devices, the restaurant was soon packed with the little black spandex dress cadre.

Phillip chuckled at the scene. Tonight's groupie leader wore hers so tight that surgical hemostats would be necessary to separate it from her skin. Closing in on Elton Brand, she armed herself by slinging her stringy straw-blond hair over her shoulders and pushing out her silicon-pumped breasts before moving in for the kill. "You are sooo cute." She fired up a killer bleach-enhanced smile.

Some of the young players hadn't been around the block long enough not to be flattered by a white chick with blond hair and big boobs. Some of the older players, Greg had told Miles, called them the IRS, short for the "Income Radar Sorority." They could spot a dollar a mile away, sniffing out money like pigs hunting truffles.

Watching this scene unfold, Miles and Phillip shook their heads. "Man, a brotha's got to be so careful these days. If homeboy breathes on that chick hard enough, she'll harvest sperm from thin air and turn up pregnant with twins," Miles said.

Phillip laughed. "Yeah. It's pretty amazing. They must wait to ovulate, then come out scouting."

"Some chicks can be just that strategic."

"Speaking of strategic chicks, what's going on with your girl Vic?" Phillip peered at Miles questioningly.

Miles looked at him out of the corner of his eye. "Nothing. Why?"

"You just need to watch your back, man."

"Last time you said I should watch the butt. Which is it?"

Without blinking Phillip said, "Both."

"What are you talking about?"

"Homegirl's got the hots for you. Haven't you seen the way she looks at you in meetings? And no matter what you say, she agrees with it. I know yo ass is tight and all, but she acts like your shit comes in flavors."

"Hots or not, it doesn't matter. I am not interested," Miles said, taking a long sip of his Pinch scotch.

"Just be careful. With chicks like that, they can be more dangerous if you aren't interested."

Miles spread his hands out in frustration. "So what am I? Damned if I do and damned if I don't?"

"All I'm saying is just stay clear."

"That's a little hard, since I do work with her."

"True, but you can keep your hands off of her ass," Phillip said, getting right to the point.

"Now you know I couldn't help that."

Phillip wasn't buying it. "Take my advice and stay away. And if you can't, make sure you're not alone with her, because chicks like Vic are usually up to no good."

"Consider me advised," Miles said, wanting to end this line of conversation. He wasn't sure where this was coming from. As far as he could see, Vic was flirtatious but cool. But to hear Morgan, and now Phillip, tell it, she was the original femme fatale.

Miles decided to turn the tables a little. "So what's going on with you and Paula?"

"Everything's cool," Phillip said, scowling.

Miles looked at him questioningly. It wasn't because of what he said, as much as what he didn't say. As long as he and Paula had been together, Phillip still didn't sound like a man anxious to walk down the aisle. "Okay, man, what's up?"

"What're you talking about?"

"Phillip, it's me. Miles. Okay? I know you well enough to know that something's wrong." When no comment was forthcoming, he added, "You've been counseling me all night, and I've got a little more experience on the female front than you do. So come clean."

Sighing, Phillip gave in. "You know, man, it's really funny, because it's nothing specific. It's just a fear that something is missing."

"Something like what?" Miles leaned back on the bar stool, crossing his arms over his chest.

Phillip shook his head. "It's that spark. That excitement of holding hands and just being together. Of course it hardly ever feels like she's truly with me anymore—always connected to her job with that damn cell phone. And it's funny, because I love Paula as a person and didn't realize until recently that something was wrong."

"Could it be cold feet, especially since I know you want to get married?"

Phillip looked thoughtful, as though searching for the source of his discontent. "I don't think so, because I don't have a problem with married. I want one woman I can spend my life with. I want the white picket fence, the two point five kids, and the dog."

Miles gave him a dig with his elbow. "I feel you on the wife, kids, and dog, but spare me the white picket fence, okay?"

Phillip didn't laugh, though. He was totally serious as he asked, "What about you? How did you know that you weren't making a mistake with Morgan? And that you wouldn't find greener grass on the next block?"

Adopting a mock philosophical tone, Miles leaned into Phillip. "Little grasshopper, you will know if the lawn is meant for you, when you no longer notice the weeds."

Finally Phillip did crack a smile. "You know, that's some deep shit, Miles."

"Yep. Love has a way of erasing imperfections—or at least blinding you to them."

Phillip sat back, absorbing Miles' words. He wasn't sure whether he was with Paula because he truly loved her and couldn't live without her, or out of habit. If he wasn't happy now, how could he expect happily ever after? The more he thought about it, the fewer answers he seemed to have.

The hostess came over to tell them their table was ready.

As they were saying good night to Greg, Miles saw that the group of b-ballers already had a casualty. One young player was now a prisoner of war, being led out the door by the blonde. Miles turned to Phillip and said, "Another one bites the dust."

17

Today was a case of everything that could go wrong was going wrong—all at the same time. And at the worst possible time. Blake's father, Dr. St. James, had sent Morgan a referral, which she considered an important test for Caché. If she passed, she and Caché would be closer to the seed money he was considering investing, as well as to a stellar list of clients. This client was from Transmodul, a small multinational consulting firm. They were hosting a dinner for seventy clients; many of which were either global corporations or well on their way to becoming global.

Before Morgan could even put her briefcase down that morning, Lisa pounced. "Tommy called saying he couldn't find the fuchsia ascocenda orchids you requested, and Henrí did an inspection of the facilities and is threatening to quit. He says that the convection oven is a relic and not fit to bake his award-winning white-chocolate chestnut soufflé." Before Morgan could respond, a body blow took her breath away. The baby had gotten comfortable right in the small of her back, and wouldn't move except to occasionally kick the inflamed nerve that he or she was resting on.

"Lisa, get Tommy on the phone right now. You tell him that if I don't see ascocenda orchids when I walk in tonight, I will personally hunt him down and yank that god-awful toupee right off of the top of his incompetent head." Glaring through the pain, she said, "Then I'll take it and sauté it in animal fat before feeding it to that weird-looking dog he calls a pet."

"Morgan?" Lisa was shocked.

"What?" Morgan winced.

"Don't you think you're overreacting—maybe just a little?" Lisa held her index finger and thumb very close together.

First Miles, now Lisa. "No. I asked him ten days ago to get those orchids. If there was a problem, I don't appreciate hearing about it the day of the event." Morgan snatched up the phone, ready for battle.

Before she could dial a digit, Lisa gently removed the phone with a worried look on her face. "Don't call him now. I'll handle it."

When she got him on the phone, Lisa began calmly, but ended, "I don't care where you get them, or if you have to grow them yourself, we expect to see those orchids tonight. On time!" She hung up the phone.

Morgan was still seething. "There's no way I'll let a few glitches ruin the evening we've planned."

"Neither will I." Lisa fixed Morgan with a penetrating look. "Promise me that you will let me handle this." When Morgan hesitated, she said in a firm tone, "Morgan?"

Just then the baby delivered another body blow. Morgan frowned through the pain. "Okay. Just make sure that it happens. This one's important."

When the phone blared again, Morgan stared at it as though it were the Antichrist. The way her day was going, she figured it had to be more bad news.

Lisa snatched it up. "Good afternoon, Caché. How may I help you?" After listening intently for a couple of moments, Lisa seemed to slump in her chair. She looked like a balloon that had just been pricked. "I'll be right there," she said before hanging up the phone.

Morgan was alarmed at her tone. "What is it?" she asked, bracing herself.

Lisa was already at the closet, grabbing her coat, halfway out the door. "Morgan, I'm sorry. I've got to go."

"Lisa."

Before Morgan could catch up to her, she was through the doorway, pulling her coat on. "I'll be there tonight. I've gotta go," she said as she sprinted to her car.

Morgan plopped down onto the sofa wearing a puzzled expression. She glanced at her Chaumet wristwatch—it was three o'clock. The dinner would begin at seven. As far as Morgan was concerned this was when she needed Lisa most. What was wrong with her? she wondered. Was something wrong with Justin? Whatever it was, she prayed that it would be fixed before seven o'clock tonight.

She and Lisa had put creative wizardry to work to transform the dining room for tonight's dinner into a work of art; it felt like a Japanese den with a European twist. Deep burgundy-velvet chairs sat around silk-draped tables dressed with bamboo mats, smooth ceramic china, chopsticks, and art-inspired flatware. The room itself was illuminated with soft lighting to give it a warm glow and flatter the guests. The menu would consist of wild mushroom gnocchi seasoned with fresh sage, followed by grilled rack of lamb with rosemary and crushed garlic flowers, served with individual crocks of spinach gratin. And of course, for dessert, Henrí's famous award-winning white-chocolate chestnut soufflé—they hoped.

Arriving at the venue at five-thirty, Morgan was greeted by eleven perfectly set tables with ascocenda orchids as their centerpieces. While she stood there enjoying the vision, she smelled the unmistakable aroma of fine cuisine wafting from the kitchen. Undoubtedly Henrí was busy at work. But there was no sign of Lisa.

Before she could speed dial her cell phone, Lisa walked through the front door. She looked exhausted.

She pepped up after seeing the orchids. "Thank God they got here," she said, shedding her coat.

"Thank God you got here. What happened today?" Morgan asked her, carefully scrutinizing Lisa.

"It's Justin. He got sick in school."

"Is he okay?" Morgan suddenly forgot about the orchids and the soufflé.

"He's better now. He's home with my grandmother."

Lisa still seemed sad and distracted to Morgan. Lisa wasn't telling her everything. This was the third time in four months that Justin had fallen ill at school. And Morgan remembered thinking that Justin didn't look well when she first met him.

"Lisa, is there something going on with Justin?" she probed gently.

"It's nothing. Just a stomach flu." Changing the subject, she said, "The room looks great. Is that a soufflé I smell?"

"Thank God, yes. Whatever you said to that prima donna chef, it worked," Morgan said, smiling.

Lisa was now glowing from a healthy dose of praise for saving the day. "I do have a few tricks up my sleeve."

"Well, keep 'em coming."

Cranston Loudel, Transmodul's senior partner, arrived and walked over. "Morgan, everything looks spectacular."

"Thank you, Mr. Loudel. We aim to please," Morgan said, including Lisa in his praise.

"It definitely shows, just look at these flowers," he said, referring to the rare orchids.

"We had those specially flown in by a local florist," Morgan said.

"Good job." He beamed Morgan an appreciative smile before turning to leave.

After he was out of earshot, Morgan said, "I'd better go check on Henrí and his precious masterpiece."

Later, after the event wrapped up, Dakota came by to meet Morgan for dessert and coffee. They walked up Park Avenue to a little café, where they settled into a corner table.

After they placed their orders, Dakota asked, "How did it go tonight?"

"It was close, but everything turned out well. The client was happy, and that's all that matters."

"What do you mean close?" The waiter brought a double

skim latte for Dakota, a cup of chamomile tea for Morgan, and one wedge of German chocolate cake, with two forks.

Morgan went on to describe the touch-and-go events that began that morning.

"Talk about sky-high stress levels!"

"Who are you telling? If that dinner had fallen apart, I could kiss Dr. St. James' money and contacts good-bye. Thank God it didn't. But I'm worried about Lisa," she confided.

"I'd watch her more closely," Dakota warned.

"Because her son is sick?"

"Maybe that was just an excuse for her to cut out on you."

"You think she'd use her son as an excuse just to leave the office?" Morgan couldn't believe that any mother would stoop to that. Besides, Lisa's reaction when she took the emergency call had been all too real.

"I don't trust her."

"Aside from a little moodiness, and poor judgment at that one client meeting, she's been really good. She did save the party tonight. She took care of Henrí and Tommy, and you can't imagine how difficult they can be." When Dakota didn't respond, Morgan asked, "What's your problem with her?"

"Did you see *All About Eve?*"

"Of course, it's one of my favorite old movies."

"Remember how Eve Harrington was always doting on Betty Davis' character, pretending to be so subservient, while the whole time the bitch was plotting to take her man and her career?" Dakota had one eyebrow raised.

Morgan just laughed at her. "Come on, Dakota, what are saying? That Lisa is planning to make off with Miles and steal Caché?"

"Don't laugh." Dakota was serious. "I'm not saying she's capable of that, but I think she's up to something. She's not being honest with you at the very least."

Stifling the unease she felt at Dakota's comments, Morgan said, "After Tyrone's scam impersonating Blake, I can't say that much would surprise me. But let's not get paranoid." Dakota was sometimes incredibly wary of people she didn't know well, which Morgan thought might be because she had been orphaned at an early age. And after Tyrone, Dakota felt extra-protective of Morgan.

"Just keep your eye on her. Didn't you tell me that she was angling to be a partner?" Recently Lisa had been dropping hints. Just last week, she'd said to Morgan, "You know, when you are out with the baby, you will need a partner in place who will care as much about Caché as you do. You know, someone with a vested interest." Morgan had tabled the discussion for later, but knew she'd have to deal with covering her maternity leave at some point. She thought she'd bring in one of her friends in the business world who had more experience and polish than Lisa.

"Just watch your back. That's all I'm saying." With that, Dakota polished off the last of the cake.

18

Blake sat in his office, counting his blessings. He felt that he had finally attained the respect and admiration of his father, and he was doing something he loved. Not to mention having a multimillion-dollar trust fund to fall back on in case his art gallery imploded. Life was good. The only thing missing was a little action in his nonexistent love life. He'd been working so hard opening the gallery that he'd neglected the pleasures of the bedroom. He wasn't necessarily looking for a big lifelong commitment or vows of fidelity, just a little fun.

Chan, Blake's newly hired Asian assistant, called through the intercom: "Blake, you've got a call on line one from a Freddie Hudson."

Blake had had several messages from Freddie since he and Spence had run into him at the X-Spot, but hadn't had a chance to return his calls. Feeling a little guilty, he said, "Put him through.

"This is Blake," he answered, his voice rich and assured.

"Hey, man, how you doin'?" Freddie asked. He was near breathless to finally get Blake on the phone.

"I'm fine. How are you?" Blake eased back in his sleekly designed leather and mahogany desk chair.

"I'd be better if I had a little company tonight," Freddie said, floating an invitation.

"Is that a fact?" Blake could hear the come-on strong in Freddie's voice.

"The fact is that I've got something real special for you," Freddie purred.

Smiling, Blake asked, "Is it bigger that a bread box?"

"It's pretty big."

"Tell me about it. Give me a hint."

"Well, let's see. It's long, stiff, and has your name written all over it."

"I don't suppose you're referring to a monogrammed pen set," Blake teased, though he was getting a little hot under the Calvins. It had been a while since he had gone down this road, especially with a rough-around-the-edges character like Freddie.

"Why don't I arrange for a personal delivery, so you can see it for yourself?"

Though Freddie wasn't the type that he would invite home for dinner, Blake thought he'd be a feisty bedmate. At least good for one night's fun. So he looked at his Audemars Piguet and said, "Can you come over around seven-thirty?" After giving Freddie his address he hung up the phone and closed his eyes, enjoying visions of a sex-filled night.

Freddie was finally being given a chance to grab the brass ring, and he did not want to miss it. For years he had watched the people who strolled up and down Madison and Fifth avenues. They wore expensive watches and designer clothes that cost more money than he'd ever stolen in his entire life. When they tired of shopping, they ate at the most expensive restaurants in the city without even thinking twice. He'd recently read about a new restaurant in the Essex House, opened by some famous French dude. He had spent more than two million dollars renovating the place, and he was charging five hundred dollars for dinner for two! And all these rich fools were lining up like refugees, waiting as long as eight months to fork it over. Didn't they know that he could buy over six hundred pieces of the Colonel's fried chicken for five hundred bones? But if he played his cards right, he too could be rolling in gourmet dough.

His preparations for tonight were extensive. He started out in the bathtub instead of the shower. Even though it was permanently ringed with various hues of rust, he closed his eyes and soaked languidly in the bubbles. Afterward, Freddie carefully lotioned his long, lean body, making sure there were no telltale signs of ghetto ash. He'd watched the way that smooth Spence dude had dressed tone-on-tone with a black shirt and black tie. He saw no reason why he couldn't look as stylish. Stepping away from the mirror, he realized that the effect wasn't quite the same with duds from the Gap. Still, it was the best he could do under the circumstances.

Outfit complete, he slammed the door of his fifth-floor walk-up and hopped on the subway downtown. He moved with purpose as he approached Blake's ritzy neighborhood on Central Park West. This was the first time he'd ever come this way with a destination and an invitation. Doing so gave him renewed confidence as he walked up to the doorman to announce his visit.

"I'm here to see Mr. Blake St. James," he said, using a regal tone.

The doorman peered at him over small rectangular glasses. "Is Mr. St. James expecting you?"

"Yes, he is," Freddie snapped.

"Just a moment." The doorman picked up the phone to call, as though he didn't believe him. Son of a bitch, Freddie thought. The doormen in these buildings were as snooty as the residents, getting off on their little sphere of power.

A minute later, he was in the elevator ascending to the kingdom above. The double doors to Blake's apartment were an imposing dark wood with a polished brass-rimmed peephole and a discreet buzzer. Freddie wiped his sweaty hands on his new pants and rang the bell. When the doors opened, Freddie had to remind himself to breathe again. He felt as though he was literally looking into another world.

"Come on in," Blake said, warmly greeting his guest.

The walls, from the expansive entry hall through the main living area of the apartment, were painted in liquid copper leaf with black-lacquered moldings. The floor was a rich, glossy hardwood where not covered by expensive Turkish wool carpets or Persian and Oriental rugs. The furniture, window treatments, and of course the art pieces were impeccable. Though he did not know exactly what he was looking at, he knew that every stick of furniture in the apartment was staggeringly expensive, and more beautiful than anything he'd ever seen up close in his entire life. With the exception of Blake himself.

"This place is awesome," Freddie couldn't help but say as he looked unabashedly around, trying to take in every opulent detail.

A little taken aback, Blake simply said, "Thank you. Can I get you something to drink? I'm having a martini." He showed Freddie to an elegant silk settee.

Freddie felt like he had in those museums that his high school would take the kids to sometimes, where there was a red velvet rope across the priceless furniture to make sure you didn't sit on it. Only here there was no rope attached. "I'll have the same."

While Cole Porter played softly in the background, Blake headed over to a 1940s-style cocktail cart to mix their drinks. A Bjorn Rye painting hung over the settee and a Steinway baby grand piano took up the corner, holding an Egyptian-style French deco vase containing three dozen garden roses in full boom.

Blake handed Freddie his drink before taking a seat next to him. "Cheers," he said, carefully clinking Freddie's crystal martini glass. Sensing his guest's discomfort, Blake started the conversation.

"What type of music do you like?" Blake asked.

"I love jazz, but R&B's my favorite. And I love Sade's new CD. It's hot." Feeling emboldened by the cocktail, he added, "But not as hot as you are."

"Is that so?" Leaning in a little closer, Blake decided to get the show on the road. "So tell me about this surprise you have for me."

Freddie was completely fixated by Blake's smooth, flawless caramel complexion and his thickly lashed eyes; the irises were a beautiful, warm brown. And Blake had the most perfect set of teeth that Freddie had ever seen. Each tooth was evenly shaped and pearly-white. And his sensuous lips looked like they'd never seen a chapped day, ever. Blake's tongue flicked out and slid over the curved top lip, then the full pouty bottom lip, leaving a moistness that beckoned to Freddie. Mesmerized, his nervousness abated, he leaned in to kiss Blake. The sensation was like his first taste of deep, rich dark chocolate. His toes curled as his loins tingled.

They kissed passionately, both men eager to journey farther down the road, certainly beyond the confines of the dainty settee. Blake moved away, pulling Freddie with him, through the living room and down the hall into his plush bedroom. Once there, they both undressed, leaving two piles of clothes strewn on the Berber carpet. Desire hung heavy in the room.

Freddie took Blake's hand and wrapped it around his own engorged member. "How do you like your gift?" he asked, his voice husky.

"I have to try it on for size first," Blake answered, before dropping to his knees to wrap Freddie's package in his mouth.

As Blake teased him with his dexterous tongue, Freddie's head was as light as air, both from the intensely building sensations within him and the incredible luxury surrounding him. He never wanted these feelings to end. Holding Blake's head, he gave him everything he had, body, soul, and seed. And Blake seemed eager to take it all.

Afterward, Freddie laid Blake on the Pratesi-covered bed and worshiped his body, from head to toes and every single inch in between, before giving himself completely to his lover. When they were both totally exhausted and satisfied, Freddie remembered his plan. He offered to go into the living room to retrieve their drinks.

The last thing Blake remembered was Freddie standing over him like a dark cloud as he took the last sip of his Belvedere martini.

19

"Hey therre, girrl!" Dakota sang as she swept into the foyer of Miles and Morgan's Harlem brownstone.

"Well, come right on in. Aren't you in a good mood?" Morgan commented, peering at her smiling friend.

"Life is *wonderful*!" Dakota declared, spinning like a top in the middle of the mahogany foyer.

"So what is Mr. Wonderful's name?" Morgan knew that the gleam in Dakota's eye was man-induced. She knew her girl all too well.

Dakota hadn't told Morgan about her new relationship with Tristan. She hadn't wanted to say anything yet, but this afternoon he had called again. He was indeed interested in her. "Tristan Lewis. We went to school together."

"School?" Morgan looked perplexed. "Does he live in Chicago?"

"We ran into each other in Chicago when I went to see Nana, but he lives here." She went on to tell Morgan about their chance encounter at the Hudson. "Girl, it was amazing. We stayed up until four in the morning having buck-wild sex. I think he's the one."

Morgan looked at Dakota like she was an extraterrestrial with two heads. "One night of hot sex and he's the *one*?"

"It wasn't just the sex. We—"

"Morgan, I have the florist on the line," Lisa interrupted, stepping into the foyer from the office. "Do you want the flowers sent to Henrí's home address or to the restaurant?"

"Send them to the restaurant. You know he'll make a big production out of receiving a beautiful arrangement in front of his coworkers. It'll be good P.R. Thanks, Lisa."

"Hello," Dakota said.

Lisa looked at Dakota like she was intruding. "Oh, hi," she said coolly, then turned back into the office.

"What is her problem? I don't know why she doesn't like me."

Morgan mouthed, *Play nice.*

"Whatever." Dakota rolled her eyes, then switched gears. "Who's Henrí?"

"He's our temperamental French chef who made that incredible meal for the Transmodul function. He likes to be stroked and I really don't mind, because it's hard to find a good chef who will do catering," Morgan said, leading Dakota into the office, where Lisa was still on the phone with the florist.

Dakota looked in Lisa's direction, then turned to Morgan. "Are you just about ready?" Dakota was there to take Morgan to the doctor's for a checkup.

"Give me a minute. I'll hit the ladies' room before we go," Morgan said.

Dakota sat on the sofa and picked up a magazine from the cocktail table. She thumbed through it and cringed as she listened to Lisa order a bouquet of pink and white roses, yellow pompons, and baby's breath. That was an arrangement befitting a suburban housewife on her birthday, not an accomplished New York City chef.

"Will they be delivered today? Okay, thank you," Lisa said, hanging up the phone.

Dakota wasn't going to say anything, but as usual she couldn't hold her tongue. "Lisa."

Lisa was writing in a notepad and didn't look up. "Yes?"

"I don't mean to intrude, but aren't those flowers you ordered a bit too pedestrian? It seems like a chef would expect something more exotic—something like birds of paradise, with tropical ginger, you know?"

Lisa's head popped up like a piece of toast. "You got a lot of nerve coming in here and telling me how to do my job," Lisa spat out.

Dakota was taken aback by Lisa's burst of anger. "Listen, I'm just trying to help."

"I don't need your help, thank you very much." She spun around in her swivel chair, giving Dakota a view of her back.

Dakota didn't want to incite her further, so she just let the subject drop. Lisa was obviously the type who had to learn the hard way.

"I'm ready," Morgan said, breezing into the room.

Driving down the Henry Hudson, Dakota was quiet. She didn't want to upset Morgan, who was chatting away about whether to have an epidural. "My doctor said most women opt for it. I still haven't decided. What do you think?"

Dakota was lost in thought and didn't hear Morgan.

"I said, what do you think?"

"About what?" Dakota glanced over at Morgan. "I'm sorry. What did you say?"

Morgan saw the distant expression on Dakota's face. "What are you thinking about? What's his name?"

"His name is Tristan, and no, I wasn't thinking, about him. Just thinking, that's all. But now that you've mentioned him"—Dakota's eyes warmed in pleasure—"I can't tell you how in sync we are."

"In sync?" Morgan shook her head. "You hardly know this guy."

"I know he's a freak," she shot back.

"The last time you got turned out by a freak, he ended up freaking somebody else, or don't you remember?" Morgan didn't want to be mean, but Dakota needed to wake up and smell the bacon. Otherwise she'd keep choosing one pig after another. "Too bad Phillip is in a relationship."

"Phillip?" Dakota scrunched up her face. "Where did that come from? Besides, isn't he in love with Ms. Lawyer?"

"I'm not pairing you with anybody. All I'm saying is you need a good brother like Phillip."

"You haven't even met Tristan. How do you know he's not a good brother?"

Morgan looked out at the murky waters of the Hudson River before answering. She didn't want to hurt Dakota's feelings. "Because I know you, and you usually gravitate toward the pretty-boy ladies'-man type. The type with a woman in every area code and no intention of settling down. And I know you want to get married and start a family, so you've got to get over that type."

Dakota couldn't deny the truth of what Morgan said, but Tristan was different. Even though he had the pretty-boy looks, he seemed sincere. She remembered how concerned he was about her when Nana had come home from the hospital. He even offered to fly back to Chicago to be with her. "I hear you, Morgan, but Tristan isn't like that. I'm telling you, he's one of the good guys. He even called to check on me when I extended my visit in Chicago," she said, in defense of her new man.

Morgan didn't want to belabor the point. "For your sake, I hope you're right."

Morgan's doctor was located near New York Presbyterian Hospital on East Sixty-eighth Street. As Dakota maneuvered through the traffic down Second Avenue, her cell rang. With the earpiece in her left ear, she hit the TALK button and spoke into the minimicrophone. "Hello? Hey, baby!" She looked over at Morgan and winked. "Oh, okay," she said, sounding disappointed. "Do you need anything? Are you sure? Okay, feel better."

"Let me guess, that was lover boy? Canceling a date?" Morgan said dryly.

"Yes, that was Tristan," she said, ignoring Morgan's tone. "We were supposed to have dinner tonight, but he's sick with a cold. I think I'll stop by the Soup Nazi after the doctor's and pick up something for him."

"Did he ask you to bring soup over?"

"No, but I'm sure he'll appreciate the gesture."

Morgan exhaled, exasperated with her lovestruck friend.
"Just be careful, Dakota," she warned.

"Thanks for caring, Morgan, but I'll be fine."

Dakota dropped Morgan off at home after her checkup
and headed west to Al's International Soup Kitchen. It was
small, but the soup was a gastronomical treat. The shop had
lines wrapped around the corner to Eighth Avenue since becoming famous on *Seinfeld*. They didn't have chicken noodle
that day, so she ordered lobster and tomato-basil bisque. With
the cartons of soup in hand, she bounced to the car on her
way to take care of her man.

She cruised along Riverside Drive, grooving to the oldies
station. "Flash Light" by Parliament Funkadelics was on the
radio. It reminded her of her pom-pom days, and she wondered if Tristan had watched her dance to that song from the
stands. She smiled at the thought.

Tristan lived in a walk-up on a tranquil tree-lined residen-
tial block between West End Avenue and Riverside Drive. She
was in luck, finding a parking space on his block. Dakota
parked her Twin Turbo 911 Carrera, which she hardly ever
drove. The car usually stayed in the garage near her loft, but
she'd offered to take Morgan to the doctor, since Miles was
out of town and she didn't want to rely on taxis. She reached
over to the passenger seat for the soup and her purse. Dakota
got out and locked the door. Since the car was an antique, it
didn't have one of those modern remote alarms.

As she strolled up the block, she noticed two people hugging on a stoop. She couldn't tell if they were on Tristan's
stoop or the one next door. Engrossed in each other, they
didn't see her walking toward them. As she approached,
Dakota thought she saw the woman's hand sneak down to
massage the man's crotch. She murmured something in his ear
that caused him to rear back, laughing.

"If you really want to rock my world," Dakota heard him
say as he kissed her on the neck, "bring one of your girlfriends."

She giggled, "You are a freak!"

"And a two-timing son of a bitch," Dakota stated.

Tristan froze like a kid caught swiping the icing off a cake with his finger. "Dakota, what are you doing here?"

Glancing pointedly at the J. Lo wanna-be, Dakota said, "I thought you were sick."

He faked a cough. "I am."

"So who's this? Your nurse?"

The woman spoke up. "No, I'm not his damn nurse. I'm his lover," she said, then pointed at the bags in Dakota's hand. "Who the hell are you? The delivery girl?"

Tristan rushed down the stairs, getting between the two women before a brawl broke out. "Look, Dakota, this is not what it seems," he whispered, then glanced back to make sure the woman didn't hear him. "She's just a friend. Come on up. She was just leaving."

"Don't even try it! Do you think I'm stupid? I'm out of here. You disappoint me, Tristan, and you're not worth it."

Dakota left Tristan standing on the sidewalk as she headed back to her car. Before she could pull off, she saw him trot up the steps and grab the woman by the waist. Doing a little damage control on the other end, Dakota thought angrily. He kissed her and patted her behind. She seemed to be pouting, but followed him back into the building as Dakota shifted gears and sped off. "So much," she fumed, "for *It's a Wonderful Life.*"

She heard beeping from her cell, indicating she had a message. She took the phone out of her purse and checked her voice mail. It was Tricia. Dakota called back and the phone rang five times until the machine picked up. Dakota called back again, and this time Tricia picked up. "Hey, Tricia, I got your message. What's going on?"

"It's Nana."

"Nana? What's wrong?" Dakota's heart paused.

"She's . . . she's gone, Kota," Tricia sobbed.

20

Life didn't get much better than this, Morgan thought as she tipped back and forth in the antique rocking chair that had just been delivered for the nursery. She had turned what was a guest room into a kiddie wonderland. It was done in soft hues of lavender, turquoise, and periwinkle—colors that were fabulous and would be great for a little boy or a little girl. She and Miles had a ledge built around the room from which a menagerie of stuffed animals now held court, awaiting the arrival of baby Nelson.

Morgan loved sitting in this room. She fingered the soft pale quilt that would soon cover her child. She also took pleasure in hanging and folding the cute little clothes that would swaddle their little bundle of joy. She felt so blessed to have it all. A promising new business, a beautiful home, a handsome husband, and the blessing of a child on the way. Being pregnant had brought her more joy than she ever would have imagined possible. In many ways it confirmed the love that she and Miles shared. It was a living symbol of their commitment to each other.

Miles stuck his head in the door. "Coming up with more decorating ideas?" he teased Morgan.

"I was thinking of a crystal chandelier, and maybe a Persian rug or two," she teased back.

He walked over to his wife and gently rubbed her stomach.

"What does baby Nelson think about all of this?" he asked softly.

"Well, we talked earlier today, and she mentioned that a few contemporary oils might add just the right touch." Morgan placed her hand over Miles'.

"Oh, really?" Miles nibbled on her neck.

"Yes, and she also thought a new Mercedes station wagon would be a good idea," she said, giving him a serious look. "You know . . . easier to maneuver her new car seat, stroller, and stuff."

Between nibbles Miles said, "She's a smart one, huh?"

"Takes after her mother." Morgan smiled.

"Okay, Mom, we'd better get going or we'll be late for dinner." Miles stood before offering his hand to help Morgan up from the rocking chair.

Dinner was at Town in celebration of Phillip's birthday. Town was on West Fifty-sixth Street between Fifth and Sixth avenues, in the Chambers Hotel. It was one of Morgan's favorite new restaurants; the chef, Geoffrey Zakarian, was brilliant. The food was consistently outstanding and the decor was sexy and sophisticated.

When they arrived, the hostess informed them that she would wait to seat them until the party was complete. They were still waiting on the fourth, Paula. Walking to the bar, they saw Phillip nursing a scotch on the rocks.

"Happy birthday!" Morgan greeted him with a hug. Miles also gave his friend a tight, one-armed hug. Morgan loved the friendship that he and Phillip shared; unlike some guys they were affectionate with each other and always there for one another, too. It reminded her of her relationship with Dakota. They were more like siblings than friends.

"I brought a gift for you." Miles smiled, stifling a grin.

"I'm taking all gifts," Phillip declared.

Miles pulled a wooden cane with a red bow wrapped around it from behind his back. "Thought you might be needing this," he laughed. Phillip was now thirty-nine, a year older than Miles, who never let him forget his age.

Phillip laughed and turned to the bartender. "I think I may be needing another one of these."

After the bartender took Miles' and Morgan's drink orders, Morgan asked, "Where is Paula?"

"She paged me just before you guys walked in. She's on her way—stuck in Midtown traffic."

"Oh." Miles could tell that this wasn't sitting well with Phillip.

After another twenty minutes, in walked Paula full of apologies. "Hi, guys, sorry I'm late. Couldn't get a cab anywhere. I practically had to walk here." She kissed Phillip on the corner of his mouth, and gave hugs and European two-cheek kisses to Miles and Morgan.

In short order, they were seated at a choice table in the center of the full dining room. Miles took the liberty of ordering a bottle of Dom Pérignon to celebrate the occasion. "That is, unless you have something else in mind," he asked Paula, unsure if she had specific plans now that the evening was under way. The whole thing was a little awkward for him. The dinner came about a couple of days ago when Miles asked Phillip what he was doing for his birthday. When he said he didn't know, Miles suggested dinner. So even though Paula was his girl, it looked like Miles was playing host.

"Morgan, how's the pregnancy going?" Paula asked, shrugging off Miles' question.

"Couldn't be better." Morgan beamed.

"I admire you." Paula shook her head. "I don't know how you do it."

Morgan gave her a puzzled look. "What do you mean?"

"You know, give up everything to have a baby." Paula made a face as though the mere thought of it was distasteful. When Morgan didn't comment, she went on. "Your business will be put on hold, you won't be able to hang out with Miles for a long time, and those designer size fours—forget it." Just then the sommelier appeared with the champagne. "You can't even enjoy a glass of Dom!" she cried, as if this new horror of being pregnant had just occurred to her and was the real deal breaker. Phillip looked as though he wanted to crawl under the table and stay awhile.

Morgan was speechless. She had never met a woman who was so selfish. To cover the awkward moment, Miles raised his glass. "Let's toast to Phillip." He looked at his friend. "Man, you're the best friend I could have. Morgan and I wish you many more years and most of all happiness." Miles, Phillip, and Paula raised their champagne, while Morgan toasted with her flute of sparkling water.

Paula said, "I'd like to propose a toast too. To the man I love and want to spend the rest of my life with. Happy birthday, honey." She leaned over and kissed Phillip, this time full on the lips, though Morgan detected a touch of chill from his end of the kiss.

After they placed their orders, Morgan pulled a festively wrapped gift from its shopping bag. "A little something from the Nelsons."

"You guys didn't have to get me anything."

"Okay," Miles teased, pretending to take the box from him.

"But since you went to so much trouble—" Phillip pulled the box back with a grin and started unwrapping it. Inside, he found a pair of brown-and-cream Santoni alligator golf shoes. "These are the bomb!" Phillip's eyes lit up like a Christmas tree.

"I can't do anything to help your handicap, but at least you'll look good," Miles joked.

"If my memory serves me—and I'm not that old yet—the last time we played it was you who needed a little help. Besides, you know I'm a tennis man at heart."

"Baby, have you taken Miles to play at Dad's club yet?" Paula asked, sipping her champagne.

"No," Phillip answered, turning back toward Miles.

"You should. You know my daddy was one of the first blacks to join Wackygyl Country Club. He can get you a tee time whenever you want." Wackygyl was a snobbish, blue-blood course up in Rochester, New York. Though Paula was black, in her mind her blood definitely ran in hues of navy.

"Do you guys belong to a club?" She directed her question at Morgan.

"In fact, we do. A very *exclusive*, very *private* club."

"Oh, really?" Paula asked, curiosity and envy sharpening her features right on cue. "Which one?"

"It's called the Nelsons. You know, it's really small, very intimate, just two members now, but it's definitely growing," she said, patting her stomach.

Paula didn't bother answering; she simply directed her attention back to the guys.

While they exchanged lies and boasts about their golf games, Morgan couldn't help but feel sorry for Phillip. It was clear to her that Paula was all about Paula. Not that she didn't love him—it just seemed that she was incapable of giving him the love and attention that he deserved and that he always seemed to admire in her marriage to Miles.

Later at home, while dressing for bed, Morgan asked Miles, "So what's up with Phillip and Paula?"

"What do you mean?" Morgan always had to pull this kind of information out of her husband. Why did men pretend that they made no observations of other people?

"I mean, what's going on? What are they doing? They've been together for three years now, and it's time to either move forward or move on."

"I'm sure they'll let us know when the time comes."

Morgan was not going to let it rest that easily. She really liked Phillip and worried about him being stuck with Paula. "But Phillip clearly wants children and Paula seems repulsed by them!"

"He's aware of that, believe me."

That was all Morgan needed to hear. "Oh, so he might break it off?"

"I didn't say that. It's just that he's having some second thoughts."

There, she knew it. She only hoped that he would see beyond Paula's pedigree before it was too late, that he would see her for exactly what she was before he woke up and found himself shackled to a spoiled, selfish, self-indulgent BAP.

21

Nana's home-going celebration was carried out to the letter. She was laid to rest in a silk-lined mahogany casket with brass inlays, and white calla lilies and roses were placed throughout the church. The choir sang "Precious Lord," as Nana had requested, but followed with a soulful rendition of "Oh, Happy Day," which dried weeping eyes and before the end of the song had the mourners on their feet, clapping and shouting with joy.

"Nana would've liked this," Tricia whispered to Dakota.

"I'm glad you suggested that song," Dakota whispered back, putting her arm around Tricia's shoulder. "I can hear her saying, 'Y'all stop all this here crying.'"

Nana accomplished in death what had eluded her in life, and that was to end the feud between her granddaughters. Despite their apparent differences, Tricia, the around-the-way girl, and Dakota, the downtown diva, had forged a friendship in their mutual grief.

"Tricia, I couldn't have made it through this without you."

"We're here for each other," Tricia said, even though a few months ago this couldn't have been further from the truth.

"Yeah, we have to be strong. You know Nana wouldn't want us breaking down."

The song set the tone for the remainder of the service, which was uplifting, with various church members speaking of the good-natured person Nana was, always giving of her time but never mincing words.

The repast was held in the church dining area. A feast of fried chicken smothered in gravy, collard greens, macaroni and cheese, potato salad, corn bread, lemon pound cake, and peach cobbler was prepared and served by the women of the church. Dakota looked around the room at the people eating and socializing. "Seems like Nana should be here overseeing this meal, making sure everybody has enough to eat," she said to Tricia.

"You can best believe she's somewhere looking down, so you better eat all of your greens," Tricia chuckled.

Dakota patted her heart. "Nana will always be here with us."

"I know, but it's gonna seem funny not havin' her round the house, cookin' catfish on Fridays."

That reminded Dakota of a problem she had thought about while flying out to Chicago. "Speaking of the house, what are you going to do with it? I'm sure Nana would want you to have it."

Tricia thought back to Nana's confession in the hospital, but decided to play dumb. "I really don't want to live there by myself. Can't you get a transfer and move back home?"

Dakota looked at her like she was speaking Swahili. "A what?"

"You know, a transfer." Tricia had known Dakota would react like that, so she put on an innocent face and really poured it on. "Doesn't your company have offices in Chicago?"

Was Tricia really asking her to move back home? "Yeah, they do, but that's totally out of the question."

"Why?" Tricia asked.

"For one, my life is in New York, and for two, I like living there."

Tricia feigned a hurt look. "Oh."

Dakota felt a twinge of guilt for being so blunt, but she had no intention of moving anywhere. She pondered for a moment, trying to come up with a reasonable solution. "I know. I got it!"

"What?" Tricia asked, puzzled. She hadn't expected Dakota to come up with a solution to her "problem."

"Let's sell the house and you can move to New York with me."

"Uh . . . uh . . . sell the house? What am I going to do in New York?" Tricia asked, surprised at the sudden turn of events.

Dakota smiled, spreading her arms wide. "What *can't* you do in New York?"

"What about beauty school?" she countered, trying to find an excuse to stay.

"They have cosmetology schools in New York," Dakota said, the idea developing as she spoke. "We can use a portion of the money from the sale of the house for a down payment on a commercial space for your shop—that is, once you finish school and build a clientele."

"I don't know . . ." Little did Dakota know that for once money was the last thing on Tricia's mind. Still, the idea of moving to big, bad New York was very appealing. "Are you sure?"

Remembering her promise to Nana to look out for her cousin, Dakota said, "Of course I'm sure. I could turn the office into a second bedroom."

This plan was sounding better by the minute. "How are we going to do this?"

"Before I go back, we'll put the house on the market. Once everything is finalized, you'll pack your bags and move to New York." She squeezed Tricia's arm. "It'll be fun. We'll be roomies. I'll show you the city. You'll love it," Dakota said, settling into the idea herself.

The following morning Dakota called a local realtor, who was delighted at the prospect of selling a late-nineteenth-century Victorian house. Her next call was to an antiques dealer, whom she informed that, with the exception of a few keepsakes, the entire contents of the house were to be appraised and sold.

When she walked through the door after running a few early-morning errands, the house was quiet.

"Come on, Tricia," Dakota called upstairs. "Let's go to the attic and decide what we want to keep." Tricia didn't answer. "Tricia?" she called again. Dakota went up the creaky stairs to Tricia's bedroom, reining in her annoyance. She couldn't believe Tricia was still asleep. She thought she told her they were going to get up early and clean out the attic. She knocked on the door, saying, "Tricia, wake up." When there was still no answer, Dakota turned the knob and opened the door.

To her surprise, Tricia's bed was empty. She went back downstairs to call Tricia on her cell. She had tucked Tricia's number inside her wallet, but when Dakota unzipped her purse, her wallet was gone. She didn't remember taking it out. Before she could drag out all of the contents of her overloaded purse, Tricia walked in.

"Where have you been? You were supposed to help me clear out the attic."

"I had a couple of errands to run. Why don't you get started?" She brushed past Dakota and dashed up to her room. "I'll change my clothes and be right there."

In fact, Tricia had just finished running a very lucrative errand. She had gotten up and driven directly to the bank. Once there, she fidgeted nervously as she stood in line. Three elderly people in front of her were engrossed in conversations with the tellers. She tapped her foot and glanced around the lobby. The branch was one of the oldest on the South Side. Marble columns flanked an expansive oak staircase and an antique chandelier hung from the center of the ceiling. She was all too aware of the rent-a-cop standing guard at the revolving door. She couldn't wait until she was on the other side of it.

"Next," said the teller, signaling Tricia to step forward.

Tricia smiled tightly as she approached the window. "Good morning," she said, trying to sound professional.

"How can I help you?"

"I'd like to close this account." She handed the teller a blue passbook.

The teller looked at the out-of-date savings account book. "I haven't seen one of these in a long time. These days most people use their ATM cards. Anyway," she said, pointing Tricia in the direction of the customer service department, "you'll have to see one of our account representatives to close this account."

"Uh, okay." Tricia took back the worn passbook and reluctantly approached a row of cubicles.

A middle-aged woman with half glasses on a gold chain around her neck sat behind a desk organizing papers. She looked up and saw Tricia standing before her. "May I help you?"

Tricia's sweaty hands clenched the passbook. "I would like to close an account."

"Have a seat."

Tricia sat perched on the edge of the chair. Reaching out, she handed over the passbook.

The woman examined the savings book, then asked, "Do you have identification?"

Tricia took Dakota's wallet out of her purse and nervously removed the driver's license.

"Oh, I see you live in New York, Ms. Cantrell," the woman said, scanning the license.

"Yes, my grandmother just passed away. That's why I'm closing the account," she explained.

The representative typed the account information into her computer. "I see this is a joint account with you and Anna Mae Cantrell."

Tricia lowered her head for effect and said softly, "That was my grandmother."

"Oh, I see. Do you have a death certificate?"

"Yes, it's right here." She presented the creased piece of paper with much more confidence because it was entirely legitimate.

The woman examined it, then said, "Will you want the full amount in a cashier's check? Or do you want the funds wired to your bank in New York?"

"A cashier's check will be fine," Tricia said quickly.

The representative looked at her computer again. "I see here that you also have a safe-deposit box. Will you be closing that out?"

"Uh, yes. Yes, I will." Tricia was pleased at the unexpected bonus. She pretended to search through the purse again. "I must have left my key in New York."

The rep peered over her half glasses. "Oh, that could be a problem."

Tricia didn't want to press the issue. The check was what she really wanted. She'd have to find the key once she got back home. "I'll just take the check and come back later for the stuff in the box."

The rep typed on the keyboard until forms began rolling off the printer. The sound of the printer might as well have been the *ka-ching* of a cash register bouncing open. "Sign here, and here."

Tricia had stayed up half the night practicing Dakota's signature, knowing she would have to forge a few documents. She scribbled on the dotted lines and handed the papers back to the representative, who checked the signature against the driver's license. It was a good thing she and Kota kinda looked alike, Tricia thought to herself.

"Go to teller number one, and she'll get your check ready, Ms. Cantrell."

"Thank you."

Tricia swiftly walked to the teller to pick up her bonanza. When the teller handed Tricia the check, she gaped at it. She had never seen that many zeros before in her life. She grinned in anticipation.

22

Freddie wearily climbed the stairs of the grimy fifth-floor walk-up that he called home. The apartment leaked as the unrelenting rain pounded the patchy tar roof of the fleabag tenement. His mood was as gloomy as the weather.

He had been out all day working, but it was impossible. Nobody kept their wallets in outside pockets of rain gear. He unlocked the triple locks on his door and shook his drenched coat on the bare floor as he entered. He kicked off his soaked tennis shoes and crossed the living room of the tiny one-bedroom apartment into the kitchenette, where he took a pot from under the rust-stained sink and put it beneath a drip near the door. He plopped down so hard on the cheap pleather sofa that it nearly tipped over.

After being in Blake's posh digs, he found his apartment hard to take. There were no imported rugs, no designer wall coverings, no custom window treatments, no obscenely expensive furniture, and no freshly cut flowers. He glared at the rickety wood-veneer cocktail table that he'd found near a Dumpster, a black vinyl beanbag chair, and a poster of Bob Marley with a spliff dangling out of his mouth that he had taped to the whitewashed concrete wall. After being exposed to Blake's lifestyle, he ached to sleep on three-hundred-thread-count sheets and drink out of crystal glasses. He craved a martini, but all he had in his tiny fridge was a Zima and two forty-ounce malt liquors. Freddie opened the cabinet above the sink only to find a plastic cup from McDonald's and a few chipped glasses from the dollar store. He twisted the cap off a forty and took a swig. After he finished the bottle, he chased it with the Zima and drifted off into a drunken slumber. He dreamed of having steamy sex with Blake and lounging around his apartment in a silk bathrobe. He dreamed of bathing in the huge marble jacuzzi, then putting on Blake's designer duds.

Freddie began snoring so hard he woke himself up. He looked around at his crummy apartment and felt a crushing disappointment that the dream wasn't real. He had tasted the good life, and now that his palate was awakened, he had to have more. Freddie reached for the refurbished cordless phone that he'd swiped from a sidewalk vendor and called Blake at the gallery.

"Blake St. James' office, may I help you?"

"Tell him it's Freddie."

Blake's assistant wasn't satisfied with just a first name. "May I have your last name, sir?"

"Hudson. Freddie Hudson." It pissed him off that Chan still didn't know who he was. He'd called often enough. Besides, he was sure that Chan didn't give Spence the third degree.

"May I ask the nature of your call?" Chan asked politely.

"He knows me," Freddie said, insulted.

"Hold on, please."

After a few minutes, Chan came back on the line. "I'm afraid he'll have to call you back."

"Oh," Freddie said, deflated, "okay."

He went back to the refrigerator and took out the last forty. He wanted to get his drink on before Blake called him back so he could muster up the courage to invite himself over. Blake might be out of his league financially, but sexually they played on the same team—the Freakazoids. They both loved wild, uninhibited sex.

The thought of Blake's lean body against his, along with the cold brew, was making Freddie horny. He unzipped his pants, pulled out his limp piece, and began to stroke it until he felt signs of life. He threw his head back on the sofa, closed his eyes, and imagined Blake's long, strong fingers massaging his soul pole. He moaned as his hand slid up and down his stiff shaft. He increased the pace until he exploded on the shiny fabric. "Damn," he said, looking down at the creamy mess. He hobbled into the bathroom with his pants twisting around his ankles, grabbed a towel off the rack, and hobbled back into the living room.

After cleaning up, he looked at his watch. It had been fifteen minutes since his call to Blake. Maybe Jackie Chan didn't give him the message. He picked up the cordless and hit the REDIAL button.

"Blake St. James' office, may I help you?"

Not him again, Freddie thought. "It's me. Freddie."

"Excuse me, sir?" Chan said, sounding put off by Freddie's abruptness.

"Freddie Hudson, I called earlier."

"Oh, yes. Well, Blake is still indisposed."

"In-what?" Freddie slurred, practically reeling from the effects of the alcohol.

Chan broke it down. "He's not available."

"Just tell him I'm on the phone. I'll wait."

Chan sighed. "Hold on, Mr. Hudson."

Beads of sweat began to roll from Freddie's underarms, dampening his T-shirt. He coughed to clear his throat. Suddenly he wished he hadn't drunk so much. He didn't want to stumble over his words.

"Hey, Freddie, what's up?" Blake said, sounding distracted.

"Hey, Blake, how you doin'?"

"I'm a tad busy at the moment. Chan said you needed to talk to me. What's up?"

"You wanna git together tonight?" Freddie asked.

"I have dinner plans tonight." Then, trying to soften the blow, he added, "Sorry."

"Why don't I meet you at yo place after yo dinner? I'll be

yo dessert tonight and yo breakfast in the morning. And if that ain't enough, I'll feed you this ten-inch rod till you're good and full," Freddie offered.

The voice over the line went stone cold. "I don't think so."

"Why not? We had fun before. This time'll be even better. I promise," Freddie pleaded.

Blake exhaled. "Look, Freddie, that was a onetime deal. I'm sorry to say there won't be a next time."

"What you mean, a onetime deal!" Freddie yelled into the receiver.

"Look, I think you're a nice guy and all, but I'm not looking for a relationship."

"I'm good enuf to lick yo damn uppity ass, but I ain't good enuf to be yo man!"

"That's not what I'm saying, Freddie," Blake said in a measured tone.

"Then what are you sayin'? Is you sayin' I can come over tonight?"

"No, you cannot come over tonight, or any night. I'm sorry, Freddie." Blake hung up.

"Hello? Hello?" Freddie said to the dial tone. "Ain't that a bitch?"

He slammed the phone back onto the cradle, got up, and marched into the bedroom. He sat on the edge of the rumpled bed, reached under the mattress, and pulled out a duffel bag. He unzipped the bag and took out a package. Holding it in his hands, he mumbled, "Onetime deal, my ass. It ain't over until *I* say it's over!"

23

Morgan watched the clock, impatiently waiting for Dakota's call. Her flight was due in from Chicago over an hour ago, and Morgan was anxious to hear from her, knowing that Nana's death had hit her hard. Because Dakota had lost both parents at an early age, it pained Morgan to see her best friend suffer yet another loss. She hoped that Dakota was right and it would, at the very least, bring her and Tricia together. Morgan decided she would take Dakota out, maybe see a play and hang out at some of the galleries downtown. That would surely cheer her spirits.

Morgan felt almost guilty that things for her were going so well. Her accountant had sent over the adjusted third-quarter report, which showed impressive stats for Caché. Their expense/income ratio was a factor of three, which was an excellent number for a new company, and their net income was respectable. Not bad for a two-person firm with no advertising or expansion budget. She had immediately sent the results to Dr. St. James, along with a cover letter promising to keep him apprised of their progress.

She had to keep the results coming, though. This quarter would make or break her chances of going from a nice income to a fabulous one. So she was pulling out all of the stops.

"Morgan, Blake's on line one," Lisa announced, pulling Morgan out of her reverie.

Morgan picked up the phone. "Hi, Blake. How are you?" She was happy to hear from him. It'd been a couple of weeks since they'd hung out. She had gone to see the hit Broadway musical *The Producers* with Blake and Spence; then the three of them had had a late dinner at Craft.

"I'm great, sweetie. How's my favorite mother-to-be?" Morgan could hear strains of classical music floating in the background. It reminded her of the first time that Tyrone called her at Global Financial. He had Bach playing in the background, pretending to be the real Blake calling from the St. James' penthouse. They later learned that he actually lived in a drug-infested flophouse on the wrong side of Harlem, and that the classical music wasn't streaming from a Bang & Olufsen system, but most likely from a dusty boom box.

"I'm really good. Just getting bigger by the day."

"And more beautiful, I'm sure." Morgan smiled. Blake always knew just the right thing to say. "How's business?"

"Things are looking good. We've been very busy lately," Morgan was glad to report.

"Not too busy for one more client, I hope."

"Never that busy," Morgan laughed. Expecting another referral, she asked, "So, who would that be?"

"You're talking to him. I'd like for you to handle a party for the gallery's official opening."

Morgan leaned forward in her chair. "Blake, that's wonderful! I'd love to." She was ecstatic. She knew that not only would it be lucrative, but the cream of New York society would be there—a whole room full of potential clients.

"Great, I'm glad to hear it. But I must confess, it was Father's idea."

"Oh?" Morgan said, puzzled.

"I was planning to do something low-key. But he advised me to make my debut in the city's art scene a big splash." Lowering his voice, he added, "And frankly, I think the other reason is so that he'd have a chance to see your magic up close and personal."

Taking a deep breath, Morgan said, "Just a little pressure . . ."

"Don't worry about that. He's heard great reports from the referral he sent, and your quarterly financials were very impressive. So consider this your opportunity to seal the deal."

"I'm looking forward to it. It'll be fabulous. I will personally make sure of it."

"I don't have any doubts."

"When can we get together to begin the planning? What's your schedule like?" Morgan asked.

"I'm free Wednesday after six."

"That sounds good for me and Lisa," Morgan said as she looked through her journal.

"Listen, honey, gotta run. Call me later to confirm."

"Will do." Morgan hung up the phone, jubilant. She leaned back in her chair, exhaling toward the vaulted ceiling.

"What's going on?" Morgan had forgotten that Lisa was still there.

"Oh, that was Blake. He's asked us to plan his gallery opening!"

"So the fag's having a coming-out party?" Lisa quipped.

"What did you say?" Morgan snapped, turning to face Lisa.

"Nothing. It's j-just—" Lisa started to stammer.

"You listen to me," Morgan said firmly. "I don't ever want to hear you say anything remotely derogatory about any of my friends, much less a client."

"I didn't mean anything by it."

"Whether you did or not, don't let it happen again." Morgan couldn't believe that Lisa was so openly prejudiced. She'd never thought so before, but then as up and down as Lisa could be, who knew?

Under her breath Lisa said, "Yes, madam."

"You have something else to say?" She gave Lisa a don't-fuck-with-me look. Because of her looks and personality, people often assumed that Morgan couldn't or wouldn't go there. They were always shocked when she took the designer gloves off.

Lisa pouted. "No."

"Don't you *ever* disrespect me like that again." Morgan was furious, but forced herself to calm down. "Listen, Lisa, I don't know what your problem is lately, but something's obviously bothering you. Is there anything you want to tell me?"

Lisa appeared to consider it for a moment. "No," she finally said, "I'm okay."

Morgan really wanted to get to the bottom of her attitude so she decided to push further. "Are you sure?"

Before Lisa could answer, the office door opened and in walked Dakota. Morgan jumped up from her seat and wrapped Dakota in a huge hug. "Hey, girl. How you doing?" She held her friend back by her shoulders to get a good look at her. Dakota was normally a ball of fire, but today she looked as though the flame had been put out.

"I have an idea. Let's go grab a bite to eat." Not waiting for an answer, she grabbed her bag and coat and was headed out the door with Dakota's arm linked with her own. "Lisa, please lock up. I won't be back today." After walking through the door, she stuck her head back in. "But I do want to finish this conversation."

After the door closed, Lisa mimicked her, "But I do want to finish this conversation." Plopping down on the sofa, she thought that if Morgan was so concerned about her, she wouldn't have run out the minute Dakota bothered to show up.

After a few minutes of sulking, she picked up the phone and dialed a local number. "Hello, this is Lisa. May I speak with Joey?" After a few seconds she said, "Joe, about that job. I'll take it."

24

Being away from New York had shown Dakota just how much she missed the Gritty City. She missed the sidewalks overcrowded with pedestrians striding to destinations unknown. She missed the song of sirens in the middle of the night. And as chaotic as it was, she missed the hectic pace of SBI. Working on the trading floor was like being caught in a time warp, with minutes melting into hours and days, dwindling away until once again it was Saturday.

Even in her down time she wanted to keep busy. When she was busy, she didn't have time to think about Nana's being gone. She had been an avid tennis player in her youth, but with the demands of work she had neglected her racket. She had not been on the court in a few years. So she scheduled a lesson for eleven o'clock with a pro at the courts in Central Park. Most of her colleagues were into golf, spouting the virtues of making a deal on the ninth hole. But Dakota had vowed to herself that as long as she could run around on the tennis court she would. She would only take up golf when her knees gave out. Then she could drive around in those spiffy golf carts.

She dashed out of the house in a white pleated tennis skirt with matching T-shirt and a navy cotton ribbed sweater tied onto the handles of her Head tennis bag. She slung the bag

over her shoulder as she stood on the corner of Cliff Street trying to hail a taxi.

"Ninety-sixth and Fifth," she said when one zoomed to a
stop and she got in. The cab cruised northbound along
the FDR, before cutting across the Upper East Side. Dakota
paid the driver, got out, and walked through the park to the
courts, where she could see tennis classes and various matches
taking place. She checked in at the clubhouse and paid for her
lesson.

"By chance, are you teaching?" she asked the handsome
hunk behind the desk, hoping to get a little "innocent" flirting
in. He reminded her of Yannick Noah, the dreadlocked
French former tennis star.

"Not today. The receptionist called in sick, so I'm stuck
behind this desk. Mel will be giving you the lesson this morning on court six. Don't worry—he's good." He flashed an
Ultra Brite smile, then winked and added, "But not as good
as me."

"Maybe next time," She winked back, then sashayed out
of the clubhouse, her short skirt swishing suggestively against
her thighs.

When she reached court six, she saw an old guy through
the fence. He was slowly picking up balls with a ball hopper.
Watching him struggle with the hopper, she hoped he wasn't
the pro.

"Come on in. What are you waiting for?" he called, waving.

Dakota looked behind her, thinking he was speaking to
someone else.

"You. Yeah, I'm talking to you," he said in a heavy New
York accent. He put down the hopper and reached into his
pocket for a piece of paper. He glanced at it, then yelled,
"Dakota Cantrell."

She opened the gate and walked reluctantly onto the court.
"That's me. Are you the pro?" she asked.

"Yep, I'm Mel," he said, extending his hand. "Take this
hopper and finish clearing the court." With that, he took a
seat on the courtside bench.

She was put off at first, but didn't want to act like a spoiled brat. Besides, she'd always been taught that picking up the balls was a part of the sport.

When she finished, Mel yelled from the bench, "What do you wanna work on today?"

"Well, I haven't played in a while, so I'd like to start with my ground strokes, then work on my serve." Coming up to the bench, she unzipped her tennis bag and took out her racket.

He rose from his seat and flexed his leg. "First, we're gonna start with a series of stretches, because we don't want any injuries."

Dakota followed his lead and began to stretch out her hamstrings. After her legs were properly warmed up, she took the racket in her right hand and stretched it across her left shoulder, then reversed the order, stretching out her left arm.

"Come on," he said, jovially picking up his racket. "Time waits for no man . . . or woman."

Dakota watched in surprise as he quickly jogged over to the net.

"Do you wanna spend your hour on the bench, or you wanna play?" he said. "Come over to my side of the net. Let's see what your coordination is like." Once she was within a few feet of Mel, he tossed a few balls at her forehand. She cleanly hit every one of them. "Good, at least we don't have to start with the basics. Now go to the far baseline and let's see what your ground strokes are like."

Dakota trotted down the court, checked her grip on her racket, and positioned herself to return the ball. The first one she hit went straight into the net. The second ball went sailing over the fence into the bushes. "Damn," she muttered in disgust.

Mel called out, "You're rushing the ball. Let it come to you." He seemed puzzled by the contrast between her good form and the results. "When was the last time you hit?"

"It's been a while, but I used to be pretty good," she said in her defense.

He nodded. "Why don't we start at the net so you can gain control of the ball? I'm gonna hit 'em to your forehand. With each ball, take a step back until you're at the baseline."

With Mel's coaching, Dakota made it back to the baseline without missing a single shot. His skills were amazing. Within an hour working on her backhand, serve, and volley, he had her game back on track.

Impressed with her improvement, Mel asked, "You've had serious lessons before, haven't you?"

"Yeah, my last tennis camp was in Killington, Vermont."

"Why didn't you say something? Had I known, I wouldn't have been so easy on you. Next time I'm gonna make you sweat."

Dakota wiped her brow with the back of her hand. "I'm sweating now," she teased. She had to admit that, for an old guy, Mel was an excellent coach. "Are you going to be here next Saturday?"

"I am, but check with the clubhouse for my schedule."

"You want me to clear the court?" she asked, indicating the chaos of tennis balls lying everywhere.

"No, leave 'em for my next victim. Most people don't like to stretch, so I make 'em pick up the balls as part of their warm-up," he chuckled.

"Aren't you the clever one? It was nice meeting you, Mel. I'll see you next week." Dakota took a towel out of her bag and wiped the remaining sweat from her face. She put a dab of clear M•A•C Lipglass on her lips before putting away her racket and leaving the court.

She was on her way back to the clubhouse when someone called out her name. She looked around but didn't see any familiar faces. "Dakota, over here." Looking to her left, she saw a guy on court two waving her over.

From a distance she didn't recognize the face, but as she approached it became clear. "Hey there," she said, stopping within a few feet of him.

"It's Phillip. Remember, I met you at Odeon with Miles and Morgan?"

Phillip wore a pair of white Nike tennis shorts exposing hairy muscular legs. His broad chest stretched out the word BROOKLYN written across his snug T-shirt.

"I remember." She then added, "How's your girlfriend?"

"Paula's fine." He glanced at his watch. "I'm waiting on her now. We're playing mixed doubles."

He's not making a play, Dakota realized. He just wanted to say hi. "Well, have a good game."

"It was good seeing you." His cell phone rang, and he added, "Maybe I'll see you around."

At the clubhouse, the cutie who was there earlier had been replaced with an older woman, who took Dakota's information and scheduled her with Mel for the following Saturday. She was bouncing down the stairs, thinking about going home and getting out of her sweaty clothes, when she heard her name called again.

"Dakota," Phillip yelled, waving to her.

She walked through the gate and saw two people on the other side of the net warming up. "Hey, Phillip, what's up?"

"That was Paula on the phone. She's stuck baby-sitting a client and will be delayed. And I need a partner," he said, eyeing Dakota desperately.

"And what do you want me to do?" she said, knowing full well what he meant.

"I want you to help me kick their butts." He motioned to the couple at the opposite end of the court and said quietly, "That's Richard Foster and his wife, Jade. They're friends of Paula's. Jade and Paula played on the junior USTA circuit and Jade thinks she's the second coming of Venus Williams." Phillip put his hands together as if praying, then mouthed to Dakota, "Please help me."

His appeal was so sweet, she smiled. "Okay, but I'm warning you, I haven't played in a while," she said, putting down her bag.

"Can you play the net?"

Dakota had just completed a few net exercises and felt confident that she could deliver. "Yeah."

"Okay, I'll serve first. Don't worry about the backcourt. Just concentrate on the net. Got it?"

"Got it, boss," she shot back.

Phillip's first serve was hard and right inside the back line. Richard tried to return it, but smacked the ball directly into the net. As Jade huffed at her husband, Dakota glanced back at Phillip. This guy could play. Phillip served to the right-hand court, and Jade sent a hard return at Dakota. With her racket out front, she popped it cross-court over the net. They rallied until Richard hit the ball out of bounds.

"Thirty, love," Phillip yelled before tossing up the ball for his next serve.

Phillip's serve whizzed past Dakota's ear, just missing her head. The serve was too fast for Richard, who swung and missed it completely.

"Forty, love," Phillip said, sounding pumped.

"We know how to keep score, Phillip," Jade yelled, clearly miffed.

Dakota crossed over to the other side of the court and stooped down a little lower to prevent another near hit. Phillip was on fire and so was his serve. Yet Jade whacked the return with such force that Dakota ducked as the little yellow sphere zipped past her. Jade smiled in triumph, but it was short-lived. Phillip ran behind Dakota and recovered the ball just before the second bounce, nailing it right on the line past Jade.

"Game!"

"That ball was out, and you know it, Phillip," Jade shouted.

Phillip looked at his partner. "It was in, wasn't it, Dakota?"

"Sure was," she said, walking over to Phillip. "Good game, partner. You were smoking that ball."

Jade turned her venom on her husband. "That ball was out, *wasn't* it, Richard?"

"Uh-huh, it was indeed."

"Richard, you know damn well that ball was in. Look," Phillip said, clearly fed up, "if you can't call it fair, let's not play."

"Actually, the ball was out," Paula said, walking onto the court. "The lines on this court are practically worn off."

Phillip and Dakota turned around in unison and stared at Paula.

"Finally, someone who can see," Jade said, smiling and waving at Paula. "I knew we should have played at the club. These public courts aren't maintained well—"

"These courts are just fine," Phillip cut her off. "If you can *play*, then you can play anywhere." He turned to Dakota and softened his tone. "Paula, you remember Dakota, don't you?"

Paula looked her up and down. "Can't say that I do."

"We met at Odeon. She's a friend of Miles and Morgan's and she agreed to pitch in for you."

"Well, I'm here now," she said, flipping her ponytail and ignoring Dakota, "so let's start the next game."

Dakota couldn't believe this woman. How rude! Dakota knew her type all too well. The snobby, upper-middle-class type. The type who felt a sense of entitlement and took kindness for weakness. Obviously, she didn't know who she was messing with. Dakota turned her back to Paula, but said loudly enough for her to hear, "Good game, Phillip. Maybe next time we can play singles."

He looked at Paula, who was pretending she hadn't heard. "Sounds like a plan," he said. "Thanks for being such a good sport."

"Anytime," Dakota said, and walked off the court.

25

It was late, and they were both exhausted. Miles had practically collapsed in a heap onto the sofa in his office, his tie askew, and Vic, shoes removed, had that disheveled look that on most women was unattractive, but on her it read fresh-from-a-romp-in-the-sack. Her long, highlighted hair was swept up in a loose French twist, but unruly tendrils had fallen around her face. Her lips were pouty, as though she had just been kissed hard, from the unconscious nibbling she had given them as she concentrated on finalizing the details that would make Ecstasy's tour a success.

She sat on the floor, leaning back against the sofa with papers strewn out between her legs. "With the girls' rantings, Cee-Cee's ravings, and our nervous sponsors, pulling this tour off will be nothing short of a miracle." She shook her head in exasperation.

"I don't know what I would have done without you," Miles said, further loosening his tie.

"Oh, don't be silly. You would have managed just fine," she said, sweeping wisps of hair behind her left ear.

"I wouldn't bet on it," he said, pleased at her modesty. "I don't know what you said to Cee-Cee to make him forget that nonsense about the girls traveling with their posse, but whatever it was, somehow I doubt it would have sounded as good coming from me."

Looking coyly out from the corner of her eye, she smiled at him. "Let's just say that I used a few diversionary tactics."

Miles' gaze wandered into the vicinity of two of the most lethal "diversionary tactics" that he had ever seen. Vic was wearing a tight-fitting cashmere deep V-neck sweater. Shaking the vision off, he said, "Whatever you did, it worked. You've got that man eating out of the palm of your hand."

"Speaking of eating, why don't we grab a bite? It's late and I'm starving."

Looking at his watch, Miles said, "Whoa." It was already nine o'clock. "I'd better get home. I'm sure that Morgan thinks I'm MIA."

Vic suddenly sounded very concerned. "You aren't going to have her cooking dinner this late, are you? I'm sure that, with the pregnancy and running her own business, she must be exhausted herself."

He hadn't thought of that. And he wasn't looking forward to microwave at all. "Yeah, you're right."

Vic sat up straight. "I know. Why don't you call her and tell her not to worry about you for dinner. I'll get us a reservation and make sure that we can be seated right away. We'll have a quick bite and call it a night." Not waiting for an answer, Vic leaned over to gather her scattered papers, providing a fuller view of her arsenal.

"Okay, you win," Miles said, throwing up his arms in mock defeat. Going out to eat was always a good plan.

Vic stood, with her backside facing Miles at eye level. Looking over her shoulder, she said, "I'll meet you in the lobby in fifteen minutes." The glazed expression in Miles' deep brown eyes told her that she had him—hook, line, and sinker.

Once she'd left his office, Miles exhaled before shaking his head. To clear it, he headed to his desk to call Morgan.

"Hey, sweetie. How's my girl?"

"Oh, hi, baby. I'm good. What time is it?" She sounded drowsy, as if she'd already nodded off. Since the pregnancy, Morgan was usually in bed as early as she could manage.

"It's about ten after nine."

"Should I warm up some dinner? I picked up Thai."

"No, don't bother. I just wanted to let you know that I'll be working a little bit later and that a couple of us are gonna grab a bite to eat."

"Okay, sweetie. Don't stay out too late." He could tell by her voice that she was already halfway back to dreamland.

"All right, honey. I love you."

"I love you too. Kisses."

"Kisses, baby," he said, smacking the air near the receiver.

Miles threw the tour file into his Hermes briefcase, straightened his tie in the gold-framed mirror over the deco credenza, and headed to the men's room. After splashing cold water on his face and washing his hands, he walked out to find Vic. He almost stopped dead in his tracks when he rounded the corner in the lobby and saw her. Gone were the gabardine slacks and Gucci loafers that she had worn just minutes earlier, replaced by a tight black miniskirt that hugged her full rear admirably and a pair of kick-ass Blahnik stilettos.

"Wow," came out of his mouth before he could stop it.

"Glad that you approve," she said, giving him a sexy smile. She strutted ahead of him toward the elevator, giving him the full benefit of her rear view.

On the ride down, Miles was reduced to stunned silence. What the hell was he doing going out to dinner with another woman? But, he argued to himself, it wasn't a date. They were just colleagues grabbing a bite. He counterargued that, if such was the case, why had he led Morgan to believe that it was more of a group thing? Only because he didn't want her to have any reason to worry, especially since she'd been so sensitive lately. Besides, he wasn't going out with "another woman." It was just Vic. When he discreetly glanced over at her, that argument lost its validity. In those fifteen minutes, not only had Vic changed clothes—she'd done a complete transformation. She had taken down the wispy updo, allowing her hair to flow freely over her shoulders.

She'd powered her face, adding blush and a warm, wet, rosy lip gloss. And spritzed a generous amount of her signature Gucci Rush perfume that seemed to float up from her ample cleavage.

"I think you'll like the spot I picked," she said as they got into a taxi.

When they pulled up in front of Mr. Chows, Miles flinched. He hadn't thought to ask where they were going. Mr. Chows was the industry hot spot, the place where music-industry executives and artists went to see and be seen. The moment they walked into Mr. Chows, Miles deeply regretted his decision to "grab a bite" with Vic. Part of the allure of dining at Mr. Chows was the sport of watching who came in with whom, checking out what they had on, and noticing which table they were given. As he and Vic entered, a slight hush fell over the noisy den of industry gossipmongers. They had just provided fresh meat for a lot of ravenous appetites.

Vic followed Charles, the maître d', sporting a beaming smile and cleavage that lit the way like a beacon on a dark night. Charles, who must have also been wrapped around Vic's manicured finger, served up one of the choicest tables in the restaurant. As the three descended the dramatic stairs leading down into the bowl-shaped dining room, eyes from the bar to the restaurant took in the attractive couple.

"Isn't that Miles Nelson?"

"Yeah. But that's certainly not his wife."

"Girrrrlllll, look who just walked in."

"Is that Miles?"

"Yep. And his wife is at home pregnant. Men ain't shit."

"You got that right."

Sensing a scene building, Charles thought it'd be good for business to help it unfold. So he made great fanfare of seating them, and signaled a team of waiters to the table to make sure that it got plenty of attention for the rest of the night.

"I'd forgotten what a scene Mr. Chows is," Miles said

mildly, after they were seated. Though he was characteristically cool on the outside, he was cringing on the inside.

"The same old industry crowd," Vic said, making light of the situation.

Just then the wine steward appeared with a silver champagne stand containing a perfectly chilled bottle of Cristal. Before Miles could protest, the server bowed regally and said, "Compliments of the house."

Vic beamed at the attention from being out with an industry player, while Miles fumed. He wanted to stand up and walk out, but knew that would have tongues wagging even more furiously. Best to play it cool, and show no signs of flirting with Vic.

Of course, the steward made a production of uncorking the bottle, and of course the cork popped so loudly that everyone in the restaurant turned to watch. After pouring a tasting glass for Miles to approve, their flutes were filled with the effervescent rosy elixir.

Not one to miss a cue, Vic raised her glass. "Here's to Ecstasy," she said. Her double entendre hung midair.

As if Miles wasn't embarrassed enough, out of the blue came a very familiar voice: "Is there a special occasion that I should know about?" It was Phillip, standing over them with a questioning expression.

Miles nearly sprang up out of his chair. Instead he manufactured a shrug that looked more like a twitch. "Oh, hey, man. Nah, we just stopped by to grab a bite." When Phillip said nothing, but raised an eyebrow as if the explanation wasn't enough, Miles went on, fumbling, "We were working late. You know, on the Ecstasy stuff." Miles was nodding his head, waiting for some affirmation, when he noticed Phillip eyeing the champagne flute in his hand. "Oh, the maître d' just sent this over," he said lamely.

"Mm-hmm. Well, have a good night," Phillip said, walking away.

Oh, shit, Miles said to himself. If his boy thought something was up, when he *knew* how much Miles loved

Morgan, there was no telling what the other nosy patrons thought.

"He's such a nice man," Vic said, leaning toward Miles and lowering her voice to a more intimate level. "Now where were we?"

In trouble, Miles wanted to shout. I'm in very deep trouble.

26

Before Morgan made it to the shower, Miles was already dressed and out the door, headed to the office with barely a good-bye. Normally he was cuddly in the morning. The early hours were usually their time to lie under the covers and dream of their new life together. Oh, well, thought Morgan, he must have a hectic day scheduled. She settled into her chaise longue with the morning paper and a cup of herbal tea. The sun was pouring in from the east-side window.

Of course, the newspaper contained all of the usual fallout from a day in the life of New York City: police chief and mayor defend cops accused of brutality, stock scheme uncovered at Wall Street's most prestigious brokerage firm, rental rates in city highest in the country, blah-blah-blah. The business section wasn't much better, with news of increasing interest rates, higher unemployment, and dire predictions for small business failures. All of this negativity caused Morgan to worry about her own company's fate. Though Caché seemed to be on the right track, she still walked a tightrope. At this point it could go either way. Their quarterly projections looked reasonable, but any unexpected expenses could swing things the other way. And of course she counted on her clients' businesses flourishing so that they could afford to hire her to plan their lavish events.

The thought of soon being out on maternity leave gave her additional cause for concern. Feeling a touch gloomy, she flipped to Talk of the Town, New York City's favorite scandal sheet. It always had tidbits of interest about who was doing whom and why.

Morgan scanned the page for the boldfaced names. Among them were the usual favorites: Donald Trump, P. Diddy, Madonna, and Gwenyth Paltrow. Just as she was skimming a blurb about Martha Stewart, a familiar name caught her eye. Her pulse quickened as she read the words:

> Sound Entertainment General Manager **Miles Nelson** was seen last night enjoying a cozy dinner for two at Mr. Chows with a bosomy babe and a bottle of vintage Cristal. Was he courting a new artist or just someone other than his pregnant wife?

Before she could expel the breath she'd been holding the phone rang. "Morgan, have you seen Talk of the Town this morning?" It was Dakota.

Morgan's tone was subdued, shell-shocked, "Ah, yeah. I was just reading it."

"Don't worry. I'm sure there's some—" She was interrupted by Morgan's call-waiting tone.

"Just a minute, Kota," Morgan said, before switching over.

"Girl, did you—"

"Yes, I've seen it," Morgan said, cutting Sheri off. She was an insipid gossiper who reveled in anybody else's drama. Most likely because she herself didn't have a life.

"So who was it?" she asked so that she could repeat it later.

"Sheri, I've got to go," Morgan said, immediately clicking back over to Dakota.

"Morgan, I'm sure there's a reasonable explanation for whatever happened last night. I just wanted to call to make sure that you hadn't gotten worked up over it."

"No, I am fine. But thanks for the concern. I'll see you later."

Morgan dropped the receiver back into its cradle and the paper onto the floor, which was where her spirits now lay. She couldn't believe what she'd just read. Hadn't Miles mentioned something about working late and grabbing a bite with a few people from the office? The scene described in the paper didn't sound at all like a group picture, nor did it sound the least bit casual. Why had he lied to her? Her lips firmed in anger. She had an idea who the bosomy babe was. And she knew why Miles had been in such a hurry to get out the door this morning.

Morgan barely made it through the rest of the day. Knowing that Miles was in an all-day label meeting, she fought the impulse to call him to demand an explanation. She repeatedly told herself that the dinner was surely a business meeting and nothing else, and the paper liked nothing more than to put the worst possible spin on it. But she also knew what a sucker Miles was for big breasts, so that and the fact that he wasn't straight with her didn't help her state of mind.

"Morgan, don't go convicting the man before he's stood trial." Dakota was Morgan's voice of reason and vice versa. They often joked that, if combined, they'd be either brilliant or hopeless, depending on which halves met.

"I'm not convicting him, but you have to admit he sounds pretty guilty," Morgan sulked. "You know, this has been my biggest fear with this pregnancy."

"What are you talking about?" Dakota asked, not making the connection. They were having dinner at Fressen, a trendy French bistro-inspired restaurant in the meatpacking district. Morgan had been close to canceling the date after the drama unfolded in this morning's paper and the calls flooded in all day, but she knew that a talk with her best friend was probably just what she needed.

"As happy as I am about having a baby, it's still hard to see your figure turn from a Coke bottle into a canteen."

"Morgan, Miles loves you, your figure, and the baby. You know that. Look how he fawns over you. He acts like you two are the only couple ever to conceive. He is such the proud father." Dakota held both of Morgan's hands and looked pleadingly into her eyes. It pained her to see her friend so down. She and Miles should be on top of the world.

"I know," Morgan conceded. "But it's probably hard for him not to be tempted. Especially given all the beautiful women he's around all day."

"Girl, now you know that what most of them have, they paid cash for."

Morgan had to laugh, since it was true. There wasn't a female R&B singer around who hadn't purchased some part of her body—from lips to nose, breasts, or hair.

"Yeah, but that's not true of everybody," Morgan said, looking solemnly at her nails. "What about Vic? Her boobs look real."

"What does Vic have to do with this?"

Morgan looked up with hurting eyes. "I'll bet she was the mystery woman."

"What makes you think that?"

"He's working with her constantly now on Ecstasy, and she definitely has the hots for him. I can smell it a mile away. The strange thing is that he doesn't or else refuses to admit that her behavior is inappropriate."

"You don't know it was her, so don't jump to conclusions."

"Oh, so am I supposed to be comforted that there may be yet another bimbo on the loose?"

The day had been pure hell for Miles. It hadn't taken long for him to learn about the Talk of the Town blurb labeling him an adulterous cheat. He suddenly understood how seemingly "normal" people ended up in fucked-up situations, all the while professing their innocence.

The chill had started with a timid but intent knock on his

office door. In walked Lauren, nervously holding something behind her back. She was all of five feet even and one hundred pounds soaking wet, but her determination was that of an eight-hundred-pound gorilla. They had worked together for years, and sometimes seemed more like siblings than coworkers—with Lauren very definitely in the older sister role.

"What's up?" As usual Miles got right to the point. He had a big meeting coming up in just thirty minutes and had no time to waste.

"Well . . ." she began hesitantly. Since when did Lauren hesitate to say anything to him?

"Lauren, what's going on? What's that behind your back?"

Finally finding her voice, she abruptly answered, "I just thought that you should see this." She laid down the paper, unfolded to Talk of the Town, squarely in the center of his desk as though it were contaminated, then crossed her arms tightly over her chest, waiting for an explanation.

Puzzled, Miles glanced down at it, then back up at her. "And?"

Lauren leaned over his desk and jabbed her finger angrily at the blurb. "I should be asking *you* that," she said.

After reading the object of her distress, he initially thought surely there was some mistake. They had to be talking about someone else. Until he remembered how Phillip had also misread last night's dinner. Then he realized that regardless of his intentions, his actions last night made him look guilty as hell.

"Well?" she asked.

Snapping out of his reverie, Miles turned toward his pissed assistant. "Well, what?"

"Well, what's this all about?" she demanded.

"It's nothing."

Shifting her weight to her other foot, Lauren said, "I'm not so sure that Morgan will agree with that."

Morgan? Oh, shit! If Lauren was this pissed off and grilling him like a burger, he hated to think what Morgan would say. Squirming nervously in the hot seat, Miles said,

"Listen, it was nothing. Vic and I decided to grab a bite to eat after working late. That's all."

Her nostrils flared. "Vic!"

"Yes, Vic. It was *nothing*. It happens all the time among colleagues."

"Miles, grabbing a bite to eat means take-out Chinese in little white cartons at your desk or conference table. Mr. Chows means having an all-out high-profile dinner," she said, pinning him with her eyes.

He looked away, defeated. "I know. You're right. But I honestly didn't know. Vic made the reservation and I didn't think to ask where."

Lauren raised her eyebrows and slowly nodded her head. "So it was her idea?"

"Yeah. But it was no big deal," he protested. "Nothing happened."

"I hate to break it to you," Lauren said, putting her hands on her small hips, "but to everyone else on the planet, an uncorked bottle of vintage Cristal is a big deal!"

"I didn't order it," Miles said.

"Oh," she answered, "so it just appeared at the table?" She was giving him that and-I-must-be-Boo-Boo-the-Fool look.

"Yeah, pretty much. The maître d' sent it over." His explanation sounded hollow, even to himself.

"Listen, I know it's none of my business, but I suggest that you watch out for Ms. Victoria."

He had had just about enough of this inquisition. "What do you mean by that?"

"Just watch your back," she said, heading for the door.

Seconds after she shut it, it reopened, revealing Phillip with a sour expression on his face. He was also holding the Talk of the Town section.

Cutting right to the chase, Phillip frowned and said, "Man, what the hell were you thinking?"

Miles shook his head. "I guess I wasn't. We were working late and—"

"Excuse me, brother," Phillip said, holding up his hand, "I

hope you don't mind me interrupting. But I'm a little confused. When I left the office yesterday—if my memory serves me correctly—Vic had on a pair of slacks and loafers. So if this was an innocent, impromptu thing, where did homegirl get the I'm-gonna-catch-a-man gear? That skirt had to hit just about here." Phillip drew a line way up his thigh. "And those heels were serious come-fuck-me skyscrapers."

Miles held up his hands in mock surrender. "Man, I don't know. All I know is that I went to the bathroom before we left, and when I came out, she had transformed like Madame Butterfly."

Phillip gave his friend a long, piercing look. "Man, I hate to tell you this, but it sounds like you were set up."

"What do you mean, set up?" Miles got up and came around to the front of his desk.

"I think honey was lying in the cut, waiting for a chance to make her moves. She probably called the maître d' and arranged to have that champagne sent over."

"You think?" Miles frowned, crossing his arms.

"Are you kidding? You'd better watch out. I smell trouble."

"But I didn't *do* anything."

"Now you sound like Clarence Thomas." Phillip clapped him on the shoulder. "Man, it doesn't matter what you did or didn't do, as long as the sound bite tastes good. And this one is pretty juicy. Now you'd best do some damage-control with your lady, Morgan."

Miles quietly said, "Listen, man, I gotta go. I've got a meeting in a couple of minutes."

Backing out the door, Phillip tipped an imaginary hat. "See ya—wouldn't want to be ya."

With a scowl Miles said, "Thanks for the support."

"Hey, man, I've got your back."

Yeah, but what about my butt? Miles thought to himself.

The rest of the day was a variation on the same theme. The look on everyone's face seemed to say, *You are* so *busted*. He hadn't realized that the gossip rag's circulation was that high. Even the office messenger had winked at Miles in the hallway

and said, "You the man." On his pager he'd even gotten a few
little ditties like:

SAVE SOME 4 THE REST OF THE BROTHERS;
CAN I JUST GET SOME OF UR LEFTOVERS?
WHO LET THE DAWGS OUT!

To make matters worse, the label meeting turned out to
be an unproductive waste of time. The only thing he could
focus on was what the hell he was going to say to Morgan.
He'd thought about conjuring up an impromptu emergency
out-of-town meeting. Since he always kept a packed bag in
the office for such occasions, he could leave town without
ever having to see her. But he talked himself out of that lame
scheme. It would only make matters worse when he finally
did have to face the music. He hoped she would call the office so he could at least break the ice over the phone before
having to walk into the Antarctic later. But no such luck.
She never called.

He worked as late as possible, and on his longer than usual
trek home that night, his shoes felt leaden and his breathing
was tight. He felt so guilty, but he hadn't done anything! That
was what he'd have to remember and what he prayed Morgan
would believe.

Bracing himself, he slipped past the doorman, who gave
him a knowing look. When Miles opened the door to their elegant duplex apartment, he could feel the chill emanating
from within. No flickering candles or mood music tonight.

"Morgan?" He decided to play the loving husband,
what's-the-big-deal role. Although the beautiful bunch of
flowers he'd picked up at the corner Korean grocer sort of be-
lied that impression. *Damn*, why had he succumed to such an
obvious cliché? He stashed them on the foyer table. When he
dropped his keys in the porcelain dish on the rolltop desk, he
noticed Morgan's were there as well. So she was at home.

"Morgan?" Still no answer.

He ventured upstairs, past the library and into the master
bedroom suite, where he found Morgan at her vanity with her

back turned to him, rubbing her favorite Mario Badescu's buttermilk moisturizer into her flawless skin.

"Morgan!" he said cheerfully, smiling as he removed his tie. "How are you, sweetheart?" Maybe she hadn't read the article. One could always hope.

She answered him with silence.

Miles started removing the cuff links from his Brioni shirt, allowing himself to think that perhaps not only hadn't she read the story, but miraculously hadn't heard about it either.

"Would you care to explain last night?" she said at last.

He stiffened. "What are you talking about?" Visions of a near miss quickly faded.

"Miles Nelson, don't you play games with me," she said, turning slowly to face him. She stood up and tossed the paper that had haunted him all day onto the floor right at his feet.

"Morgan, it's not what you think," he said, backing up.

"Oh? And what do I think?" He could see the hurt beneath the anger in her eyes.

"It *was* just a couple of us." He wished that he could take that lame reply back. He'd known when he said it last night that he was skirting the truth. But then it felt like an easy out that would prevent exactly the drama he found himself in now.

"Miles, don't get cute with me," she snapped. "You know damn well that 'a couple of us' sounds like a group thing. But you and honey were cozied up together over a bottle of vintage champagne. That couldn't be farther from the lie you told me. So don't you stand here and further insult me with your hairsplitting and half-truths."

"Morgan, I know it sounds really fucked up, but that's not how it happened." He proceeded to give her a blow-by-blow of how the night had unfolded.

She heard him out, then said sharply, "I knew it."

"Knew what?"

"That it was Vic, or should I say, Victoria. There seems to be a history of you omitting pertinent facts where she is concerned—starting right off the bat with her gender."

He threw up his hands in defense. "I never said that Vic

was a guy! In fact, I didn't know myself until she showed up in my office for our first meeting."

"She seems to show up a lot lately." Morgan turned her back to him, resuming her seat at the vanity.

"Morgan, the relationship is strictly professional."

"My only concern is *which* profession." She met his eyes in her mirror.

Holding his breath, Miles came up behind Morgan and encircled her in his arms. Though he could feel her tense, she didn't pull away. "Morgan, I love you more than anything in this world. And I would never do anything to hurt you or to destroy our marriage and our family." As he talked, he began gently rubbing the swell of her stomach. He could feel her shoulders quiver with the effort to contain her deepening sorrow. He held her tighter, wanting to comfort her and assure her that this was all a big mistake and had nothing to do with his feelings for her. "Baby, you know how much I love you. You can't let some uninformed gossip column poison what we have."

"But you must be tempted." She turned to face him, tears streaming silently down her face. "I feel like a cow!"

Gazing deep into her eyes, he said, "When I look at you, I see the most beautiful woman in the world, whose amazing body is preparing to deliver God's ultimate gift. Nothing that Vic could ever do could come close to the love and beauty that we share."

Instead of softening, however, her face turned hard again. "You're full of great lines these days, Miles. Tell me, what did you use on Vic last night?"

27

Dakota sat on the sofa in front of the television, mindlessly clicking channels. She was beginning to have reservations about Tricia moving in. She hadn't shared her living space with anyone since she lived in a college dorm. She thought she would have more time to get used to the idea, but Nana's neighborhood was in the middle of gentrification with suburbanites making a reverse exodus back into the city, so the house was only on the market two weeks before it sold. To Dakota's surprise, Tricia didn't have any second thoughts about moving to New York. She seemed all set to fit in with Dakota's high-rolling lifestyle.

As promised, Dakota moved her office equipment and converted the space into a cozy bedroom, buying new furniture, stereo equipment, and a television set so Tricia would feel at home. She also had the cleaning woman come and scour the entire loft. One of the drawbacks of living in the city was the amount of grit that seeped through the windows, doors, and vents, whether they were opened or not.

Dakota ordered a car to pick up Tricia, who was arriving on the seven-ten at Penn Station. She looked at her watch and figured Tricia should be there in thirty minutes. Dakota looked around the loft. Everything was perfect, just as she'd thought. She decided to call Morgan. When the mechanical voice of the answering machine picked up, she hung up and dialed Morgan's cell.

"Hey, girl, can you hear me?" Dakota asked through the static.

"Barely. Hold on, I'm going through the Park Avenue tunnel." After a few seconds Morgan came back on the line. "Hello. Is that better?"

"Much."

"What's going on?"

"Just a little stressed. Tricia will be here any minute. I hope I didn't make the wrong decision."

Morgan didn't sound hopeful. "You guys are getting along better, right?"

"Yeah, but I'm still nervous," Dakota said, running her hands through her hair. "I've been so busy making sure the loft was spotless, I forgot to stock the fridge."

"Listen, why don't I stop by Popeyes and bring over dinner."

Dakota laughed. "You and your chicken. That baby's going to come out with wings if you keep eating Popeyes."

"Girl, it's what I crave. I can't get enough. I'll be there in about twenty minutes."

"Thanks. See you then."

Dakota wanted Morgan and Tricia to get better acquainted, and was glad she would be there to help welcome Tricia to town. The three of them could sit around and have a good old-fashioned gabfest. That would help pick Morgan up out of her blues about Miles.

Just as Dakota hung up the phone, she heard a beep-beep from the street and looked out the window. There was Tricia, standing next to a black town car, waving for Dakota to come down.

"Good Lord, Tricia, what didn't you bring?" Dakota asked, when she came out of her building. She peered in the backseat, which was jam-packed with at least six pieces of Louis Vuitton luggage.

"That ain't nothing. I got more back there," Tricia announced proudly.

Dakota walked around to the open trunk and dropped her jaw at the sight of two Louis Vuitton steamer trunks. "Where did you get this luggage?"

"It ain't real," Tricia lied.

Dakota's expert eye surveyed the merchandise. She would have sworn the luggage was genuine, but no way could Tricia afford that. Hell, *Dakota* couldn't afford it.

After several trips up the stairs, the car was finally unloaded. "I need to call a contractor to build more closet space," Dakota said, looking at the luggage in the middle of her living room floor.

"I had to bring *all* my stuff," Tricia snapped. "It's not like I'm here on vacation. I did relocate, or don't you remember?"

Dakota didn't get riled. Tricia must be tired from the long train ride. "Don't get me wrong. I just wasn't expecting all of this." Dakota headed toward the back of the loft. "I'm going to clean out another closet—it shouldn't take long."

"You need some help?"

"No, relax yourself."

Tricia looked around at the richly decorated loft, with its polyurethane hardwood floors, eighteen-foot-high windows with custom rose-and-gray metallic drapes that matched the gray velvet art deco furniture. All this must have cost a fortune, especially the silver flat-screen television with towering speakers on both sides. "I'm going to like living here," she said softly. Too bad she had to share it with Dakota.

She picked up the slim television remote. Just as she settled in to watch, the doorbell rang.

"Kota, somebody's at the door!" she yelled out.

"Answer it—that should be Morgan," she yelled back.

Tricia clicked off the TV and walked to the door. "Who is it?"

"It's Morgan."

Tricia opened the door and stared in shock at Morgan's protruding belly. Dakota hadn't told her Morgan was pregnant. The last time she saw Morgan, she was as slim as a model. Tricia stood aside as Morgan entered the loft.

"Welcome to New York, Tricia."

"Damn, who blew you up?" Tricia said, pointing rudely at Morgan's midsection.

"Excuse me?" Morgan said, holding bags of Popeyes chicken.

"Last time I saw you . . . well, let's just say now you look like a blimp!" Tricia laughed.

"And the last time I saw you, you were Tacky Ann, and I see you still are," Morgan retaliated, commenting on Tricia's red polyester miniskirt, animal-print midriff sweater, and black thigh highs that stopped just short of her skirt. To complete the ensemble she wore candy-apple-red, spike-heeled ankle boots.

"Who you calling tacky? You just mad 'cause yo ass is fat and I don't mean *phat*," she said, sucking her teeth.

On the verge of blowing her cool, Morgan said, "I'm not going to stand here and trade insults with you. If you're going to live here, you're going to be seeing me a lot." She turned and walked away.

After storming into the kitchen, she put the bags down and leaned her forehead against the fridge, closing her eyes.

Dakota appeared in the doorway and, eyeing Morgan, said, "What's wrong?"

"Nothing," Morgan said, grabbing some dishes and nearly flinging them on the table.

"If it's nothing, then why are you trying to break my dishes? Come on, Morgan, what is it?"

"You better tell your tacky cousin she's barking up the wrong tree."

So much for sitting around for a friendly chat, Dakota thought. "What happened?"

Morgan recapped the incident.

"I'll be right back," Dakota said, and marched into the living room.

Tricia was curled up on the sofa watching television. Dakota grabbed up the remote and clicked off the set.

"Hey! I was watching that."

"Listen up, Tricia. Morgan went out of her way to bring us dinner and your insults were totally out of line. You know she is my best friend, so I would really appreciate it if you would at least try to get along with her."

"All I said was, she blew up."

"Look, keep your insults to yourself." Dakota put the remote back on the cocktail table. "Now come on, let's eat."

"I ain't hungry." Tricia sucked her teeth, then added, "Why you takin' her side, anyway."

" 'Cause I know you, and I know Morgan doesn't get upset over nothing. Now come on," Dakota pleaded, "let's not ruin your first night."

"Naw, I'm going to bed." Tricia huffed off toward her room.

Dakota went back into the kitchen and sat at the table with Morgan. "I'm sorry, girl," Dakota said, noticing Morgan's dark mood.

"Thanks, but it's not just Tricia. It's Miles, you know?"

"Well, like I said before, I wouldn't worry about that Vic. She's not even in your league. Pregnant or not, you could run circles around that hooch."

Morgan weighed Dakota's words for a moment. "It's just so embarrassing having my husband in Talk of the Town. Never in my wildest dreams did I think I'd read about Miles in that scandal sheet."

Dakota reached across the table and touched Morgan's hand. "Girl, today's news is tomorrow's trash."

"You're right. That paper is probably lining somebody's cat litter as we speak." Morgan yawned. "God, I'm exhausted. I'm going home to bed."

At the front door, Morgan noticed Tricia's LV luggage. "Did you lend her those trunks?"

"No, she brought them with her."

Morgan ran her hand across a trunk that was standing upright. "Where did she get the money for Louis Vuitton?"

"She said they're fake."

Morgan leaned over and looked closely at the shiny brass lock. "Looks real to me."

"Trust me, Tricia can't afford Samsonite, let alone Vuitton," Dakota said, then hugged her friend good night.

28

Plans for Blake's gallery opening were coming along well. In addition to hiring Caché, he'd also hired a publicist, Hanna Mates, from Genesis Strategies. The investment was already paying big dividends. The idea of a sophisticated young black art dealer and his equally worldly black clientele intrigued the media. It was as though a new species of human beings had been found roaming the planet. Blake had joked to Morgan that no matter how many well-educated, well-to-do black people whites met, each new one seemed an anomaly. He couldn't count the number of times he'd been told, "You're so different" or "You're the exception," by white people who thought it was a compliment.

As the face behind this insurgence of black sophistication, Blake was sure to get even more attention. After seeing the stunning build-up about the gallery, *Architectural Digest* had already interviewed him for a feature story, and he was scheduled to appear on the *Today Show* and *David Letterman* after the opening. Still, both producers were holding out until after the big splash, just to make sure it was more than a ripple.

The next morning, chaos shrieked in his ear. After rolling over and reaching blindly in the general direction of the phone, he grappled with it before finally picking it up. "Hello," Blake said in a gravelly voice.

His father's baritone boomed through the receiver. "Good

morning, Blake. What are you doing still in bed at eight o'clock? Didn't I teach you that the early bird gets the worm?"

"Good morning, Dad," Blake said, ignoring the rest of his father's unsolicited commentary. He was grateful to have his own place so he could do what he wanted to do when he wanted to do it. He couldn't figure out what had taken him so long to make the move.

"I'll be stopping by in about an hour. Need to discuss something with you." It was not a request, but more like a command.

Blake sat up in a panic. "Why don't you come by the gallery? Or better yet, let's meet somewhere for lunch."

"Not to worry. I have a meeting in Midtown, so I have to pass your building anyway. I'll be there in an hour."

His father's tone caused Blake to remove his black silk eye-shades. "Sure, Dad. I'll see you then."

What now? he thought, looking over at his bedmate. Although he had won a measure of his father's respect, he still had a long way to go.

"Freddie, Freddie, wake *up*!" Blake said, nudging him urgently. Blake had been horny the night before and thought with his little head instead of the one on his shoulders. He'd called Freddie over for one last romp. But now he had to get Freddie, and all signs of him, out of there before his father arrived.

Freddie stirred, then stretched before finally opening his eyes. "What is it?" he asked groggily. He'd been in a deep sleep, dreaming he was on a sandy white beach, getting a massage from a buff dude in a Hawaiian hula skirt.

"Get up. You've got to go. My dad's coming over." Blake's tone was brusque. He was already out of bed, gathering Freddie's things.

"Why I got to go? Why can't I meet him?" Freddie pouted. He had expected to lounge around all day while Blake went to the gallery, then serve him again once he got home.

"Because I don't want my father in my business like that."

"He's met Spence," Freddie reminded Blake. He was beginning to really feel used. He was good enough to suck Blake's dick, but not good enough to meet his family.

"Spence is different," Blake said, immediately wishing he could take the words back.

"Oh, really!" Freddie sat up pissed. "Is it because he has money, or is his dick just bigger?"

Thinking fast, Blake said, "No, it's nothing like that. Spence has been a friend of the family for a long time. So it's not suspicious to my father when we are together." It wasn't a complete lie. Spence's aunt and Blake's mother had been in the same sorority chapter of Delta Sigma Theta back in their day.

"I don't know what you think you're hiding," Freddie said scornfully. "I'm sure your father already knows you're gay."

Getting annoyed, Blake said, "That may be, but that doesn't mean that I have to rub his nose in it."

Blake walked naked into his huge California closet. There was even a chair in it for him to sit in while pondering which of his many expensive garments to wear. All of his suits hung like soldiers, shoulder to shoulder on oak hangers. Slacks and shirts were also lined up in separate sections. His shoes even had their own long shelf, where they stood at attention with wooden shoe trees inserted into each pair.

"I'm sick of feeling like a piece of toilet tissue. You just use me, then toss me away without a second thought."

Blake walked out of his closet, tying the belt of his silk Armani bathrobe. "If you feel that way, don't come back."

Freddie felt like he'd been slapped in the face with a two-by-four. "You bastard!" he screamed. Jumping from the bed, he threw on his clothes so fast that the buttons on his shirt were misaligned. "You think you can just fuck me and keep on steppin'? I'll show you. Who do you think you are? King Tut? I've given you everything, and what do you do? Toss me a bone, pat me on the head, and dismiss me like your slave?"

Blake stood there stunned. This was a side of Freddie that he'd never seen before. He had to get him out of here before his father arrived. If his father got a whiff of this mess, all the points he'd accrued up to now would be forfeited.

"Freddie, just calm down," Blake said, coming closer. "We can talk about this later."

"I want to talk about it *now*." He stood in the middle of the room with his arms folded stubbornly across his chest. He wasn't budging.

Blake was anxious to defuse this situation and get Freddie out of his apartment. Then get him out of his life for good. "Just tell me what you want," Blake said calmly, mentally taking out his checkbook. Surely he could buy his way out of this debacle.

Yet Freddie's next words floored him. "I want to move in with you. You've got plenty of room." When he saw Blake's mouth drop open, he went on. "Besides, I could help out around here. I could cook for you and take care of all your needs," he added suggestively.

"I'm sorry, Freddie, but that's just not possible." The mere thought mortified Blake.

"Of course it is," Freddie pleaded.

"I'm sorry, but no," Blake said definitively, turning to show Freddie the door.

"If that's the case," Freddie spat out, "then deal with this." He reached into the breast pocket of his jacket and removed a set of color pictures, which he shoved into Blake's hand.

Reaching for them, Blake was stunned to see himself lying on his own bed naked with another man's erect penis in his mouth. Feeling sick, he dropped the photos and sat heavily on his bed.

Freddie gathered up the pictures. "I suggest you think about this. Just let me know when I can pick up my key." Enough said, he walked by Blake and saw his way out.

Blake was in a state of shock. How had he let this situation spiral so far out of control? What started out as a night's fun was now a living nightmare.

Blake sat with his elbows on his knees holding his head, willing himself to wake up from this god-awful dream. Just when he finally had his life on the right track, some two-bit piece of ass was threatening to derail all of his plans. Why hadn't he seen this coming? This wasn't the first time that his physical yearnings had gotten him in hot water, but it was the first time that he'd had so much to lose. Images of being interviewed on TV, photographed at events, and quoted in papers flashed through Blake's mind, juxtaposed with the sordid image of him splayed out naked, stripped of all dignity, lying on his back sucking another man's penis. How had it come to this?

Then he remembered the first night that he and Freddie had been together and how after the last sip of his martini he had had no memory of the rest of the night. He figured he'd just passed out from the alcohol and sex, but now it appeared as though there was a lot more to it than that. He remembered Freddie had volunteered to go into the other room to get their drinks. There, he must have slipped something into Blake's martini. Maybe he had some kind of date-rape drug hidden in his jacket along with a small camera. Given Freddie's behavior this morning, Blake wouldn't put it past him.

He had to find a way to put a stop to this. There was no way he could allow Freddie to move in with him. What would his father think? More important, what would his father think if he saw those lurid pictures?! Blake could never allow that to happen. Suddenly he remembered that his father was on the way over. He only had about twenty minutes to shower, dress, and attempt to compose himself. How on earth did he get himself into these crazy situations? It was reminiscent of his days with Tyrone, who always had some drama playing out. Only this time, he was the star of the show.

29

Dakota was spending a lonely Friday night at home doing her nails. And Tricia was spending the same Friday night at the Seaport Mall. Dakota assumed window-shopping, since Tricia had yet to find a part-time job. After catching Tristan trying to have his cake and icing too, Dakota was lying low, licking her wounds. While her nails dried, her phone rang.

"Hello?"

"Hello, may I speak to Dakota?"

She didn't recognize the sexy male voice. It wasn't Tristan, and besides, he knew better than to call her. "Speaking."

"Hi, Dakota, it's Phillip."

She stopped fanning her hand. "Oh, hi." She had forgotten that she had virtually invited him to get in touch with her on the tennis court.

"Are you busy? Did I disturb you? I got your number from Miles."

"No, just doing my nails." She didn't know what it was about Phillip, but she didn't feel the need to build herself up with him.

"How about dinner tonight? Nothing formal, just a little takeout. I just ordered enough Thai to feed a family of four."

"I don't know. I . . ."

"You're hungry, aren't you?" he said, determined to sway her.

"Look, Phillip, I think you're cool, but I'm not into hunting on someone else's territory," she said.

"You're talking about Paula, aren't you?"

"Yes, your girlfriend. She's still your girlfriend, isn't she?"

Phillip hesitated before answering. "Actually, I've been rethinking my relationship with Paula. You saw a little bit of it that day on the tennis court. Her priority at the moment is her career, and our relationship seems to always take a backseat. I thought I loved her, but now I don't know . . ."

Dakota couldn't believe how honest he was being. Men rarely opened up to her like this. It was as if they were girlfriends having a conversation about relationships. "Well, have you told her you want to cool it?"

"Not yet, she's in London on business. But I plan to have a heart-to-heart with her as soon as she gets back. To be honest, Dakota, I'm ready to settle down, and I don't think Paula's on the same page." Phillip exhaled heavily, as if a burden had been lifted. "I don't know why I'm telling you all of this. My plan was to call and invite you over for dinner, not spill my guts."

Dakota smiled. Most men she knew would have lied and said that they had already broken up. "I don't mind. It's actually refreshing to hear a man speak about his feelings."

"Okay, enough of true confessions. Why don't you hop in a taxi and come on over? I live at 922 Hudson, near White Street," he said, with a hint of excitement in his voice.

Her stomach growled loudly. Why not? she thought. He was Miles' friend forever, so it wasn't like she didn't know anything about him. "Yeah okay, I'm starving," she finally admitted.

"Great. Then I'll feed you and send you on your merry way," he laughed.

She hung up and touched her nails to make sure they were completely dry before changing her clothes. She dressed casually in jeans, a cashmere sweater, and loafers. That surely wouldn't send any wrong signals.

She caught a taxi and soon pulled up in front of a modest six-story apartment building. Dakota was mildly surprised.

She had assumed that since his address was in Tribeca, he lived in a loft.

"Dakota Cantrell to see Phillip Anderson," she told the doorman.

"Just a second, please," he said, picking up the house phone, announcing her. "Go on up. He's in P-three."

Better and better, she thought. When she stepped off the elevator into a small hallway with only three apartment doors, she pushed the bell on number three.

Phillip greeted her with chopsticks in hand. He was dressed in gray sweatpants and a white T-shirt. "Hey, hungry woman, come on in."

As Dakota stepped into his apartment, she was blown away. The black hardwood floors were polished to a mirror finish. The furniture was straight out of Roche-Bobois. Two identical tan nubuck sofas faced each other in front of a massive fireplace. To the right was a long dining table with stark white leather chairs. The wall at the rear had extra wide French doors that led to a terrace.

"Nice place," she said, looking around.

"Thanks," he said proudly. "I had it gutted and totally remodeled."

"Can I see more?" she asked, craning her neck to get a better look down the hall.

"Come on, let me give you the two-dollar tour," he joked. Opening the first doors, he said, "This is my office." It was your typical home office with computer, fax, and scanner all on a handsome teak desk.

The next room was a beautiful guest suite.

"Nice color combination," she said, referring to the cappuccino-hued walls and teal bed linen.

"I wish I could take all the credit. To be honest, I had Sheila Bridges, an interior designer, come in and hook it up." He proceeded to another room. "And this is my kingdom."

And what a kingdom it was! His bed was most unusual. It appeared to be king-sized, but from the proportions, Dakota knew it was larger. The headboard was about five feet tall, and curved slightly around the head of the bed.

"What's this made of?" she said, running her hand over the surface.

"It's a bark from West Africa."

"Really? It feels amazing," she said, admiring the texture. "What size bed is this?"

He smiled at the question. "I had it customized. It's about a foot wider and longer than the average king."

"Oh, I see. Big bed for a big man," she teased.

"Let's eat, 'cause this big man is hungry," he said, grabbing her hand and leading her back to the living area.

He had two bamboo mats laid out on a cocktail table, and cartons of Thai food in the center. He sat down on one of two large pillows on the floor, and Dakota did the same.

Phillip offered her a pair of chopsticks. "I hope you don't mind sitting Indian style. If so, we can eat at the table."

"Actually, I like to sit on the floor. Reminds me of when I was a kid. What's this?" she asked, looking into a carton.

"Chicken Panang. I hope you like curry. It's a little spicy."

"I love Chicken Panang. It's my favorite."

"Good. Like I said, I ordered plenty, so help yourself," he said. "That one has lemongrass pork chops."

They ate mostly in silence. Dakota glanced over at him, as he was busy chowing down. She chuckled to herself. Most of the guys she dated wouldn't be caught dead with a pork chop hanging out the side of their mouths. Watching Phillip enjoying his food increased her appetite and soon she polished off her dish and leaned back on the sofa.

"Here, I'll take that," Phillip said, reaching for her empty carton and going into the kitchen. He came back with a tray of sake and two cups. "You like sake?"

"I love it. I haven't had it in a long time."

She was reaching up for the cup when she felt a sharp muscle spasm. She winced at the pain.

"What's wrong?"

"I don't know. It's my shoulder. It was fine earlier." She rubbed the sore spot. "It's probably from tennis. When we played Saturday, I must have pulled a muscle going for a backhand."

He sat on the sofa and nudged Dakota with his knees until she was positioned between his legs. "You probably just need a good massage," he said, putting his hands on her shoulders. "I give the best."

Dakota immediately stiffened. She hadn't expected him to move in so fast, and she didn't know what to say. The old I-give-good-massages line was too tired.

Feeling her tense up, Phillip removed his hands. As she looked up at him, he said, "Look, I am not trying to put the moves on you. I just want to smooth out this knot in your shoulder." He waited until she nodded, then put his hand on her sore spot. He started digging in with his thumbs. "Tell me if you want me to stop."

"No, it's cool." She leaned forward, reasoning that it did feel like he knew what he was doing. In fact, she couldn't believe how good his hands felt. He had a firm but gentle touch. She closed her eyes and relaxed into his caress. Pretty soon she laid her head on his knee and drifted off.

He looked down and realized she was asleep. He didn't want to disturb her, she seemed so peaceful. Curious, he stroked her hair and the side of her cheek, which was smooth as velvet. She was a classy woman, and he liked how comfortable he was with her. He closed his eyes and imagined making love to her. He felt himself getting excited at the thought, then opened his eyes and said silently, Come on, man, calm down, calm down.

It was one in the morning when Dakota woke up. She found herself lying on the floor. Phillip was seated across from her, and seeing her stir, he came over to help her sit up. "Your magic hands put me to sleep! I guess it's been a hard week," she said, apologizing. Stretching her arms out, she accidentally brushed his thigh. "Excuse me." She stood up and looked at the imprint of his six pack through his T-shirt. Her eyes wandered farther south and stopped at the bulge beneath his sweats. Their eyes met, holding for long seconds. She felt her nipples harden as she watched the mound under the soft cotton fabric grow. She wanted to straddle him and feel his rock-hard penis against her. She licked her lips at the thought.

Phillip licked his full lips in return and reached for her narrow hips, pulling her close for a hug. Her breath caught. She couldn't go back down that road. Not so soon after the Tristan misadventure. She wanted to make love to him, but knew this was happening way too fast. He still had a girlfriend, and she wasn't into being the other woman. She was poised to say no, but to her surprise he didn't push it farther. Instead he said, "I can see that you're tired. Why don't you stay the night? You can have the guest room."

"I don't know, Phillip."

He took her hand. "Come on, I'm harmless. Really." He spread his arms and smiled sweetly to disarm her.

Dakota thought about it for a second, then decided it would be in her best interest to hightail it out of Dodge. This was, after all, another woman's man. As much as she disliked the other woman, she had to respect their relationship. So she thanked him for dinner and the massage. On the way home she couldn't help but think how good she felt in his hands. Like clay to a master sculptor.

30

If sexual intoxication were an illegal substance, this night would have been like crack cocaine to a drug addict. Though supply was readily available, the customers were still unable to get enough of it. The women oozed toe-curling, heart-pounding, spine-shuddering sex through every pore. Every sexual fantasy imaginable was played out on the seductively lit stage in the main room of Scores, a strip club located in Midtown Manhattan.

Juerg, Dakota's most profitable Swiss client, sat mouth agape in a sexual daze. His Nordic blue-green eyes shone like orbs of melting ice. "Oh, oh . . ." That seemed to be the limit of his vocabulary as he let a chesty brunette ride him, undulating like a rattlesnake uncoiling from her enclave. He sat hypnotized by her smooth, melodic movements.

Dakota's deskmate, Paul, sitting opposite her, leaned in to whisper, "I hope he doesn't have any heart problems, 'cause he is about to blow a fuse."

"Don't worry. He's a big boy."

"Even if he isn't, she's certainly a big girl," Paul said, holding two cupped hands in front of his chest.

"Down, boy," Dakota teased.

They both had clients visiting and decided to take them out on the town in the Big Apple. A part of the male-dominated world of Wall Street revolved around big cigars, bigger bankrolls, and women with store-bought boobs. A true modern woman, Dakota was not the least bit put off by it. In fact, whenever she accompanied her colleagues on these sex-cursions, she sat back and took notes. She had to admit that over the years she'd even picked up a trick or two. Her favorite one was walking away from a man while wearing just a thong, then glancing over her shoulder with a come-hither look. It never failed to get the man up and running, so to speak. As obvious as such ploys were, she found them quite empowering.

When the song ended, the slithering temptress transformed into a no-nonsense bill collector. She stuck her hand out for the twenty-dollar cost of her lap dance. Dakota handed it to her, plus a five-dollar tip. After all, Juerg was her guest and this was a business expense. The brunette took the money and held on to Dakota's hand. "Can I dance for you?" she asked, licking her red lacquered lips.

"No, but thanks," Dakota replied. It wasn't the first time that a woman had come on to her—especially in a strip club.

"You sure? You're very beautiful," the brunette cooed.

Before Dakota could answer, Juerg and Paul began egging her on. "Come on, Dakota, don't deprive us of the ultimate fantasy!" For some reason seeing two women together seemed to be every heterosexual male's wet dream.

"Let's see how liberal you really are. Come on, Dakota. What's a little dance among friends?" She shot Paul a warning look, but before she could protest, the dancer stood between Dakota's legs, spreading her knees apart to make room for the private show that was about to be performed up close and personal. She proceeded to bump, grind, and swivel in time to the music. Then she turned around and shook her ample ass lewdly in Dakota's face, while smacking her own butt cheeks to make them jiggle. When she turned back around, she bent forward at the waist with her arms stretched out to jiggle her enormous breasts within an inch of Dakota's face. Juerg, Paul, and all the nearby patrons were riveted like salivating dogs.

When the dance was finally over, Dakota gamely placed a twenty under the dancer's g-string, causing the onlookers to clap and hoot raucously.

The DJ called for all of the dancers to gather behind the stage for the legendary Scores review. It was like an X-rated Miss America pageant, during which the audience had a chance to appraise all of the merchandise at once before clamoring for their favorite. There was every size and flavor—the blonde in the extra-short cheerleader outfit, the bobbed brunette wearing a crotch-high Catholic schoolgirl uniform, a redhead in a gypsy harem costume, and the clichés went on. There were so many, but only two black girls, Dakota noted.

One wore a skintight Lycra dress that stopped just after the round of her behind. A garter around her thigh was stuffed with twenties. She wore a pair of five-inch come-fuck-me pumps and a wig that was longer than the dress. The other black chick had on a weave that should have been outlawed, the way it stuck up from her scalp. She wore a sexy maid's outfit. Dakota had wondered before what type of woman would do this for a living. The standard excuse was, "I'm in school and need to pay my tuition. So I'm really using them." *Riiiiggghht*, Dakota thought. A likely lie. Not that she intended to pass judgment, but it seemed pretty clear to her that these women simply had to have loose morals.

While the guys were ogling their choices, Dakota took out her two-way pager to see if she had any messages. Although this was great entertainment for the guys, for Dakota it was starting to get old. She didn't understand why they were so fixated. After all, it was pure fantasy: silicone, makeup, wigs, and plastic surgery. But it still looked good under the dimmed lights.

She was surprised to see a message from Phillip.

Her heart was now the one thumping. She hadn't spoken to him since that odd night at his apartment. She'd often thought of him in the past two days.

HEY, STRANGER, his message read.

Dakota typed back, STRANGER DANGER.

Within a few seconds he responded, YES U R DANGEROUS.

ME? DANGEROUS! U R THE 1 WITH THE LETHAL HANDS, she typed, remembering his massage and the strong hands that had so relaxed her mind and body.

U HAVEN'T SEEN ANYTHING YET. I'VE JUST GOTTEN WARMED UP.

I'M SURE PAULA COULD TELL ME ALL ABOUT IT.

His response wasn't immediate. He'd obviously been caught off guard. TOUCHÉ.

Her attraction to Phillip had taken her by surprise, but she couldn't lose sight of the fact that he was somebody else's man and so far he hadn't told her they'd broken up. So she typed her final response: GOTTA RUN.

She stashed her pager into the side pocket of her Marc Jacobs bag, and turned her attention to Juerg's favorite dancer. She was built like an Amazon, and had him worked into a frenzy. His eyes were literally rolled back in his head. Laughing, Dakota glanced at Paul, but he too was otherwise engaged.

One of the black strippers was down on her knees between his legs, squeezing her boobs. He seemed mesmerized by the size and color of her nipples. Dakota was ready to hand him a bib to catch the drool.

Dakota sat back in her chair and took a long sip of her grappa, satisfied that everyone was having a good time.

"Oh . . . oh. . . ." Juerg was at it again, that witty conversationalist. Just then Paul's dancer stood up and turned to give him a good view of her hindquarters. Using Dakota's trick she was looking over her shoulder while he focused like a laser on her ass. When she faced forward to grab her boobs for the all-over body shake move, she froze, staring in disbelief at Dakota.

Dakota stared right back. Her mind was slow in processing what her eyes clearly saw. "Lisa?"

Mortified, Lisa ran from the room, leaving Paul in a sexual lurch. Dakota sat there with her mouth open.

Oh, my God, she thought. Wait till I tell Morgan.

31

Sterling Cappricio, a Los Angeles–based clothing designer who was showcasing his couture line in New York, had hired Caché to plan the event in the upstairs lobby of 60 Thompson, a boutique hotel in SoHo. The lobby and bar had been transformed into an offsite boutique with ornate circular racks of exquisite gowns dispersed throughout the lobby. A twenty-foot-long, crimson-carpeted catwalk ran the length of the space. Flat-screen monitors had replaced bottles of liquor on the shelves behind the bar and Morgan had had Lisa pull slides from Sterling's ready-to-wear line to be shown on the monitors during the cocktail hour. With Morgan's pregnancy advancing, Dakota had agreed to help out.

By the time Dakota reached the hotel, everybody was in motion. Workers were setting up folding chairs on either side of the catwalk. Makeup artists were busy applying layers of war paint to the faces of models. Waiters were uncorking bottles of wine. And Morgan was orchestrating it all.

"Hey, girl," Dakota greeted Morgan.

"I am so glad you're here. Put your purse down, roll up your sleeves, and get ready to work," she said.

"I'm fine, thanks for asking."

"Girl, I'm sorry. I'm just a bit frazzled. Lisa isn't here yet with the slides, and without them we're screwed. I can't have ten blank screens staring at the guests!"

Dakota wanted to tell Morgan right then and there that her trusty sidekick was probably somewhere hiding underneath a rock, afraid to show her face now that she had been busted. Seeing the stress lines form across Morgan's forehead, Dakota knew this wasn't the right time to pile more on. Instead she said, "What can I help with?"

"Sterling's been asking me every five minutes where the slides are so he can preview them and make adjustments if necessary. I need you to find Lisa—here's my Palm with all her numbers. Then I need you to schmooze Sterling and buy me some more time," Morgan said, jotting a note about something else on her clipboard.

Dakota went out on the terrace for a little privacy. She dialed Lisa's cell first. She couldn't wait to hear her explanation for last night, but the slides took priority. The phone rang three times before Lisa answered in a hoarse voice. "Hello?"

"Lisa, this is Dakota. Where the hell are you?"

There was a long pause, and Dakota thought she heard a sob. "Um . . . Dakota? I really don't feel well. . . . I have a cold," Lisa said sheepishly.

"From overexposure, no doubt," Dakota snapped, suddenly furious at the bitch for jeopardizing Morgan's event like this. "I don't care if you have the bubonic plague. You better get over here with those slides, *now*, because the show is scheduled to start in an hour."

"Dakota, I *can't*. Please tell Morgan I'll be out for a few days," Lisa said, sniveling. "I'll make it up to her, I promise."

Dakota exhaled. She knew what the real problem was. Lisa didn't want to face Morgan. Well, she should have thought about that before she decided to moonlight as a stripper. This also explained her coming on to Ken. It was probably what came naturally to her after hours!

"Look, Lisa, even if you have to come by ambulance, you'd better get those slides here in the next thirty minutes. Otherwise Caché is going to look like a rinky-dink company unable to pull off a simple fashion show."

"On one condition," Lisa said, suddenly sounding wide-awake.

Dakota couldn't believe the gall of this girl. "I don't think you're in a position to negotiate anything."

"You want the slides or not?"

"You little, blackmailing—" Dakota stopped herself. She had to think about Morgan and Caché first. "What do you want?"

"Don't tell Morgan about last night. I want to explain the situation myself."

Dakota thought about it for a second. "Yeah, all right, it's none of my business anyway. Just get those slides here pronto. And if you don't—" Dakota heard a dial tone before she had a chance to finish.

Dakota found Morgan in the lobby, overseeing the lighting of the catwalk. "Lisa's on her way," she said.

"What happened? Is she all right?" Morgan quizzed.

Dakota would let her girl Friday talk her way out of this one. "She'll explain when she gets here," she said. "Meanwhile I've got another mission to accomplish." Dakota headed in the direction of Sterling, the temperamental designer. She schmoozed impatient investors with millions of dollars at stake for a living, so buttering up this prima donna would be a piece of cake.

Forty minutes later, Lisa slunk in looking guilty as sin. Dakota watched as she talked to Morgan, probably blaming her tardiness on something that came up with her son—a definite soft spot for Morgan.

"Lisa, where have you been?" Morgan asked frantically after handing the slides to a tech assistant.

"Morgan, I need to talk to you."

"Can it wait until after the show?" Morgan began to turn away. "We're already running behind schedule."

Lisa lightly touched her arm. "I need to talk to you now. It won't take long."

Morgan led Lisa downstairs away from the pandemonium. The restaurant on the ground floor was empty except for the wait staff. She looked into Lisa's face once they were seated.

Lisa's moods had been swinging lately, but Morgan had never seen this helpless look in her eyes before. "What's going on?"

"I don't know how to say this . . ." Lisa dropped her head. "I'm . . . I'm a—" She began to cry softly.

Morgan touched her hand. "Lisa, what is it?" She unfolded one of the napkins on the table and handed it to Lisa. "Come on, tell me. It can't be that bad."

"I'm a stripper," she blurted out.

Morgan thought she had misunderstood. "What did you say?"

"I work part-time at Scores," Lisa said through sobs.

Morgan was speechless. Scores was one of the upscale gentlemen establishments in the city, but it was still after all a strip club. "Why on earth are you working there?"

"I'm desperate for the money."

"Lisa, I know you're a single parent, but I thought you were satisfied with your salary? And the bonus we agreed on after the first quarter results? And what about your reputation? After all, you have a young impressionable son."

At the mention of her son, Lisa began to cry again. "He's why I'm working at Scores."

Morgan thought, Here it comes, the same lame "education" excuse most strippers used. "Come on, Lisa, don't insult my intelligence. Don't sit here and tell me you're working in a strip club to put your son through school."

"No, I'm working there to save his life," she said flatly.

"What are you talking about?"

"He has leukemia, Morgan, and he needs a bone marrow transplant. My insurance covers only the bare basics, and now that he's been diagnosed with cancer, I can't get any more insurance. The only way he can have the transplant is if I pay for it out of pocket."

Morgan could literally feel Lisa's pain. Instinctively, she folded her arms around her belly as if protecting her unborn child. "When does he need the operation?" she asked solemnly.

"He's in remission and they've located a match. So now's

the perfect time"—Lisa hung her head—"except I don't have all the money."

Morgan's maternal instinct was fully engaged and she wanted to help. She began flipping different scenarios in her head. She didn't have a lot of money in her personal account and she didn't dare dip into her and Miles' joint account. There was the Caché account—the last quarter had been profitable and they were in the black. That's it, she thought. She would use the money in that account. Every business-savvy cell in her body protested the decision, but she took Lisa's hand and smiled at her. "Lisa, go ahead and schedule the operation."

"Morgan, haven't you been listening? I can't schedule anything. I don't have all the money."

"I'll lend it to you."

Lisa looked shocked. "I can't let you do this. It's not your problem."

"I know it's not my problem, but I want to help." Morgan looked steadily into her eyes. "Please take the money."

"Thank you. Oh, God, I can't believe this. I promise I'll pay you back," Lisa said, wiping her eyes.

As she went back to work, Morgan's smile began to dissipate. Was she completely crazy? The money in Caché's account was earmarked for Blake's gallery opening. She had vendors and subcontractors to pay. But what choice did she have—it was either the life of her company or the life of an innocent little boy.

32

Ecstasy's tour opened in Los Angeles to a sold-out crowd at the Staple Center's nineteen-thousand-seat arena. After sultry vocalist Jennifer Freeman opened the show, the lights went down. The crowd buzzed with anticipation as spotlights came up on each girl. They floated in midair near the top of the arena, singing the opening number, "You Make Me High," while being lowered one by one to the stage on invisible harnesses. The crowd went wild—singing, screaming, and chanting the song's hook:

> Touch me, tease me, make me cry.
> Don't stop it, baby, 'cause you makin' me high.

They each wore see-through silver mesh halters with matching hot pants.

Meanwhile, their uncle/manager Cee-Cee was backstage looking like the new-millennium pimp. He had on a silver polyester zoot suit, a black-and-gray leopard-print shirt opened to his navel, and an assortment of platinum chains with medallions. His hat was a white two-tone Stetson with a silver iridescent band. He also wore a pair of silver sunglasses, causing him to periodically bump into things since it was dark. Halfway through the concert, he made his way among the backstage crew, strutting like a rooster with a full hen-house.

"Girl, you sho look good," he said, shaking his head as though he couldn't believe the vision that stood before him.

"You don't look too bad yourself." Vic looked him up and down, thinking he looked atrocious.

Buffing his nails on the wide, seventies-era lapel of his jacket, Cee-Cee reared back on his silver gaiters and said, "I do okay for an old man."

Vic came close enough for the old man to peer right down her ample cleavage. Though she was repulsed by him, she never knew when she might need to work him, so it was best to keep him within clawing distance.

By the second half of the show, it was clear to everyone, from the wildly enthusiastic audience response, that the tour had gotten off to an excellent start, which was reason enough for corks to pop resoundingly from champagne bottles.

"Congratulations, man. The girls are awesome," Phillip toasted Miles.

"Thanks, man." Miles smiled broadly. He was ecstatic that all of their hard work was paying off in such a big way.

"I think we're looking at the new-age Supremes."

"So does that make me Barry Gordy?"

"Only if you're sleeping with Keisha," Phillip laughed. "Are you going to the after-party at the Sky Bar?"

"I'll stop in for a minute. Gotta show my support to the girls. They kicked ass tonight."

"Cool, I'll see you there."

Just as Phillip left, Mr. Lindenhoff, the president of Millennium Music Worldwide, the parent company of Sound Entertainment, walked up with an extended hand. "Miles, you have done an outstanding job." He beamed. "Congratulations."

"Thank you, but it was with the help of a lot of people. I've got a great team."

The German smiled through yellowed teeth. "You're too modest."

"Will I see you at the after-party?"

"Afraid not. I'm on the red-eye back to Gotham. But I didn't want to leave before speaking to you."

"Thank you, sir."

"Keep up the good work."

Miles could have floated off the ground. Mr. Lindenhoff didn't give compliments often, so praise from him made the night that much more special.

By the time he got to the after-party, it was in full swing. The girls, high from adrenaline and all the adulation, were in full party mode. They even did an impromptu a cappella set standing on the outside bar, swaying to their own beat, while the Cristal flowed like water over Niagara Falls. Cee-Cee stood in front of the bar, keeping time with his silver cane.

Phillip saw Miles standing near the back and made his way over. "It looks like your girls are having a good time."

"They deserve it," Miles said, thinking about all of the hard work they had put into the tour.

Phillip looked at his wrist to check his watch, but he had absentmindedly left it on the nightstand in the hotel room. He stifled a yawn. "I'm outta here. I've been up since five this morning, Eastern time, so I'm beat."

"I'm right behind you. I've just got a couple of rounds to make and I'm gone too."

"Check you later, man."

As Phillip left, Miles remembered that they were both staying at the Four Seasons. He was about to try to catch up with him to suggest they share a car to the airport in the morning when he felt a touch on the arm of his Prada jacket. Smelling the vapor of Gucci Rush perfume, he knew who it was before he turned to see.

"Vic, oh, hi. How are you?" Before she could reply, he had his question answered. He could see that she was three sheets to the wind.

"Better now," she said, her heavily made-up eyes at half-mast. She wore a little Genie top that buttoned, then tied at the waist with a pair of hip huggers that rode very low. Only one of the buttons on her blouse was fastened now, and she was listing on her stilettos.

Smelling danger, Miles decided to excuse himself. He could make the social rounds another time. "I've got to go. I'll see you later," he said, making his escape.

Nearly tripping after him, Vic said, "Me too. I just need my car keys." She fumbled drunkenly through her handbag. "W-w-where are they?" she slurred, still searching.

"Vic, you are in no condition to drive," Miles said sternly.

"I'm fine," she proclaimed primly, before a hiccup sent her into a giggling fit.

"Come with me. Where are you staying?" Miles sighed. He had to make sure she got back to her hotel safely. The last thing he needed on his conscience was her having an accident that he could have prevented.

"I'm at the Four Seasons."

"Let's go." He grabbed her arm and guided her carefully down the stairs and out of the bar.

When they got to the hotel lobby, Vic had no idea what room she was staying in. She found the whole matter hilariously funny. "I could stay in yours," she teased, brushing seductively against him.

Seeing that he was getting nowhere with her, he went to the desk clerk and asked him for her room number, but was given a song and dance about privacy policies and walked away empty-handed. According to the rule book, Vic had to request it herself, and since Miles wanted to spare her the embarrassment of being seen so inebriated, he decided to check out her handbag, hoping that the card she had received at check-in was still there.

Fortunately, it was. When he got her upstairs, half carrying her into her suite, he was turning to leave when she said, "Wait one second . . . *please*," and disappeared into the bedroom.

She was probably going to be sick. "That's just great," he muttered softly.

As he waited, he remembered he wanted to call Phillip about the next morning. He pulled out his cell and dialed the number, but got his voice mail. Just as he was finishing his message, Vic materialized from the bedroom. She was dressed in nothing but a sheer thong and stiletto mules. Her arms were folded underneath her large, firm breasts, provocatively displaying them. Miles was shocked, but couldn't help staring at her erect nipples. "Vic," he said, finding his voice, "I don't know what you have in mind, but I'm outta here."

Closing in, she tried to grab him for a kiss. "Don't be such a party pooper," she slurred.

Miles grabbed her arms and said, "You've obviously had too much to drink. I suggest you do the same thing that I'm about to do. Go to bed."

"That's exactly what I had in mind," she said, reaching for his crotch. When he caught her hand to remove it, she pulled backward and fell onto the sofa, with Miles tumbling down on top of her.

She gazed into his eyes and purred, "Miles, you are an incredibly sexy man." Before he could respond, she cupped his face between her hands and kissed him with teasing wet and warm lips. She could feel him pulling away and she opened her legs and wrapped them around his back, pinning him against her.

Miles knew he should stand up and walk—no, run—out of the room, and never look back. But his body began to respond to the soft ripeness of her breasts, the taste of champagne that lingered on her tongue, and the slow seductive grind of her crotch against his hungry sex. Without planning to, his hips began to grind into hers. His tongue began to duel with hers. The heat was intense. The temptation was unbearable. The smell of her perfume was . . . the perfume Morgan used to wear.

As though ice water had been thrown on him, Miles' head cleared and he pulled away, panting. He stood up abruptly, looking down at Vic, her legs splayed out, her chest heaving. "I've got to go," Miles said, turning hastily for the door.

Vic raised herself from the couch. "Miles, don't go now." Lust burned bright in her eyes and gave her voice a raspy quality.

"Vic, this is wrong. I love my wife. I have no business here."

Not one to give up easily, she began cupping and massaging her breasts and nipples, tempting him further.

But he had found his resolve. He reached for the doorknob.

"Miles, don't," she pleaded. In a flash she sprang up from the couch and ran around to block his exit. She screeched, "Don't you walk out on me!"

Miles met her angry stare head-on. "Good night, Vic."

"What? Are you too good for me?" she sneered.

The lust had been replaced by the outrage of rejection.

"It's called being married."

"No one walks out on me," she fumed, slinging her hair back.

"Excuse me," he said, firmly pushing her aside and opening the door.

"You'll regret this," she threatened as he walked out. "Count on it."

33

Morgan and Dakota were meeting at Serafina for lunch. Morgan arrived first, and as she walked up the stairs into the Italian eatery, she savored the aroma of pizza cooking in the open brick ovens. The hostess sat her at a quiet table along the wall. Morgan welcomed the break. She needed to collect her thoughts. She had just come from the bank, where she withdrew the money for Justin's operation. Though she felt compelled to help, she didn't know what she was going to do now that she had drained Caché's account.

Dakota arrived as Morgan was pondering her situation. "What's the matter? You look like you just lost your best friend." Dakota sat across from Morgan. "It's Lisa, isn't it? Can you believe that about her moonlighting gig?"

Morgan thought about telling Dakota about Lisa's son, but decided against it. She didn't want to invade Lisa's privacy. Besides, it was bad enough that Dakota had caught Lisa literally with her pants down. She'd tell her after the operation and after she'd had a chance to think about how she was going to recoup the money. "Yeah, it's pretty surprising."

"Well, did you fire her yet?"

"No," Morgan said, looking over the menu.

"What!" Dakota nearly exploded. "Why not?"

Morgan put down the menu. "She has her reasons, Dakota. Look, I really don't want to talk about it. Anyway"—Morgan changed the subject—"how's Miss Tricia adjusting to New York? Or should I ask, how is New York adjusting to her?"

Dakota hunched her shoulders. "Okay, I guess. She's hardly ever home. She seems to live over at the Seaport Mall."

Morgan looked surprised. "Doing what?" Just then the waiter arrived to take their order.

"Shopping apparently," Dakota said, after he'd gone. "She's constantly coming home with shopping bags full of clothes from the Gap, Victoria's Secret, Express, and The Limited."

"How can she afford to shop?" Morgan asked. "Tricia is still in cosmetology school, and she has no source of income, right?"

Dakota looked perplexed, "I have no idea where she's getting all this money from. Most of what we got from the house is in a money-market account."

"Maybe she has a sugar daddy stashed away somewhere," Morgan chuckled.

"I don't think so. At least she hasn't talked about one. She's only been here a couple of weeks." Dakota thought for a second. "Knowing Tricia, she probably applied for credit cards and plans to use them until they're maxed out."

Morgan looked up with sudden concern. "Are all of your cards accounted for?"

"Yes, Mom," Dakota teased. "We'll see what girlfriend does when the bills start rolling in."

"All I can say is, you better watch out. You may end up paying for them." The waiter brought their lunch. Dakota had ordered the porcini ravioli with leeks and a Caesar salad, while Morgan had the margharita pizza and a mixed green salad.

While they ate, Dakota's two-way went off. She reached inside her purse, opened the pager and read the message.

WHAT R U UP 2?

Morgan looked at her quizzically, and Dakota said, "It's Phillip. He wants to know what I'm doing." Dakota typed, HAVING LUNCH.

Phillip answered back, WHAT ABOUT DINNER?

Morgan watched a smile spread across Dakota's face. It was obvious to her that her friend liked this guy and she knew from Miles that Phillip was having second thoughts about his relationship with Paula.

HAVE U HAD THAT TALK YET? Dakota responded.

HAVEN'T HAD THE CHANCE. SHE'S MIA AGAIN. Her smile disappeared. She wondered if Phillip was just trying to have his cake and eat it too. Dakota thought she had better steer clear until he straightened out his relationship. CALL ME AFTER YOU DO, she typed.

PLEASE DON'T MAKE ME EAT ALONE, he pleaded.

I DON'T KNOW.

PLEEAASSE!!!

Dakota could just picture his handsome face pleading with her, much like he had on the tennis court. ALL RIGHT. WHAT PLACE AND WHAT TIME?

LOU'S AT 8. SEE U THEN, read his last message.

"Well?" Morgan asked anxiously.

"He invited me out for dinner tonight."

Knowing how gun-shy Dakota was about relationships, Morgan decided to reveal what she knew. "Girl, I shouldn't tell you this, but even though theoretically they're the perfect pair, Phillip feels Paula treats her clients better than she treats him." Morgan leaned in closer. "And ever since you guys played tennis, he can't stop thinking about you."

Dakota's jaw dropped. "You're kidding? He said that?"

"You can't breathe a word of this to Phillip. Miles will kill me," she warned.

"Scout's honor," Dakota said, holding up two fingers. Yet then her mood shifted. "Girl, he's not going to leave her. Not Ms. Buppy."

Morgan didn't like the defeat in Dakota's tone. "Paula's family may be from Westchester and she may have gone to Ivy League schools, but it's not like you're living on skid row, Ms. Wall Street," Morgan said, reassuring her friend.

"I'm from a working-class neighborhood on the South Side

of Chicago. My grandmother had to work two jobs just to send me to college."

"Which gives you more character, since you didn't have family money to rely on. Now snap out of it." Morgan snapped her fingers, as if bringing Dakota out of a trance.

"I guess you're right."

"I know I'm right."

Morgan made a good point, but Dakota couldn't help but compare herself to Paula, even though she didn't know her well. She knew her type, with that air of entitlement.

Morgan continued. "Don't give Paula a second thought. You're only having dinner with him."

"That's true," Dakota said, weighing Morgan's words. She would have a friendly dinner with a friend, then go home and watch a late-night movie on cable.

When Dakota returned to her loft, Tricia was camped out on the sofa, slumped underneath one of Dakota's expensive chenille throws in some ratty sweats watching *Love Jones* on DVD. If she wasn't out shopping or at beauty school, she was a world-class couch potato. Dakota looked around the room and rolled her eyes in disgust. A grease-stained pizza box sat cockeyed on her cocktail table with two cartons of leftover Chinese food on top of it, and an empty pint of Ben & Jerry's Chunky Monkey was capsized on the floor next to the sofa.

"Damn, is Larenz Tate fine or what?" Tricia remarked, licking her lips.

"He was fine the first twenty times you saw the movie," Dakota said sarcastically.

"Girl, I don't care how old this movie is or how many times I've seen it, I could watch it every day."

"And you do," Dakota mumbled.

"What?"

"Nothing." Dakota thought to herself, God give me strength. Keeping her promise to Nana was proving to be a hard lesson in patience, and she was no saint. "Maybe you didn't notice, but there is a garbage compactor in the kitchen. Or do you plan on letting this stuff grow and multiply?"

"Why you trippin'? Isn't the cleaning lady coming tomorrow?" Tricia said, never taking her eyes off the screen.

"Yeah, she is, but that doesn't mean that I want to sit around all afternoon watching this mess."

"I'll pick it up. As soon as the movie goes off." Her eyes were still glued to the screen.

"Whatever," Dakota said, trying to avoid an argument. "Anyway, have you seen my laptop?"

"It's in my room. I was using it for a homework assignment," Tricia said nonchalantly.

A saint, Dakota told herself, you are indeed a saint. Without saying another word, she marched into her once-immaculate office, which was now Tricia's bedroom. Clothes were strewn everywhere. Pants and skirts were draped across wire hangers, and jackets hung on the doorknob instead of inside the closet. She gritted her teeth in frustration and went to the desk to find her laptop. She nearly gasped; another empty carton of ice cream was sitting on top of her computer. Her first impulse was to storm in there and give Tricia her walking papers, sending her packing back to Chicago, but she held back. This was her idea and she had to try to make it work. She refused to become estranged from her last living relative. She picked up the empty carton with two fingers and took it into the kitchen to toss it out.

Sick of the mess, Dakota got some boxes out of the storage closet for Tricia to organize her things. Inside, she noticed a small box marked NANA'S STUFF. She remembered going through Nana's attic and putting her personal belongings in a box. At the time she was too emotional to sort through it all, but now, feeling melancholy, she took the box off the shelf and brought it into her bedroom. Sitting Indian style in the middle of her bed, she opened the flaps and peeked inside. She had forgotten about the small wooden treasure box, set on top of a stack of papers. She tenderly rubbed the inlaid surface before lifting the lid. Inside were yellowing pictures of Nana as a girl, along with a silver-framed wedding picture of Dakota's parents. How could she have forgotten that? Dakota kissed the frame, then placed it on her nightstand. A few pieces of costume jewelry were scattered at the bottom of the box, plus an odd-looking key. She picked it up and examined it. On a round paper key ring the words SEAWAY NAT'L BANK were written in Nana's handwriting. I bet this is a safe-deposit key, she thought, intrigued. She quickly searched through the papers to confirm her hunch. Though she didn't find documentation to identify the key, she did find insurance papers with her father as the policyholder and Nana and herself as the beneficiaries. The policy was in the amount of two hundred fifty thousand dollars. There were also old bank statements—that held her name alongside Nana's. "Why didn't Nana tell me we had a joint account?" she said softly.

After Dakota recovered from the shock of the discovery, she picked up the phone and called Morgan. "Hey, girl, listen to this. You won't believe what I found."

Dakota told her about the box and the strange items in it.

There was a long pause. Finally Morgan said, "Why don't you catch a flight to Chicago in the morning, go to the bank, and close out the account? Then you can find out what's in the box too."

"That's a good idea. I'm dying of curiosity," Dakota said, rubbing the key between her thumb and index finger. "But I don't think I'm going to tell Tricia about this."

"You don't have to explain anything to her. It's your account."

"True. And you know she'll have her hand out," Dakota said. "She wants to open her salon right after school, you know. I suggested she rent a booth at an established salon to build a clientele first, but of course Ms. Thang wants to come right out of the gate running with the big dogs. She plans to use the money from Nana's estate to open her shop. She's acting like we sold the house for half a mil. If she knew about this money, she would want me to use it to bankroll her dream shop—"

"And did I ask you for one red cent?" Tricia blurted out. She had been standing in the doorway.

Dakota looked up, shocked. "Uh, all I meant was—"

Tricia cut her off. "And who you telling my damn business to anyway?"

"Morgan, let me call you back."

"Oh, I should have known you was talking to *her*," Tricia said, and stormed out of the room.

Dakota quickly hung up and followed her. "Tricia, I'm sorry. All I meant was—"

Tricia snapped at her again. "Yeah, I know what you meant."

"Would you let me finish? All I meant was, before you jump out there you need a solid client base and enough funding for your shop. Otherwise, you won't survive longer than a couple of months. I'm one hundred percent behind you. I just want you to be realistic. After all, this is New York and the competition is stiff."

"I'm not worried about the clients or the funding," Tricia said, turning her attention back to the television.

"Come on, Tricia, don't be mad. I'm sorry. Okay?"

Before she could respond, the telephone rang again. The cordless was on the sofa near Tricia, so Dakota asked, "Are you going to answer that?"

"Yeah?" Tricia spat rudely into the receiver. "Yeah, she here. Hold on," she said and tossed the phone to Dakota.

Dakota fumbled with the handset in midair before getting a firm grasp on it. "Hello. Oh, hey, Phillip. Yeah, I'll be there at eight. Okay, see you in a few." She pressed the END CALL button and looked at Tricia, who was still sulking. Dakota sighed, then said out of guilt, "Do you want to go out to dinner with me and Phillip?"

"No."

"Come on, Tricia, all you do is shop and go to school. You haven't been out on the town yet."

Tricia weighed her options. She could stay and watch *Love Jones* for the umpteenth time or she could check out Dakota's new friend. She turned off the movie and went to her room to change. Dakota nodded to herself as her cousin disappeared. Having Tricia along wasn't a bad idea. That way Phillip couldn't suggest any nightcaps.

Dakota took her time getting dressed and fixing her hair and makeup. She tried to treat seeing Phillip casually, but somehow couldn't help herself.

"Tricia, are you ready yet?" Dakota yelled from the living room. "Come on, we're running late."

"Just a second."

Dakota looked at her watch—it was seven-twenty-five. Just as she was about to call out to Tricia again, she walked into the room wearing a simple navy dress with an ivory beaded sweater tied around her shoulders. "Wow, you look great." Dakota had never seen her so polished, not one thing askew. "Come on, let's go."

"Where are we going?" Tricia asked as they exited the loft.

"Twenty-second Street between Broadway and Park South." Dakota knew Tricia had no clue where that was since she spent most of her time downtown.

Lou's, a bar and restaurant, used red as its primary color. Red lighting illuminated recesses in the wall near the booths as well as the ceiling above the ebony-colored communal dining table.

The owner greeted Dakota with a kiss on the cheek. "How have you been?"

"I'm good, Louis. How are you?"

"Well, thanks. Will it just be the two of you tonight?" he asked, referring to Tricia.

"No, we're meeting a friend," she said, glancing around the restaurant. She spotted Phillip among the hip eclectic crowd at the bar. "I see him over there."

"Let me know when you're ready for your table," Louis said.

Dakota gave Phillip a kiss on the cheek. "Sorry I'm late. I brought Tricia. Hope you don't mind."

Phillip looked briefly disappointed, but he said, "No problem." He had spoken to Tricia over the phone, but had never met her. "It's good to finally meet you."

Tricia scanned him from head to toe. "Nice to meet you too."

"What can I get you ladies to drink?"

"I'll have a Cosmo," Dakota said.

"What about you, Tricia?"

"Uh." Tricia thought for a second, then said, "I'll have the same." The name was foreign to her, but she knew that, if her snooty cousin was drinking it, it must be good. When the drinks came, she looked at the pink concoction in the martini glass, sneered, and said, "This look like a Shirley Temple without the cherry."

"Just try it," Dakota said, taking a sip.

Tricia gingerly touched the cocktail to her lips. "Mmm . . . tastes, like punch."

"Don't be fooled," Dakota said, and put her drink on the bar.

"Please, I can handle this little girly drink," she said, taking a big gulp.

Dakota was about to warn her again, when Phillip interjected, "So, Tricia, how do you like living in New York?"

"It's all right." She tipped the drink bottoms up. Wiping her lips, she said, "I'll have another one of those. What'd you call it? A Cosmic?"

"Cosmopolitan. Cosmo for short," Phillip said, signaling the bartender. "Dakota, do you need a refill?"

"No, I'm good."

Phillip glanced at his watch. "I'm going to check on our table, make sure they can change it to three. I'll be right back."

"I like these Cosmics," Tricia said, taking a healthy swallow from the second drink.

"Cosmos, and you'd better slow down because they will sneak up on you," Dakota warned.

"I don't taste no alcohol. Girl, I could drink these all night."

Dakota shot her a look of disapproval, which Tricia ignored.

"Follow me, ladies. Our table is ready," Phillip announced.

Once they were settled in the booth the waiter arrived to take their drink orders.

Tricia said, "Yeah, gimme another one of them Cosmics."

The waiter didn't hide his pained expression. "Excuse me?"

"The lady would like a Cosmopolitan," Phillip said.

Dakota could feel her cheeks flushing. She wanted to stop this fiasco of an evening before it escalated further, but leaving now would be awkward, after they were already seated. The most she could do was try to make the best of an embarrassing situation. She turned her attention to Phillip. "So how's work going?"

"In a word, hectic. N2Deep is in the studio, and Zulu Rhymthz is on the road touring. I tell you—"

Tricia jumped right in. "You know N2Deep?"

"Yes, they're one of the groups I work—-"

"They's tight, especially that fine-ass Trey." She gave Phillip a huge wink. "Why don't you hook a sistah up? I could definitely rock his world."

Dakota wished she could vanish in midair or, better yet, make Tricia disappear. Why had she thought this was a good idea?

"Well, uh . . ."

Dakota came to Phillip's rescue. "Tricia, the music industry is a business just like any other business, and when the artists are in the studio or on tour, they are working. It's not a party like it appears in the videos."

Tricia turned on her. "Oh, so now you in the record business too? Earlier you was in the hair business, telling me when to open *my* shop. You such a damn know-it-all," Tricia said, "but there's one damn thing you don't know."

Dakota couldn't help but think that no one in Paula's family would ever make a scene like this. She glared at Tricia, as if to shut her up, then said quietly to Phillip, "I'm sorry."

"Don't be sorry for me," Tricia spat out, her voice rising a few decibels higher, " 'cause my shit is 'bout to blow up."

Dakota glanced nervously around them, hoping no one overheard.

As if on cue, the waiter arrived with their menus and Dakota mouthed to Phillip, *Let's get through this quickly*.

Seeing the mortified look on Dakota's face, Phillip patted

her hand. "Relax. We're just having a friendly chat before dinner, that's all."

"That's right!" Tricia chimed in.

Thinking about Paula and her upper-crusty friends, Phillip said, "Anyway, it's refreshing to hear someone speak plain English, instead of listening to a walking thesaurus or a one-sided cell conversation."

Dakota leaned back in the booth and listened to Phillip and Tricia talk animatedly about the music business. He seemed to genuinely enjoy the conversation. For the life of her, Dakota thought, she would never understand men.

34

Blake didn't know where to turn. He had too much at stake to lose it all over a little indiscretion—actually it wasn't an indiscretion, it was a flat-out *scandal*. He clutched the compromising pictures Freddie had mailed as a reminder. As he paced the living room floor, his grip became tighter and tighter until the photos were a mangled mass in his hands. He dropped them and picked up the phone to call his publicist to explain the situation. Maybe she could do damage control before the pictures hit the tabloids, as Freddie had threatened.

"Hello, hello," Blake said repeatedly when he heard no dial tone.

"Hey, lover boy," said the other voice on the line.

"Who is this?" Blake yelled into the receiver.

In contrast to Blake's volatile emotions, Freddie was as cool as a frosty Frappuccino. "How soon we forget. Were you picking up the phone to give me my move-in date?"

"I was calling—" Blake stopped midsentence, thinking twice about divulging any more information to this lowlife. "I was *not* calling you. And I refuse to be blackmailed!"

"Look, you got three days to make up yo mind, or else yo black ass gonna be all over Talk of the Town, and this time it won't have nothin' to do with yo damn gallery."

Before Blake could respond he heard the phone slam in his

ear. "*Son of a bitch!*" he screamed, and ground his shoe down on the pictures. Blake couldn't believe he had gotten himself into this predicament. How could he have been so stupid? He knew Freddie wasn't in his league, but it was hard to turn down sex that was by anyone's account a homerun. This was the last time he would let his dick mess up his life.

The phone rang again before Blake had a chance to re-cover. "*What?*" he screamed into the receiver, thinking it was Freddie calling again.

"That's not what I'd call a warm hello." It was Spence.

Blake exhaled, relieved it wasn't his blackmailer. "Hey, Spence, what's up?"

"My question exactly. I was calling to see if you wanted to go to lunch. But I gather you have something besides food on your plate," Spence said.

"You could say that." Blake didn't want to get into details.

"Come on, spill the beans. What's going on? You sound . . . desperate." Spence sensed Blake's hesitance. "Don't worry. Whatever it is, it's safe with me."

Blake *was* desperate. Besides, he reasoned, Spence was his proven friend and maybe he could help him find a solution to his Freddie problem. "It's terrible, Spence. You won't believe what's happening to me." Blake went on to tell Spence the gory details.

"Sounds like our boy Freddie is a pro. I bet my career he's done this before."

"Whether he has or not is beside the point. I just can't allow him to move in here." Blake rubbed his temples. "I know, maybe you could find him an apartment. I'll pay for it of course," Blake said, grasping at straws.

"Well, I just got a listing for a large one-bedroom on Seventy-ninth and First. It's a doorman building with a roof terrace."

Blake's voice brightened. "Sounds great. Why don't I—"

"Wait a minute, Blake. Trust me, this is not the solution. Like I said before, this guy is probably a pro, and if that's the case, I bet he has a rap sheet."

"You think?"

"Yep. His kind always does. Let me make a couple of calls. I have a few connections in law enforcement."

"Thanks, Spence," Blake said, sounding hopeful.

"Don't thank me yet. I'll call you as soon as I have some info," Spence said, before hanging up.

Blake sat on his sofa with his head in his hands. He prayed that Spence turned up something on Freddie, because the last thing he needed was his private life splashed across the pages of Talk of the Town.

35

The Monday morning following Ecstasy's triumphant tour debut, Miles strode into Sound Entertainment's office like a conquering hero returning home with the spoils of victory. Had his chest stuck out any farther, the elevator door wouldn't have closed. His Testoni-clad feet were barely touching the carpeted floor as he floated along, absorbing praise like a dry loofah in a bubble bath.

"Miles, you the man!" Followed by slaps of high-five.

"Great job, Miles!"

"The girls were fierce!"

The entire staff was counting Christmas bonuses already. Since the concert was televised on Pay-Per-View, the audience was well beyond the thousands at the Staple Center, and the album sales had already begun to reflect the huge success.

It was all Miles could do to keep from yelling in triumph. But of course, it went against his nature to be anything other than cool and collected, so he didn't. Even so, his staff could see how pumped he was.

As he walked past Lauren's desk, she said with a bemused smile, "The construction contractor will be in later today."

Miles stopped, puzzled. "Construction? What for?"

"Well, I figured it would be hard to fit your head through the door after this weekend, so I thought I'd arrange to have it widened." She snickered good-naturedly before getting up to come around and give him a big congratulatory hug.

He laughed. Aside from Morgan, who knew him better than Lauren? Still chuckling, he walked into his office. He stopped in his tracks as he was greeted by a loud chorus of "*Surprise!*" Fifteen of his direct reports and a couple of executives from the corporate office all wore big smiles and T-shirts that read, MILES, YOU DA MAN. Everyone knew that if it wasn't for his vision, Ecstasy would be just another girl group.

"I can't believe you guys! You could have given me a heart attack," he said, holding his chest.

Phillip stepped forward; he had obviously been behind this. "We just wanted to go on the record and let you know how dope you are, and to say"—he raised one of the T-shirts. "You da man!" They all laughed.

"So what would have happened if the concert had flopped?" Miles asked, smiling.

"This office would be as empty as the Mojave," Phillip teased.

"Thanks, guys," Miles said, greeting them individually as they filed past him out of his office.

Phillip lingered behind. "I just want you to know that I'm proud of you," he said, giving Miles a guy hug, their fists clasped between them.

"Thanks, man, but it's not like I did it alone."

"True, but without your leadership, all the help in the word wouldn't've mattered."

"What can I say? I've got a great team," Miles was anxious to deflect some of the glowing praise. "Speaking of my team, where is Vic?" It hadn't escaped him that she hadn't been among those gathered in his office.

Phillip shrugged his shoulders. "I don't know. Haven't seen her." He turned to leave.

Miles had a flashback to the ugly scene that had unfolded Saturday night in Vic's hotel room. He figured she was probably too embarrassed to show her face. "By the way, did you get my message Saturday night? I was hoping we could've shared a car to the airport."

"No, I didn't. In fact, I haven't been able to find my cell phone. Until I find or replace it, be sure to hit me on the two-way instead."

Miles waved him away. "Man, you'd lose your butt if it wasn't attached."

When Phillip left, Miles sat at his desk basking in the glory. Not only was his career soaring, but things at home were getting better too. When he returned from La-La Land with the news of Ecstasy's success, Morgan was genuinely happy for him. They'd shared a celebratory dinner that ended in some of the best sex they'd ever had. Life was good. He had a beautiful wife and a child on the way. What more could he ask for?

Morgan had shown him the first sonogram of their baby. It took his breath away. The idea that he and Morgan had created another life was miraculous to him, and Morgan had never looked more beautiful. Her slim figure had blossomed into a womanly vessel, confidently carrying a precious new life.

Lauren stuck her head in his office. "Miles, Mr. Lindenhoff just called. He wants to see you in his office at one o'clock."

"What does he want?"

"Didn't say."

Probably an extra bonus, Miles thought, smiling his satisfaction.

The rest of the morning flew by in a flurry of phone calls, meetings, and a quick bite to eat at his desk for lunch. A few minutes before one o'clock, Miles gathered his portfolio in case Mr. Lindenhoff wanted a quick state-of-the-business report and headed to the elevator.

Walking down the long hallway to Mr. Lindenhoff's office, Miles was still flying high on success. It almost felt like a cape billowed out behind him. When he reached the office, Inga, Mr. Lindenhoff's icy assistant, peered up at him over rectangular reading glasses.

"Hi, Inga. I'm here to see Mr. Lindenhoff."

Without any sort of social pleasantry, she said, "He's expecting you," and motioned with her eyes toward his office door. She was known for the frigidity of the blood that coursed through her veins, and Miles couldn't help but think that what she really needed was a good, headboard-banging fuck.

He walked through the double mahogany doors with a warm smile spread across his face, fully expecting compliments for a job well done. Instead, the coolness of his reception was palpable. Instead of a chummy one-on-one with Mr. Lindenhoff, he was confronted with an unsmiling Bob Townes, the Vice President of Human Resources, and a scowling Vic Pellam. Miles didn't need a crystal ball to tell him this was not good.

Without preamble, Mr. Lindenhoff closed the door and gestured to a chair. "Have a seat," he said tersely. He sat opposite the boss's massive desk, while Vic and Bob sat on either side.

His mind raced to understand what this assembly was about. He hadn't told anyone about Saturday night's fiasco and couldn't see why Vic would. But of course, that was exactly what she'd done.

"Miles, a very disturbing matter has been brought to our attention. One concerning you and Ms. Pellam."

Miles said, "I know what you're referring to, but I'm willing to let the matter drop. It was quite a celebration, and everyone has a bit too much to drink from time to time."

Anger flashed in Mr. Lindenhoff's icy blue eyes, and his hands clasped the arms of his desk chair. He looked as though he would launch himself right out of it, directly at Miles. "Sexual harassment may not be a big deal to you, but it certainly is to us!"

"Sexual harassment?" Miles was stunned. But in the frosty silence, he saw what Vic meant by revenge with an otherworldly clarity. Vic sat to his left with a wounded-victim expression and the most modest set of clothes she'd probably worn since preschool. Not an ounce of flesh showed beyond her hands and face. Even her neck was wrapped in a Hermes scarf. Bob sat to his right, looking indignant, his mind no doubt conjuring up angles to distance the corporate office from this impending scandal. So Vic had turned the tables and got her story out first. He *knew* he should have reported her behavior that very same night.

"You've got this all wrong," Miles insisted, looking from Mr. Lindenhoff to Bob and back. "In fact, the situation happened in completely the opposite way. Vic had too much to drink at the after-party and needed help getting back to her room. Once there, she came on to me."

Bob turned his nose up in disgust. "This is so typical. Blame the victim. For your information, we have a desk clerk at the Four Seasons who can attest to the fact that you showed up at two o'clock in the morning asking for Ms. Pellam's room number."

"Because she was too drunk to remember it herself!" Turning to Vic, Miles pleaded with her. "Vic, please, tell them the truth."

Without batting an eye, Vic said to him, "The truth is that your behavior was reprehensible. Yes, I had too much to drink, but that does not entitle anyone, least of all a colleague, to take advantage of that. I never would have believed you to be capable of what you did, had it not happened to me." On cue, tears streamed down her cheeks.

Clearing his throat, Mr. Lindenhoff said, "Rather than draw this out needlessly, why don't you simply admit your mistake and we'll settle on some form of severance to keep this unsavory business out of the press?"

Seeing the full implication of Vic's lies, Miles stood to leave. He wouldn't continue to play Vic's game with the deck stacked against him. Calmly he said to Mr. Lindenhoff, "You've got the wrong guy. Not only did I not harass Ms. Pellam, but I will not sit here while she plays out this despicable charade." Miles headed for the door. Before turning the knob, he looked back at the group and said, "You'll be hearing from my attorney."

"Oh, Miles?" Facing Mr. Lindenhoff once more, Miles was hit dead-center with a parting shot. "Until this matter is resolved, you are suspended. Be out of your office within the hour."

36

Caché's plans for Blake's gallery opening were moving along splendidly. The event would be the company's shining and most critical moment. Not only because of the large scale of the celebration, and the who's-who guest list involved, but more important it would determine the level of support Dr. St. James would give to the company's future. Morgan and Lisa had made multiple lists and checked them twice. There was no room for error this Saturday night.

"Morgan, Henrí's on hold. He wants his check for the Lincoln Center event messengered over today. What should I tell him?" Lisa asked.

Morgan kept her head buried in the budget that she'd been poring over. "Tell him you'll have to get back to him."

"That's what I told him the last two times he called," Lisa informed her.

"Well"—Morgan glanced up—"you'll have to tell him again."

"Just a moment, Henrí," Lisa said, before putting the call back on hold. "Morgan, he says that, if he doesn't have payment by the end of this week, he won't show up for the event on Saturday night." Lisa's expression was pained as she relayed this bad news to Morgan.

It got Morgan's undivided attention. "You're kidding me?"

If the temperamental chef boycotted Blake's gallery opening, it would ruin everything that Morgan had worked for!

"I wish I were," Lisa said, slowly shaking her head.

"Shit, we'll be ruined!" The look of panic on Morgan's face worried Lisa.

"Listen, I'll buy us some time." She picked up the phone. "Henrí, not to worry. You'll have your check by the end of the week." She listened for a couple of minutes, nodding occasionally. "You'll have it. I'll see you on Saturday." She hung up the phone, before collapsing into her chair.

Afraid to ask, Morgan did anyway. "What did he say?"

"He said that if he didn't have his money by Friday at five o'clock, we could start learning to cook ourselves, because he wouldn't be there."

Morgan dropped her head into her hands. "How much do we owe him?"

"Fifteen thousand dollars." When Morgan had made the decision to give Lisa the money for her son's operation, there were two events on the calendar that had since been canceled. Their fees would have been enough to cover accounts payable. She knew then that she was cutting it close, but the life of a child was much more important to her than the margins on her balance sheet.

"What am I going to do?" Morgan asked, closing her eyes in defeat.

"Can we hire someone else?" Lisa asked hopefully.

Morgan shook her head. "It's too short notice to get a decent chef in New York on a Saturday night. Plus, if word of this gets out, my reputation is ruined anyway. There's no way Dr. St. James would back a company that can't even pay its vendors."

"Morgan, I'm so sorry." Lisa looked as though she were about to break down in tears.

"What are you talking about?"

"If it weren't for me and my problems you wouldn't be in this predicament."

Morgan sat up straight, realizing she had to show more

confidence in front of Lisa. "Listen to me. Don't you worry about this. We'll manage."

Lisa wasn't convinced. "But how?"

An idea popped into Morgan's head. "Worst case, Miles and I will call our banker and get a loan for the money."

"Do you think he'll do it?"

"Of course he will." All of a sudden, Morgan felt better. She dialed the phone to check in with him, but neither he nor his assistant picked up. Puzzled, Morgan replaced the receiver without leaving a message.

37

Dakota had taken an early-morning flight to Chicago for a day trip. It was eerie coming back without anticipating a big hug from Nana or her soulful home-cooked food. Even after she had moved to New York, the Windy City had always been her home. Now it was just another city. Dakota fought the urge to drive by the old house. She couldn't bear the thought of Nana not being there, whipping up catfish and spaghetti. Tears began to roll down her cheeks as she thought about her grandmother. She and Nana had been so close. That was why Dakota couldn't understand why Nana never mentioned the insurance money.

Heading down King Drive, she took in the familiar surroundings. The corner drugstore she had gone to as a child was now boarded up. The family-owned toy store where Nana bought her Barbie dolls for Christmas was now a liquor store. And the neighborhood play lot was now a gas station. It occurred to her that this was probably the last time she would see the old neighborhood. Now that Nana was gone, she had no reason to visit. Dakota pulled the rental car into the bank's parking lot and reached into the backseat for her briefcase. It held Nana's death certificate, insurance papers, bank statements, and the safe-deposit key. She knew that the bank would not relinquish the contents of the box unless she had the matching key and proper identification. Approaching the entrance, she felt as if Nana were with her. She had gone to this same branch as a child with Nana so many times.

She walked in and marveled at how the lobby matched her memories so exactly. The chandelier that loomed over her head as a child seemed smaller now, but she still had the urge to slide down the polished mahogany banisters that flanked the grand staircase. She used to beg Nana to let her do it, at least once. Of course Nana said, "Chile, this ain't no playground. It's a place of business." Thanks to Nana, Dakota felt she always knew the proper way to behave in any situation, even if she sometimes chose not to.

With that in mind, she stepped up to the customer service desk to take care of her business.

"May I help you?" asked an older woman with glasses on a gold chain around her neck.

"Yes, I'm here to close out an account," Dakota said, entering the woman's cubicle.

The customer service rep looked at Dakota oddly, as if she were familiar. "Come in and have a seat. Have we met before?"

"No, I don't think so. I haven't been in this bank for years," she said. Opening her briefcase, Dakota handed the paperwork to the rep. "I'd like to close this account and have the funds wired to my account in New York."

The woman put the half glasses on the bridge of her nose and examined the statements. "These account statements are dated. Do you have the savings passbook?"

"No, that's all I have, but it was a joint account with my grandmother and she recently passed."

"Oh, I see. Well, I'll need some identification before I can look up any account information."

Dakota handed over her driver's license. "It's out of state."

"That doesn't matter." She studied the license carefully. "Oh, I see you're from New York."

"I'm actually a native Chicagoan. I moved to New York about ten years ago," Dakota said, starting to feel impatient. Chicago was a big city, but sometimes it moved like a small town compared to the pace of New York.

The rep removed her glasses. "You know, I've always wanted to see a Broadway play and have dinner at Tavern on the Green. My sister and I had planned a trip last year, but she took ill."

Dakota had had enough. Why was the woman revealing her personal life?

"Ah, well. Maybe we'll take that trip next year," she said, putting her glasses back on the bridge of her nose. "So let's get down to business." She typed something into her computer.

After frowning at the screen for what seemed like forever, she said, "This account has been closed."

"Closed?" Dakota asked, wondering if Nana had closed it. "When was it closed?"

"Over a month ago. A cashier's check was issued to you for the full amount." Suspicion replaced the friendly tone of her voice.

It hit Dakota like a ton of bricks. *Tricia!*

"What's going on here, young lady? Are you trying to receive another check?"

"No, of course not. I-I'm not the one who closed out the account," Dakota said, shocked at Tricia's nerve. "It had to be my cousin impersonating me." She now recalled how her wallet went missing the day after Nana's funeral. And this also explained Tricia's sudden windfall, Dakota thought, picturing all the shopping bags of new clothes and the designer luggage.

The bank representative pulled a manila folder out of her filing cabinet and opened it on her desk. She removed the signature page and compared it to that on Dakota's license. There was a slight difference in the way the "D" was written. She asked Dakota to sign her name on a piece of scrap paper. Her signature was identical to the one on the license. She shook her head. "I'm sorry, Ms. Cantrell. It looks like there is a discrepancy here. I need to speak to the branch manager." She reached for her phone.

"Wait," Dakota said. She was fuming. "Before you bring any charges against my cousin, I'd like to speak with her first. We may be able to resolve this privately, without bringing un-

deserved negative publicity down on you or the bank."
Dakota couldn't wait to confront Tricia. She had a mind to
call her right here and now, but wanted to see her face-to-face.

She took a key out of her briefcase. "I'd like to collect the
contents of my grandmother's safe-deposit box—if they're
still there."

At the vault area, the representative requested a duplicate
key from the manager. They each inserted a key to take the
box out of the vault. The representative showed Dakota to a
private room and gently closed the door.

Dakota placed the box on the table and sat down. Her
heart was racing. She had no idea what to expect. She held her
breath and lifted the metal lid on the strongbox. Her anger at
Tricia instantly dissipated when she saw Nana's handwriting,
printed on a tattered-edged envelope. She gingerly opened the
envelope and took out a note written on Nana's floral sta-
tionery.

Kota,
These are your parents' wedding rings. I saved them for you.

Dakota reached inside the envelope and took out two gold
filigree bands. One was smaller with a solitaire diamond in
the center. She put her father's ring on first and secured it
with her mother's ring. Tears began to stream down her face.
She hadn't been this close to her parents since their deaths.
Dakota held the rings close to her heart and cried for the parents she barely remembered, and the grandmother she loved
and missed so much.

38

He felt like the walking wounded as he returned to his Sound Entertainment office on V-Day. The once-victorious Miles Nelson who had sauntered into work earlier that day now drifted past Lauren in a daze, without a word or a glance.

Inside, Miles threw a few miscellaneous files absently into his briefcase. He wasn't exactly "cleaning out his office" because he'd be back . . . right? Or would he? Along with the files, he tossed in his cell phone, his two-way pager, and his Palm Pilot. As he gathered his things, his eyes fell on the silver frame at the corner of his desk that held a picture of Morgan. When he picked it up and looked at her smiling face, the enormity of his situation hit home. Not only were his career and reputation at risk, but so was the security of his family. And it wasn't just the two of them anymore to be concerned about. Now he also had their unborn child.

The buzzing from his intercom slowed his spiraling thoughts. "Miles, Inga's on line one," Lauren announced.

"Put her through," Miles answered in a hollow tone. That conversation proved as unfriendly as his earlier encounter with the boss's secretary had been. This one was to inform him that Mr. Lindenhoff had called an emergency meeting, scheduled for Friday, to hear the case against him. They would then determine a final course of action. So he and his attorney had been summoned to appear.

He could hear in Inga's tone that she had already tried and convicted him. It would only be a matter of time—and not very much—before every assistant in the company knew of Vic's scandalous charges. The inner-office gossip network was more efficient at delivering the news than CNN. To spare himself, Miles quickly finished packing and headed for the door.

Lauren wore a puzzled look as he passed her desk. "Miles, where are you off to?" He didn't have any appointments scheduled outside the office as far as she knew.

"I'm sorry, Lauren, but I can't explain now. I'll touch base later today or tomorrow. Meanwhile, you're going to hear some disturbing things . . . Don't believe it, okay? We've known each other too long, and you've always had my back." He smiled sadly and headed for the elevator, leaving her gaping in astonishment.

Before making it home, Miles received two calls on his cell phone. One was from a concerned Lauren, demanding to know what was going on. The other from Phillip, whom Lauren must have called the minute Miles left the office. Both were on the war path. Lauren's solution to the problem was to assemble a posse of her homegirls, spread on some Vaseline, and show Vic the true meaning of "harassment," but Phillip's solution was a lot more strategic. "I want you to make two phone calls immediately," he instructed Miles, "one to Denise Brown, and the other to Sam Jones, a private investigator I know."

"Denise, I understand. I was planning to call her anyway. But a private investigator?"

"Miles, trust me. Vic is playing dirty pool, and for someone to know the rules as well as she does, this can't be the first time she's cued up. You're gonna need all the ammunition you can get to return her fire."

"You're right," Miles said, shaking his head.

"Where are you headed?"

"I'm on the way home."

"I'll be right over."

"No . . . really. I'll be okay. I just need some time to think." Miles had never felt as alone and helpless as he did at that moment. But now was not the time for self-pity. "I don't know what I'm gonna say to Morgan."

"You'll tell her just what you told me—the truth."

"All of it?" Miles asked quietly.

"Man, you've got to be honest with her. You had a moment of weakness and it passed."

"Yeah, but not before I ended up on top of Vic with my tongue planted in her mouth."

"Miles, contrary to popular opinion . . . you *are* human. Most men put in that situation would find it hard not to be lured in. But to your credit, you didn't let it go farther than that."

"But I should have known better than to even put myself in that position."

"If you are waiting for me to say, 'I told you so,' I'm not doin' it. Your only offense is naivete in the first degree."

"Guilty as charged," Miles conceded. "You said Vic was trouble from day one."

"Yeah. But even I had no idea how much."

"Well, Morgan did."

"Listen, Miles, you've got to trust Morgan. She's not some shallow chick who's only there for the good times. She loves you and she believes in you. Call me later, okay?"

"I'll reach out. I may need somewhere to stay after Morgan gets wind of this . . ."

"I'll be here in the office until seven. After that hit me on the two-way."

"If you don't hear from me, send in the cavalry."

Once home, Miles phoned Denise Brown, his lawyer for the past eight years. She was known throughout the entertainment industry for being fiercely protective of her clients. Though sexual harassment matters were not her forte, she insisted on working closely with a human resource attorney she knew who specialized in such cases.

"Don't you worry about a thing. By the time we're finished with Ms. Pellam, she'll be lucky to make it out of town with all her silicone intact."

Miles laughed weakly. "I hope you're right."

"Have I ever let you down?"

After setting a course of action with her, Miles hung up, feeling a little better. At least now he was getting some reinforcements.

His next call was to Sam Jones. He was an ex-cop who knew all the rules and how best to break them. After hearing the history of his relationship with Vic, Sam assured Miles that he would get back to him by Wednesday with some information. That done, Miles sat down in the office, tried to collect his thoughts, and prayed.

Morgan arrived home late to find her husband sitting silently in the darkening office, staring out the picture window that faced the beautiful but frigid East River. Though Miles was still wearing his suit, his tie was askew and his shoes had been kicked off. His usual handsome face looked desolate.

"Hi, sweetie. What's going on?" Morgan asked with rising concern. Miles was always in motion, so the mere fact that he was still and in the dark was cause for alarm. His uncharacteristically disheveled appearance heightened her worry further. When he didn't answer, she dropped her briefcase and purse to rush to his side. "Baby, what's wrong? You're scaring me."

Miles took a deep breath and faced Morgan with a look so sad it pierced her heart. At that moment she was sure someone close to them had died. "I've been set up," he said. "My career may be over." Unable to look at her anymore, he buried his face in his hands.

Hugging him tightly, Morgan said, "Baby, just tell me what happened."

He recounted the evening in L.A. in detail, his voice strong with the conviction that his actions were justified. Until he got to the part where Vic walked out of her hotel bedroom practically naked, and Miles knew he had crossed a line. He explained to Morgan that he tried to leave immediately and that was when Vic pulled him on top of her and they fell on the sofa. Morgan could tell by the pleading look in his eyes that he was afraid she wouldn't believe him.

"What happened next?" Morgan's tone was remote, as though she didn't really want to hear the reply.

Miles stood up and began pacing slowly in front of the window. The moon cast a dull, ominous glow over the river. "Morgan, we've always been truthful with each other. And we've always respected and trusted each other. I am going to count on that trust now and tell you exactly what happened. Because I don't want any secrets between us."

Morgan felt as though her very existence had been put on pause, awaiting the outcome of his next words.

"When Vic pulled me on top of her, I tried to get up. She wrapped her legs around my back and . . . and . . ." He found it difficult to allow the words to come from his mouth. His head was hung low, the pain clear in every line of his body.

"And what?" Her breathing was shallow but rapid, as though she were unable to take in a full complete breath.

"And she kissed me."

"And?"

"And for a brief moment, I did respond," he admitted, looked pleadingly into Morgan's eyes.

Morgan felt as though she had been hit hard in the pit of her stomach, where her baby was. In a barely audible voice she asked, "What *exactly* does that mean?"

Inhaling deeply, Miles said, "I don't know. My initial reaction was purely physical. I allowed her to kiss me and I kissed her back for a few seconds—until my mind caught up to my body and I was repulsed by what had happened." He shook his head. "I stood up and told her that it was wrong. That I loved you and I was leaving. That's when she chased me to the door and threatened me, but I never thought that she'd stoop to accusing me of initiating it."

Morgan didn't answer. Tears rolled down her cheeks.

"Morgan, you have to know that I love you. More than life itself. Nothing means anything to me without you, our child, and your happiness. Please forgive me for being stupid, gullible, and weak." He reached out to touch her shoulder.

She pulled away from him, and ran from the office, desperate to escape the image of her husband locked in a torrid embrace with Vic Pellam.

39

Dakota made a beeline from the airport straight home to deal with Tricia. She knew Tricia had a shady employment past, but she didn't think she was capable of forgery. Dakota planned on getting every red cent back—not because she needed the money, but because Tricia needed a good, hard lesson in how to conduct her life. For starters, Dakota would make her return any unused clothes. Then she would work out a repayment plan, no matter how many years it took Tricia. If she refused to cooperate, Dakota would ask the bank to prosecute. It was time for tough love.

As the taxi pulled up in front of her building, Dakota looked up at the loft for any signs of Tricia, but all the windows were dark. Sure enough, when she opened the door, there were no signs of life. Tricia's campsite—the living room—was empty. Dakota checked her bedroom on the off chance she was there, but it too was empty. Back in the living room, she planted herself on the sofa and waited.

Dakota sat in the dark for an hour before she heard a key in the door. "Good, she ain't here," Tricia mumbled.

Just as she turned to relock the door, Dakota turned on the lights. Tricia jumped with fright and dropped the shopping bags she held. "Damn! You scared me."

"I see you've been shopping again," Dakota said through clenched teeth.

"So what's it to you?" Tricia said. "Like you and Morgan don't go shopping every chance you get."

Dakota got up from the sofa and walked toward Tricia. "At least we use our own money."

Tricia looked uneasy. "Well, I gots my own money."

"No, you have *my* money," Dakota said, shoving the bank records in Tricia's face.

Tricia looked down and stiffened at the sight of the evidence. "What—what's this?" she stuttered.

"All I want to know is, why did you steal the money, Tricia?" Dakota said on the verge of tears. "I would have given it to you. You didn't have to steal from me. We're family."

"You always had everything," Tricia said, backing away, waving her arms all around. "Look at this place. It's the bomb. You rollin'. I just wanted to see how it felt not to have to worry about money."

"Tricia, I work every day for my money. You act like it's served up on a silver platter. You have no idea what I have to deal with in the 'white world' just to get a check. If you ever finish school, you'll be making money too." She folded her arms in front of her. "I want to know how you found out about the joint account and the insurance money."

Tricia looked down, ashamed of herself at last. "The nurse had given Nana morphine, and she started driftin' off. Before she fell asleep, she told me the whole story. She thought she was talkin' to you. And I figured you didn't need the money," she said softly, "so I took it."

Dakota pinned her with a no-nonsense stare. "You realize that's a felony, don't you?"

Tricia began to fidget. "You ain't gonna call the police, are you?"

"I should and teach you a lesson." Seeing Tricia cringe, Dakota let out a long, tired breath. "But Nana would roll over in her grave. So I'll tell you what I am going to do, or should I say, what you're going to do." She outlined the basic repayment plan.

"But—I need this stuff!" Tricia protested, snatching up the shopping bags.

"Listen, Tricia, this isn't open for negotiation." Dakota stepped forward and took the bags out of Tricia's hands. "You're going to get a part-time job after school—"

Tricia cut her off. "How am I gonna work and go to school?"

"Most people manage it. Besides, you should have thought about that before stealing from me."

"I ain't stole from you. It was Nana's money!"

How could she say that? It took all the willpower Dakota had not to lunge at her and wring her scheming little neck. "I suggest you change your attitude before I change my mind and call the cops."

Tricia sucked her teeth. She knew Dakota had her over a barrel. She would do whatever was necessary to stay out of jail. She retreated toward her bedroom in silence.

Dakota called out to her, "And one more thing."

Tricia stopped in her tracks. Without turning around, she asked, "What's that?"

"Put that Louis Vuitton luggage in my room." She grinned. "I've been dying for a set."

40

It was the call that Freddie had been waiting for his entire life. All of his hopes and dreams were on the line. "Freddie, it's Blake."

"I hope you've got some good news for me." Freddie was tired of Blake putting him off, trying to buy some time. Quite frankly, Freddie didn't see what the big deal was. It wasn't as though Blake didn't have enough space in that huge three-bedroom apartment. Either he let him move in or his nasty pictures would be all over Talk of the Town. They'd crop the X-rated bits, of course, but the uncensored versions would be all over the Internet. He hoped that Blake realized that it was time for him to face the music. He and Freddie were about to become roommates.

What made Blake think he could get away with using him, then tossing him to the curb when it was time for him to be with his highfalutin friends? Now Freddie planned to be highfalutin too. He only regretted that it'd taken blackmail for Blake to agree to be his boyfriend. But he was sure once Blake got to know him and see him dressed in all the nice things he would have—which of course Blake would buy—that he would fall in love with him.

"Can you stop by this afternoon?" Blake must have resigned himself to his fate because he didn't have the attitude that Freddie had been hearing in his voice lately.

"You got my key ready?"

"I sure do," Blake answered. Finally, Freddie would get what was coming to him. He was about to enter into the good life. Not with a day pass, earned by picking the right pocket, but as a lifelong member.

"I'll be right there." Freddie dressed quickly. He slowed his pace only to pack up a few things to take over to his new place. That way he could stay there tonight, and pick up his other stuff later. He wouldn't bother with most of it. Shit, he would just buy all new stuff. He hadn't discussed it with Blake yet, but of course Blake would give him his own credit card. After all, wasn't that what sharing your life with someone was all about?

Freddie walked along Central Park West with a new pep to his step. He strolled like someone who belonged there, instead of someone with his nose pressed to the glass. Exhilarated by his new neighborhood, he scouted out the dry cleaners, newspaper stands, coffee shops, and quaint cafés where he would soon be a regular.

Approaching his new building, he was tempted to let that snobby doorman know right away that he was now a resident. Thank you very much. But he decided to save the pleasure for when he could sail right by with his own key. That would fix him. "I'm here to see Mr. St. James. He's expecting me."

He hated the way this uniformed servant looked down his nose at him, as though he smelled something foul. "I'll let him know that you're here." He dialed Blake's apartment before sending Freddie up.

Blake answered the door wearing one of his beautiful smoking jackets. It was burgundy silk with a black velvet collar. He wore the matching silk pajama pants and a pair of black velvet lounge shoes. Freddie decided that he'd get a set just like it.

"Hey, roomie," he said, walking by Blake into his new home.

"Come on in," Blake said sarcastically to Freddie's back. He was already halfway down the foyer. "Can I get you something to drink?"

"No need to be so formal," Freddie said, removing his jacket. "After all, I do live here now."

"May I have the pictures and negatives, before I give you your key?"

"I don't have them with me. They're at my apartment. I'll give them to you later, though," Freddie lied; he had no intention of giving up those pictures. He'd take the negatives and put them in a safe-deposit box or something.

"In that case, don't you think we should toast to our new relationship?" Blake was already at the bar shaking up a pitcher of martinis.

Freddie loved the sound of that. "Toasting to our new relationship." That warmed his heart. "Sure," he said, plopping down onto the sofa.

After the drinks were poured, Blake proposed a toast. "To the beginning of a wonderful new arrangement." His smile dazzled Freddie.

"Cheers," Blake said before taking a long, slow sip.

Before Blake could join him on the couch, the phone rang. While Blake took the call in the kitchen, Freddie continued to enjoy his cocktail. Blake returned shortly, sitting down next to Freddie, putting his arm over his shoulders. "Do you remember the first time we did this here? Had martinis and got to know each other?"

"How could I forget?" That was the night that made this all possible for him.

Blake began rubbing the back of Freddie's neck. "That was the night of the infamous photo shoot." Blake nodded his head with a slight smile, as though it was the cutest trick he'd ever known.

"That was it," Freddie proudly acknowledged, enjoying the feel of Blake's strong hand.

"You know what's funny?" Blake asked without stopping his massage.

"What's that?" Freddie asked with his eyes closed.

"I don't remember any of it. How did you manage that?"

"It was easy." Freddie never raised his head or opened his eyes. "I just slipped a roofy into your last martini." Freddie's conscience never bothered him about doing that. He figured that Blake had put himself in those compromising positions, so it wasn't like he was making it up. He just caught it on camera, that was all.

"I thought it had to have been something like that."

Freddie turned to face Blake. "I hope you're not still mad at me. That's the only way I could get you to take me seriously."

"And this is the only way I can get you to take me seriously." Blake stood abruptly and crossed to the door that led into the dining room. When he opened it, Spence was standing on the other side.

"What are you doing here?" Freddie asked, shocked to see him.

"Just stopped by." Spence entered the room and stood before Freddie, holding a tape recorder.

"What's going on here?" Freddie stood up to face Blake.

"Like he said, Spence just stopped by. He's got some information that you'll find quite interesting. Show him, Spence." Blake stood before him with his arms crossed at his chest.

Spence pulled a sheet of paper from his breast pocket, tossing it into Freddie's hand. It was a copy of a police report. Freddie was wanted in New Jersey for a counterfeiting scheme that had gone awry a couple of years ago. "What the fuck is this?"

"It's pretty obvious," Blake said, setting his drink down on the coffee table.

"This changes nothing," Freddie hissed. "If I don't leave here with my key, I'll see you in the funny papers."

"I don't think so," Blake answered. "If you do, not only will you face time for these charges, but add blackmail and assault to your rap sheet. I'd guess you'd be spending the next twenty years with a whole slew of new roommates."

"You bastard."

Blake just looked at him then shoved his coat into his chest before showing him the door. Freddie was furious. He'd fix that smug son of a bitch. He headed home, fuming with outrage that Blake and that asshole Spence would treat him this way. Well, he'd fix them.

When he got to his apartment, the door was already open. In shock, he ran immediately to the bed, where he lifted the mattress to discover that nothing was under it. No pictures or negatives. Before he could curse out loud, there was a knock at his door. Enraged, he headed back to the front room, where two uniformed officers met him in the doorway.

Instead of a posh new apartment on Central Park West, Freddie was facing new accommodations all right. Just not the kind he'd envisioned.

41

At a time in Morgan's life when she should have been on top of the world, she was sinking quickly into a pit of despair. Her husband had been unfaithful to her, her business was teetering on the brink of ruin, and at this very moment, an innocent young child lay in a hospital fighting for his life. It couldn't get much worse. At least she hoped not.

She sat alone in her office racking her brain for answers to a list of insurmountable problems. Morgan had until tomorrow at five o'clock to get fifteen thousand dollars to Henrí, or Caché would be history. That was only a little more than twenty-four hours from now. After everything she'd sacrificed for the company, including her position at Global Financial and almost her marriage, it would be a devastating loss to her. But it was one she'd have to prepare herself for, since at the moment no lightbulbs were going off. She hadn't had a sudden stroke of insight, nor had she hit the lottery. Besides, with Miles' career hanging in the balance, she really had even bigger fish to fry.

The phone rang, interrupting her thoughts. "Good afternoon, Caché."

"It's me." Morgan's heart skipped a beat. It was Lisa calling from the hospital. She sounded exhausted and drained. The doctors had started Justin's bone-marrow transplant at eight o'clock that morning, and since that time Morgan had been sick with worry about him, on top of everything else.

"How is he?" she asked anxiously, quickly forgetting her other problems.

Lisa began to sob, causing Morgan's breath to catch in her throat. "He's going to be fine," she finally managed to say. Though Lisa was relieved, the tears were from the release of months of built-up anxiety, and worry over the health of her only child.

Morgan finally exhaled, causing her to collapse in her chair. "Thank God!" Morgan was so happy for Lisa and Justin. Lisa composed herself enough to give Morgan some of the details about the procedure. Apparently everything had gone well in the O.R. and his doctors hoped for a real recovery after a round of chemotherapy.

"Morgan, I don't know how I'll ever be able to repay you for what you've done for us."

"Lisa, don't mention it. Really. The most important thing is that Justin now has a fighting chance."

"I know what you've sacrificed. Caché is in trouble because of this." Morgan could hear the tears welling up again.

"No company is worth the life of a child. Though I love Caché, I would never put it ahead of Justin's life."

"Thank you, Morgan. From both of us." When Morgan hung up the phone she felt better about life, even if her own was crashing down around her. Just knowing that Justin would probably be all right gave her the strength to get through the remainder of the day. Her conversation with Lisa reminded her of how precious life was, and also how fleeting it could be. Regardless of what happened this coming Saturday night, she realized how blessed she was to have her health, a child on the way—and yes, Miles.

As disappointed as she was in some of his actions, she knew Miles was a good man. Not perfect, but a good man nonetheless. She also realized that, if he had slept with Vic, chances were he wouldn't be in the trouble he was in, since she would have gotten exactly what she wanted. Morgan felt certain that he'd been completely honest with her in his confession, leaving nothing out, and she appreciated that.

Suddenly clear on the solution to at least one of her problems, she grabbed her coat and purse, and headed out the door.

When Morgan got home she found Miles sitting at his desk in his pajamas and house slippers. Morgan had *never* seen him wearing pajamas in the afternoon, except of course when he was sick. It was clear that he'd been suffering, not from a physical ailment, but in many ways, one much worse. With his career on the line, his reputation in question, and the threat of criminal charges, she felt bad that he also carried the weight of her anger on top of it all.

Miles turned expectantly to face her, and she could see the plea for forgiveness in his eyes. Without saying a word, she walked over to him and held him to her breast. He clutched her like he wanted to hold on to her and his child forever, never letting go.

Miles felt the tears burning behind his eyes. The thought that he'd nearly compromised this for a little titillation was beyond him. Though he never intended to sleep with Vic, he admitted to himself that he had enjoyed a mild flirtation, thinking that no one would get hurt. Boy, had he been wrong.

"Morgan, please forgive me," he said. "I am so sorry that I hurt you. I want you to know that I've learned something very important here—about myself and about what really matters. It'll never happen again."

"I know, baby," Morgan said. It felt good to embrace her husband again.

Miles led her to the sofa, where he sat facing her. He held her hands and gazed into her eyes. "Morgan, your love and trust mean everything in the world to me. I cannot imagine my life without them."

"Miles, I'll always love you."

"But do you trust me?"

"I do," she answered, her gaze steadfast.

"Then I can face anything." Over the last few days, he had begun to doubt if he had the strength to go up against Vic and the company. He felt like a condemned man, simply waiting for judgment. But now he had hope.

"I'm going to fight this, honey. Phillip and Denise and a lot of other people are in my corner. Everything's going to be fine," he assured Morgan.

Morgan stood from the sofa. "Maybe not," she said, pacing the floor.

"What do you mean?" Miles was confused.

Morgan told him all about Lisa and her stripping, Justin and his leukemia, and finally about Henrí and his money.

"Wow!" He headed over to Morgan. "Baby, I'm so sorry. I had no idea all of this was going on."

"It's not your fault."

"I'll call the bank. Maybe they'll loan us the money."

"What about your job reference? Plus there isn't enough time." Morgan held her head low.

It pained Miles to see Morgan so defeated. But it pained him even more that there wasn't a thing he could do about it.

42

Dakota opened her Sub-Zero refrigerator, looking for something to throw together for dinner. Tricia was still sulking in her room and probably wouldn't resurface until she got really hungry. While she was gathering ingredients for a salad, the telephone rang.

"Hello?"

"Hey, you." It was Phillip.

"Hey, yourself," she smiled. She hadn't seen him since that surreal night with Tricia at Lou's.

"Have you had dinner yet?"

"Look, Phillip, let's not go there," she said, without pre-amble. As far as she knew, he still had a girlfriend, and that was that.

"Wait, Dakota. I know how you feel. I'm calling because Paula and I finally called it quits. She admitted that she's try-ing to make partner and her career is her top priority."

Dakota heard the dejection in his voice. "I'm sorry."

"There's nothing to be sorry about. It's just that Paula and I were together for such a long time and I do care about her as a person."

"I understand." Dakota didn't want to appear paranoid, but she had to ask. "Are you sure you're over her?" She needed to know exactly where she stood with Phillip. She didn't want just casual sex. She wanted a relationship. A committed, monogamous relationship. She braced herself for his answer.

"Absolutely sure. I want a relationship with you, Dakota. I'm not into casual sex. I hope that's okay with you."

She nearly dropped the phone. Dakota couldn't believe Phillip had just verbalized her thoughts. "It's more than okay," she beamed through the phone. Her doubts about him choosing Paula over her were finally put to rest.

"So now that we've got that settled, will you come over for dinner?" He paused, waiting for her answer, then added, "I'm cooking."

Dakota didn't know many guys who could boil water, let alone orchestrate a meal. "Can you cook?"

"Well, I guess you'll just have to find out for yourself."

There were a lot of things about this man that she wanted to find out, Dakota thought happily. "See you in a few." She rushed into her room and changed into a Baby Phat T-shirt with rhinestones, and a pair of snug jeans. She was so elated she could have floated over to his place. Instead, she grabbed her purse and a bottle of wine, and headed out the door to catch a taxi.

When she stepped off the elevator in Phillip's building, she smelled something burning. "I hope that's not dinner!" she said, ringing the bell.

Phillip came to the door in a panic; he was holding a scorched dish towel and a whisk. "Come on in," he said, and dashed off to the kitchen.

The kitchen was an open galley with appliances along one wall and an island counter separating the kitchen from the dining room. Dakota leaned against the island and watched Phillip lose his usual composure. Two large pots on the back burners were bubbling over, while smoke seeped from the oven and water ran in the sink, threatening to overflow. Dakota stifled a laugh, shook her head, and took charge. She removed the dish towel from Phillip's hand and gave him the wine. "Here, open this. Then go sit. Let me handle the rest." She turned off the water and the burners, then took out of the oven what appeared to be a roasted chicken.

"Damn. Everything was going fine. Then all of a sudden the chicken started smoking," Phillip said, wiping his forehead with the back of his hand.

Dakota looked at the setting on the stove. "Four-fifty!" she exclaimed. "No wonder it's smoking," she said, turning it off. She gave him a wry smile. "What were you trying to cook?"

"Baked chicken, whipped potatoes, and spinach," he said, sounding defeated.

Dakota did an inspection of the lost goods. From what she could make out, the potatoes were hopelessly waterlogged, and the spinach was too dry, stuck to the pan, and charred beyond recognition.

"Just drink your wine and relax. I'll salvage some of this chicken," she said, poking the bird with a fork.

Dakota cut away the burned outer skin and found enough moist meat to make chicken salad. Luckily Phillip had mayonnaise, onions, and celery. There was a head of slightly wilted lettuce in the fridge and no bread. She searched his cupboards and found an unopened bag of Ruffles. She peeled off the outer layers of lettuce, uncovering a few crisp leaves, and arranged them in the center of a plate. She mounded the chicken salad in the middle and arranged the chips around the perimeter. Bringing the plate into the living room, where Phillip was collapsed on the sofa, she said, "Ta-da! Dinner is served."

"Wow," he said, looking at the presentation before him. "This is like a page from *Bon Appetit*. How did you manage it?"

"Contrary to popular belief, I can cook. Most people assume that because I don't have a family and love the restaurant scene, I don't know my way around the kitchen," she said, sitting next to him on the sofa.

He took a chip and scooped up some chicken salad. "Well, they're wrong. This is good."

They ate every morsel of the salad and chips. Phillip took the plate into the kitchen and came back with the wine. He refilled their glasses and toasted, "Here's to improvising."

They chatted over wine about work, their favorite vacation

spots, current events, and sports. After an hour Dakota decided it was time for her to go home. She didn't want to wear out her welcome so soon. "Thanks for dinner, Phillip. I'm going to head home now."

He stood up. "No. Thank you." He walked her to the door. "You are incredible," he said, kissing her on the cheek.

Dakota could feel chill bumps run up her spine as his lips touched her face.

"Give me a hug," he said, reaching out for her.

Phillip's strong arms encircled Dakota. He held her so close that she could feel his heart beating against her chest. She felt as if she could stay there forever. Holding on, her hands traveled up his back, enjoying the ropes of muscle on either side of his spine. Needing to get even closer, he moved his groin rhythmically against hers. She could feel him hardening against her. As his hips rotated seductively, he bent to kiss her passionately. Parting her lips, she accepted his tongue, returning the heat of the delicious French kiss, their tongues dancing with desire. When her knees buckled Phillip picked her up to carry her to his bedroom.

Before reaching the threshold, he paused. "You know how much I want you, but we don't have to do this if you're not comfortable. I want you to be completely ready."

His concern touched her and brought tears to her eyes. The men she had known always put their wants first. "Phillip, I've never been more comfortable in my life."

He laid her in the middle of his bed and raised her T-shirt, planting kisses on her flat stomach. He traveled south with gentle, wet kisses until he came to her low-cut jeans and slipped them over her hips. Dakota moaned in ecstasy as his mouth found her core and his tongue worked its magic. "I want you," Phillip groaned, in between licks and kisses that made her tremble and shudder on the verge of exploding.

When she nodded her readiness, Phillip reached to the nightstand and took out a condom. Dakota watched in a sexual daze as he stood to remove his pants and underwear, and smoothed the condom over his erect sex without taking his eyes off her. Dakota did a seductive stretch, luxuriating in the big bed and luring him in until he gazed at her naked body like a parched man seeing an oasis in the Sahara. "I want you," he said again, his voice heavy with lust.

"I'm right here, baby," she said, spreading her legs and touching herself.

Phillip's eyes widened and he nearly leapt on her, hungry for her love. He kissed her shoulders, trailing his tongue down to her firm nipples. He sucked and nipped them until she gasped with pleasure, arching her spine and throwing her head back. He rolled onto his side so that they lay facing each other, their eyes saying what their mouths didn't have to. Dakota then turned him over to his back and straddled him, feeling the tip of his penis just kissing her vagina. Phillip reached around for the flesh of her backside and pulled her closer, sliding into her wet heat until he was totally connected to her, mind, body, and soul. He began to thrust and she rode him with wild abandon, at last bringing them both to a shattering orgasm. They lay in the afterglow without saying a word, just holding each other like two lost souls who had found their way home.

43

Miles woke up on Friday morning feeling like a con-demned man. Normally the beat of raindrops tapping on their bedroom window was soothing to him, but not today. Instead they sounded like ricocheting bullets searching for a target. He looked over at Morgan, still sound asleep, one arm resting protectively across her stomach.

Miles stepped into a steaming hot shower, wishing that his troubles could be washed away as easily. Even though his tension was more than just physical, the heat did relax his constricted muscles, allowing blood to circulate more freely, and helping his mind to focus on the details from his briefing with Sam Jones, the private detective.

He and Denise had met Sam on Wednesday over lunch at Della Femina. Miles was surprised when he was introduced. He had expected a slouchy dude in a disheveled khaki suit, sucking on a cigar. He'd obviously watched too many B movies as a kid, because Sam Jones could easily have been an executive at Procter & Gamble. He was about five feet eleven, with a slim but tight build, olive complexion, and close-cropped, curly dark hair. His suit wasn't couture, but it had a nice cut and was well pressed, and his shoes were buffed to a high shine. So much for images of Columbo.

After they were seated, Sam said, "I have good news and I have bad news."

Bracing himself, Miles said, "I'll take the bad first."

"Unfortunately, there were three witnesses who saw you attempt to get Ms. Pellam's room number from the front desk. And none of them remember seeing the two of you together then. So obviously that doesn't help your story about helping her to her room."

"It's not a story," Miles said, fixing Sam with a pointed stare. "It's the truth."

Sam held up open palms. "Hey, man, I'm on your side. Remember?"

Miles shook his head, checking his aggressiveness. "I'm sorry. It's just that I can't believe that I was so stupid," he said, smacking his temple with the palm of his hand.

"Don't be so hard on yourself," Denise said, "I understand exactly what happened."

Interrupting, Sam continued. "The other problem is at the Sky Bar. There are several people who saw you two leave together, with your arm around her."

"I was supporting her. She was drunk," Miles insisted.

"What I'm sure her attorney will say is that you two picked up the flirtation that started at Mr. Chows. It got a little heated. She said no. And you insisted."

"That's bullshit!" Miles cried. People at nearby tables turned to stare.

"Miles, listen to me," Denise said, in the low tone she used when all kidding was aside. "Regardless of what they say on Friday, you must not show *any* emotion whatsoever." When he didn't respond immediately, she said, "You got that? The last thing we need is for you to come across like a man who has a temper when things don't go his way."

Miles still didn't like the idea of sitting there passively, listening to Vic's lies. "What am I supposed to do? Just sit back twiddling my thumbs while they assassinate my character?"

"That's what you've got me for."

Realizing that everything was riding on the outcome of today's meeting, he stepped out of the shower and began dressing like a knight suiting up in armor for a jousting tournament.

Before heading out the door, he leaned over the bed and kissed Morgan awake.

She smiled and reached up to gently touch his face. "Miles, you know that I love you. No matter what happens today."

"I know, baby. I love you too," he said, and straightened to go.

Phillip passed Vic and her lawyer in the hallway, no doubt on their way to ruin Miles' life and career. If his parents—God rest their souls—hadn't raised him right, Phillip would have smacked the smug look right off her face. The impulse to introduce his fist to her nose was so strong that he had to consciously uncoil his fingers. Still, the tension traveled up his arms and over his shoulders, coming to rest squarely in his neck and upper back. It pained him physically to see Miles persecuted for something he hadn't done.

It always seemed to him that the good brothers were the ones to get jacked up, while the thugs went about their merry way. And Miles Nelson was as good as they got. He should have let Vic, drunk or not, find her own way back to the hotel. Growing up in Brooklyn, Phillip had seen every type, so he could spot a con a mile away, on a rainy day, wearing sunglasses. He had warned Miles, unfortunately to no avail.

Phillip had done all he could to help. Calling in the private detective had borne some fruit. They had found out that Vic's employment history was dodgy at best. Every man that she had ever worked for, since graduating from Pasadena City College in Los Angeles, had ended up as her lover, married or not. These relationships always yielded quick promotions that she parlayed into even better jobs. Vic was like an ambitious monkey, swinging from limb to higher limb before she landed on Miles' team.

Phillip exhaled. Banishing images of her from his mind, he made himself focus on his desk, which was bordering on chaos. He had seriously neglected his work these past few days of Miles' crisis.

Breaking through his thoughts, Cheryl, his secretary, said,

"Phillip, Hallack Cleaners just called. They found your cell phone in the breast pocket of your black suit."

So that was where it was. He remembered wearing the suit the night of the concert and must have turned off the ringer and stuffed it in the pocket without ever thinking another thing about it.

"Have them deliver it here with the rest of my cleaning."

While trying to get some work done, he couldn't help but watch the clock like a fellow inmate might on the date of his buddy's execution. The "hearing" was scheduled for one o'clock. It was actually more like a kangaroo court. The top rung of management was as solid as a weather vane—they went any which way the wind blew, and right now it was blowing hard against his boy Miles.

At ten after one, Cheryl walked into his office to hang his dry cleaning on the hook behind the door. Then she handed him his cell phone.

"Thanks."

"I'm just glad you found it. You know what a pain dealing with Verizon is. And I'd be the one having to do it." She sighed like she carried the weight of the world on her shoulders. Cheryl enjoyed playing the martyr, but she was totally devoted to Phillip and they both knew it.

Once she left his office, he powered the phone on and began listening to the electronic voice inform him that he had fifty-two unheard messages. "Oh, great," he said, kicking back in his chair for the onslaught. But when he got to number nine, he almost fell over backward onto the carpet.

Miles had always loved walking through the impressive lobby of Sound Entertainment's building and ascending in the wood-paneled elevator to the floors above. He remembered how proud his mother had been when she first came to visit him. His pride was now replaced by a sense of doom, but he'd never show it. He still looked like a man in charge of his destiny, though that sentiment couldn't have been further from the truth. In fact, his destiny now lay in the hands of the five unsmiling people he encountered when he and Denise walked into the fifty-fifth-floor conference room.

Mr. Lindenhoff sat at the head of the long table, looking even more joyless than usual. He was flanked by four hatchet men: the president of human resources, two of their fleet of corporate attorneys, and the chairman of the board. The only things missing were a gallows, a black hood, and a noose. At the other end of the table sat Vic, wearing a somber blue business suit and a white blouse with a strand of pearls. Her blond-streaked hair was pulled back in a chignon, and her makeup was subtle and tasteful. She looked more like an injured lamb than the sultry sex kitten who had clawed her way to the top.

Miles and Denise's arrival brought the low murmur of conversation to a complete stop. All eyes focused on him, as though a piranha had been let loose in a school of goldfish. Determined not to let them see him sweat, Miles calmly sat at one of the two seats that were obviously intended for Denise and him.

The lead corporate attorney, Mr. Lowenstein, cleared his throat and all eyes turned to him. "For the record, I'd like to tape these proceedings. Unless there are objections," he said, looking at Denise.

"None whatsoever," she said, removing her own tape recorder from her bag and placing it toward the center of the table.

"In that case, let's get started." In a drone he stated the date and time and place, and named everyone present, even taking the time to spell names out for the record. After his prelude, he turned to Miles and Denise, asking them to provide an overview of the situation from their point of view.

Denise recounted how Miles and Vic had met, vividly describing the cleavage-enhancing outfits in detail that she wore then and to subsequent meetings. She had a long list of employees who would corroborate this, and for visual impact she pulled out a photograph taken at a company cocktail party, where Vic looked like a Pamela Anderson wanna-be in a scanty excuse for a dress. She then moved on to the infamous Mr. Chows incident, recounting the sudden change of clothes and how Vic orchestrated an innocent agreement to "grab a bite to eat" into a full-blown media opportunity. She had statements from the maître d' proving that Vic had called in advance to order the champagne and ask for a high-profile table, promising to tip him heavily later. Next she laid into Vic's sudden appearance at the Knicks game in a seat right next to Miles, which she had procured by enticing its original occupant to give her for the last ten minutes of the game in exchange for a dinner date with her afterward. All this led up to the fateful night at the Four Seasons. As an encore, Denise gave them a blow-by-blow chronology of Vic's sordid and twisted career path, which had unfortunately led to her client's door. By the time Denise was finished, Vic looked like a deranged stalker, or at the very least a sexual climber of the first order.

Through all of this, Vic showed minimal embarrassment, as though she knew that the end game belonged to her. So what if there was some unpleasant squeamishness along the way? Besides, her lawyer hadn't even gotten started.

Denise concluded, "Gentlemen, it is obvious to me that Ms. Pellam is a seasoned manipulator whose plans include soiling the reputation of a proven professional, while further-ing her own self-interest. I ask each of you to take a look at the woman sitting in this room, look at this picture, review the facts, then tell me how you could reconcile the startling difference." She looked each man in the eye. "My client, Mr. Miles Nelson, has a near-perfect personnel record, without the slightest whisper of misconduct toward female colleagues, past or present. In fact, he inspires affection and loyalty in everyone he works with, to which they will readily attest. No. In this case this man is guilty of only one thing—trusting this scheming and conniving excuse for a woman." Vehe-mence dripped from Denise's voice, though she never once raised her tone.

When she was finished, all eyes were on Vic, as though in a Perry Mason moment she might stand and confess to it all.

When that didn't happen, Mr. Lindenhoff cleared his throat, before asking Vic's lawyer, Mr. Ronald Smith, to make his own comments.

When he was sure that he had a captive audience, Smith shook his head and let out a small chuckle. "You know it was with controlled hilarity that I sat here and listened to Ms. Brown so eloquently, yet blasphemously blame the victim for a crime committed by her client." Then the smile faded, and a different demeanor came over his chalk-white complexion. "And yes, I did say crime. It is a crime in all fifty states for a man to force himself on a woman. It's called rape."

Miles felt every atom in his body about to propel him across the table in the direction of Vic's pearl-clad throat. Knowing her client well, Denise quietly patted his hand, which had a death grip on the armchair, signaling him to calm down.

"It matters not what Ms. Pellam chooses to wear, whether to the office, a party, or to church. It does not give Mr. Nelson free rein to sample the menu. As you well know, we are in the entertainment industry and she violated no dress codes. To hear Ms. Brown tell it, my client dragged Mr. Nelson to Mr. Chows and force-fed him, putting a gun to his head to make him drink champagne. And since we are talking about a crime, I'll remind you that preordering champagne to celebrate a business success doesn't qualify." Vic sat smugly as her lawyer valiantly reclaimed some of her dignity.

"But it's obvious that Mr. Nelson misread Ms. Pellam's intentions from the start, leading up to the humiliating incident that took place at the Four Seasons in Beverly Hills." He looked to Vic as though to be sure that she was emotionally stable enough for him to continue. On cue, she lowered her head, inhaling deeply as though the incident were so fresh in her mind that at any moment she might erupt in tears.

Miles looked at Denise with incredulity written on his face. Never had he seen such a convincing act in his life. *He* almost believed her!

"My client admits to having a few celebratory drinks too many. So when Mr. Nelson offered to take her back to the hotel, she never gave it a second thought. She knew it wouldn't be responsible to drive and she thought it was nice, one colleague looking after another. Now we all know that Mr. Nelson was only looking after himself." Mr. Smith turned his disgusted expression on Miles, as though he were the lowest form of subhuman matter. "Once inside her room, he wasted no time forcing himself on her, ending up on top of Ms. Pellam, pinning her to the sofa. My client"—he clasped her shoulder protectively—"was forced to fight him off as he struggled to remove her clothing." With that, Vic did burst into tears, causing her lawyer to fish the preplanted handkerchief from the breast pocket of his suit.

"As despicable as this man's behavior was, there is more." They all looked at him expectantly. "Miles Nelson's wife is pregnant."

He sat back in his chair heavily, as though profoundly saddened by this example of man's depravity. Before Denise could react, Miles bolted from his seat. "You lying son of a bitch. You leave my wife out of this!" Denise jumped up, grabbing his arm. Mr. Smith leaned in front of Vic, as though protecting his client from the volatile Miles Nelson.

Mr. Lindenhoff, alarmed by the outburst, pounded on the table. "You *will* be seated. Now!" He stared Miles down until he again took his seat. "I think I've heard enough. This is not a criminal trial, at least not here today," he added, looking accusingly at Miles. "But I've heard enough to decide that—"

The door burst open before he could complete his sentence. Phillip stood there, panting. "You . . . you've got to hear this," he said. They all stared at him like he was an extra who'd walked onto the wrong movie set.

Ignoring the questioning looks and murmured protests, he walked to the speakerphone in the middle of the conference table and dialed his cell phone number. "This is important new evidence—it proves Miles is innocent." As they listened to the beginning of his recorded message, Phillip entered his code, giving him access to his stored messages. After forwarding through the first eight, they all heard Miles say, *"Hey, man, give me a buzz on the cell. I'm headed to the airport first* thing in the morning. *Let's share a car.*" Then there was a long beep as though a random key had been pressed, but the line was not disconnected.

The next thing they heard was Miles' voice again, saying, "*Vic, I don't know what you have in mind, but I'm outta here.*" Though the volume was remote, he could still be heard clearly.

Next came Vic's voice: "*Don't be such a party pooper.*"

Miles said, "*You've obviously had too much to drink. I suggest you do the same thing that I'm about to do. Go to bed.*" By now, all eyes were on Vic.

"*That's exactly what I had in mind,*" her tape-recorded voice seductively answered. There were tussling sounds, followed by "*Miles, you are an incredibly sexy man,*" followed by more tussling.

A few seconds later, they heard an obviously agitated Miles say, "*I've got to go.*"

A panting Vic pleaded, "*Miles, don't go now.*"

"*Vic, this is wrong. I love my wife. I have no business here.*"

A second passed. "*Miles, don't!*" A few seconds later she screamed, "*Don't you walk out on me!*"

Her voice was now laced with a hint of anger.

"*Good night, Vic.*"

"*What? Are you too good for me?*"

"*It's called being married.*"

"*No one walks out on me.*"

"*Excuse me,*" Miles said.

"*You'll regret this,*" Vic threatened. "*Count on it.*"

As the room sat in stunned silence, Miles' and Phillip's eyes' met. Miles felt overwhelmed with gratitude and love for his friend, but the look he sent him simply said, *Thank you, man.*

44

At that very moment, Morgan sat in her Harlem office still grappling with what to say when Henrí called, wanting to know where his money was. She hadn't slept much at all the night before knowing that there wasn't a white knight anywhere on the horizon. She figured she could avert total calamity by asking Blake to lend her the money, since it was unfair to let his big event be totally ruined because she was unable to manage her cashflow. Unfortunately, that would undoubtedly cause his father to lose confidence in the company, and withhold his investment. Help that she'd been sorely counting on, especially now that Miles' career was in jeopardy.

Besides, she also needed those funds to give Lisa a raise and expand her staff, so during her maternity leave the company would continue and grow. Within a year, she'd hoped to have an office in D.C. So much for the best-laid plans. The way things were looking now, after she had the baby she would probably have to close the office. Putting off the inevitable, she decided to wait until the last moment to call Blake, just in case a white knight was circling the block, delayed by parking.

"Hey, girl!" Dakota bounced through the door, wearing a huge smile on her face.

"What are you doing here?"

"It's good to see you too," Dakota said sarcastically. She

was there to share her news about her relationship with Phillip. But sensing Morgan's ill mood, she held back.

"I'm sorry. It's just one of those days." Morgan got up to hug Dakota before taking her coat. "Miles' inquisition is today. I am just so worried about him."

Dakota took Morgan's hand. "Morgan, you've got to do what Nana always told me to do: 'Let go and let God.' Besides, karma is a bitch and witches like Vic never get away with these things for long."

"Well, I hope that karma is on a schedule and she's got today circled in red."

"Let me tell you about karma and things catching up to people. . . ." Dakota told Morgan the details of how she had busted Tricia, who had tried to steal her inheritance.

"No, she didn't!" Morgan was horrified by Tricia's dishonesty.

"Yes, she did. Homegirl was buying up the South Street Seaport."

"What are you gonna do?" Morgan asked. It had to be a tough position for Dakota.

"Keep her under my thumb and make her pay me back every cent she spent."

"That's nice of you. I thought you were going to say you kicked her out, right after calling the police."

"I couldn't do that. It's not what Nana would have wanted. Besides, like you learned with Lisa, sometimes people do things as a cry for help, not because they really want to. I think Tricia is genuinely remorseful and is going to try to change."

"Speaking of Lisa, Justin will be home from the hospital in a few days." She'd finally told Dakota about the operation last week.

"That's great news!"

"The only good news I've had lately." Morgan looked so desolate that Dakota wrapped her arms around her friend's shoulders.

"Things will get better." Dakota wished she could help Morgan through this rough time with Miles.

Morgan looked at her watch. It was two o'clock. "I've been putting this off long enough. Excuse me while I make a call." Morgan looked as though she'd rather have bamboo shoots stuck under her fingernails than pick up the phone.

"What is it?" Dakota's expression was troubled.

"I've got to borrow from Blake to pay Henrí. Otherwise he won't show up tomorrow."

"*What?*" Dakota was puzzled. She knew Morgan to be an excellent manager and couldn't imagine her letting her business get so out of hand.

Morgan sighed. "I lent the money to Lisa for Justin's operation," she said, finally coming clean.

Dakota knew about the operation, but she had no idea that Morgan had fronted the cash. "That was a noble thing to do, girl." Dakota looked at her with newfound admiration.

"Noble with no company." She picked up the receiver.

"How much is it?"

"Fifteen thousand dollars," Morgan answered as she started dialing.

"Is that all?" It was Morgan's turn to look puzzled. Dakota acted like she had that kind of money lying around in a checking account. In fact, she did.

Dakota reached over to take the phone from Morgan's hand. "I just told you that I have an inheritance."

"I know, but—" She couldn't imagine it being much money the way Dakota always described her upbringing. And after Tricia's shopping spree, there couldn't be much left.

"It's a quarter of a million dollars," Dakota said with a straight face.

Morgan was shocked. "Did you just say a quarter of a million dollars?" They both screamed simultaneously, and then fell into a hug while hopping up and down.

Dakota grabbed her coat and bag. "Come on, Morgan. We've got to get to the bank and over to Henrí's in a hurry."

As they dashed out the door to Dakota's car, Morgan thought to herself, So there was a white knight looking for parking.

45

After nine months of grueling renovations and three fired interior designers, the St. James Gallery on Fifty-seventh Street was finally ready for its opening. The premiere party had gotten lots of advance press thanks to the strong influence of Dr. Richard St. James, whose business and U.N. connections were vast and far-reaching. There wasn't a politician or person of influence in the world that he couldn't tap, if need be. And of course his wife, the other Dr. St. James, a leading neurosurgeon and active participant in numerous charitable organizations in New York, was at the epicenter of the city's social upper crust. To this already rich assemblage was added the young, hip Wall Street and entertainment crowd with which Morgan, Miles, and Dakota rubbed elbows. As if that weren't enough to generate a high-octane P.R. machine, the fact that this was the first black-owned fine arts gallery to ever open in Midtown added fuel to the combustion.

The gallery housed a wide-ranging collection of contemporary, modern, and surrealist art combined with raw talent by yet-undiscovered artists from Harlem, Atlanta, Jersey City, and various wellsprings of creativity not regularly tapped by the art establishment. The effect was what Blake termed Art Uncovered. To him the essence of art was hidden by bogus and prefabricated labels: Black Art, Contemporary Art,

American or Traditional Art. In his gallery it all became a part of a hybrid of beauty and shared expression.

To convey this philosophy Caché sent each of the three hundred invited guests an unconstructed ten-piece puzzle. Each cardboard piece was covered with a different textured fabric, ranging from a magenta-hued raw silk to a featherlight beige burlap. Once assembled, the eight-by-six-inch invitation was a tapestried work of art itself.

This same fabric had been purchased in bulk and swagged across the twenty-two-foot-high ceilings of the gallery. Fans placed in the corners on rafters were turned on low to create a fluid, floaty effect. Artwork was hung on retractable walls that slid in and out of the main room like pocket doors, so as the evening progressed, the art exhibit would too. Shortly before showtime, the center lights were finally dimmed to a golden glow and halogen pinpoint lights were directed and brightened. Morgan surveyed the room and finally allowed herself to breathe a sigh of relief. So far, so good.

"Morgan, not to worry. All systems are go," Lisa reported.

"Henrí and staff are in the kitchen?"

"In the flesh," Lisa was happy to say.

"Did the black truffles make it in from France?" Morgan asked, holding her breath.

"*Absolument*," Lisa answered in a bad but enthusiastic French accent.

Morgan moved about the gallery double-checking every small detail with Lisa at her side. "Has the guest list been updated?"

"Twice," Lisa answered, keeping up with her. Morgan could scarcely believe the transformation in Lisa since the burden of paying for her son's treatment had been lifted. She had always been a good but erratic worker; now she was phenomenal, and Morgan's absolute rock. It was the best money she had ever spent.

Many in the art scene came, fully expecting to see walls filled with works only by black artists such as Romare Bearden, Jacob Lawrence, or Vernette Honeywood. So they were surprised to find an eclectic collection of works, such as an engaging oil on canvas laid down on masonite by Alexej von Jawlensky, an abstract marble sculpture by Jacques Lipchitz with bright nonnaturalistic colors, and a piece by Fernand Leger on painted ceramic relief.

. "Blake, the exhibit is fabulous," a distinguished-looking gentleman paused to compliment him.

"Thank you, Mr. Rubenstein. I'm so glad that you and Mrs. Rubenstein were able to come." Blake was aglow. He wore a cranberry velvet tuxedo by Armani over a cream silk French-cuffed shirt with diamond-encrusted studs and a black thickly ribbed ascot.

He strolled among his stylishly clad guests with a sparkling glass of Veuve Clicquot in hand, a brilliant smile on his face, and just the right words ready on his lips. He charmed everyone— men, women, the young, the old, white and black. The party was in full swing and everyone was having a grand time.

In addition to the free-flowing champagne, guests were offered select vintages of French red and Californian white wines. Waiters in black monk sheaths served an assortment of delicious appetizers, from scallops with thin truffle shavings perched atop a mini-lobster ravioli, to foie gras in a puff pastry, succulent prosciutto-wrapped melon, and countless other mouthwatering concoctions.

"Congratulations, Blake," Morgan said, greeting him with a big hug and European-style kisses on each cheek.

"Thank you, darling. You look incredible."

Morgan wore a cream wool crepe sleeveless shift that hugged her breasts before falling fluidly past the swell of her stomach down to the floor, where it whispered around cream beaded mules by Gun Metal. The matching shawl draped languidly over her arms.

"Why, thank you," Morgan blushed. "I guess I'll do for a pregnant woman."

"You make even pregnancy look glamorous. I've seen women who were pregnant who shouldn't be seen in public at all, let alone at a black-tie gathering."

"You haven't seen me trying to rise up out of a chair. Trust me, there's nothing glamorous about it," she confided.

"Speaking of chairs, don't overdo it tonight on my behalf. If you need to cut out, go ahead. After all Lisa's here."

"Thanks for the concern, but I'll be fine. I love watching your success!"

"Well, for the record you have done an outstanding job," he said, looking around at the festive crowd. Just then Dr. and Mrs. St. James approached, arm in arm. He wore his immaculately tailored tuxedo with the ease that spoke of old money and sheer class. His wife was regal in a red fitted gown by Dior that was a work of art displayed against her rich ebony skin and white hair, which she wore swept into a French twist.

"Blake, we are so proud of you." Dr. St. James beamed at his son.

Those seven words represented everything that Blake had ever wanted in life: to shine in the eyes of his father. "Thank you, Father."

Dr. St. James then turned to Morgan, took her hand, and bowed to touch his lips to the backs of her fingers. It was such an elegant gesture that she felt like the most important woman in the room. "Good evening, Morgan, and don't you look splendid! Let me introduce you to my wife, Dr. St. James."

Morgan felt as though she should curtsy, but in her current condition she might never make it back up. "Dr. St. James, it's such a pleasure to meet you."

"And you, my dear. I've heard such good things about you." Blake's mother had such extraordinary bearing. She looked like a queen standing next to her king.

"Thank you," Morgan replied.

"Morgan, tonight's affair is a triumph," Dr. St. James said. "Just as I knew it would be. In fact, I received your second quarterly report last week, and my accountant just responded this morning. We are ready to move forward with the investment."

Morgan's breath caught upon hearing the news. "Dr. St. James, I am honored."

"You've earned it." He smiled broadly. Morgan had a vision of her father, who'd passed away several years ago after working himself up the ladder to a very senior position at Coca-Cola in Atlanta. He always said, "Work hard, do the right thing, and you will succeed." In the last couple of months she'd begun to doubt his motto. But not anymore.

Blake excused himself as he saw Spence enter the gallery. He looked marvelous in a three-button suit-cut tuxedo with a black shirt and a black necktie. One couldn't help but notice him as he made his way through the crowd toward Blake.

"Not too shabby," Spence said, taking in the scene. He gave Blake a big hug. "Congratulations, I am so proud of you."

"Thank you." Blake smiled at him. He felt so lucky to have a friend like Spence. With him Blake never had to worry about double agendas, or being double-crossed. "Thanks to you, the press tonight will be strictly PG."

"What are friends for?" Spence grinned, lifting a glass of champagne from a passing waiter.

After a pause, Blake said, "You know, in a way I can't help but feel sorry for Freddie. He reminds me so much of Tyrone. Always looking for a shortcut."

"Have you heard from Tyrone lately?"

"Not directly. But I hear from his mom, Mattie, that he's somewhere up in Canada. I think Montreal. He sends her these long letters, protesting his innocence. And apparently he now goes by the name Tess."

"Tess?"

"Go figure."

"Hey, there's Dakota. And who's that fine male specimen with her?" Spence asked, eyeing him mischievously. Dakota wore a black silk crepe skirt that trailed in a long V behind her, with a silver mesh handkerchief top and a pair of silver Robert Clergerie evening sandals.

Blake and Spence joined Dakota and Phillip, who stood talking to Morgan and a circle of their friends. Minutes later

Miles walked up with a big hug for Morgan and a warm smile beamed at Phillip. "You two are the greatest," he said, looking like he'd won the lottery.

Picking up on the private jubilation, Blake asked, "What's this all about? Did I miss something?"

Others in their little group also wore questioning looks. Miles said, "I'd like to toast to the true meaning of friendship. Friends are people who have your back, even when you don't know it's exposed. Friends are people who find a way to give you advice, even when you're full of yourself." He then turned to face Phillip. "Friends are those who cringe when you make mistakes, but will never say I told you so. . . . Here's to you, Phillip." The toast had special meaning to four other friends standing there also. Blake was forever grateful for Spence's helping him out of a very sticky situation and Morgan could never repay Dakota for saving her company and her reputation.

After recounting the story of his dramatic eleventh-hour rescue, Miles held up his hand to get their attention again. "But I do have one small complaint," he said to Phillip with a teasing smirk. "Couldn't you have come just a little sooner?" Everyone laughed.

"All I know is, when I ran into that room it felt like Siberia." Phillip now faced Miles. "I guess I could've come a little sooner, but I wanted for once"—he held up one finger—"to see the cool and collected Miles Nelson sweat." Everyone laughed even harder, because Miles had the reputation of a cool customer.

Enjoying the happy mood, Phillip took the opportunity to make a toast of his own. Raising his glass, he said, "This toast is for two people who have always been an inspiration to me. Their relationship epitomizes the kind of love that we all dream of—only for them it's real. Like everybody else, they've had good times and trying times, but no matter how challenging, they've always been able to put their love for each other first, and that solid foundation has withstood everything they've faced. This toast is for Miles and Morgan. And let's not forget the little Nelson on the way." Everyone again raised their glasses with smiles and nods and murmurs of agreement.

Phillip added, "I just hope that my girl and I can nurture our love the way you two have." He looked at Dakota, giving her shoulders a squeeze. "Here's to us, baby."

Morgan leaned in to whisper to Dakota, "Am I hearing this right?" She had been so caught up in her quest to save Caché that she'd only gotten the bare-bones story on Dakota and Phillip. The two friends had yet to settle in and fully dissect the exciting new relationship.

"You heard right"—Dakota smiled—"it's real."

Although Morgan knew the answer, she asked anyway, "Is this what you want?"

Dakota looked up at Phillip. "I've never wanted anything more in my life."

Morgan clinked her crystal flute of ginger ale against Dakota's champagne. "To realizing our dreams."

Epilogue

Morgan had been insistent that Dakota not give her a shower, at least not until after the baby was born. She reasoned that if guests didn't know the sex they'd play it safe and buy boring yellow or puke green—colors thought to work for boys or girls, but which in truth didn't necessarily flatter either. No, Morgan wanted her daughter in pink, or her son in blue. Miles had no idea why women made such a fuss over showers to begin with. Even so, bursting with pride, he attended the coed baby shower with his bundle of joy strapped to his chest in a baby harness.

When he and Morgan entered the downstairs dining room of Aquavit, all of the women cooed, oohhed and aahhed, while the men lay in wait to tease Miles about his doting behavior. He was proving to be a true Renaissance man. He could come home from a high-pressure day at Sound Entertainment and change a diaper—even the bad ones—and later on make slow, exquisite, love to his amazing wife.

Before Morgan could take the baby from the harness, they were circled by their friends, each taking a good long look at Zoe, who lay contently curled against her father's chest. "She is beautiful!" Lisa exclaimed, marveling at the perfectly formed little girl swathed in a pink cashmere receiving blanket. Young Justin looked on in awe at the tiny baby.

"Thank you." Miles was so happy that his glow rivaled

Morgan's during pregnancy. He could spend hours watching Zoe, fascinated by her every breath. Morgan settled her daughter into a beautiful wicker bassinet, set in the middle of a large table surrounded by gifts.

"You'd think Miles had the baby by himself," Phillip teased, before giving Miles a big hug.

"Where is my godchild?" Dakota bounced into the room. She had been conferring with Aquavit's renowned chef, Marcus Samuelson, about the brunch menu. Before anyone could answer, she joined the chorus of *oohhs* and *aahhs*.

Laughing at Dakota's baby talk, Morgan said, "That's one thing about having a baby. You are automatically put in your place." To the room at large, Morgan said, "My best friend enters a room and doesn't so much as glance in my direction!"

By now Dakota was cradling the baby and gently rocking her. Watching her, Miles nudged Phillip. "Watch out, man. You know, it's contagious."

Phillip smiled in Dakota's direction. "That's not necessarily a bad thing."

As the guests sat around drinking mimosas and helping Morgan open one designer baby outfit after the other, Lisa joined Dakota in the ladies' room. "This has turned out really well."

"It has." Dakota was all smiles over Zoe, Morgan, and Miles, and yes, over Phillip too. This was the first time in a relationship that love came easy. It wasn't forced, orchestrated, or arranged—it just flowed.

"Thanks for letting me help. I know how protective you are of Morgan."

"Thanks for offering. It seems that when we work together, it's all good." She was about to turn to leave the ladies' room, but stopped. "Lisa, I never officially apologized for the horrible things I said to you."

"It's all forgotten. Actually I want to thank you for giving Morgan the money. If she had lost Caché I would never have been able to forgive myself."

"I'm just glad that Justin is doing well." They hugged each other tightly.

When they returned to the room, Morgan was opening the last of the gifts. The St. Jameses had sent a sterling silver baby serving set. Miles said, "What's a silver spoon if she can't have the cup, saucer, knife, fork, and tray?"

"Only the best for my baby," Morgan said, kissing Zoe's soft cheek.

"That's obvious, considering she's wearing a pink cashmere set at two weeks old," Dakota joked.

The last gift was an exquisite crystal piggy bank with Zoe's name hand-painted in soft pastels. "That's beautiful," Dakota remarked. "Who is it from?"

Morgan frowned. "I don't know." Her troubled expression deepened as she read the card.

Dear Zoe,
    May you always have everything you deserve in life, especially love.

Your Aunt Tess

ACKNOWLEDGMENTS

They say it takes a village to raise a child. While *Revenge Is Best Served Cold* was my firstborn, *Talk of The Town* is its rival sibling. As you might guess there are many people that I must acknowledge for their inspiration and support with the conception and development of both books, as well as my writing career. Starting with my family. Love and gratitude to my mom, Gloria Freeman for years of support and nurturing; thanks to my talented sisters, Alison Howard-Smith and Jennifer Freeman, and my two beautiful nieces, Chealsae "The Track Star" Smith and Korian Young. To Scott Folks, hugs, kisses and always my undying love. I also give special thanks to my cousin April Phillips and her handsome hubby, Ted, and their work of art, Saxton, for harboring me during my many visits to my hometown, Atlanta, Georgia. I also thank Margaret Mroz, my stepfather, Edsel Freeman, and my brothers-in-law, Donny and Tony Smith, for their support. Though your family often doesn't have a choice about being a part of your life, friends do. And I've been blessed to have some very special people who choose to do so. Starting with Karen and Oswald Morgan (kisses to Zoe!), Judith and Juan Montier, Greg Fierce, Vannessa Baylor, Anne Simmons, Veronica Chambers, Debra Jackson, Antonio and Erica Reid, Rose Salem, Len Burnette, Julie Borders, Harriette Cole, Mike and

Diane Frierson, Robin Lawson, Eula Smith, Denise Brown and Saunte Lowe.

To round out my village there are other people and organizations that have also supported my dreams and aspirations, including the Atlanta Sister, Sistah book club (thanks Vaunda!), the Shrine of the Black Madonna bookstore, Eso Won Books, OurStory Bookstore, the African American Bookstore, the staff at *Savoy* magazine for giving me a forum for my musings with my Tongue 'N Chic style column, Kenneth Chenault for being an inspiration, Keith Clinkscales for being a mentor and friend, and to Atlanta publicist CoAnne Wilshire for always getting the word out. And special thanks to Russell and Kimora Simmons for hosting and supporting the launch party for *Revenge Is Best Served Cold*. And to my coauthor, Danita Carter: We did it again! And of course without my editor, Audrey LaFehr, and her assistant, Jennifer Jahner, *Revenge* would never have been served and there'd be nothing to *Talk* about!

To God Almighty I give reverence for every breath and for the miracle of life. And to Steve Salem, Buddy Crofton and Minnie Bullock, Rest In Peace . . .

Tracie

As always I give praise to God for His love and endless blessings. I would like to collectively thank all of the people from coast to coast who assisted Tracie and me with *Talk* as well as *Revenge*. Without you, the dream would be just that— a dream. For you I write this poem

> Friends are your chosen family.
> A gift from God above,
> offering unconditional love.
> Friends don't judge you by the size
> of your bank account, or lack thereof.
> Friends bring you back to reality

when you start believing your own press.
Sharing in your dreams
even when they're far-fetched.
Though the miles may separate you,
a true friend remains true.
And like a good wine,
friendship mellows with time.
So sit back and let it breathe.

To our editorial team, Audrey LaFehr and Jennifer Jahner, thank you for your dedication. To our publicist, Hillary Schupf, thank you for the "product placement." To William Boyd Jr. and his wife, Delisa, thank you for your friendship, and, Bill, thanks for an awesome photo session. To Denise Milloy, thanks for the "magic" you wield with those makeup brushes. And to the African-American booksellers whose support is unwavering.

Danita

ABOUT THE AUTHORS

Tracie Howard is the former Director of Sales for American Express. A graduate of Georgia State University with a degree in marketing, she also worked for the Atlanta Committee for the Olympic Games, Xerox Corporation, and Johnson & Johnson. She is the Lifestyle correspondent for *Savoy* magazine, and divides her time between Manhattan and Los Angeles. Visit her Web site at www.traciehoward.com.

A jewelry designer who secured a stockbroker's license while working on Wall Street, **Danita Carter** is constantly reinventing herself. A native of Chicago, she has had her work featured in *Essence* magazine as well as in international jewelry competitions. She currently lives in Manhattan. Visit her Web site at www.danitacarter.com.